ECHOES ON A FRACTAL LINE

LEE-ANNE MCAULAY

Wee Writing Bureau Publishing

Second edition

Paperback ISBN: 978-1-0683747-3-9

Ebook ISBN: 978-1-0683747-1-5

Kind permission and access to the archives at Alloa Tower were granted by the Right Honourable Earl of Mar and the staff team for the National Trust for Scotland.

Credit for cover design belongs to Ken Dawson at Creative Covers

Credit for developmental editing goes to Samantha Nimmo of Serpents and Swords Editing

I owe so much to my family and friends for their unwavering support and positivity.

Also, to my husband Alan, without whom this would not have been possible.

This book is dedicated to my grandparents, Heather and Bill Finlay, who always believed I was meant to be a writer. I hope I've made you proud.

CHAPTER 1

HAZEL

Another cursed tower house and ghostly apparition proposal slammed onto the rejection pile. Hazel sighed, removed her green-framed glasses then placed them on the desk. Rolling her shoulders, she sat back in the taupe leather chair and pressed her palms into her eyes. *Was a little originality too much to ask?* After months of work to secure a research grant and fund from the World Heritage Foundation, she wouldn't see it wasted on curses and populist paranormal nonsense.

As the newly appointed Lead Engagement Officer, Hazel knew a different approach was needed to bring the trust's offering into the present and keep it relevant. It had been a tough sell to the notoriously conservative board of trustees, but with the support of the trust's finance and marketing leads, she had presented case studies from around the world and the board agreed to part fund a collaborative project. Her idea to develop a new program around the historic buildings and locations in

Central Scotland. The area was so rich in history right back to the Picts and had been the northern frontier of the Roman empire in Scotland until 211AD. Time and time again, the fate of Scotland had been decided in this landscape. Bringing fresh lenses to the well-known stories of Wallace, Bruce, and the Jacobites was the way to bring the tourists and members in. Hazel knew that if they got this right, they could secure the future of the buildings and sites for a generation. Without a significant boost to visitor numbers, the History of Scotland Trust would have to start mothballing properties. If that happened, these beautiful and important places would fade. That was the challenge Hazel had chosen.

Visitors came to this part of Scotland in their thousands. They flocked to Edinburgh and Stirling Castles for bloody battles, royal intrigues, and a fruit scone in the tearoom. They could, Hazel believed, be persuaded to explore more of the area if there was a compelling story to follow or a mystery to solve. She understood why the proposals had hooked onto the hauntings and macabre elements. These places had been in their prime during the most brutal episodes of history. The paranormal was also popular again thanks to several novels, documentaries, and films set in Scotland. It was the Braveheart effect. For the project to have the impact and longevity that the History of Scotland Trust needed, it would have to be more than a ghost tour.

A soft tap on the door interrupted Hazel's thoughts. Recognising Marcus by his tall wiry silhouette in the frosted glass pane, she called to him to come in.

'You looked in need of a distraction,' Marcus said, handing her a cup of tea balanced delicately on a mismatched saucer. 'Don't worry, it's the good stuff.'

The delicate China cup rattled alarmingly as Hazel took it. She placed the saucer on the desk, wrapping her hands around the blue and white pattern. Lifting it to her nose, she sighed and then grinned. Although it wasn't her beloved coffee, at this time of the afternoon it was an acceptable alternative.

'Oolong?' she asked, noting the slightly tangy scent before she took a sip and sighed. 'Mmm, it's heavenly. Mei is a wonder.'

Marcus nodded and grinned. Mei had made it her mission to convert everyone she came across to the delights of real tea. Her friendship with Hazel meant Mei had put years into this endeavour and may, at last, be winning the war.

'I'll tell her you approve,' he said. Gesturing to the piles of papers on her desk he asked, 'How's it going?'

'It isn't,' she sighed. 'This is all clan feuds and vengeful clergy. Or worse,' she gestured contemptuously to the file on her right, 'unidentified women dressed in black wailing in towers. Not a serious historical proposal so far.'

Hazel grimaced and swept the piles of offending papers across the polished wooden desk as though they might be contagious.

'There's time yet, Hazel. The call for proposals doesn't close for a few days,' he said soothingly. 'Mei tells me that the History Department at Stirling is awash with rumours. Both Dr McDonald and Dr Leinster are working on proposals.'

'Are they?' Hazel's green eyes flashed with interest. 'Are they indeed? I wonder why? The research grant is significant but not really in their league I imagine.'

'Bitter rivals from what I hear.' Marcus leaned forward and dropped his voice to a conspiratorial whisper. 'Dr Leinster has been looking for a chance to regain the advantage since McDonald took apart his work on the Douglas papers last year.'

'Oh yes, I remember that now,' Hazel replied thoughtfully. 'It was a pretty ruthless thing to do to a colleague but by all accounts, Dr McDonald made a good argument.'

'Yes,' Marcus said, 'it won't have won her any friends on the faculty or in other universities, but it certainly made an impression.'

'Eggs and omelettes.' Hazel shrugged.

Marcus laughed and as he turned to leave threw back over his shoulder, 'A kindred spirit perhaps Hazel? Another trailblazer shaking up the establishment!'

This last sentence earned him a glacial stare under her blunt-cut fringe to which he raised his hands in a gesture of surrender. He laughed to himself as she shooed him out of the door and across to his own office.

The academic world in Scotland was small but prestigious. Positions on the faculty of any of the universities were fiercely contested. Klaus Leinster was a respected and established historian whose work centred around Scotland's place in Europe in the 18th century. On the other hand, Lauren McDonald was a rising star. Her appointment was part of the drive to establish Stirling as a centre for innovation and research. Known for taking a leading-edge approach, she had earned a reputation for being brilliant but controversial.

Either of those names would add significant prestige to the project. Hazel gazed out of the window and up towards Stirling Castle with the great hall glowing gold in the afternoon sun. It was a fortress and had always been the true key to power in Scotland. After all, that was why the History of Scotland Trust had chosen this location for its head office. Under the grey stone of the vaulted ceiling, she sipped her tea thoughtfully.

Hazel worked her way through the remaining proposals. Her initial sifts had left three possibilities, one around the Iron Age Settlements looked particularly promising. The archaeology digs sitting alongside a series of 'citizen science' events at the HoST sites had real potential to grab the public imagination. It was easy to picture welly booted visitors peering into the trenches and coaches of school children eagerly sifting through mounds of earth for fragments of bone or pottery. She made some notes and clicked the lid back on her Parker fountain pen. Checking her watch, Hazel was surprised to see it was nearly 5 p.m.

Her phone vibrated and she balanced the teacup on the saucer as she pulled it from her pocket. True to routine, it was a message from Mei. On Thursdays, she met Mei, and they went for a long steady run. It was a chance to de-stress and catch up, and a part of the week they both looked forward to. The pair had met at university as part of the athletics team and remained friends despite living, for a time, in separate countries. Hazel tapped out her reply confirming that she would be at the Blairlogie car park in thirty minutes then took her bag from her locker and went to change.

Mei's electric blue Mini convertible was recognisable anywhere. Hazel smiled as she drew level with it and Mei gave a little wave. The women climbed out of their cars and began their pre-run rituals of clipping on hydration belts, tightening ponytails and setting sports watches. Hazel did her warm-up stretches and watched as her friend took a selfie to post to Instagram. The contrast between the two of them wasn't lost on Hazel, who was in a pair of functional black shorts and a khaki green vest top whilst Mei wore a neon bright set in the latest pattern from Sweaty Betty. Even without the bright Lycra, Mei stood out with her glossy black hair and deep brown eyes. At four foot eleven, Mei was tiny, but her effervescence and effortless grace filled every space she entered. Next to her, Hazel felt awkward and inelegant.

They fell into an easy tempo as they began to run. Their route would take them up onto the hillside behind the university and along towards Bridge of Allan. The golds and pinks of the early evening light across the Forth Valley set the colours in the turning leaves blazing. Hazel settled into her rhythm as they climbed the first steep section of the hill, and the friends ran in companionable silence. Although they were opposites in so many ways, the two were equally competitive and their twenty year friendship was an anchor they both cherished. Over the years these runs had been a way for them to leave behind the stress of academia and, later, work. Giving them space and time to work through the challenges and dilemmas life threw at them.

As the path evened out and the women's breathing steadied, they began to chat. Mei shared her exasperation that Suki showed no interest at all in music and art, preferring instead to paddle board with Marcus or play rugby with the school team. At nine years old, she was already demonstrating she had her mother's independent spirit although not, so far, her love of dresses and shoes. Hazel was fond of Suki and enjoyed being an honorary auntie. Amused by her friend's chagrin and unable to resist, she asked if she should plan a trip to Murrayfield, home of the Scotland rugby team, instead of the usual theatre trip as a Christmas treat.

As they began to run along the hillside with the loch and campus of the university below them, Mei eyed her friend shrewdly. This route, although the shortest, was the most challenging of their regular circuits. It had the most spectacular views but was also Hazel's go-to when she was frustrated or needed to work on a problem.

'So,' Mei began, 'how are you feeling about the project? Marcus says the pressure is on to find the right theme.'

'There are a couple of promising ideas around the Iron Age and following the journey of the lesser-known clans. I could work with either of those and they are a change from the usual Bruce and Wallace stories. It'll be interesting to see how the academics want to research it and then how that shapes the way we present it,' Hazel said, trying to sound confident.

The truth was that she was starting to wonder if her risk would pay off. Would either of these topics bring history to life and capture the public's imagination? Would it have the depth to keep them coming back? The trustees had agreed to fund the project, but they had been clear that the investment needed to be worth it. The grant from the World Heritage Fund would give the project a fighting chance but it would be down to her and the academic that the trustees selected to make it work.

'Marcus tells me that the rumour mill has both Dr Leinster and Dr McDonald writing research proposals. Do you think there's any truth to it?' Hazel asked.

'Yes,' Mei said confidently. 'They're both working on research that could link to your brief and with yet more budget cuts coming, that funding will be useful. They're both good historians and the post-grad and PhD programmes at the university are always oversubscribed.'

'Well, that is positive. The local link will appeal to the trustees too I think,' Hazel remarked. 'Do you know them both?'

'Only a little. Our paths don't cross often. Dr Leinster is a traditional academic, part of the old guard. One of the university's 'big hitters' as the new dean keeps calling them. You know? The ones that are consulted for films and TV shows. Dr McDonald is more of a big character. She does things her own way I hear. Not really a part of the faculty core.' Mei hesitated before adding, 'They really don't get on. Not after that business with the Clan Douglas research last year. I wonder what happened between them that Dr McDonald chose to raise the issues the way she did.'

Now on the second hill section of the run, the women fell silent as the path became stony. Looking up towards the outcrop, Hazel picked out the place where the trees opened out onto the bluff. She turned to Mei gave her a wicked grin and accelerated. Mei groaned and followed. Hazel enjoyed the effort and felt the frustrations of the day melt away as she focused only on the next few steps.

They stopped at the edge of the tree line and stood breathing hard, hands-on hips. Hazel reached across and gave Mei a high five before taking a gulp of her water. From this vantage point, she could see for miles with the Wallace Monument in front of them and Stirling Castle in the distance. The sun, beginning to dip behind them, caught the winding ribbon of the River

Forth making it shimmer and sparkle. For a long moment neither spoke, taking in the view across the valley. It was breathtaking and so worth the climb. There was something in this landscape that called to Hazel, a sense of belonging and connection. It was home.

CHAPTER 2

HAZEL

Hazel placed the chrome cup on the desk and flipped open the lid. The rich and bitter aroma filled the space. She inhaled deeply, closing her eyes and savouring the moment before letting out a long, slow exhale and reaching forward to switch on her laptop. As the machine powered up, Hazel opened the planner on her desk. There was only one appointment on the page, written in red ink and underlined twice: a call with the Chief Executive Officer of the History Trust of Scotland and the chair of the board of trustees at 3 p.m. Today was the deadline for submissions and Hazel would need to have a shortlist of collaboration proposals for the board to select from.

As the email server loaded, Hazel took a sip of the coffee. It was black and the bitter edge sharpened her focus another couple of degrees. She scanned the subject titles in her inbox and flagged four containing proposals. Glancing through the sender names she saw three different universities. From Stirling, there were two submissions, one from Dundee and one from the Highlands and Islands. There was a flutter of excitement as she noted both Dr Leinster and Dr McDonald's names.

She downloaded the proposals and sent them to the printer. It was the academic in her, she supposed, that preferred to read from paper. Being able to highlight and annotate as she worked just wasn't the same on a screen. This brought to mind her father's opinion that not all technological advancement was progress. As a research chemist, he often voiced this to provoke a reaction from colleagues, but Hazel silently agreed with him.

Heading to the communal office printer, she passed the glass panels of Marcus' office and saw he had his headphones on, already engaged in a video call. He never remembered to close the privacy blinds. Hazel teased him about this being because he was afraid of missing any office excitement or home baking. Catching his eye, she waved, and he acknowledged her with a nod.

Returning to her own office, Hazel pulled the cord that closed her blinds over, a signal to her colleagues that she was unavailable. Taking her glasses from their case and the final sip of her coffee, she settled down to read. At the top of the pile was a proposal named *Landscapes and Loyalties: What Shaped the Identities of the Scottish Clans?* Dr Leinster's proposal was ambitious and aimed to draw on the modern links to the old clans across the trust's sites with a mixture of military, feudal and rural elements for the visitors to explore. It would, Hazel knew, appeal to the international tourists drawn to the lands of their ancestors to explore their family trees. Small teams of researchers under the supervision of the students on his doctoral programme would identify the key theme for each site linked to their own area of academic interest.

Hazel made notes in the margins of the proposal with ideas for how to pull in visitors and create experiences around the themes. Her pen moved swiftly, circling the keywords and underlining points to tease out for discussion with the professor. She glanced at the clock reassuring herself there still plenty of time to make her decision. This idea had real potential to create pockets of interest across the country. They could be linked to answer the big question of how the clans saw themselves and what legacies they left behind.

Standing to stretch her back and legs, Hazel walked towards the window and it's view of the old town. The clock tower stood out against the dreich sky like a sentinel for the castle above. On the north side of the building, her office was cold and dark with exposed brick and steelwork that gave it a utilitarian feel. It often bore the brunt of the wind and rain, but she didn't mind that because it offered the best views. Those with a sunnier and warmer space to work had to endure views of the cinema and budget hotel or the monstrous shopping centre in the new part of the town.

The clock chimed the hour and with a jolt Hazel returned her attention to the documents. She shuffled the three remaining proposals around, conscious that her knowledge of the rivalry between the two Stirling University historians might lead her to draw irrelevant comparisons. She put Dr McDonald's piece to the side to read last.

Lifting the next paper, Hazel began to read through the proposal from the Highlands and Islands. She made her way through it making notes. This was a collective submission from several historians based throughout the north and the islands. They proposed to explore the history of the Celtic people from the Shetland Isles downwards through Scotland. It was called *Celtic Connections: Music, Art, and Mystery*. She tapped her pen lightly on her thigh and wondered what the trustees would make of the idea of holding festivals at key sites across the country. A smile tugged at her lips as an image popped into her mind. She pictured one or two of the more serious trustees presiding over food trucks and portable toilets, up to their knees in mud in a field full of tents.

Pushing the thought aside, she continued. The idea of celebrating the connection to the Celtic people and culture was another promising option. It could perhaps become a regular event and bring in repeat revenue. *Was it* the *idea*? she wondered. She tapped her pen on the paper as she worked through the pros and cons. Thoughtfully she placed the proposal on the 'maybe' pile.

Hazel glanced down at her watch and was surprised to see it was 11.45 a.m. already. Her shoulders tightened, anxiety buzzing through her. With two more proposals to read and a briefing of the top three to prepare before her call at 3 p.m., time was of the essence. Hazel rolled her shoulders back and returned her focus to Dundee's proposal. Titled *The Weaving of a Nation: Scotland's Place on the World Stage*, the idea was to tell the story of how Scotland's relationships with the rest of the world shaped the country. The proposal looked at the Norse, Pict, and Celtic influences right through to relations with Europe and America.

Hazel was impressed by the scale of the project and made notes on the directions it might take across the sites owned and cared for by HoST. The more Hazel considered this, the less convinced she became of how manageable this would be in practice and how much interest it would actually spark for visitors. She placed it decisively on the 'no' pile, glancing again at the clock. Time was running away and she still didn't have a proposal she felt truly confident in.

The tapping of Hazel's pen had increased in speed as she finally came to Dr McDonald's paper and realised that alongside the hum of anxiety about the impending deadline there was also a prickle of anticipation. She pushed her glasses back up the bridge of her nose and began to read. Her pen raced across the page circling and underlining the key points. On the first reading at least *Fractal Lines* was a simple idea, looking at the events and places from the well-known historical events through a different lens. What drew Hazel in was the organic nature of the proposal. The research team would go through the archives and records for a particular site at an interesting point in history and look for individual stories to tell about life at that time. This would then link to other places and stories at other sites across the trust and create a sort of trail for people to follow. Her mind danced from possibility to possibility as she made the links. Dr McDonald's proposal also suggested telling these stories in diverse ways using local artists and creators.

Hazel rolled her eyes when she saw the success of the Culross Witch events being cited. At Culross, they had created a series of events with painters, poets, musicians, and storytellers bringing the events of the witch trials to life. It continued to be hugely popular and had become a focal point for remembering those who were persecuted during those dark times. The comparison was compelling, and she knew it was a strong proposal.

Hazel was surprised by how understated it was, not at all what she had expected although she couldn't pinpoint exactly why that was. The focus on individual stories and themes more intimately linked to the specific trust sites was a sharp contrast to the lofty ideas and broad-brush strokes of the other proposals. She knew presenting this as an option to the board might be harder to sell than some of the others. Yet this idea truly excited her and put it decisively in the space she had reserved for the 'yes' pile.

After a hasty lunch she barely touched, Hazel returned to her desk with another black coffee, this time from the office filter machine. It was now 1:15 p.m. and she needed to focus. Coffee at this time would help her concentration but she would pay for it with a sleepless night. *I'll need to run later*, she thought, *to get rid of both the caffeine and the nerves.* The project was her best shot at boosting visitor numbers and balancing the books. Her chance to prove herself. Pulling the 'maybe' pile towards her for a final sift Hazel reached again for her pen and notebook.

Fifteen minutes later Hazel knew what her recommendations to the board would be and she was confident in her choices. This was the last hurdle to jump to get the project off the ground. Nine months of work and careful preparation came down to this phone call. A treacherous thought crept in and caught her off guard. If she could make this a success, would she be able to put the events in York behind her? Would the doubt be gone? The current of nerves grew in intensity as it pulsed through her and collected as a tight knot in her stomach. She closed the door in her mind on those thoughts and forced herself back to the present.

Back to the task at hand and winning over the trustees, Hazel knew that if the CEO and chair of the board could see the potential in the ideas then the rest of the trustees would be easier to persuade. She looked down the list for a final time:

Brochs and Mountains: Life in Iron Age Scotland led by Dr Leonard of St Andrews University

Landscapes and Loyalties: What Shaped the Identities of Scottish Clans? Led by Dr Leinster of Stirling University

Fractal Lines led by Dr McDonald of Stirling University

In front of her was a set of bullet points with the central ideas from each proposal and notes of what Hazel saw as the benefits and challenges for the trust. She read them through again deliberately slowing herself down. Marcus tapped gently on the door, and she smiled at him.

'Okay?' he asked.

'Yes.' She nodded. 'I've narrowed it down to three of them,' she said, gesturing at the pile of papers on the edge of her desk.

Marcus lifted the papers and flicked through them, scanning the synopsis on the front of each. He looked up at her eyebrows raised.

'Fractal Lines?' he asked the surprise evident in his tone. 'Not a bit airy-fairy for your tastes?'

'It's a good idea.' Hazel met his gaze and kept her tone level despite a spike of defensiveness. 'And there is a lot of potential across the sites. I think it might attract other opportunities to collaborate and diversify.'

Hazel gave him an overview of the strengths of each proposal. She suspected that her friend had known that running through the list out loud would help to prepare her for the meeting. She was grateful for it. Over the years of their friendship, Hazel had noticed that Marcus had a way with people. He just knew what they needed and offered it quietly without fuss or grand gestures. For all his humour and easy-going nature, he was a very astute man and observed far more than he let show. *Sharp* was how her father described him. He brought the best out of people by just being there. *It would be hard to dislike Marcus*, she thought, *unlike me*. Hazel seemed to raise hackles when she tried to help. It had been the same as long as she could remember.

The thought sent Hazel's mind back to the office in York. The bright white walls and fluorescent lights had her nerves on edge as she faced Matt across the beech-topped desk. She had only wanted the best outcome for the project and her question about the integrity of the research had been logical in her mind. The reaction it provoked in him had been explosive. No matter how Hazel tried to reframe the issue it just made it worse, and she had become aware that the whole place had gone silent. Listening. Their voices, amplified by the bare walls and tiled floors, carried clearly across the open space. Within the room, the atmosphere became suffocating and neither of them could bear it any longer.

As the door had banged shut behind her colleague a wave of frustration had risen within her bringing tears that stung. Why couldn't he be logical about it and just listen? Could he not see that being honed into the details would leave the team better prepared in the next phases of the project? Hazel felt her cheeks burning now and she released her breath, forcing the memory away.

Noticing how dark it had become under the gathering cloud Hazel reached across and put on the lamp, she much preferred its soft yellow to the harsh glare of the overhead strip light. The warm glow pooled around her, inviting and comforting, as she took stock. Marcus had agreed that she had three strong proposals to pitch and that it was clear she could take any of them forward. He had left her feeling ready and reassured. Hazel filled her glass with water and arranged her notes, book, and pen in front of her. A little ritual that helped her ground herself. Rolling her shoulders back and down, she opened the meeting app and started the call.

An hour and a half later the meeting ended, and Hazel sat back into her chair letting out a sigh of relief. She had surprised herself with how animated she became whilst arguing for the potential in Dr McDonald's proposal. For a while, it had seemed that the proposal would be overlooked because it wasn't as traditional as the other two. The trust had stayed with traditional exhibitions and experiences in the past and visitor numbers were still falling. It was time to try something new and fresh, she had told them. Hazel really could see how the ideas within Fractal Lines might appeal to visitors. Then there was the fact that of all the proposals it had the most obvious longevity.

In the end, her passionate defence of the principles in Fractal Lines won over the Chair. The next step was to present the project outline to all the trustees at the board meeting in two weeks. Hazel glanced down at her watch, 4.37 p.m., she had time to call Dr McDonald to arrange to meet and then she'd go for a run.

Chapter 3

Lauren

As the heavy door opened, a peel of laughter escaped down the beige corridor and the spicy scent of oud and amber perfume warmed the air. Lauren held the door for Tom as he left his supervision session. She genuinely enjoyed this part of her job. Teaching the undergraduates was rewarding, she thought of it as preparing the ground, but mentoring the postgraduate and doctoral students was a different experience. It was a more collaborative process and Lauren liked to challenge the thinking of her students, opening up room for discussion and debate. Tom had real potential but lacked confidence and Lauren thought he needed more fieldwork experience. 'Get out and get muddy in the landscapes and places,' she had advised, 'it might shift your perspective.'

The buzz of her phone began from under the stacks of essays on her desk. Following the noise, she lifted a pile and found it.

The number wasn't stored in her phone and so she answered it with a note of caution.

'Lauren McDonald speaking,' she said, tucking an unruly auburn curl behind her ear.

'Dr McDonald? This is Hazel Rankin from the History of Scotland Trust. I presented your proposal to our CEO and Chair of the Board, and they would like to hear more. Could we meet to discuss this?'

'Of course, that would be lovely'. Lauren felt a flutter of excitement and she leant forward to grab her pen to take down the details. 'I'm delighted that Fractal Lines is being considered.'

'I can really see the potential in this project.' Hazel's tone was all business and Lauren frowned slightly. 'When we meet we can work it into a solid business plan. Then we all know where we stand'

'Great,' Lauren said at the first pause in Hazel's flow. 'I look forward to working with you.'

Lauren was thoughtful when the call ended. She sat on the edge of the orange sofa and considered the conversation. It was clear that Hazel Rankin intended to have an active role in the project and would be bringing her own ideas to the table. They had arranged to meet on Friday to begin mapping out the project and preparing their presentation.

As a historian, Lauren was trained to look for the little details and she had picked up on a coolness coming from the other woman. Something in the brusque tone sparked her interest. It was almost challenging. *Was Ms Rankin just naturally reserved,* she wondered, *or was there perhaps more to it?* Lauren tapped her nails on the back of her phone case as she followed her train of thought. She would find out soon enough she supposed and was looking forward to this meeting.

The early evening was cool, and the steady rain had eased to a fine mist. Lauren put her hands into the deep pockets of her wax jacket as she walked. The walk from the Pathfoot Building, where the University of Stirling's history department was located, took around twenty minutes. The high road wound steadily from the university's campus to her house above the neighbouring village, Bridge of Allan, and during the lighter months was her favourite part of the day.

Tiny droplets of rain collected on her hair and her cheeks were flushed by the time she opened the door at the side of the house and entered. Siggi, the black labrador, padded through from the kitchen to greet her with his tail wagging. She rubbed his ears and asked him about his day as she bent to take off her Doc Martin boots. In the kitchen, she put on the radio and removed the stopper from the bottle of Merlot they started last night. She sat at the breakfast bar and pulled her notebook with her ideas for the Fractal Lines proposal from her backpack. *Where was the hook,* she asked herself, *the interesting story waiting to be brought to light?*

Lauren was swaying in time to the music, barefoot on the terracotta tiled floor when she caught her wife watching her from the doorway, smiling softly. The smell of tomatoes and garlic filled the room as Lauren stirred the bubbling pot and then tapped out the rhythm of 'Rhiannon' by Fleetwood Mac on its cast iron lid. Lauren thought of herself as an intuitive cook which, to her, meant cooking what she felt like eating with what they had. To everyone else, particularly Annie, it meant cooking without a recipe and with a flagrant disregard for convention. Call it flair or call it intuition, more often than not it worked, and it meant they never had the same meal twice if Lauren was cooking.

'Hmm, smells wonderful,' Annie said, 'dare I ask what it is?'

'Hello love.' Lauren turned to greet her with a kiss on the cheek. 'It's a chicken and capers pasta thing and it will be ready in fifteen minutes.'

Every creation was a 'thing' to Lauren, who held up the wine bottle and gave it a questioning shake towards Annie. As Lauren handed her the glass of wine, Annie leaned back against the table and took an appreciative sip. They chatted over dinner, as they always did, about their respective days.

With the table cleared and the kitchen tidied, Annie joined Lauren on the dark leather sofa. Siggi sprawled in front of the wood burner, snoring gently. The light flickered and the herby scent of balsam wood drifted around them as Lauren sighed contentedly. She tucked her feet up under her resting her head on Annie's shoulder. Evenings like this were her idea of heaven with the wood burner more for ambience than heat. Lauren shared her news about the phone call from Hazel Rankin and the plan to meet and prepare the presentation. Annie frowned as Lauren described the cool tone she detected during the call and her thoughts on what may be behind it.

'Since when did somebody being a little standoffish worry you?' Annie asked, laughing and then added, 'You normally see that as a challenge and thoroughly enjoy winding them up.'

'I don't know. It was odd... I expected more...' Lauren began waving her hand as she searched for the right word.

'Enthusiasm?' Annie supplied.

'Well, yes frankly,' Lauren laughed. 'Given how much is at stake with this project. It's as important for the History of Scotland Trust as it is for the academics.' Then she caught her wife's raised eyebrows. 'What?' she demanded.

'I do believe,' Annie declared incredulously, 'you are genuinely committed to this cause.' Seeing the tight smile on Lauren's face, she continued more seriously, 'Keep an open mind and give the woman a chance. You're the one who's always saying that there must be room for other opinions and ideas.'

Lauren pondered that last comment. She didn't want to admit that deep down she hoped Hazel wasn't being influenced by rumour and speculation. The thought of facing that yet again was exhausting.

Lauren knew her professional clash with Klaus Leinster had played out very publicly and she had come out of it looking like the villain. She had no choice though. Leinster's behaviour wasn't right. Lauren could not sit by and allow the careers of young historians to be sacrificed to the hubris of Leinster and his ilk. How could she when it had taken nearly ten years for her own to recover back in the early days? Heavens knew she'd tried to handle it through the university channels first. The bitter disappointment when the 'old guard' had closed ranks still stung. It shouldn't have surprised her though. Protecting their own was what they always did. That had left only one route open to her. She knew her academic argument had been sound and, in the end, was proven right. It had been the quality of her own research which secured her offer of tenure to the faculty. Although that hadn't mattered. It suited some people to paint her as a harpy. The damage was done, and some now believed she was only interested in furthering her career ambitions. They were wrong.

At the time, she said nothing to defend herself. Annie had been furious with her, but Lauren knew it would only make things worse. She had taken the high ground and told herself that her professional integrity and the quality of her work spoke for itself. She wasn't going to justify herself to anybody. Where Hazel Rankin was concerned though, Annie had given her good advice. An open mind was needed, and she was, she had to admit, looking forward to this meeting. Lauren could see the innovation in Hazel's project and the woman had certainly taken on a real challenge in her role. She knew a couple of the academics on the trust board and wondered what 'the establishment' would make of it. Together, perhaps, they could create something special.

CHAPTER 4

HAZEL

Hazel paused on the turn of the stairs to look at her reflection. She straightened the roll on the neck of her camel cashmere sweater and pushed the sleeves up her forearms before striding confidently down the final flight of stairs and into the atrium. The History of Scotland offices were converted military barracks and the sparse exposed brick in the corridors contrasted with the elegance of modern steel and dark wood of the reception. She noted the woman standing looking at the map. It showed all the sites owned or managed by the trust and was etched on reinforced glass, suspended on steel tension cables. She looked questioningly at the receptionist who nodded to confirm that this was her visitor.

She walked towards the woman, taking in the riot of auburn curls held back with a silk scarf and long floral skirt under an old green wax jacket. As her footsteps approached, the woman turned to face Hazel. The woman's mouth curved in a smile, but her eyes swept over Hazel in open appraisal, taking in her immaculate glossy bob, expensive sweater and sensible loafers. Hazel met her gaze and offered a handshake, making the woman's bracelets tinkle.

'Doctor McDonald, I'm Hazel Rankin, it's good to meet you,' Hazel started. 'Let's go up to my office, can I offer you a tea or coffee on the way?'

'Just Lauren, please. It's good to meet you too,' she replied. 'Is the coffee any good?'

Hazel laughed, surprised by the bluntness of the question but nodded approvingly. Hazel led the way up the stairs and into the kitchenette at the centre of the office.

'Is Columbian okay?' Hazel asked as she lifted the filter pot from the warmer. 'We run on caffeine here, so it is usually the good stuff.

'Perfect.' Lauren took the proffered mug and took an appreciative sniff. 'My wife limits me to two cups a day so this really is a treat.'

'There might even be a tin of homemade shortbread if we're lucky,' Hazel said taking the tin and giving it an experimental shake. 'Success!'

'Red carpet treatment, eh?' Lauren reached into the tin and took a rectangle of the crumbly golden biscuit. 'No such luxuries at the university these days.'

Hazel caught sight of Marcus watching them through the glass and he gave her a questioning waggle of his eyebrows. She sighed inwardly. He could be such a child, trying to make her laugh just as she was trying to make a good impression.

The women sat facing each other in Hazel's office with coffees in their hands and a small plate of shortbread on the table between them. The table was formed of a single slice of wood, and it had been varnished to a high sheen which caught the pale sunlight and glowed. The solidly square chairs had, evidently, been chosen for their aesthetic and not for comfort as both women shifted in their seats trying to settle in. Hazel began by outlining what the trustees were looking for as outcomes from the project and Lauren nodded along. Attracting an increase of eleven per cent in visitor numbers and a seven per cent increase in revenue across the sites selected for the project was Hazel's task, but finding the stories that would attract this was Lauren's.

Lauren reached into her backpack and brought out her folder with her notes. She opened out a folded sheet of A3 paper and placed it on the table between them, explaining that she had sketched out a few ideas. Hazel leaned forward, arms resting on her knees, listening intently and following the flow of the other woman's thinking on the mind map. It was a kind of timeline of pivotal periods in Scottish history and branching out from that were the key places, events and people.

Rising thoughtfully, Hazel moved to her desk where she unlocked her laptop and typed a few words. She swivelled the screen around to show Lauren an overview of the locations of all of the sites and properties managed by HoST. The map showed that there was a higher density of them right in the middle of the country. The other hot spots were on the West Coast and up in the North-East. All areas associated with tourism and the places Hazel thought might have the most potential. Lauren studied the map and then returned to her notes. She was silent for a moment before tapping her nail on a name. John Erskine.

'An interesting character was John Erskine,' Lauren said. 'Went from Secretary of State for the British Government to rebel leader in less than a year.'

'Yes. Something of a local legend in Alloa,' Hazel agreed. 'He renovated the family seat into a tower house inspired by the great palaces of Venice and Versailles. Not a man short of ambition.'

'It must have come as a shock to his allies when he switched sides,' Lauren said, 'all those marriages and intricate relationships all designed to strengthen the Clan and their loyalties to the government. Gone in one fell swoop.'

'I believe they call it political adaptability these days,' Hazel mused. 'It's all the rage again.'

'Oh it certainly seems to be,' Lauren agreed and then added thoughtfully, 'I guess he had his reasons though. It was a huge gamble for him and his family.'

The women agreed to build a pitch that started with Lord Erskine, Sixth Earl of Mar, at Alloa Tower. It gave them options for a trail to follow locally but also links to Aberdeenshire and the Mar Estates there. They divided up the aspects of the presentation between them and agreed to meet again to pull it together the following week.

Hazel watched as Lauren gathered up her papers and packed them away. She took in the bohemian style, wild hair and air of self-assurance. A woman who gave the impression of being at ease with herself, but there was an edge there too. She had been engaging and quick-witted, although not exactly warm. Dr McDonald was also very direct and came across as unconcerned about how others perceived her. It was unsettling.

The 1715 Jacobite Uprising, Hazel thought as she made her way back to her office, *we might be on to something here*. After all, what started with John Erskine that autumn would ultimately lead to the fields of Culloden thirty years later. It would change the Highland way of life. She met her own eyes in the mirror at the turn on the stairs. The hairs on the back of her neck and arms rose and she felt herself shiver with... what? Excitement or apprehension, Hazel wasn't sure.

CHAPTER 5

JEANNIE

J eannie watched the flames dance in the grate. They glowed orange and yellow, almost too bright in contrast to the grey light from the hole in the thatch that let the thick curls of black smoke rise and leave. The sand remained on the table where Jeannie had paused in her scouring and although it worked its way into the cracks on her fingers, the woman barely noticed the sting. Just as her Grannie had taught her, Jeannie always threw a pine log onto the peat fire when she cleaned. Despite the way the wood smoked, the earthy scent freshened and cleared the air.

The earthy smell of the resin always reminded her of her late husband. His quiet and thoughtful presence was so at odds with his huge frame and his strength. Jeannie remembered the time Duncan had strode into their house to find her heavy with child scouring their table, back aching and fingers bleeding. He'd taken in the scene and wordlessly moved her into the chair, rolled back his shirt sleeve, and taken over the task. It was through a thousand of these little kindnesses they showed a deep love and respect for each other. A true partnership. She missed him still. Even after four years, the ache in her heart at the memories rose to burn her throat and her eyes stung with tears.

Frantic hammering on the door snapped Jeannie back to the present. She stood quickly, shaking her head free of the memories and wiped her hands on her apron as she crossed the earth floor. The boy shuffled impatiently from foot to foot as the door opened and from the pale horror on his face, she knew it was her healing box he had been sent for.

'You'd better come, Widow Kellie,' the lad wailed. 'He's hit his head, and the blood is all over the hearth.'

Jeannie nodded and, realising she'd get no sense about who and why from the terrified kitchen boy, she lifted her healing box from the shelf. Turning back, she handed it to the boy who had followed her anxiously. She then reached for the basket of linens and fabric scraps she kept at hand for cleaning and bandaging wounds.

'Show me!' she commanded, hurrying behind as the lad ran across the open space between the village and the tower house.

The women paused at their looms and washboards at the sight of Jeannie, skirts held up, bunched in one hand, and tendrils of blonde hair flying as she followed. They exchanged worried glances, knowing that something was amiss and watched as the lad led her through the kitchens. The lad froze at the doorway and Jeannie, knowing he was too afraid to go back in, took her box of herbs and ointments from him gently. She sent him on with a message to the women at the well to get extra water boiling. He nodded in acknowledgement and hurried away, his relief palpable.

Across the large table covered with half-peeled root vegetables and cooling bannocks, Alais, the cook, nodded urgently at Jeannie. As she approached, Jeannie could see the man lying on the floor. The source of the thick pool of blood on the hearth and stones was a wound on the side of his head. It was Alan, one of the laird's secretaries. Alan was part of the core group of retainers who attended the Earl of Mar as he travelled to fulfil his role of secretary of state. Alan had returned with him to Alloa when his laird's services to the crown and government were no longer required by the new King George.

Jeannie dropped to her knees at his side, suddenly aware of the stillness in the room. The usual bustle of the kitchen was gone. Aside from the crackle of the fire, the only sound was the low moan of the man in front of her as he drew each breath. Jeannie leaned forward to get a closer look at the wound. It didn't look too deep, but until it was cleaned it would be hard to tell. Turning to Alais, she asked softly for a bowl of water and returned to her careful examination of Alan's face.

He was tall and lean, his features almost gaunt so as her fingers moved gently around the swollen cheekbone it was easy to feel the damage. The shifting lump deep under the skin told her the bone was broken. He hadn't reacted at all to the pain, and his bright green eyes stared fixedly ahead, one black pupil much larger than the other. Jeannie took a breath to steady herself and rose to arrange what was needed.

The kitchens leapt back into action at a stern word from the cook, although everyone moved quietly and edged around the hearth where the man lay. Alais gave instructions in a clear and sharp tone, and they were obeyed instantly. The kitchen boys were sent scurrying with messages. Their haste as much about relief at escaping the heavy atmosphere of the room as eagerness to obey their mistress. The kitchen was Alais' domain and her authority within it was absolute.

Short minutes later, men came rushing in from the stables to move Alan to one of the rooms off the great hall used by the laird's guards. They lifted his limp body gently from the floor and the work of cleaning the kitchen began. The two women moved to the relative privacy of a small stone alcove where the vegetables and berries were stored out of the heat and light of the fires.

'What happened, Alais? Did he trip?' Jeannie asked softly.

'No, he...' Alais started and squeezed her eyes shut against the memory. 'He was asking for food to be prepared for the laird's journey then his voice became strange. Like he was drunk. His face sagged and he tried to walk...'

Jeannie reached out and squeezed the other woman's shoulder, offering comfort and encouraging her to continue.

'His legs gave way under him, and he fell. His head hit the hearth. The noise... a loud crack. Then the blood everywhere...' the cook continued in anguished whisper.

'Did he wake after the fall? Did he speak?' Jeannie asked.

Alais shook her head and buried her face in her apron, weeping.

Jeannie made her way through the kitchen past the kilns and grey stone cooking hearths to the servery with its oak sideboards and earthenware plates. She stopped to collect a pitcher of water from the stone basin by the door to the icehouse. She crossed the flagstone floor feeling it cool beneath her damp cloth slippers which she'd forgotten to change in her rush to leave the house. As she approached the archway leading into the great hall, she lifted a wooden dipper from the hooks of cutlery and a small pewter spoon from the cutlery stand. Crossing the large hall with its lime-washed walls and long low benches, Jeannie steeled herself for the guarded and curious stares of the clansmen who made up the laird's guards.

As she entered the makeshift healing room, James, nephew of the laird, inclined his curly brown head to her. He stood at the end of the table by Alan's head. His hands clasped behind his back and his eyes hooded.

'Have you all you need, mistress?' he asked, voice thick with concern for the man who had once been his mentor.

Jeannie surveyed the room, noting that her healing box and basket of linens had been brought and placed on a bench by the fire along with a mortar and pestle and an assortment of bowls. All cooks knew the basics of healing for cuts and burns and Alais had made sure she had what she needed to start.

'Aye for now, but I'll be needing fresh water brought through the night. Boiled for the bandages and cool for the cloths.' Jeannie looked around again and added, 'Light to work by too.'

James left her to her task, and she heard him issue instructions to the man at the entrance to the room. Widow Kellie was to be attended and all she needed brought to her.

Jeannie soaked a strip of cloth in water and began to clean the wound on Alan's head. It wasn't deep but the skin around it was already turning a livid purple. As she worked, she watched the man's eyes carefully for any flicker or sign of pain. There was nothing. *That at least*, she thought, *was a blessing*. All she could do for him now was keep him company. From her stool beside the table, Jeannie watched through the window as the sky faded from grey to black and she held Alan's hand. Occasionally another of the guards or laird's men would visit and look at her questioningly. Those who had seen war or clan fighting knew what death looked like. She would gently shake her head and they would leave again quietly, some offering a prayer before they went. In the great hall behind her, the evening meal was served as usual, but the conversation was muted, and the household ate quickly and did not linger.

A shadow alerted her to a figure standing hesitantly in the doorway. Jeannie turned to see John, Earl of Mar and Laird of the Erskine Clan. She rose to greet him and he waved her back to the chair.

'I've sent for the surgeon from Stirling, Will he last the night?' the laird asked.

'I dinnae think that he will,' she answered and added gently, 'he's not in pain but his breathing is slowing. I don't think it will be much longer now.'

John Erskine stepped forward and looked down at his secretary, emotion clear on his face. No longer the fierce clan chief or the aloof politician, instead there were deep lines of sadness and worry. Jeannie rose and busied herself tidying the bandages and adding another slab of peat to the fire, her back to the men. The laird spoke softly to his friend of their adventures in London and on the roads. He thanked him for his service, promising him a fine burial. John whispered a prayer head bowed and with his hand laid over Alan's breast.

A cough from outside the room broke the spell and Jeannie saw all trace of vulnerability leave as he drew himself up to his full height and become the stern leader again. His face was inscrutable as he left the room with one last long look at Alan and a nod to Jeannie.

Outside, she heard the earl give orders to his nephew and James reply angrily. The eerie quiet of the tower carried their words to her. The exchange continued in voices tight with tension until the elder had enough.

'Those are my orders, lad, like it or no. See to it,' he growled.

As the echo of the laird's furious footsteps echoed across the hall, Jeannie shivered. A sense of foreboding stole over her. The laird and his retinue were going to Braemar. James was to take command of Alloa Tower and call in the Erskine bannermen which could only mean they were preparing for a fight.

As the darkness softened in readiness for the dawn, Jeannie heard the change in Alan's breath. His chest rose and fell more slowly now, and his features slackened. She'd watched at enough sickbeds to know that death was close now. With a quiet step, she moved to the door and sent the guard waiting there to fetch the minister.

Returning to his side Jeannie took the man's hand and began to hum '*cdul gu lo*'. The old lullaby was sung at cradles and if it were true that the soul could still hear to the end, she hoped it might bring some comfort. The minister stepped into the room and Jeannie moved aside. Bringing out his cross, he placed it in Alan's hands which were now folded on his chest and began to deliver the last rights. His strong voice was steady as he recited the words and commended Alan's soul to God's keeping. Within a few moments, the sounds of Alan's laboured breathing stopped. He was gone. The peat shifted in the hearth and the flames blazed red sending a plume of sparks into the air. A breath of ice touched the back of Jeannie's neck.

CHAPTER 6

HAZEL

The meeting room felt airless with so many bodies, even with the sun streaming in through the windows. Marcus, shirt sleeves rolled up to his elbows, twisted the rod to close the blinds. Hazel gave him a grateful look and returned to scanning the room trying to gauge the responses from the trustees. Some followed the discussion with heads bent over their briefing papers, but most had their attention firmly fixed on Lauren.

Dr McDonald was delivering her part of the presentation, speaking about how her team of PhD and graduate students would combine their knowledge and academic fields of interest to explore the layers of history at key History of Scotland Trust sites. Hazel was quietly impressed by how Lauren had taken the rough mind map of ideas sketched on the sheet of paper they discussed last week and turned it into this. The flow of the presentation felt seamless so far. Hazel moved to the front of the room to join Lauren for questions and discussion.

Hazel hadn't expected it but took it in her stride when she learned that a select group of academics would be joining the presentation. A subgroup of the board had been assembled for the duration of the project and some of the academics would sit on it in an advisory capacity. It was hoped, the CEO explained, that this level of rigour might well attract more funding and perhaps even some media attention. The greater surprise had come when Dr Leinster had entered the room. He was a trustee of the National Library and they had an interest because they held the historical records. Hazel had watched Lauren closely during the introductions and noticed the almost feline smile when the rivals greeted one another. If Lauren had been discomfited, Hazel hadn't been able to tell.

The questioning was robust but nothing that Hazel hadn't expected from the trustees. Marcus gave her a wide smile and subtle thumbs-up as she caught his eye when looking around the table to see if there were more questions. The Chair, satisfied that his fellow trustees had had ample opportunity to gather further information, opened the floor to their guests for comment and questions. Hazel's pulse jumped. She had prepared thoroughly for today but not for this. She put her forearms on the table before her to brace herself as Dr Leinster was invited to speak.

'May I begin by congratulating my colleague...' He paused, casting a cold smile at Lauren. 'And Miss Rankin on a compelling presentation.'

Here we go, thought Hazel, *'there'll be a 'but' attached to this*. She waited as he leaned back in his chair, pink shirt under his blue wool blazer with the top button undone and shuffled the papers in his hand.

'I think we can all see the potential of this project for the History of Scotland Trust and the historians involved. I wonder if you might already be considering how this may play out beyond the scope of the project, Dr McDonald?' he said, tone even and voice carrying clearly across the room.

Hazel felt Lauren tense ever so slightly beside her.

'Well of course the research may be used in the academic world by any of the historians involved or by the university,' Lauren replied, her tone light and her smile serene. 'There may well be other opportunities for exposure that arise as a result of this work, or it may simply be an excellent learning platform.'

'Exposure indeed,' Dr Leinster interjected, cutting her off. 'Potential for a book or perhaps even a television series? The next 'Dr Lucy Worsley'. Ladies and gentlemen, we may well witness the birth of a star.' His tone was light, and he smiled but his eyes never left Lauren's face.

There was polite laughter in the room and Hazel heard Lauren draw a slow breath in. It had been a low blow. An iron fist in a velvet glove.

'Come now Klaus, let's establish when our story will be set before we start selling the TV rights,' Lauren said softly, a mere hint of reproach in her tone. 'With a little bit of luck, this could be a springboard for many ideas that will ultimately engage people in the history of Scotland. Uncover the stories of its unsung heroes... and its villains.'

The buzz in the room at the tea break was palpable. A heaviness spread through Hazel as she realised that the expectations of many of the board had gone up several notches at the possibility of books and series. The other big Scottish cultural organisations would be watching closely too. Marcus, seeing her alone, swept in before she was forced to make polite conversation with anyone else.

'Well done,' he said, saluting her with his teacup. 'That was excellent. The board are thoroughly charmed by Dr McDonald and the two of you work well together.'

Hazel gave a forced a smile in return.

'Leinster was openly goading her, Hazel. You saw that. I think she deflected it brilliantly,' he said guessing accurately at the cause of her angst.

'Yes, I know he was. All dressed up as friendly banter. Snake!' Hazel spat the last word and Marcus eyes widened at the sharpness.

Hazel sighed and ran her hand across her face. Removing her glasses to polish on the cuff of her cream silk blouse, she avoided meeting her friend's eye. *Where did that come from?* she wondered, the venom in her tone had taken her by surprise too. It was partly the casual way in which the man had attacked Lauren that riled her. He was hiding behind his position as a trustee of a well-respected institution. She had read the subtext in his jest. The implication that they were not serious professionals; they were playing at being historians to promote themselves. She'd come across men like him before and had no interest in being caught in a power struggle or trying to prove herself worthy because it was never enough. If it looked like she would succeed, then goal posts would move. She simply wasn't going to let that happen again. Marcus saying her name returned Hazel to the room.

'I want the focus to be on the basics. On doing this the right way for the properties. For the employees and the communities. Not the agendas of individuals and glory hunting. Not this time,' she said quietly.

Marcus nodded and said, 'This is a different set of circumstances, Hazel. You need to let that go. It's behind you. Give Lauren a fair chance.' He gave her arm a squeeze and they returned to their seats for the next part of the meeting.

The meeting resumed with a vote. Hazel looked around the table as one by one the trustees voted to endorse the project. She relaxed the pressure in her clasped hands and felt the tension leave and she let out the breath she hadn't even realised she was holding. Relief flooded her body.

'Excellent,' the chairperson began. 'I'm very much looking forward to following this project wherever it may lead.' He paused and beamed at Hazel.

'Yes,' another of the members agreed, 'the organic nature of it is going to be fun. How can it be anything but a success with this dynamic pair at the helm?'

The excitement in the room lifted her and Hazel heard Lauren's warm laugh beside her. It was infectious and she found herself grinning broadly at Marcus who winked.

She stood beside Lauren as people began to leave. They accepted congratulations and words of encouragement from the trustees. Lauren looked at ease, as though in her natural habitat, a contrast to Hazel who had always found situations like this uncomfortable and was tugging at her sleeve awkwardly. Beside her Lauren laughed at a comment from Marcus as Klaus Leinster approached them. He waited politely to allow Marcus to say goodbye and then stepped forward.

'Congratulations, Miss Rankin,' he said, offering his hand which Hazel took to shake. 'This promises to be an exciting project. Very innovative. My colleagues and I will be watching with interest.'

He turned then to Lauren and acknowledged her with a small bow before making his way out of the room. Hazel watched him leave with a feeling of unease. That man set her nerves on edge. Deep in thought, she twisted the thin gold band she wore on her thumb.

Lauren turned to her and said, her voice low, 'By the pricking of my thumb, something wicked this way comes? Or, in his case, goes. Which is one hundred per cent preferable.'

Hazel stopped twisting her ring and dropped her hands to her sides.

'Don't let him rattle you,' Lauren continued.

'Do as you say and not as you do then?' Hazel's tone was sharper than she intended. *What is wrong with me today?*

'I will not be belittled like that by anyone. I earned my professional qualifications and position the hard way,' Lauren said firmly.

'Fractal Lines is about bringing history to life for people and preserving these properties for the future,' Hazel said. 'It cannot be about personalities and rivalries.'

Lauren shook her head.

'What you permit, you promote, Hazel. I am well aware of the brief here and of the stakes for the trust *and* for my students with the scrutiny. Is this how we are going to start? Are we going to let that man push us into proving ourselves or are we going to work in partnership to deliver this project?'

'As long as we understand each other,' Hazel said, her tone brisk and verging on rude.

She was annoyed at herself for being so prickly and tried to smile and soften. All she had wanted was for them to make a good impression and highlight the strengths of their project. Now it had become about them and having to prove themselves. As much as she didn't want to admit it, Lauren was right. This was no way for them to begin the project. It seemed as though the pressure of the presentation was bringing back the past to both of them.

CHAPTER 7

HAZEL

The sun glinted on the quartz within the stonework of Alloa Tower and the wind whistled around the ornate crenelations crowning the building. Hazel walked along the tree-lined avenue towards the tower, which couldn't completely block out the supermarket to the left or the council offices to the right, but they did at least focus the eye on the destination. The tower was more of a home than a fortress, but it was still an imposing building that commanded the landscape around it. She entered through the large wooden door and stood for a moment on the threshold, taking in the thickness of the walls and the vaulted ceiling.

Lauren had already arrived and it seemed she had commandeered the charter room on the first floor. The large oak table was already strewn with papers. She stood at the far end with a lady in the tweed waistcoat of a History Trust of Scotland property guide and a young man with a serious expression who looked to be in his twenties. They were deep in discussion, clustered around a laptop screen. Hazel took in the portraits lining the walls. Despite the grandeur and size of the pieces there was one which seemed to dominate the room – it was a particularly imposing figure of a woman, white streaks of hair at her temples. She watched them imperiously with green eyes. Hazel removed her wool coat and put it over the back of a chair leaning in.

The paper laid out on the table in front of her was an enlarged copy of the Erskine family tree with branches stretching wide. She leant in to take a closer look, tucking her hair behind her ear as it fell onto her face. The Earldom of Mar was held by the senior branch of the clan but as Hazel followed it out across the breadth of the branches there were marriages and strategically placed clansmen spread across Scotland. Hazel's eyes were drawn back to the portrait of the woman and, Lauren, following her gaze pointed to a name on the family tree.

'Lady Frances Pierrepont, John Erskine's second wife,' she said. 'This would have been their private family room before the mansion house was built. Not exactly cosy, is it?'

'No,' Hazel agreed, wrapping her scarf more tightly around her neck. 'But probably less frigid with a fire in both grates. That portrait is so life-like, she looks as though somebody is about to get a piece of her mind. What is her story?'

'Not a very happy one,' Lauren explained. 'Frances was an English aristocrat. She married John at the height of his political power. He was the secretary of state in the British government and a favourite of Queen Anne. She would have been used to a life at court and being in the centre of the action. It seems she returned to England when the earl was exiled in France and died there in 1767.'

'I wonder what she made of this place after the palaces of London,' Hazel said, looking around her. 'Although this was renovated to be the epitome of luxury.'

'Yes,' Lauren agreed, 'and it was probably her fortune that paid for it.'

The discussion moved to the family tree and the leather-bound books and papers, yellowing pages uneven and curling at the edges spread out on the table. As Lauren opened one of the books, a musky and almost sweet smell escaped. Hazel breathed it in. It reminded her of the vintage book shops in Hay on Wye that she used to visit with her father during family holidays – he loved to search for old scientific books.

An image came to her of the shelves stacked from the ceiling to the floor of a shop with a well-worn red and gold rug. The light filtering along the gap between the shelves filled with dust as she sat on the floor turning the pages of a book about flowers. It had the most beautiful hand-drawn illustrations and kept her occupied whilst her father passed the time of day with the owner. She loved the smell of old books, and her attention returned to the page open in front of her. It was a list of purchases by the looks of it and Hazel leaned in close to make out the handwriting.

A young man Hazel judged to be in his twenties stepped forward.

'I'm Tom.' He held out his hand. 'I'm a doctoral student with Lauren.'

'Hazel Rankin. Pleasure to meet you.' Hazel shook the proffered hand

Tom stepped round her to look at the book and caught her with his elbow.

'Oh no!' he said running his fingers through his hair nervously. 'I'm so sorry,'.

Hazel felt a pang of sympathy for him and tried to soften her expression to reassure him that she wasn't as formidable as all that. Tom, with the support of a small group of postgraduate students, would go through all of the records and documents to look for evidence of what changed for the inhabitants of the tower house and the village around it around the time of the 1715 uprising.

'This is a book of domestic accounts from the time of the tower's refurbishment. Unfortunately for us, a lot of the domestic and household documents were lost in 1801 during the fire,' Tom said.

'Along with the mansion house built by our antagonist Bobbing John,' Lauren added looking around her. 'Legend had it that the fire was foretold. Part of a good old-fashioned curse placed on the Erskines by an angry monk.' Her voice had dropped to a dramatic whisper.

'The Doom of Mar,' Hazel cut Lauren off, her irritation rising. She remembered this story from a visit here when she was at school. 'Conveniently, this seems to have been a fairly comprehensive curse covering almost all eventualities. Things very likely to happen if given enough time.'

'You've got a point there I suppose,' Tom said. 'Fires, misfortune and the deaths of children were hardly rare occurrences.'

'Oh, neither of you have got any sense of the dramatic,' Lauren complained. 'If an ancient and powerful clan didn't pick up the odd curse or two across the generations, then they probably weren't doing it right. Bound to upset a few rivals along the way. It all adds to the atmosphere.'

'A good tale of treachery and intrigue is the fashion in historic properties. Something to spook the visitors is practically a requirement it seems,' Tom said with a hint of mischief in his voice.

'Oh, don't you side with Hazel!' Lauren gasped, hand over her heart pretending to be wounded. 'Anyway, it doesn't matter what we believe from our detached and scientific perspective. It matters what the people believed at the time.'

'Well, Dr McDonald, we call a statement like that confirmation bias these days,' Tom quipped.

'Yes, we do indeed,' Lauren replied.

Her rich, deep laugh was surprising coming from her small frame. It engulfed them all and was infectious. Even Hazel found herself giggling as the tension dissipated.

'Putting curses aside, what have we got to get us started?' Hazel asked, trying to bring them back to the task at hand.

'A letter from the earl containing instructions for the garrisoning of the tower and order of provisions dated a few weeks before the Battle of Sherrifmuir. It was sent from Perth,' Tom said and opened the file on his laptop.

As the guide returned with the faded box of documents Lauren had requested, they pulled up chairs ready to work. Lauren pulled the box towards her and blew a layer of dust from the top as she opened it. Hazel read through the letter with Tom. The writing was neat and flowing. Pen strokes made by a decisive hand, a man who expected the orders he gave would be obeyed without question: a constant watch on the road and river was to be set with a rider ready to take news to the earl in Perth. If Argyll was mustering to come north or if King George sent a regiment from England, he wanted to know about it. The man charged with holding the tower would have been in no doubt about his job and the earl's expectations.

A document like this hinted at what life was like for those living here during that time. Threads that could be pulled to see where they would lead. This is what they were here for. Hazel felt a thrill of excitement.

The afternoon brought a meeting with the property staff and managers from the area offices of the trust. It was here that some of the practical challenges of researching on-site would have to be worked through. A mismatch of chairs formed a circle with the table in the centre. The final participants who arrived a few minutes late were faced with the choice of perching on a particularly ornate Queen Anne chair or a fold-out metal chair that rocked slightly on the uneven floor. *This*, Hazel thought, *demonstrated the point beautifully*. It also had the unanticipated benefit of keeping the meeting brief and to the point.

It had been agreed that the research teams would be based here in the charter room and their progress would be on display on a series of boards that would arrive the following week. The room would remain open to the public to begin to build some interest. Tom looked uncomfortable at the thought but was gently cajoled by Lauren and Elizabeth, the curator, into embracing the chance to make the work of historians real to the public. He had been mollified, at least to some extent, by the fact that the property was only open Friday to Monday and there would be a guide stationed in the room to manage the tours and field any of the more general questions. Like most of the smaller properties, the tower would close to visitors from the end of October until April so this first phase wouldn't be for too long.

The next phase of planning would depend on what the research turned up, but the trustees had agreed to temporary structures being put in the grounds of the tower should they be needed. A delicate balance was being struck between the need to 'poke around in the dusty corners' as Lauren had put it and having a minimal impact on the property.

Hazel felt drained and her neck was stiff with tension by the time they finished. She now had much greater sympathy for those who negotiated treaties for a living. As she made herself a coffee in the staff break room, she contemplated the progress they had made. The next ordeal of the day was to contribute to an article for the local newspaper. It was good publicity, she knew, but she couldn't pretend to be looking forward to it. Anything that drew attention to her career like this made her anxious.

There were still a few minutes until the journalist and photographer were due to arrive and she planned to let Lauren and Elizabeth do most of the talking. Her coffee was made with instant granules, and she grimaced as she lifted the chipped white mug to drink. It was every bit as grim as she feared but it was caffeine and needs must.

After the interview had finished, Hazel and Lauren wound their way up the narrow spiral case to the roof of the tower. The door to the rampart was stiff and Hazel had to put her weight behind the push. It gave suddenly and she stumbled, caught off guard. Her heart hammered and her head reeled as she became aware of how high and exposed the roof top was. She felt off-kilter, as though she was on the deck of a ship on a rolling sea. The wind from the morning had dropped to a steady breeze and cooled her cheeks as she held onto the stone of the door frame trying to ground herself. Glancing behind her, she was relieved to see Lauren just rounding the last curve of the stair, too absorbed by the exertion of the climb to notice her discomfort.

Hazel moved out onto the roof walk and made a loop around the top. Lauren joined her and they stood side by side taking in the landscape each lost in her own thoughts. It was clear from this vantage point just why this tower had been so strategically important, standing watch over the ferry crossing at the Forth and with clear views on all sides. Hazel couldn't help but wonder what it must have been like to be here during 1715. To be stood right here watching. Waiting to see if it was reinforcement or retribution approaching.

The door opened and the photographer stepped out onto the roof, breaking the spell of the moment.

'Perfect!' he called to them. 'Don't move. That's a lovely shot.'

He held the camera out to show them the image on the little screen. It was certainly powerful. The two women stood in profile looking out over the distant hills. A stray curl from Lauren's head caught the light as it blew in the breeze. Hazel's collar pulled up against the wind and her hands in her pockets. Dressed as they both were in earth tones, they were timeless as they stood side by side, looking back into the past.

CHAPTER 8

MAIREAD

As the horses crested the hill, the green and gold expanse of the valley opened out from the sweep of the Ochil hills to the distant Trossachs. Mairead pulled the reins, her legs numb from days in the saddle. Wiggling her toes, she tried to bring some life back into them as she took in the landscape before her. In the late afternoon sun, Mairead could make out Stirling Castle on the rise to the east, the town below visible with the grey stone of the buildings a shadow.

The castle stood proud on the hill, guarded on three sides by rocky cliff faces. The fortress commanded a view over the Forth and her father always told her it was the true seat of power in Scotland. Whoever controlled Stirling Castle could control the crossings of the river and so the access to the Highlands and wilds in the north. Clan Erskine's seat of power had always been in this area and Alloa Tower stood watch over the crossing to Fife. Now, she would be at the very heart of the Erskine lands, and she smiled knowing that this was her chance to prove her worth as the mistress of a large household.

The summons had come unexpectedly, delivered by a messenger to the lodge on the edge of the Mar Estates. A letter from her husband James asking that she make haste to join him. He had been given stewardship of his uncle's family home, and she was needed to run the household. Mairead had been delighted, as the third daughter in a Campbell household, her marriage to James had been made to strengthen the ties of alliance between the two clans. She had made a good match and being the laird's representative in a small town had offered her comfort and security.

Raised to understand the rules of hospitality, duty and honour, James had been impressed by his wife's grace and composure. She was more than capable of running a household too. Her ability to read, write and reckon had been useful when the tithes were to be collected. This brought her to the attention of John Erskine, the clan chieftain, a man who recognised potential and knew how to turn it to his advantage. James was an experienced soldier and had proven himself able to lead the men. Together, they were a useful asset to the Erskines. This new elevation was unexpected but it honoured them both and she meant to play her part well. For James, to show his uncle their worth and make him proud.

Riding in the company of two of the Erskine household guards and her serving woman, Murren, they had been able to make the journey from the Mar Estates in the northeast quickly. In her saddle bags, she had the essentials along with her best cloak and gown. Mairead had arranged for the rest of their belongings to follow. Eager to take up her new duties, she had kept pressure on the guards to move with haste. Her body ached and her eyes were gritty with dust from the road, but she was almost there. Another hour or so of riding and they would be within sight of the tower house. She sat a little straighter in the saddle and kicked the roan mare into a canter, determined to make a good impression at her new home. The guards still flanking the women became more relaxed now they were in friendly territory, moving their swords to their backs as they matched her pace.

The village around the tower was bustling as Mairead arrived. The doors of the forge were wide open and in the orange glow of the furnace the smith was working a blade, the ringing of the hammer carried clearly through the night air. The boys at the bellows gave her curious glances as she slowed her horse to a walk. The familiar sounds of the village and smells of peat smoke and midden soothed the flutter in her stomach. A woman feeding geese and chickens scrambled to move them, squawking indignantly, from the path of the horse. She dipped Mairead a curtsey. Mairead smiled warmly in response as she switched her reins to one hand and smoothed a red curl back behind her ear.

As the party came to a halt and the guards dismounted, Mairead had time to take in the size of the tower and the extent of the house behind it. The house had only been finished a couple of years ago and was said to be as fine as any in Scotland. James had told her about the design for it and that his uncle had been inspired by the buildings he had seen in London and Versailles. It was a much larger household than she had left in Kildrummy and similar to the size of her family home in Argyll, where her father oversaw the Campbell Estates along the western coast as brother to the chieftain.

James strode out to the courtyard and gave his wife a childish grin. She was pleased to see it. Being, as she was two days earlier than expected, she had hoped he would not be angry at her impatience. It was that smile that had won her over in the days before their wedding and she returned it with her own shy smile. For all his broad shoulders and height, he was still awkward and nervous around her. Keen to please and make her laugh. They had grown to like each other quickly and over the early months of their marriage, it had developed into an easy playful affection which was now deep love and respect.

At nineteen, Mairead was only two years younger than James and they looked well together. Both tall and red-haired, Mairead's slight frame was a contrast to James' strong and muscular one. He took her waist, lifted her down from the horse, and then steadied her for a moment as the feeling returned to her feet. Holding her hand, James led her towards the wooden arched door of the tower.

'Welcome to your new home,' he murmured, handing her the large bunch of keys on an ornate silver ring.

The keys to the store cupboards and coffers were hers to keep and wear as a symbol of her authority. She took them eagerly, feeling their weight and admiring the pattern of thistles winding around a Celtic knot. James smiled proudly as he saw her delight in the new responsibilities.

In the great hall, the tables were being laid for the evening meal. The fires were laid ready to provide warmth against the chill of the evening and the yellow tallow candles waited to be lit. The hall was lime-washed and had wood-panelled floors which echoed as they walked. Used to the draughty expanse of the great hall in Kildrummy Castle and the cold stone floors of their home, this felt different. Warmer and less like a fortress. A woman approached and curtsied to Mairead. Her hair was tied back with a piece of cloth, blond apart from a wide streak from the left temple which was the colour of birch bark. The woman raised her eyes to meet Mairead's and she smiled.

'I can show your woman to your rooms and help her unpack, mistress. I've water coming for a bath too. You'll be wanting a soak after your journey?' she asked.

'Yes, thank you,' Mairead replied and turning to Murren said, 'You can go with...?'

'I'm Widow Kellie, mistress, but the Lady Frances called me Jeannie,' she supplied.

Mairead nodded and gave instructions for Murren to lay out her gown for the evening meal.

Her attention returned to the hall, and she moved toward the tapestries. Embroidered with rich threads of green and red, those along the left and right of the hall bore the Erskine Crest and the words of the family motto 'Je Pense Plus,' *I think more*, in a thread of cream. At the end of the great hall behind the dais, the tapestries depicted a boar hunt. A maiden stood watching the knight on his white horse throw a spear and then the boar lying prone surrounded by dogs and men. This, Mairead knew, had been a gift to John Erskine from the late Queen Anne. A sign of favour from the Royal household to their secretary of state. She wondered if it remained here now because of the Chieftain's affection for the Queen or as a reminder of the power he had held. James often described his uncle as a canny old fox. She decided to wait until she was alone with her husband to ask why it was, she who now held the keys to Alloa Tower.

The curious glances continued as James led her through the hall to the house beyond. The candlelight flickered as James led them along the corridor, his frame obscuring the light from the room at the end. Mairead held her skirts up as dust and mud dried and flaked away from them. She was aware in this close proximity to James that she smelled earthy from the horse with a sour undertone from the exertion of the riding. Her back ached and she thought longingly of the warm water in the bath that awaited her. As they entered the room, a man approached to inform James of a messenger arriving.

'Mistress,' the man said, acknowledging her with a bow of his head before striding back across the room.

'I'll show you your room and leave you to rest,' James said, taking her hand.

He was quiet as he led the way to the east side of the building and Mairead watched him carefully, concerned at the change. He held himself tight, shoulders squared as if bracing himself. Gone now was the boyish smile, she thought that he looked older somehow. The dark circles under his eyes deepened and his jaw clenched, showing a strain she hadn't noticed in her joy at arriving. At the door, he stopped to allow her to enter ahead of him. Stepping forward, she was met by Murren who said the bath was almost drawn and described all of the luxuries within the room. The words came spilling out so quickly in her excitement that they sounded to Mairead like the buzz of a bee. She was barely listening anyway and looked over her shoulder for James, who had gone.

A wave of exhaustion swept over her, and her legs became weak. Making her way to the bed, she sat down and took in the room. The bed and furniture were made of a dark and highly polished wood that shone a deep, rich red in the light. The walls were covered in paper the colour of a clear spring sky, and in the pillars of light from the candle sticks, Mairead could make out the shape of leaves appearing to climb the wall. She reached out to touch the velvet smoothness in wonder as she had never seen a room so fine.

Two portraits hung on the walls, but the light was too faint to make out anything other than the outlines of a seated figure, with what looked like a child resting on her knee. This was the room of the lady of the house. It was now her responsibility to see her new home run well. Mairead pulled her knees up to her chest and rested her head on them, feeling for a moment very alone. [OBJ]

CHAPTER 9

JEANNIE

Carrying the last of the buckets of warm water into the room, Jeannie saw the young woman sat on the bed, curled in on herself. *So slight and delicate, barely more than a child*, Jeannie thought with a pang of sympathy. The wooden tub in front of the fire steamed gently as she lifted the linen sheet back and tipped in the water. Jeannie had positioned herself discreetly with her back turned towards the girl, offering her some privacy to prepare for the bath and to compose herself.

She reached then into the pocket of her apron and brought out a small bag of fragrant herbs, adding them to the water. The smell of bog myrtle rose with the steam, fragrant and slightly woody. It would help ease the aching muscles and relax the mind. Jeannie pulled the linen back across the top of the bath to keep the water warm and turned to Mairead.

'I sent Murren along to the kitchens for a meal and a rest, mistress,' she said. 'The cook, Alais, will see she's fed, and I can help you wash your hair or dress if you would like.'

'Thank you,' replied Mairead, then hesitated.

Jeannie had seen the flicker of irritation in the other woman's face when she had spoken and thought she might refuse the offer of help. Then Mairead drew herself up, raising her chin slightly.

'Some help to wash my hair is all I need. Murren can be fetched to help me dress,' she said guardedly.

Jeannie nodded in acknowledgement of the instruction. Whilst Mairead stepped into the bath, Jeannie returned to the fire where she lifted an iron kettle onto the hook above the flames, setting the water to boil for tea or to top up the bath if needed. She gathered the soap, jug, and comb in thoughtful silence, wondering how much this young woman knew about why she had been summoned to take over the running of this household.

With a gentle word to Mairead, she scooped a jug of water and poured it over the thick red hair and began to work the soap into a rich lather. The woman sat with her arms wrapped around her knees as her hair was rinsed over and over. The cascading water broke the quiet and removed the need for any conversation. When the water ran clear, Jeannie touched Mairead's shoulder before taking the hair and twisting it at the nape of her neck. Jeannie held the hair up as Mairead sat back against the side of the tub and Jeannie let the hair flow over the side as she worked the comb through from scalp to ends, teasing out the knots. At last, Jeannie saw the tension begin to leave. With herbs and heat of the water doing their job the young woman's shoulders softened and she sighed gently.

On the fire, the kettle began to hiss. Jeannie stood and reached for the cloths to cover her hand as she removed it and set it on the hearthstone. The new stone was still smooth and the same grey hue as the others on surrounding the fireplace. A contrast to the blackened stones in the tower which were pitted and worn with use. Jeannie prepared an infusion of chamomile flowers and leaves which she left to steep.

'Will I fetch your woman now, mistress?' Jeannie asked.

Mairead's eyes fluttered open as she replied, 'I'll soak here a while yet. At least whilst the water is hot.'

'Drink this,' Jeannie said, handing a cup of the infusion to Mairead who sniffed at it and wrinkled her nose. 'Chamomile flowers and leaves from the Myrtle. It'll help the aches better than wine or ale will.'

Jeannie was aware of Mairead's eyes on her as she set about airing the linen for drying in front of the fire and tidying away the jug and soap. She crossed the room to place the comb beside the clean shift and dress laid out ready for the younger woman.

'You are from the clan estates in the north, Widow Kellie?' Mairead asked. 'Your speech is like those in Kildrummy.'

'Aye.' Jeannie nodded. 'My husband Duncan and I came with the laird and Lady Margaret, the laird's first wife. When Duncan passed, my place was here.'

'What is your place here?' Mairead asked.

'I attended to Lady Frances and the laird. I help the old and the sick. Mind the herb garden and the still.'

'A healer then?' Mairead asked.

Jeannie followed the other woman's gaze to the tea and herbs in the bath and gave a small shrug of her shoulders. It was not a title she claimed with strangers. That word could be dangerous still. Even in these parts. Especially to a widow living alone and favoured by the laird.

Mairead handed the cup back to Jeannie and stood up abruptly, clearly discomfited. In her haste to step out of the bath her leg caught in her chemise, and she pitched forward. Jeannie caught the top of her arm with a tight grip.

'Steady now, lass,' she said, bracing Mairead as the woman recovered and stepped from the tub. 'You've had a long ride and you'll likely be ready for a meal.'

Mairead gave her a weak smile as she stepped behind the screen. Jeannie handed over the warmed linen sheet for Mairead to dry herself and, taking the wet line shift, noticed the bright red mark just above the hem. Wordlessly she poured the cooling water from the kettle into the bowl for washing and put in a cloth ready to clean the wound made by the edge of the tub. She picked up the fresh chemise and draped it over the side of the screen. Mairead reached for it and pulled it over her head.

'I'll see to that cut before I fetch Murren,' Jeannie said. It wasn't a question, and she saw Mairead stiffen slightly at the note of command.

Jeannie put a chair in front of the fire and beckoned Mairead to sit. The younger woman lifted the soft chemise to her knees exposing a raised welt and a deep graze. The blood was still streaming from the area where the skin had lifted. Jeannie held the cloth firmly to the cut and tightened her hold on the back of the leg as Mairead winced. For a few minutes, the women both watched the flames in silence broken only by the crackle of the log as it burned down.

Jeannie removed the cloth and checked the leg to see that the bleeding had stopped. She nodded with satisfaction. The blood-stained cloth dripped as she placed it into the bowl. Three dots landed on the hearthstone and drew together, forming a crimson pool against the cold stone. A chill spread through the room and a thorn of fear prickled in Jeannie's heart. The moment passed and Jeannie wiped the stone clean, trying to erase the lingering oddness. She glanced anxiously at Mairead who remained staring into the fire, lost deep in her own thoughts.

Jeannie thought again how young the lass looked sat in the chair with a shawl pulled tight around her shoulders and wondered how she would cope with what was ahead of her. The men were stationed around the tower on watches and messengers arrived at all hours of the day and night. It wasn't a household the girl would have charge of, but a garrison. She threw another log on the fire, sending up a shower of red sparks that jolted Mairead from her thoughts.

'I'll send your woman along now to help you dress and be back later to bandage the leg,' Jeannie said.

'It is fine. Don't trouble yourself,' Mairead replied.

'It will be slower to heal if it catches on your skirts and rubs.' Jeannie waved away her protest. 'More painful too.'

Mairead thanked her for the bath as she was collecting the bowl and wet linens. Pausing at the door, Jeannie turned back to the fire.

'If you'll heed my advice, mistress,' she said, gesturing to the bath, 'take such comforts as you can now.'

Mairead met Jeannie's eye, her expression set into a hard glare.

'It might be wise, Widow Kellie, to keep your counsel for those that ask for it,' she said.

Jeannie reeled from the anger in the words. She tried to read the other woman's face, but she had turned it back toward the fire.

'As you say, mistress,' Jeannie said, keeping her voice level.

Leaving the room and pulling the door closed behind her Jeannie's mind raced. Had she imagined the venom in the word 'wise'? She had only been trying to help the lass.

Handing the bowl and linens to a passing maid, she walked slowly towards the kitchen where Alais was busily preparing the platters to send out to the great hall. The cook greeted her with a nod before returning to the preparations. Jeannie entered the still room at the back of the kitchen. The room where soaps, medicines and herbs were prepared. She didn't need a light to find her way. It was her place. She knew exactly where to find what she needed and reached into a willow basket on the shelf for a bandage.

A quiet word with one of the kitchen maids led her to Murren who was sitting tucked in a corner, taking in the scene, all but forgotten. Jeannie approached and gave instruction for Mairead's leg to be bandaged and then bathed again in the morning. The woman went gratefully back to her mistress, awed by the bustle of the large kitchen and Jeannie, pulling her bottom lip between her teeth, watched as she went.

Jeannie leant with her back against the table, massaging her temples when Alais approached her.

'Is all well, Jeannie?' she asked, wiping her hands on her apron.

'Aye. The new mistress has a wee cut on her leg is all,' she replied, adding, 'I've a sore head and no mind to sit in the hall tonight,' to forestall any further questions from Alais.

'Sit here a while, when the young Erskine comes down to his dinner the kitchen will be quiet. We can eat together then,' said Alais.

'I'll not put you to any trouble, you've a household to feed,' Jeannie replied and squeezed her friend's hand. 'I've broth at home. Early to bed will do me good I think.'

Alais motioned for Jeannie to stay put a moment as she took a loaf from the basket and a hunk of cheese from the board on the table. Handing them over, she gave her friend a long look before the sight of a man in riding breeches trailing mud across the floor sent her hurrying to scold him and chase him away. Jeannie took the chance to slip out, needing time to be alone and to think.

It had been long years since the tower had been garrisoned like this. Not since before the union of the crowns had there been so many clansmen and men at arms stationed here. The laird had fallen out of favour with the new King George, that much she knew. He was never a man to be underestimated but the wheel would surely turn, as it always did, and see him back on top. Her mind drifted back to the angry exchange between the earl and young James. He had assumed command as he'd been told and the weight of it had taken the easy nature and smile of the lad turning into a furrow of worry on his brow. Anger at being left behind? The talk in the village was that it must be hard on the lad to be left here when his kin and friends went north with the earl. Jeannie didn't think so. James was a lad who knew his duty to his laird and he looked like a man wrestling with it.

Jeannie banked the fire and sat in the high-backed chair with a solid wooden seat and carved back. She had eaten her supper of broth and cheese at the table, but her mind was too full now to rest. The chair had been Duncan's and although not as comfortable as her own, sitting in it made her feel closer to him. Beside her she had placed her basket of yarn and needles. Knitting kept her hands busy and allowed her mind to work at a problem.

The words of Mairead, the young mistress, had been turning over and over in her head since leaving the bed chamber. *The lassie had looked so dainty and alone curled up on the bed*, Jeannie thought. She had felt sorry for the young woman and meant to offer comfort. A friendly face amongst the strangers. Perhaps even help the lass find her feet. Taking on a big household must be daunting, but it seemed that wee body contained a spirit of iron. The girl had a bite like a midge. Jeannie knew she'd have to try and smooth the water and tread lightly. The last thing she wanted was the new mistress to think she was an interfering besom.

Jeannie looked around her home, it was simple but dry and warm. When she and Duncan had come here to serve the laird, they had been given the house in the centre of the village. Duncan was the Tacksman collecting the rents and managing the estate around the tower. Not an Erskine by blood but instead by fealty. The Kellie and Erskine families were part of the same line whose roots ran deep in the wild Highlands. Duncan and the laird had been lads together, their loyalty went deeper than their oaths. It was in honour of this bond that Jeannie had been allowed to stay in the house. Her home for twenty-four winters. It was her lot as the wife of the Tacksman to help those on the estate. More than once, the information gleaned from the women had proved useful to Duncan. He had been a fair man and with Jeannie's help, he made sure nobody gave more than they could afford, and the clan folk got what help was needed. Little disputes were managed before they became big ones and so the estate worked no matter where their laird was.

Over the years Jeannie had carved out her own place within the tower and the community of villages around it. Duncan often called her 'sharp as a tack' because she was quick to learn, and her keen eyes missed nothing. She had some skill with herbs and was called upon to tend to the wounded and the sick. John Erskine was a man who valued wit and skill, and so Jeannie had become a part of the inner circle within the family. She had attended First Lady Margaret and then Lady Frances, proving herself to be both useful and level-headed. A woman known to keep her word and tell a hard truth. It had won her the respect of some, but others were wary believing that she had too much influence and freedom.

She'd been young enough to marry again when Duncan died, and still was, but when the Lady Frances had offered to speak for her, Jeannie had been firm. She wanted no other. Her two sons, now grown men, would see her provided for, of that she was certain. *And what other protection did she need in the household of John Erskine?* she had reasoned. Lady Frances had pushed the matter no further and the laird had let it be as a kindness to the widow of his friend.

With the harsh words from the young mistress, Jeannie had realised that her position may be less than certain. Her needles clicked as her thoughts raced. The laird and his lady had gone, and now the long shadow of another war was creeping closer to the tower. She had all this to lose. Her home, her position, and the small freedoms she had bought for herself through hard work and service. For the first time since Duncan had gone, Jeannie felt fear about the future.

CHAPTER 10

MAIREAD

The great hall was a wall of noise as Mairead entered. The hum of conversation and scraping of benches quietened as her presence was noticed. Elbows nudged neighbours and whispers sent a wave of hush from the dais that rolled down the length of the three long tables at which the villagers and household were seated. She felt the heat rise in her cheeks and willed herself to move forwards without haste. Heads turned and eyes watched with open curiosity as she approached the smaller of the two chairs in the centre of the family table. Mairead looked around for James, but he was not in the hall. A man approached from the left of the table with a small bow of greeting. He was the Erskine retainer for the tower and attended on James. His name was Gavin. He was a short and swarthy man who walked with a slight limp. His role was to see that messages were answered, and orders were relayed.

'James sends his apologies, mistress,' he said quietly. 'He is writing a report for his uncle which must return with the messenger. It would be best to start the meal.'

Mairead gave him a small smile of thanks as Gavin gestured for her chair to be pulled out. She nodded to those waiting to serve the meal and then sat down.

The large platters of roast venison, baskets of domed wholemeal loaves and steaming root vegetables were placed first on the family table. Jugs of ale and red wine were offered by the serving lads who weaved around those carrying the food. This was the well-rehearsed routine of a household used to large gatherings. When the earl was in residence the family ate meals cooked in the French fashions as they did at court and in London. James had told Mairead of the visits from English nobility to the tower since the house had been completed.

According to stories, the Stewart king had once stayed here too as a boy. Tonight, they ate a hearty meal, simply prepared, to welcome the new mistress. This was a gesture that fit her new position and Mairead felt a tingle of pride and excitement in her spine. For the folk living on the laird's estate, meals like this came only on feast days or for celebrations.

Purple and yellow carrots glazed with honey and roasted added colour to the tables. The rich smell of roast mutton mingled with the oily tallow of the candles and the mass of bodies in the hall. The benches were full this evening. Here and there families sat, children on their laps, waiting patiently. Once the platters had been arranged on the table, the minister stood from his seat next to her. The hall fell silent but for a crying baby, and heads bowed respectfully as he led a short prayer of thanks for the food. Mairead picked up her knife and the family began to eat. The noise of conversation and laughter rose again as the platters were served to the rest of the hall.

Mairead shuffled herself back in the chair a little, trying not to draw attention to her discomfort. She sipped her wine and took in the sight of her new household. As she looked along the family table at the other senior members of the household, Mairead saw one or two faces of men who had come with James. As he was rising in position in the clan, so were they. Her husband had a good-natured way about him and was always at the centre of any game or contest. His warmth drew others, and she was glad he had these familiar faces around him now. This is how the bonds of kinship and loyalty were made amongst the men of the clan.

It was different amongst the women. She would make a point of thanking the cook tomorrow she thought, knowing that was an alliance she needed if the household was to be run well. As a young lad appeared to fill her cup, she pointed to James' empty plate and gave instructions for it to be filled and kept warm for him. The young lad bobbed between two of the men to spear slices of meat with a fork whilst they teased him by pulling it out of his way laughing. Gavin cuffed the closest around the ear playfully.

'Let the lad alone, he needs to get James a dish filled whilst there is still some left. Mind your manners now,' he said, pointing his fork towards Mairead as reminder to them.

Having filled the plate, the lad retreated to the relative safety of the kitchen.

Mairead lingered over the food, hoping that James would join her. The minister, John Dunn, asked politely of her journey and where her kinsfolk was from. She answered him and looked out over the hall. She could not see the Widow Kellie among the tables. Mairead had a moment of satisfaction at that. Although, she thought, she would have liked for the woman to see her now – in her place of honour at the family table. Casting her mind back to the conversation she wondered what the woman had meant by her advice to enjoy such comforts whilst she was able. The Lady Frances may have allowed the woman to offer advice and speak to her in such a forward manner, but she would not. She was a woman grown and not a child to be scolded or coddled.

The noise in the hall dulled as tables began to empty. People made their way to their beds or back to their duties. It was dark now and more candles were brought to the raised platform at the top of the hall, bathing it in a soft yellow glow that made the rest of the hall seem cavernous. Mairead saw James round the bottom of the spiral stair and called for his dinner. He had not yet seen her, his progress into the room halted by another of the men from his garrison, and she noted the shadow of fatigue on his face. As he approached, she smiled at him and handed him his cup.

Gavin had engaged the younger men at the table in a game of cards and they were deep in concentration. With the minister gone to his prayers, they had a moment together at last. As her husband ate, Mairead told him of her journey down from Kildrummy and the news from the houses they had stayed in. James pulled her chair toward him, so their heads were close together. His plate now cleared Mairead watched thoughtfully as he cleaned his hands in the lavender scented bowl, she offered. James reached out and gently touched the end of her braid draped across her shoulder leaning closer to breathe the floral scent. Her heart swelled at the moment of softness in the growing dark of the hall.

'You smell like a lady of court,' he said. 'That'll be Jeannie's soap. She's known for it.'

'It's a fine soap I'm sure,' Mairead said with a hint of annoyance.

James caught the tone and frowned at his young wife.

'We have had no time to talk,' he said, 'we can go up to the solar and sit by the fire. You can tell me your news.'

'Aye, I'd like that,' she said, sensing her opportunity to ask the question that had been on her mind since James had summoned her here.

In the solar, two chairs were set beside the fire. A brown speckled earthenware jug sat on the table with two matching beakers so simple in their design. It reminded Mairead of the shell of a hen egg. There was no sign of the silver goblets they had drank from in the hall up here. The tapestries that lined the walls were in rich hues of greens, browns and reds that echoed the heathers and hillsides she had ridden through today. The light of the candles was not enough to make out the details of the scenes, but it felt more homely and less grand than anywhere else in the tower or house had seemed. This was a space for the family to gather at rest and play. A place they did not need to show off the wealth and standing of the Earldom of Mar. It reminded Mairead of their home in Kildrummy and for a moment she wondered when she would see it again.

Seated by the fire with their wine served warmed and smelling of cloves, they both looked into the flames, content for now just to be together. Mairead lifted her feet onto the small, embroidered stool in front of her and her skirts rose away from her ankles. The bandage had a dark stain where the wound underneath had been leaking. James noticed it and knelt to take a look. Mairead winced as he lifted her leg and seeing that he had caused her pain he placed her foot back on the stool and stood.

'What is amiss?' he asked.

'It is nothing' she said dismissively. 'A cut. I caught in on the tub after my bath.'

'It needs care, Mairead, the bandage is bloody. I'll send for Jeannie to clean and dress it for you.' He turned to leave.

'You'll do no such thing!' Mairead said her temper rising. 'I'm sure there is no need to bother the Widow Kellie at this hour.'

'Mairead...' he began, his own voice rising in response.

'She's seen it. She was there when I stumbled.' Mairead's tone was clipped.

James looked at the untidy bandage and back at the face of his wife his confusion evident.

Mairead's cheeks burned as she remembered the way she had sent the woman away. Murren had returned with a bandage and had done her best, but Mairead had been so impatient that she'd made it hard for her to dress the leg well. She had berated Murren for leaving her unattended for so long. The bandage had been working its way loose since and Mairead could feel the cut as she walked.

'I can manage,' she said, trying to reassure him.

'What is this about?' James asked sharply. 'Jeannie has the knowing of healing and the herbs. For as long as I can remember she's dressed cuts and looked after the sick. She set my leg when I fell from my horse as a lad. I'll send for her in the morning.'

He stood over her with his hand on her shoulder. Mairead jumped to her feet and raised her chin defiantly, her temper blazing.

'You sent for me to run this household.' She took the ring of keys from her belt and held them out, voice louder with every word. 'I have said I can manage and manage I will. The Widow

Kellie will be sent for if I need her. It is clear that she should know her place!'

'It seems she is not the only one. Enough woman!' James shouted, his face cold and stern. He ran his hand across his face wearily. 'I don't want to quarrel with you, wife,' he said softly.

James reached out to her, but she turned away. Embarrassment and fury warred within her, leaving her shaking and with tears stinging her eyes. She fought them back and stood straight and resolute.

James picked up the jug and refilled his glass as he watched his wife. He began to explain how Jeannie's husband, Duncan, had collected the rents and managed the estate. The Tacksman here when his uncle served in the English parliament. Jeannie had looked after the bairns and the elderly. She'd delivered most of the babies born here including wee Frances, the laird's daughter. He moved gently to stand behind Mairead, wrapping his arms around her narrow shoulders and kissed her on the top of the head.

'There is no harm in Jeannie,' he said soothingly. 'She knows every inch of this estate. The families. Seek her out for information and help. It'll go easier for you that way.'

James seemed satisfied that her silence was agreement and the end of their argument. Mairead allowed her spine to soften into his embrace unwilling to push him further for now. There was nothing to be gained from it she knew. *What hold*, she wondered, *did this woman have on the Erskine's? Why was she of such value?*

As the clock ticked forward Mairead's thoughts returned to the question nagging at her since the letter from James had arrived. *Why were they here and what was happening?* She could contain it no longer and cleared her throat.

'What is amiss with the laird? she asked softly.

'He's fallen out of favour with King George,' James replied and with a deep sigh continued, 'My uncle couldnae bear the insult.'

Mairead listened carefully as James explained that the wheel of politics had turned again and as a favourite of the old Queen and a tory peer, the laird was cast aside. No longer the secretary of state for Scotland or a member of the privy council, his influence and power waned. Then the King had gone so far as to snub the earl publicly.

'His pride will be the ruin of him,' James said sadly and shook his head.

James fell into silence as fresh wine was brought and the candles changed. Such caution in her husband was new to her but she held her tongue. It gave Mairead time to consider what she had heard. Her husband's uncle was thrawn and she could imagine only too well his anger at the insult. A man who had lent his support to the Act of Union, uniting the Scottish and English crowns, only eight years before. A laird whose clan was one of the most ancient and powerful in Scotland. She thought she understood now why they were here. Having senior members of the family in residence at all the great estates of the Earldom and the clan lands was a reminder to the parliament and so to the King just how much power he held. The complicated weaving of oaths and alliances between clans stretched back generations. The warp formed through centuries of coming together for profit or defence. The weave was made through marriages that, like her own, strengthened the ties. Her own uncle was the Duke of Argyll and Chief of the Campbell clan. Although, as she knew well, the power of the clans was not absolute and depended on the monarch.

Her thoughts turned for a moment to her home on the western coast. Saddell Castle had been a stronghold of the MacDonalds but had been taken from them by James VI and given to the Campbells. The Campbells kept it occupied to deter any attempt to reclaim it. Mairead had lived there until her marriage to James. She was the youngest of three sisters and they had gone to their new households before her. Mairead remembered the open skies around her home and still missed the salty tang of the sea and the waves crashing against the shore.

When they were alone again, James picked up the thread of his tale. He too had been lost in his thoughts and his words came slowly, his voice thick with tiredness. They spoke of Lady Frances and the children being safely in Braemar and of the endless lists of commands and requests that came by messenger almost daily now. Mairead rose and lifted the jug to refill their cups, and James placed his hand on her arm to stop her.

'I'll need a clear head tomorrow,' he said quietly. 'My uncle has called in the clansmen.'

The statement was delivered softly but Mairead could see the clenching and unclenching of his fist at his side. Her heart lurched and her mouth went dry.

'To what end?' she said, her voice sounded shrill to her own ears, and she swallowed hard.

'A show of strength. A reminder to the King that Scotland is a long way from London and that the Scots first loyalty is to their clan and kin,' James replied.

'The laird is baiting the King?' she asked, thinking aloud. 'Surely he'll not be so rash?'

It was the way of the clans that an insult to the laird was an insult to them all and something as grave as this must not go unanswered. John Erskine was a man who understood the game of power and politics. Surely, he wouldn't risk it all to make a point.

'My uncle is wily. He will have more than one plan.'

Outside, Mairead heard the approach of horses, hooves clattering on the cobbled stones and the shout of guards demanding the rider identify himself. James stood quickly and moved to the window. The light of the torches showed two riders, their horses stamping and steaming eager for the water trough and stable. With an apologetic look, he straightened his shirt stays and went down to receive the messenger. Mairead lifted a candle and made her way quietly down the stairs. At the turn on the stair on the floor below, she heard voices in an urgent and hushed debate. She couldn't quite make out the words and lingered a moment, caught in her rising anxiety. Her candle flickered in the breeze, casting her shadow on the wall and Gavin's face appeared in the doorway to the charter room.

'Mistress,' he said loudly, causing silence to fall in the room beyond. 'I'll see you to your room.'

Mairead hurried behind him trying to keep up with his striding pace and was relieved when she saw Murren rushing towards them. She thanked Gavin curtly and, arriving at her room, closed the door behind her with relief.

With Murren's help she undressed and changed into her night shift before sending the woman to her bed. Mairead sat down on the bed and undid the bandage on her leg. The skin around her cut was red but it didn't seem, as far as she could see in this light, to be bleeding. Making a pad from a folded handkerchief, she rebound the cut with a clean strip of cloth. She would need to see to it in the morning.

Tired though she was, Mairead's head raced with the events of the day. Her first day as the Mistress of Alloa Tower had been trying. Tomorrow she would begin as she intended to continue by taking charge. *James had his own troubles to carry*, she thought, he looked older than he had when she had seen him last, he would need her to keep the household in order. She could perhaps take some of that weight from his shoulders.

CHAPTER 11

LAUREN

L auren sat in her office at the university and watched as the crowds of students milled around from the window. The university campus with its green spaces, shaded woodland and loch was at its most splendid during this time of the year. The leaves and shrubs were still in full foliage but the vibrant red of the acers reflected on the mercurial surface of the loch was breathtaking. The cygnets whose nests sat in the reeds were still fluffy and grey but becoming more curious about the humans in their environment. The sun shone and the students had brought a renewed energy to the place. Some chattered excitedly to their friends and others wandered more uncertainly looking down at their maps of the campus.

Orientation days were always like this, a mix of people keen to start university life and be away from their families and those who were resigned to simply making the most of it. There would be plenty of graduate and final-year students who had been conscripted to help with directions and support in exchange for vouchers for the food court. She saw one of her own students standing at the edge of the car park wearing his bright green 'volunteer' t-shirt which declared that he was 'here to help' but apparently nobody had told him that. He looked thoroughly disinterested with his shoulders slumped leaning against a lamp post.

She thought back to her own days in halls of residence when they were divided by gender. House masters or house mistresses lived in the ground floor accommodation to safeguard the physical and moral welfare of the students. That had been the 1980s and such things were unthinkable now. Besides, they had not exactly prevented the shenanigans they were intended to deter. *Well at least not in my case*, Lauren thought, smiling to herself at the memories of those early relationships and discovery.

Still, she would miss teaching the first years this semester. Not the general chaos of the first couple of weeks as the timetables settled, and the students stopped switching modules around. That drove her to distraction. The faculty had taken her off the course list for undergraduates to enable her to focus on the Fractal Lines project. She would keep her post-graduate students and deliver a fieldwork module on the historic sites. Retaining the supervision of the doctorate students had been a non-negotiable for her. She thought of Tom; he deserved this opportunity after all he had been through around the Douglas papers. He had the makings of a truly talented historian. Thankfully the legacy work had been the part of her proposal the dean particularly liked. High-profile opportunities were few and far between, but this would benefit the current cohort and attract other candidates. So, the funding wheel turned, and the faculty budget survived another round of cuts. It benefitted them all.

Her email inbox pinged, and Lauren opened the tab. It was from the National Library of Scotland and was a zip file containing copies of correspondence to and from the Earl of Mar during the latter part of 1715. She downloaded the file and scanned down the line of little yellow folder headings. Those concerning Scotland she would send on to Tom and his team for analysis and adding to the detailed timeline they were building.

The name of the final file caught her eye, *Personal Papers: Lady Frances*, and, intrigued, she clicked to open it. Thumbnail images appeared in a neat grid on her screen. A tingle of excitement swept through Lauren; this was the part of being a historian she loved. The anticipation. The hours spent pouring over documents, gathering fragments of detail, and chasing whisps of information, following their trail like fey lights through a forest. Pulling this together unravelled time and brought to life the people, places, and events as they had been. So much deeper than the bare dates and family trees.

She recalled the portrait hanging on the charter room wall. The painter had captured a frank expression and a sense of energy, Lady Frances Erskine looked as though she were about to stand and step out of the frame. So much more than the children she had borne, or dates of birth and death on a page. More than the family she came from and the one she was married into. Who was the real woman behind those intelligent eyes and aristocratic cheekbones? What was her story?

Lauren plugged her laptop into the large screen on the desk and opened the first image. It was a letter from another society lady. The handwriting on the embellished paper was neat and precise. It spoke of the small domestic news that such ladies shared in their correspondence. Of marriages made and babies safely delivered. The progress of a new garden taking shape and at the bottom, a small sketch of a dress, worn by a French courtier, which, having previously scandalised the court, was now the height of fashion. Only the final lines of the letter revealed anything of interest to the project. It read:

We continue to pray for your swift return to the court and that the earl may regain the King's favour.

It seemed that in July 1715 the earl, or Lady Frances at least, still had friends at the court in London. Had Frances known by then what was coming? How had she felt? Lauren tried to imagine a modern equivalent to the situation Frances had found herself in. How would it feel if Annie made a choice that would completely upend their lives from which there was no going back? Where everything and everyone they cared about was at risk. The stakes could not be higher, and Lauren found she couldn't think herself into that scenario. It was not something Annie would do, not in her nature, not how their relationship worked. Annie was her rock and her safe place. That had proved to be more valuable to Lauren these last few years than she had ever known it could. Sadly, it was all too easy to imagine it in other places. Other parts of her life. She shook her head, trying to free herself from the thought and the wash of heat that rose inside her at the injustice of it all.

The job of a historian, of course, was to be objective. To arrive at conclusions having fully considered all the facts and evidence. Lauren knew only too well that it was never that simple. Understanding what had happened also meant understanding why. Context was everything. Events were driven by a series of decisions made by people. People with all their messy and powerful emotions. There had to be room for curiosity and a deep empathy for all it means to be human. You had to think yourself into the situation facing another person and consider it from that perspective. Lauren knew that when you did this it opened the story from a completely different angle.

It was this that Klaus Leinster didn't seem to understand. Empathy and instinct were tools that were just as important as knowledge and reason. That was the difference between them, and he just couldn't see it. She could remain open to the possibility that she might be wrong, that she might not know as much as she thought. That changed the perspective and sometimes, just sometimes, it changed the narrative. Re-cast the characters in new roles where heroes became villains.

Lauren rubbed the small of her back and pulled her elbows back towards each other to stretch. *Too much sitting*, she thought as she scanned across the grid of images in front of her. On the third row down a file name caught her eye and she leant forward with interest. It read 'From Frances to 'Niece' at Alloa Tower'.

'Ah,' she said, thinking out loud, 'here we go. Let's see what you have to say for yourself, my lady, shall we?'

The image that appeared on the screen was another letter. The handwriting looked quite different from that in the other – it was larger, and the pen strokes were bolder. A more confident and flowing hand with flamboyant style in the letter at the start of each sentence. Delicate curls contrasted with the thicker and more defined lines and angles. The paper's mark could still be seen clearly in the centre at the top of the page, Lauren recognised it as the Erskine family crest.

Her bracelets tinkled as she shook them back from her wrists, leaning forward on her elbows to better see the screen. It was dated the first day of September 1715 and addressed simply to 'Dear Niece'. That struck Lauren as odd, and she pulled her notebook and pen towards her to make note of it. The first paragraph was pleasantries as would start any letter, although perhaps a little brief. At first glance, the letter was simply a list of things to remember and unsolicited advice about which merchants to use whilst Lady Frances was elsewhere. That in itself was odd. Surely a household of that size would have a steward and a cook who knew those things. There was little warmth or personal detail in the letter to imply a close connection between the two women. It read much more like a set of instructions.

Lauren tapped her biro on the notepad and then pulled up her timeline. On the 6 September 1715 John Erskine, Earl of Mar, raised the standard of the 'Old Pretender' and declared to the world that James VIII was the rightful King of Scotland. The call to arms for the Jacobites and the beginning of the uprising.

Lauren, frowning at the screen in puzzlement, read the letter again working through the problem in her head. There would have been messengers flying up and down Scotland gathering support, relaying information, and gathering intelligence. Messages that Erskine would not have wanted to be read by unfriendly eyes. This letter was so bland as to be of no real importance and yet it was sent and delivered.

'Why?' she asked aloud. 'Why would you send this letter, Frances?'

At the bottom of the page, Lady Frances had reminded her 'niece' of the responsibility of running the household at the clan family seat and wished her well. The letter had a stilted flow, as though much was being left unsaid, which Lauren couldn't reconcile with the poised handwriting. Not a single smudge or mistake. This had been penned with deliberate care and attention. On the personalised family stationery too. She scrolled back up to the top of the page and looked again at the crest she stopped. A slow dawning of realisation crept into her awareness.

'*Je Pense Plus. I think more,*' she read aloud. 'It's the motto!'

Her heart raced as she searched the clutter of her desk for her phone. The motto was the message! It was a warning and an instruction to James and his wife. Locating the phone in her cardigan pocket, she flicked through the contacts until she found Hazel.

'Hello? Listen, I think we've got something here. It's in a letter from your friend in the portrait,' Lauren said breathlessly. 'I'm sending an image of a document to your email. Where are you?'

Lauren held the phone sandwiched between her shoulder and her chin as she stuffed the folders back into her bag.

'At the tower? OK, I'm on my way.'

She uploaded the file to her email and sent it to Hazel and Tom. As she lifted her laptop into her bag she noticed, unfolded on the desk, the Earl of Mar's family tree. Scanning down the page she found James, the young nephew who had been stationed at Alloa Tower to watch over the crossing at the river Forth, and next to it the name of his wife, Mairead.

Well, my dear, she thought, *what did you make of that letter then?*

CHAPTER 12

JEANNIE

Jeannie knelt in the garden under the shade of the tower wall with a small knife in her hand and a cloth bag open. She leant forward and cut a stalk of comfrey, the woody stem thick with large green leaves and crowned with delicate lilac flowers. She placed it on the ground beside the bag, careful not to bruise the leaves which gave off a pungent smell and tainted the more delicate plants.

She had risen with the sun this morning to gather what she needed for a day in the still room. Her supplies of salves and ointments were getting low and the garden, now in full bloom, was ready for her to harvest. Jeannie always sent a small kist containing little jars and bottles of remedies to cure common ailments and illnesses with the laird and the lady when they travelled. Their unexpected journey north had left spaces on the shelves and cabinets. A day of preparing the plants for drying or boiling lay ahead of her and she sighed contentedly.

The herbal garden lay on the opposite side of the house to the kitchen garden and was mostly in shade for the warmest part of the day. It was cool and peaceful today and a welcome relief from the busyness within. Before coming outside, she had asked one of the lads in the kitchen to set the fire for her and fetch water fresh from the well. By now the room should be ready for her, although she was in no hurry to return to the heat.

As she entered through the door at the side of the kitchen, she placed her bag on the table and poured some water from the waiting bucket into the kettle then lifted it onto the hook over the fire. She saw Murren hovering in the doorway, peering into the back of the room. A dark tendril of hair had escaped from the white cap on her head, and she reached thin fingers up to tuck it back as Murren approached.

'Can you come and see to the mistress?' Murren asked. 'The cut on her leg is weeping and painful.'

Jeannie gave a quick nod and began to gather bandages, cloths, and little pots of ointment.

'Does the wound smell?' she asked.

'No, but it is very red and hot to the touch,' Murren answered.

The woman's colour was high and by the way she was wringing her hands in her apron, Jeannie judged she needed to keep them busy. She handed Murren a wooden bowl and instructed her to collect a jug of boiled water from the kitchens to take back with her. Murren nodded and as she turned to leave Jeannie caught her arm.

'The cut was not too deep. It will heal. Dinnae worry yourself, your mistress will be fine,' Jeannie said gently.

Murren chewed her bottom lip and nodded. Jeannie guessed that the other woman had been given a hard time of it over the bandaging and took pity on her.

'The skin will be easily irritated by anything that rubs it. There might be a wee bit of swelling too. It needs good padding and to be kept clean. You go on and I'll be along to tend to it,' she said gently.

When Murren had gone, Jeannie opened the cabinet and took out a small pot, the fabric of the lid held tightly in place with twine. Then she took the small knife and carefully removed a few of the leaves from the comfrey she had cut earlier. That would be useful steeped in water to help clean the wound again and cool the leg around it.

As Jeannie made her way across the house to the family living quarters, there was a change in the atmosphere of the garrison. The small groups she passed were in quiet conversation and not the usual cheerful trading of insults or games of cards and dice. As she passed a knot of clansmen dressed in their plaid and leather jerkins, she caught the gist of a hushed conversation with one man talking animatedly to the others. Jeannie heard him utter the word *cursed* before he was firmly shushed into silence by another who crossed himself. Jeannie didn't recognise the men and quickened her pace as she moved past them. There was a new watchfulness to those on guard duty as they stood straighter and more alert. Jeannie had seen this tower face threat before and recognised the tension in the faces of the men. An uneasy feeling crept along the back of her neck.

Jeannie knocked at the door to the lady's room, and Murren answered with a small smile before opening the door fully. Jeannie saw Mairead, with a ledger in her hands, sitting in the chair by the writing bureau. The bright morning light coming through the window created a pool of warmth around her. Her leg rested on a small wooden stool. Jeannie wished Mairead a good morning and took in the dark shadows under her eyes and her pale skin.

As she got closer, Jeannie could see the livid edges of the flap of skin torn by the rough edge of the wooden bathing tub. There was nothing to the young mistress and so the bone of the leg had borne the brunt of the knock. The area around it was raised with the beginnings of a purple bruise forming down the shin. Between the aches and pains from days of being jolted around on horseback and the stinging of the cut, it was easy to see why Mairead had found little rest the previous night. Jeannie took the comfrey leaves and crushed them gently against the side of the wooden bowl with a spoon. Next, she added the cooled water from the jug and placed a cloth in it to soak. She knelt by the chair placing the cloth gently on Mairead's leg and felt the woman stiffen. Her own nose wrinkled in distaste as a smell like horse manure engulfed her.

'The comfrey leaves are fresh this morning and the smell is stronger,' Jeannie said catching the other woman's horrified expression. 'It'll fade soon.'

Lifting the cloth away, Jeannie carefully checked the wound. There was no sign of the telltale greenish tinge or sickly-sweet smell that showed the wound had started to fester. Content that it was clean, she patted it dry as gently as she could and brought the small jar from her pocket. Removing the lid, she applied a greasy brown layer of the ointment to the shin bone. With as light a touch as she could manage, she went across the cut itself. Jeannie heard the small whimper and Mairead gripped the sides of chair. Looking up, she saw the woman's eyes closed and face turned away.

'I've just to dress it now,' Jeannie said as she stood and went to clean her hands. 'It will heal well I think.'

'Thank you,' the young woman replied. 'James tells me you have knack for mending bones and soothing bruises.'

Jeannie recognised this as an olive branch and laughed as she returned with the linens to pad and wrap the leg.

'Just as well with all these lads charging around the country getting themselves into mischief. Barely a week went by when they were young without a bloody nose or a knock to the ribs that needed tending,' Jeannie said, remembering fondly the long-limbed and clumsy young lad James had once been playing in the dirt and fields with her own sons.

Her thoughts returned to the shade of uncertainty growing around her in the tower and then back to her sons. Her eldest Angus, who was so like his father in stature, solid and strong, but more like her in his determination and quick mouth. Collum, on the other hand, was a gentler soul, thoughtful and steady. She wondered where they were and what this all meant for them. They had followed their laird to England. Angus was serving in the army and Collum as a clerk to the Courts of Justice. Unwilling to dwell on the niggling worry of a mother for her grown sons, she wound the bandage firmly round the leg and secured it tightly. It would need to be changed again in a few days and by then it would be much improved, Jeannie was sure.

A loud rap on the door revealed Gavin and Alais. Murren glanced over her shoulder to her mistress who held her hand up to indicate she needed a moment to prepare herself. Jeannie, understanding the unspoken dismay, smoothed Mairead's dress down to her ankles and placed the slippers onto her feet. Hooking the stool out of the way, she pushed it out of sight. Mairead gave her a grateful look and motioned to Murren to admit the waiting steward and cook.

As Jeannie collected her bowls and prepared to leave, she heard Mairead thank Alais for the meal the previous evening and enquire after the stores and provisions for the estate and for the men forming the garrison. Gavin, now seated at the small table behind the two women, made a list of the orders and instructions that were given by Mairead in a clear and authoritative tone. As Jeannie returned to the still room, she found herself approving of the way their young mistress had taken charge of the room. It was good that her thoughts had been of the strain on the household with so many extra mouths to feed. Perhaps she had judged Mairead Erskine too harshly.

Jeannie began to prepare the herbs she had gathered that morning with the quiet of the room allowing her to concentrate on the task at hand. She unhooked the rope at the wall and lowered the pulley rack down above the table. From it, she untied the stalks of meadowsweet now dried out. She took the pestle and mortar from the workbench and ground the leaves and sweet-smelling white flowers down into a powder that would help with pain. The rhythmic thump of the pestle soothed Jeannie's frayed nerves a little as work like this always did. Absorbing her worries and sending her frustrations down into the mortar to be ground away with the herbs. What she needed now was nutmeg to grate into the powder.

The kitchen was a hive of activity with the midday meal being prepared. A flash of red hair caught Jeannie's eye, and she saw Alais over by the spice cupboard showing their new mistress the stores. Unwilling to draw attention to herself, Jeannie went instead towards the well. The fine weather meant that square was busy with villagers and men from the garrison working outside to make the most of the sunshine. A group of women sat together on stools. They were bent over their washing tubs and chattered loudly as they worked. A cluster of small children played with sticks and stones at their feet.

The thud of hooves could be heard, and Jeannie stopped to watch as the horses galloped towards them. The rider in the lead pulled his reins to slow his mount but had left it too late. The horse snorted and danced sideways as it tried to avoid the livestock and people. A small lad of about four in a blue tunic took fright and fled towards his mother crossing the path of the horse. The horse reared up onto his hind legs, sides heaving with effort and foaming at the bit. The rider, caught off guard, was unseated and fell with a cry to the ground. The second horseman turned his horse sharply to avoid riding over his companion. For a heartbeat, everything went still as the fierce heat of the sun beat down on the scene. A scream galvanised Jeannie into action. The scream had come from a woman, the mother of the small lad, who sat stunned and silent on the floor holding his arm. Blood ran down his face. Jeannie hurried towards him.

Another woman came to comfort the mother who was sobbing whilst Jeannie checked the child over. Behind her, the horse was brought under control, and the rider helped to his feet. Furious, he strode towards them.

'What did ye think you were doing, boy?' he shouted sending spittle flying.

The boy's terrified silence infuriated him further and he raised his hand to strike. Jeannie shot to her feet and put herself between the man and the child who remained pale and silent behind her skirts.

'That lad should be whipped!' the man roared, now beyond all reason.

'He got a fright is all, he's a bairn for heaven's sake,' Jeannie said as calmly as she could.

The man's face was a livid red and he was so close she could smell the sourness on his breath. His knuckles were white on the leather of his belt.

'Out of the way, woman!' he shouted.

Jeannie stood her ground, eyes locked defiantly with his. The man's lip curled in a snarl, and he lifted his hand again bringing it down across Jeannie's cheek. The force of it threw Jeannie's head back and a ringing began in her ears, she probed the inside of her mouth with her tongue and tasted the sharp metallic tang of blood. There were gasps and shocked cries from the watching crowd and then a voice, high and clear carried across the space.

'What is the meaning of this?' Mairead demanded as she made her way towards, them taking in the scene.

The rider turned to her ready with an angry retort and stopped short when he recognised her.

'Mistress Erskine,' he said. 'I've come with a message from the earl.' He pointed to the leather pouch he wore over his shoulder. 'This boy spooked my horse, and it threw me. The horse near broke a leg!' The anger was returning to the man's voice.

'He took a fright, mistress, and ran to his Mammy. He meant...' began Jeannie.

'I mean to see his hide tanned,' the man continued.

'You rode in here like all the devils of hell were behind you, don't you dare blame the lad!' Jeannie's voice rose in outrage.

'Enough,' said Mairead sharply. 'I'll hear no more. The lad will be dealt with.'

'Take this man and his companion to James at once please,' Mairead said turning over her shoulder to Gavin.

'Mistress...' began Jeannie.

'Enough, Widow Kellie. See to the lad and his mother.' With that, Mairead turned on her heel and walked away.

Jeannie remained rooted to the spot. Her eyes filled with stinging tears that she blinked back, determined she would not allow them to fall. She drew a breath in to steady herself as the wave of prickling heat swept through her body. The group of women began to move. They picked up their washing and herded the children back towards their homes. One of the younger women, heavy with child, handed Jeannie a cool handkerchief that she had soaked in the well and pressed it into her hand. She gestured to Jeannie's face and squeezed her hand again in sympathy before hurrying away.

A whimper from the child, now cradled in his mother's arms, brought the world back into focus. Jeannie shook her head, trying to dislodge the ringing in her ears. Cupping the boy's chin, she turned his face from side to side gently trying to see where the blood, now dark and sticky, was coming from. Using the handkerchief, she wiped away a smudge of it from his temple and was relieved to see it was coming from a graze above his ear. That was good as it looked to be from the fall on the stony ground rather than a blow to the head from the horse's hooves. The wrist, however, was almost certainly broken and would need to be set.

Jeannie had been about to send the mother and child along to the still room to see to him there but hesitated. To do that would risk him coming to the attention of the messenger again or to Mairead. Instead, she instructed the lad's anxious mother to take him home and she would treat him there. The woman, close to tears again, was ushered gently along by one of her friends. *The lad's injuries were a heavy enough price*, thought Jeannie, *and I'll see to it that he pays nothing further.*

CHAPTER 13

MAIREAD

With a worried look over her shoulder, Mairead stepped back through the doorway to the tower. The villagers had returned to their work, but the atmosphere was heavy with tension and conversations were hushed. The Widow Kellie was seeing to the child now but the blow the messenger had struck would leave a bruise and her anger was justified. A knot of anxiety twisted deep in Mairead's stomach. What other choice had she had? For messengers to ride that hard into the village, their errand must be urgent and could be a warning of danger for them all. She had been decisive and brought the altercation to an end. That was her duty and should, at least, earn the respect of the household. She would see that James was aware of the man's actions and leave it to him to decide what is to be done. She could look in on the lad later and send Murren to enquire after Widow Kellie.

Mairead climbed the staircase towards the solar on the top floor of the tower. As it wound its way past the door to the charter room, she heard voices raised in anger. A crash of steel echoed through the stairwell, and she recognised James' deep voice.

'You swore fealty to this clan!' he roared.

The echo bounced off the walls of the staircase and silence within the great hall below her. The response, if there was one, was lost to Mairead as her heart pounded so hard she could hear it. Putting a hand out to steady herself, she braced against the turn in the stair as her stomach lurched and her head reeled. The stone was cool and reassuringly solid, and she composed herself quickly, not wishing to be caught listening on the stairs again. Mairead picked up her skirts and ran to the solar. Breathless, she stood by the window, hands slick with sweat as she grasped the silver cross around her neck.

She had never heard James so angry and that added to the black dread closing in around her. *Are we in danger*, she wondered, *is there to be an attack*? Would the message James had received take him away from her again and leave her here in a strange place with only Murren? Afraid and alone, Mairead took a moment to gather herself. She must be calm, she told herself, make herself presentable and go down to the midday meal. It was what was expected of her – to carry on as though all was well.

She sat in the high-backed chair looking out towards the distant hills just visible through the tiny window. The hillsides blazed with the yellow gorse and orange heather. She pulled her hair over her shoulder and began to brush it. She ran her fingers through the lengths, coarse with the heat of the day and began slowly weaving it into a neat braid The movement as she wound strand over strand helped steady her racing heart. Then, once she was sure her legs had stopped shaking, she stood and straightened her skirts.

In the great hall, the tables were set out with bread baskets and bowls of fruit. On the fire, a large black pot was suspended containing brose, a meal similar to stew and made from whatever foods needed to be used. It was filling and easy to keep warm on the fire. Unlike the evening meal, this was less formal, and people came and went when time and work allowed. They sat at an empty seat and served themselves. As Mairead entered the hall there were groups of men sitting in twos and threes talking quietly amongst themselves as they ate quickly. Most of them were men from the garrison and she stopped at each group she passed to bid them a good day or ask after the wives and children of those she knew. The men were polite but circumspect in their answers as if they simply wanted to get back to their meal. The room had the feeling of uneasy watchfulness, as though waiting for something to begin.

Passing the cooking pot, she peered in. She wrinkled her nose as a waft of steam told her the brose today was leek, cabbage, and beef shank. In the far corner, Mairead saw Murren and made her way over. Murren rose quickly to her feet but Mairead motioned for her to sit back down and finish her meal as she sat opposite from her

'I'll have bread and a few of these,' Mairead said, pulling a bowl towards her and picking a few juicy red berries. 'It is too hot for brose.'

'The talk of the kitchen is that a wee laddie was trampled by the messenger's horse this morning and the man was determined to beat him,' Murren said, her voice an urgent whisper. 'They say that Widow Kellie stood up to him and was thrashed for her troubles.'

'The boy is being seen to by Widow Kellie. If it were very serious, I would have been told by now.' Mairead ensured her voice was calm but pitched loud enough to be overheard by those sitting nearest.

'You will go along after your meal to the kitchens and ask Alais for a basket of food to take to the lad's mother,' Mairead continued. 'On the way back, you can look in on Widow Kellie and ask her to attend me later today.'

Murren dipped her head in acknowledgment and finished her drink. She rose quickly – Murren did everything quickly. Her fluttering movements always reminded Mairead of a blackbird. She was forever flitting hither and thither. Always busy. Mairead thought the woman had about as much sense as a blackbird too and watched as she dashed off into the kitchens. No doubt eager to share the titbit of information she had gleaned with the kitchen girls. Such was the currency of women. Still, it had helped Murren find a place within the household and, thinking of her own loneliness, she did not begrudge the girl that.

Mairead glanced up at the wooden shutter of the charter room which overlooked the hall. It was firmly shut and whatever was unfolding behind it remained, for now, within its walls. Gavin crossed the hall with his stiff gait and unreadable expression, although up close she could see the creases of tiredness in his eyes.

'James asks if you'll join him in the solar, mistress,' he said gently.

Glancing over his shoulder, she could see a group of his closest kinsmen and senior guards making their way into the hall. Silent and grim, they sat down and poured themselves ale from the jugs. Mairead made her way back up the stairs to the solar where James sat in the chair by the fire, head in his hands. He hadn't heard her approach and tensed when she laid a gentle hand on his shoulder. He turned his head to look at her and his dark eyes held such anguish that her heart ached for him. She put her hand to his cheek, it was rough and unshaven under her fingertips. She stood for a moment in quiet solidarity, holding the silence for him until he was able to speak.

'My uncle,' he began, hoarse with raw emotion, 'has called in the clans and is preparing to march on Inverness.'

'On Inverness? Why has... What happened?' The questions came tumbling out.

Foreboding slithered down her spine. James took her hand and pulled her close until her ear was level with his mouth.

'He intends to declare for James Stuart,' he whispered.

Her hand flew to her mouth and their eyes met. He nodded slowly, jaw tight and lips pressed together in anger.

The room around her swam as panic rose in a rush of heat. John Erskine, a friend of the late king and favourite of the Queen, was leading an uprising to put a Stuart king on the throne of Scotland. That would mean being at war with the government. At war with their friends. At war with her family. She swayed backwards and James held her arm to steady her. He lowered her gently into the chair and held her hand, watching as she fought for mastery of herself.

'We are commanded to watch the crossing from the south and for any muster at Stirling,' James said softly, not wishing to be overheard.

'Are we safe?' she asked, voice barely above a murmur.

'Aye, for now. The commander of the government soldiers in Scotland will know something is amiss but I dinnae think he'll know what. Not yet,' James whispered slowly. 'They'll ken soon enough though.'

Mairead nodded and swallowed hard. Her throat felt tight and her mouth dry.

'We must make it seem all is as normal,' James said. 'Go about our business until word reaches Stirling.'

'But we must be ready.' Mairead forced the words from her dry mouth.

'Aye, we must,' he agreed. 'But with caution.'

From the table at his side, James lifted a letter and handed it to her. The seal was unbroken.

Mairead stared at it, the red of the wax seal on the back and the large confident handwriting. A letter from Lady Frances. She cracked the seal and unfolded the letter. It was written on thick paper with the family crest at the top. She read slowly, then put it in her lap frowning. This was a list of merchants and people who were to be visited. It bore neither her name nor her position in the family, addressing her only as 'niece'. Widow Kellie, on the other hand, was not only mentioned but named as Jeannie. She felt a stab of irritation as she read on. Her aunt by marriage advised her to trust the woman's counsel, bidding Mairead to remind Jeannie to look in on Isobel Murray, the wine merchant's wife.

'What message for you?' James asked as he noted her frown.

Mairead looked at his tired face and made the choice not to burden him with her worries on top of his own.

'From the Lady Frances, our aunt reminds me of my responsibilities to the household and to the family purse,' she said mildly trying to smile. 'I'll be going to the market in Stirling tomorrow and so I'll be sure to get a good price.'

'You'll not be going to the market—' James began.

'Aye I will,' Mairead interrupted, her hand raised to silence his protest. 'You said yourself we must keep up appearances.'

'But I didnae mean for you...' James tried again.

'There will be more mouths to feed with the men garrisoned here and the estates can only grow so much. Gavin and Alais have a list of what is needed. Besides, it would look strange if the new mistress of the house didn't visit the market would it not?' she said, hoping reason would prevail.

James shook his head, a wry smile playing on his lips. He'd been out manoeuvred by his wife and they both knew it. Mairead, victorious, stood up and kissed the top of his head lightly.

'You have your orders,' she said, 'and I have mine. Now you must eat something, I'll have Gavin bring it here.'

'I must go make sure the men know their duties,' he said, trying to rise.

'Aye you do,' Mairead said, pushing her luck a little further, 'but not before you've eaten.'

As she walked away from him, she looked back. He stood now by the window looking out over the fields towards the ferry crossing at the bend of the River Forth. His hands were behind his back and legs planted wide. Watchful and waiting. She felt a sob of worry and sorrow for his burden begin to rise in her throat. Forcing it down, she lifted her chin and descended back to the hall with the folded letter still in her hand.

Back in her rooms, Mairead looked at the portrait of Lady Frances on the wall. It was, she knew, a good likeness of the woman. They had been introduced at her wedding and again when the earl had visited Kildrummy on a tour of his estates. Those clever eyes saw much but said little. Mairead had never known the woman make small talk or idle gossip to pass the time. It was that which made the letter so strange.

Sitting down at the writing desk in front of the window, she opened the letter again and read it over. It had come with a messenger whose haste had almost killed a child and his horse into the bargain. It had been sent alongside the news that John Erskine served a new king and was marching north to Inverness. It was not a letter written in haste, there were no smudges of ink or crossings out. *This is more than just a letter*, Mairead thought, *it is a message to me*. A message for the protection of the clan and the estates.

She placed the letter down on the dark polished wood of the desk and her eyes fell on the box which held the ink and the wax. It was marked with Erskine family crest. She looked again at the letter and the motto, *Je Pense Plus*, embossed into the paper. The words her aunt by marriage had spoken on the day of her wedding returned to her now. The laird had been complimenting her learning and accomplishments, and Frances had regarded her shrewdly. *'The women of this family must keep their wits about them, girl.'* Then it came to her and the message made sense. *I spoke true when I said I had my orders*, she thought. Were the merchants and people to visit in the letter also supporters of the Stuart King? Was she to place her trust in Widow Kellie? Were these her allies now?

Je Pense Plus, she thought again, *that is what I must do now. Think and keep my wits about me.*

CHAPTER 14

JEANNIE

The lad, Johnny, lay sleeping on the pallet. He had blue smudges of exhaustion under his eyes, but his face was smooth and his sleep peaceful. His tiny wrist was set and bound tight between two wooden staves. The willow bark had eased the pain and Jeannie had reassured his mother, hovering restlessly at his side, that the arm would heal just fine.

'Bairns heal quickly,' Jeannie said as she picked up her basket. 'The hard part will be getting him to keep the splint on. I'll look in again tomorrow.'

'My thanks, Widow Kellie,' the mother said, her eyes fixed on the blooming bruise on Jeannie's face. 'You paid a heavy price for a kindness today.'

Jeannie managed a smile and then took her leave.

The skin of her face felt hot and tight. She was certain one of the teeth at the top of her mouth had loosened. A cold compress would help the swelling but would do little to calm the anger she still felt towards the messenger and the mistress. Lady Frances would never have stood for violence such as that and certainly not for a child, a babe really, to be punished for it. As she ran a finger along her gum, one of her back teeth throbbed in response. Her own injuries to her face and her pride would fade with time but she doubted the tooth could be saved. A whiskey later to help her pull it may be needed. There was a fine bottle on the shelf in her house for just such need. Lost deep in her own thoughts, she almost walked right into Murren.

'Oh, Widow Kellie!' Murren called out. 'My mistress has asked if you will attend her.'

Jeannie looked at her coldly and the woman, taking in the bruising, blushed and looked down at her feet.

'When you have a moment to spare.' Murren's voice was barely audible, and she shifted the basket she carried to her other arm.

Jeannie was about to give the woman a sharp word when she caught herself. It was not her fault the mistress behaved as she did. Murren was a wee mouse of a woman, and it would be cruel to treat her so. Instead, she nodded in response.

'Are those for Johnny and his mother?' she asked, pointing to the basket over Murren's arm. It was filled with bread, berries, and a jug of milk. 'That's a kind thought.'

'There is a wee treat for the lad too,' Murren said, pointing to the sweet bannock cakes and smiling shyly.

Jeannie returned the smile and promised that she would change her stained apron and then attend to Mistress Erskine.

Mairead was seated at the writing desk but rose to her feet as Jeannie entered. Jeannie remained just inside the doorway, silent. The women faced each other across the expanse of the room with its Berber carpet and blue linen wallpaper. Their eyes locked and Jeannie, determined not to look away first, felt a flicker of satisfaction in the other's discomfort and in her own defiance. Mairead broke the deadlock with a small cough and moved toward the centre of the room.

'How is the boy?' Mairead asked, and Jeannie was surprised to hear a note of genuine concern in her voice.

'He'll mend,' she replied. 'The wound on his head is not serious, but the arm will take longer.'

'And you?' Mairead continued. 'Your face...'

An angry retort flew to Jeannie's lips, but the other woman spoke again.

'I am told that the smith did not take kindly to the rider striking you,' Mairead said quickly. 'I believe he will have reason to think twice before doing such a thing again.'

Jeannie's eyes widened and she let out a harsh laugh that had nothing to do with mirth.

'How can I help you, mistress?' Jeannie asked, feeling the tension begin to ease.

Jeannie listened as Mairead spoke of the need to visit the market in Stirling. She offered a list of household items, linens and medicines that were normally purchased there for Lady Frances. Mairead asked that she speak to Gavin of any such items that were needed. The woman hesitated and with her head tipped to one side she gave Jeannie a long look. She seemed to reach a decision and took another step forwards.

'Lady Frances has written to me and asks that you look in on the wife of the wine merchant,' Mairead said. 'Why would that be?'

'Isobel Murray?' Jeannie asked. 'She had a hard time delivering her babe and in the days that followed got the milk fever. When the surgeon advised Murray to call for the Minister, Lady Frances sent me to see what else might be done.'

'You healed her?' Mairead asked in surprise.

'Some women survive.' Jeannie shrugged. 'I just changed her poultices and gave her teas for the pain. These things are in the hands of God, but I'll look in on Isobel gladly.'

Jeannie sensed that there was more the other woman might say and waited, hands folded on her apron, for her to find the words. A dark cloud of worry passed over the young woman's face and Jeannie felt the hairs on her neck and arms rise as if a cold breeze blew through the room. Their eyes met again, and Jeannie saw the moment Mairead let down her guard. The other woman tilted back her head then squeezed her eyes shut tight as though sending up a prayer. She beckoned Jeannie closer.

In a small voice barely above a whisper, Mairead told Jeannie of the letter from Lady Frances and the warning it contained.

Jeannie could make no sense of it, why was a warning needed? There must be more to the tale.

'Where does the laird expect the threat to come from?' Jeannie asked puzzled.

She saw a flush begin on the pale skin of Mairead's throat and the woman swallowed hard.

'I threw my lot in with Erskine's long ago, mistress,' Jeanie said steadily taking Mairead's arm. 'All I have I owe to my position in this household. You've nothing to fear from me, lass.'

Mairead nodded.

'The laird will declare himself for the Stuart king,' Mairead said, her voice quavering. 'He's preparing to march on Inverness.'

Jeannie remained silent as the thoughts swirled round her head and Mairead watched her closely. It seemed there was more courage in Mairead Erskine than her small frame suggested. The words now spoken, and the decision made, the young mistress had regained her composure. There was no trace of the frightened girl in the stance of the woman before her. It seemed that there was no time for fear or dismay. They must do what they could to prepare for whatever they must face.

CHAPTER 15

HAZEL

L ost in her own world Hazel sat again in the charter room. Gentle lamplight made it feel cosy and comfortable. With tiny windows and wooden shutters that overlooked the great hall natural light was limited. Thick walls meant that only a dull hum could be heard from the town beyond. She had been completely absorbed in her engagement strategy and time had flown. Checking her watch, she was surprised to see that it was late afternoon already. Many of these properties, she reflected, had the same effect; they were almost timeless. Having stood for so long and witnessed so much, it was as though they stood separate from the modern world. That was part of their charm and made them special. There were certainly worse places to work. She looked around the room feeling lucky that she got to have access to this.

If they could begin to gather some interest in the project now with special events for members and locals, then it would hopefully carry the momentum through the winter period when the tower was closed to the public. If all went to plan then by the time it reopened at the end of March next year, there would be a story to tell here. Then her focus would move to the next location and the cycle would begin again. She shifted in her chair to stretch out her legs, re-reading the list of options and ideas, satisfying herself that it gave the folks in marketing enough to work with to start planning events and developing materials. They had a meeting scheduled at the end of the week to discuss the strategy and time was of the essence.

Lost deep in her work the buzzing of her phone broke the spell.

'Hi Lauren...' Hazel began. She had never heard Lauren so animated and listened, with a slight frown as she tried to understand the importance of the letter from Lady Frances.

'Yes, I'm still at the tower,' she continued and refreshed her email account. 'Yep. Got it. OK, I'll wait here. See you soon.'

Intrigued to see what had Lauren so excited about, she opened the email and downloaded the image of the letter. The handwriting caught her eye immediately. It was beautiful and, as somebody who adored writing with a proper pen and ink, Hazel always appreciated that. She enlarged the image to focus on the way the letters were formed and the flourishes at the start of sentences. Looking up at the portrait of Lady Frances, it was easy to imagine her at her writing bureau, enjoying sharing letters and news with her circle of acquaintances. Hazel still loved to send and receive handwritten letters. Thanks to email and messenger apps they were a dying art form but to her they were special. She began to read the text and had to admit that something about the letter didn't feel right. She leant closer and tracked the words across the screen with the end of her pen. It felt cold and stilted as though the words on the page didn't match up to the person who had written them.

Hazel sat puzzled in front of the screen as Lauren entered the room and with a rattle of bracelets and a waft of oud. Hazel didn't need to turn round to know who it was.

'What do you make of it then?' Lauren asked.

'It doesn't really say very much but the handwriting is beautiful,' Hazel said, pointing to the screen.

'I think it might be a kind of warning, look at the date – 1 September,' Lauren said. 'Just days before her husband declared for the Stuart King and sent from Braemar.'

Hazel frowned and looked again at the letter. She couldn't see how Lauren had made that leap from the words on the image in front of her.

'I don't follow your logic Lauren, what makes you say that?' she asked.

Lauren pulled a chair out and sat down. Opening her laptop, she pulled up the letter to Lady Frances, putting the two screens side by side.

'Look at this... it's a letter from Lady De La War to Frances.' Lauren sat back to give Hazel a better view of the screen.

Hazel read through the other letter. It was full of news of mutual acquaintances, court gossip and an update on the latest fashion. *The tone was certainly different, less formal, almost chatty*, Hazel thought. It had a few smudges and even a little drawing and the writing was smaller, more compact and functional. It was a letter to a friend and Hazel could easily imagine it today as a social media post or a message. Lady De La War expected a reply, it was good old-fashioned correspondence between women who were friends. Hazel was aware of Lauren's gaze on her and looked up to see an expectant expression.

'Yes, it does have a different tone,' Hazel said carefully, 'and there are a few smudges and mistakes. It's a different kind of letter.'

'Exactly!' Lauren said.

She switched the laptops around so that Lady Frances' letter was now in front of her and scrolled back to the top. Picking up a pencil from the table, she pointed to the greeting at the top.

'*Dear Niece*,' she read. 'Don't you think that's odd? Not dearest, not a name?'

Lauren made her way through the letter line by line, pointing out the irregularities and the odd turns of phrase. She waved her hands and pointed emphatically at the screen as she made her points. Hazel sat, head to one side trying and failing to keep up with the other woman's train of thought.

'Why would this be sent at a time it must have been vital to keep what was planned secret? A letter about visiting merchants and where to buy wine?' Lauren looked expectantly at Hazel.

That made a degree of sense. Messages between Jacobites across Scotland and down into England had been sent in code. Anyone who had studied the Tudors or the Gunpowder Plot knew that code was all part and parcel of any intrigue.

'Okay...' Hazel said, 'but how does that make the letter a warning?'

Lauren stood up abruptly, wincing as her chair scraped the floor. She strode to the fireplace and tapped the carving of the family crest set into the mantle then pointed back to the screen.

'The last line,' Lauren said, '*I remind you Niece, that your first responsibility is to the clan, the tower and manor house represent the pride of the Erskine.*'

Hazel read the line again and looked back to Lauren.

'*Je Pense Plus*... the motto. *I think more.*' Lauren strode back across the room and sat arms folded looking at Hazel.

'That's a bit of a leap Lauren...' Hazel began, radiating disapproval.

'Not a leap, a hunch. An educated one at that. I mean, look at her.' Lauren gestured to the portrait. 'Does she look like a woman who sat at home mending socks whilst her husband led a rebellion?'

Hazel sighed, her thumb and forefinger massaging her temples as she looked down at the table in front of her. *Here we go again*, she thought. Jumping to conclusions without all the facts. Not again. Not another humiliation because other people's egos were more important than the facts.

Hazel stood and paced the floor between the table and the stone entranceway at the stairs. The soles of her black loafers squeaked as she turned around. No, she decided, this was not going to happen again.

'Lauren,' she said, pointing to the portrait, 'that is a piece of art. He was commissioned to paint it, and it is his interpretation of a woman who died nearly 300 years ago.'

'It isn't a vanity portrait though. It doesn't record her status and wealth.' Lauren gestured to the portraits of other Erskine clan chiefs.

The walls contained several more pictures of men in their long white wigs and full regalia of state, others astride horses looking manfully into the distance. Other ladies were also featured depicted in beautiful gowns or in full family scenes. There were even some of the more contemporary lairds in military uniform with their medals displayed. Frances was sat at a small table with her child on her knee and a country scene in the background. It was a picture for the family to enjoy.

'I think the lead is worth exploring and we know who the niece was. Her name was Mairead and she was married to John's nephew, James.' Lauren walked to the family tree and pointed to the name.

Hazel returned to her seat and looked at the family tree. The information could be triangulated at least and making the links between the information and the people was the job of the historians. Hazel saw the confusion and beginnings of anger in Lauren's creased brow and narrowed eyes. She shifted uncomfortably in her chair.

'Look Lauren,' Hazel said, 'I just want this project to be a success. I want it to tell the real stories of the people here and not...'

'Not what, Hazel?' Lauren's hands hit the table with a thud, and she stood waiting for the answer.

The two women faced each other across the table, the air around them thick with tension

'Not the story we want it to be,' Hazel said quietly and looked away with a sigh.

Lauren drew in a breath and straightened herself. Hazel braced herself for the storm of anger.

'I'm not doing this.' Lauren's tone was icy, 'I'm not becoming that version of me. I'm better than that. *You* are better than this.' Lauren threw her hands up in the air and reached for the papers on the desk.

'It's my professional reputation too. I know what I'm doing,' Lauren said evenly.

She packed her bag and as she turned to leave, she paused beside Hazel.

'Whatever issue you have going on here needs to be dealt with. You are so afraid of making a mistake that you won't take any risks at all.' Lauren shook her head sadly. 'That only ends one way.'

Hazel remained silent with her face turned away, unable to respond. It was, she knew, the truth and hearing it from a woman like Lauren didn't make it any easier to swallow. Lauren made her way to the staircase before she paused again.

'If you'll take my advice,' Lauren began gently, 'you'll get out of your own way.'

Hazel sat looking down at the pool of light reflected on the rug on the floor from the window as Lauren's footsteps echoed down the staircase. The patch of light illuminated a vine of roses in the pattern.

Hazel's mind drifted back to York and her home in one of the tiny, terraced houses in the city centre. The duck egg blue front door with its stained-glass panel showing a white rose against a river background. The panel had always reflected colour onto the oak floor of the narrow hallway in the afternoon sun and it was a favourite spot for Artemis, her black cat, to nap lying stretched out in the heat. She had bought the house when she took the position with the Yorkshire Museums Association. It had been her dream role as an exhibition manager and York was a beautiful city. Easier to live in than some of the bigger cities with an academic vibe that her father said reminded him of Oxford.

Her cottage in Alva was sweet and had a beautiful view of the hills but she missed her home in York and all it represented.

A polite cough woke her from her daydream and the caretaker, with his keys in hand, wondered if she would be much longer. Taking the hint, she collected her things and made her way out of the building.

CHAPTER 16

HAZEL

Mei was already waiting, leaning against the car as Hazel pulled up on the roadside. They had arranged to run east along the hill footpaths. It was an out-and-back route but a good run to work on speed. The pools at the bottom of the waterfall offered them the option of a cool dip on a warm evening. Hazel climbed out of the car and began to work through her warmup stretches, her body stiff and tense.

'I needed this tonight,' Mei said, 'it's been a hell of a day'.

'Me too, want to talk about it?' Hazel asked.

'Nope, I want to run off the rage!' her friend said.

As if to emphasise the point, Mei pulled the zip up her reflective vest so forcefully she almost tore it clean off. Hazel raised her eyebrow and gave her friend a wicked grin. They waited for a gap in the traffic and darted across the road.

'Race you!' Hazel called over her shoulder as she broke into a run.

From behind her, Mei squealed in surprise and Hazel upped the pace again.

At the end of the first kilometre they slowed to a gentle jog, sipping their water. This part of the path was in the shade of a line of old ash trees and the breeze that danced through the leaves was cool and refreshing.

'Better now?' Hazel asked.

Mei nodded as she took another mouthful of water. She began to tell Hazel about her day and her frustration with the new interns in the laboratories. It was always hectic at the start of the new academic term, trying to get all the new starts up to speed on the work they were doing and drilling in the lab protocols. Mei's current research study looked at the relationship between water sources and the diversity of pollinators in hill streams in Scotland.

'I must be getting older,' Mei said, 'I'm complaining about the work ethic of the younger generation. I thought *I* was the younger generation!'

'It's depressing,' Hazel agreed as she tightened the loop on her sunglasses. 'We aren't quite the older generation though either.'

'No. We're stuck in the middle with all the responsibilities and none of the glory,' Mei complained. 'We used to have fun!'

Mei sounded so plaintive that Hazel laughed and caught a bit of dandelion fluff in her mouth. She stopped abruptly blowing and trying to wipe it off her tongue, pulling a face.

'This is fun!' Hazel said as they picked up the pace again. 'Just keep telling ourselves that this is fun.'

Reaching the end of the footpath, they turned and began the run back to the cars. Ahead of them, the sun started to sink behind the peak of Dumyat and the air began to cool raising goosebumps on their arms. The path was busy with walkers and cyclists on such a beautiful evening, and they ran in silence as they weaved their way along. Hazel settled into a steady rhythm that allowed her mind to open and process the events of the day. Hazel realised she had been holding on too tight. Trying to keep control. Her fear of history repeating itself clouding her thinking. Lauren was right, she was getting in her own way. This wasn't how it was supposed to have been. She tried to do the right thing and instead she'd lost everything. Her job, her friends and her home. *Will I ever be free of it?* Anger welled up and hitched in her throat, she wanted to beat her fists on the ground and scream.

Instead, she turned to Mei and asked if she was ready for another sprint. She pushed herself into a hard run and let the anger ebb away as she pounded along the pathway with Mei beside her. Sweat formed on her top lip and her vest top stuck to her back. Her ragged breathing was loud in her ears. She made no effort to try and control it, she needed it to be hard – to override the anger and the pain.

As the cars came into view, Mei began to slow down but Hazel kept pushing. At the edge of the road, she stopped. Holding onto the gate she sucked huge mouthfuls of air into her lungs and let her heart rate slow. Her cheeks felt raw with the sun and salt from her sweat. She suspected they would be an unattractive scarlet too. She peeled the back of her top away from her skin and wafted it trying to cool down. Mei came to a graceful stop beside her, glowing beautifully and still looking fresh.

'Do *you* want to talk about it?' she asked pulling her ankle up behind her to stretch her quad.

She waited silently for Hazel to speak.

'I've been thinking a lot about what happened in York,' Hazel began. 'The project has stirred it all up again.'

'Yes, I can see why,' Mei said, 'but you must let that go. It's over and done with. You did the right thing.'

She couldn't seem to move on. Coming back to Scotland and picking up the pieces of her life had been so hard. The settlement money had been more than enough to buy a new house, and she had her family and friends. It still felt like a defeat. She'd lost her beautiful home. Her professional reputation was tainted. Worse, though, was the emptiness. York had cost her a piece of herself, and deep-down Hazel feared it had gone forever. How had she been so stupid?

Only her parents knew the full story. She'd never been able to bring herself to tell Mei or anyone else. She was ashamed because no matter how many people told her otherwise, she feared that it *had* all been her own fault.

She had been introduced to Matt at the opening evening of a new art exhibition at a gallery. He was a runner like her and played tennis. They had hit it off and one thing had led to another. It had been fun for a while but when they had been put onto the same project team, Hazel started to feel uneasy. Too much time together, perhaps, or she just saw a different side of him at work. He liked the easy option and being the centre of attention. All of that was a huge turn off for Hazel. She knew it wasn't going anywhere and so she ended it. His reaction took her by surprise, she had thought he understood that it was nothing heavy between them. Matt took it hard and spiralled, going out drinking and taking risks. She could ignore that, it wasn't her problem, and she hoped he could be professional. That changed when he started cutting corners on the project.

They were curating an exhibition of art, literature and pottery linked to the Yorkshire Dales, the pieces would be sold, and the aim was to raise the profile of the galleries and local creatives. The financial target was ambitious, and the team were under pressure to secure items that would attract buyers. Matt had sourced an unknown painting by a local artist which could easily take them past the target if its provenance was sound. It was a big *if*.

Hazel had been horrified the day she saw it appear in the exhibition marketing attributed to the artist. She had confronted Matt and they'd argued. Feeling she had no choice, Hazel raised her concern that the painting was a fake and became a whistleblower. Although her boss had promised to look into it, Hazel had been put on gardening leave. Her colleagues distanced themselves from her. Not Matt. He just wouldn't leave her alone. That had just been the beginning of her nightmare.

On autopilot, Hazel worked through her cool down, as she raised her arms skyward stretching out her back, she became aware that Mei was speaking.

'Hmm...?' Hazel said. 'Sorry, I was miles away and I missed that.'

'I asked how you and Dr McDonald are getting along,' Mei repeated. 'Are you OK?'

'Just a bit frustrated. I don't know what it is about Lauren, it just gets so...' Hazel made fists with her hands and continued, 'Tense.'

'What do you mean?' Mei asked as they crossed the road.

'Whenever I'm around her I become a total control freak,' Hazel said. 'I try not to be, but she just brings out the worst in me. I don't even know what it is... she's just so... formidable.'

'Uh-huh,' Mei said with a glint of amusement.

They lent against their cars, enjoying the last of the evening sun and Hazel turned to look at her friend.

'Uh-huh? What does that mean?' she asked defensively.

'Has it occurred to you that perhaps you make her feel the same way?'

'What?!' Hazel was affronted. 'No!'

Hazel thought back to their conversation at the tower. What was it Lauren said again? *I'm not going to become that version of me'.* Although it was a strange thing to say to somebody, Hazel knew exactly what it meant, she felt the same sometimes. She didn't want to become what other people expected her to be. What they projected on to her to suit their own narratives. She sighed and turned back to Mei, who stood looking expectant as Hazel considered it all from this new point of view.

'I think you're probably right,' Hazel said. 'I've been so focused on the project being perfectly planned and executed that I haven't left room for it to grow organically.'

Mei smiled and reached over to pat her friend's arm reassuringly.

'Ugh, why can you always see these things when I can't?' Hazel asked.

'I know you.' Mei shrugged. 'And I manage a bunch of egotistical maniacs let loose in a lab all day. Then of course there is Marcus...'

They both laughed and Mei hugged her friend.

'You're too hard on yourself,' she said gently as she let Hazel go.

As she drove home, Hazel wondered how she could start to build a bridge with Lauren. She could stop trying to micromanage it all and let Lauren do what she did best.

Letting herself into the house, she was greeted by Artemis who gave her a round scolding of meows for the lateness of her dinner and padded through to the kitchen tail aloft to wait to be served. She followed, apologising and promising to make it up to her. Once the cat was fed and had returned to her favourite past time of sleeping, Hazel made her own dinner of salmon and vegetable parcels. She wrapped the parcel in tin foil, popped it into the air fryer and poured herself a gin and tonic.

As she sat waiting for her meal to cook, she opened her phone and saw a message from her mother – it was a link to an article on the Scotsman newsfeed. As she opened it, she saw the picture of herself and Lauren on the roof of the tower. It was a striking picture of them in profile looking out across the valley. The caption read 'A bridge to the past'. The Scotsman had evidently picked up the story from the local paper. This was good news for the project's profile and could mean more media coverage. Looking again at the picture Hazel felt the same flutter of excitement she had when she read Lauren's proposal. This could be something so special and she knew it needed them both.

CHAPTER 17

LAUREN

The smell of toast wafted through the kitchen and drew Lauren, yawning, to the table. Annie had laid out the jams and butter ready and stood turning the toast over with a two-pronged iron fork. On the aga, the kettle began to whistle. The sun streamed through the windows, warming the stone floor and making the kitchen look like a photo from a country living magazine. It was moments like this that made all the idiosyncrasies of an ancient wood-fired stove worth it. Lauren put on the oven glove and retrieved the kettle. Lifting the lid on the teapot, she poured water in. Some tea would help her feel more human, she hoped. Annie dropped a kiss on her head and reached over to place the hot toast down. As Lauren reached for a slice, Annie sat beside her and placed a copy of The Scotsman newspaper down in front of her with a look of triumph. Lauren eyed her wife, who, with a sigh, tapped the photo on the folded page.

'You've made the broadsheets,' Annie said.

Lauren, who would be the first to admit it, was not a morning person and glared down at the newspaper. Although she never wanted to entertain a conversation until she had consumed at least two cups of tea, Annie had a determined look about her this morning and there would be no avoiding it.

'What are they saying?' Lauren asked as she heaped marmalade onto her toast.

'Highlighting the project and the international funding grant. It is a fabulous picture of you!' Annie said.

'Hmm.' Lauren remained unconvinced.

'This is Hazel that you're with, is it?' Annie said. 'She's like a model, all high cheekbones and angles.'

Lauren rolled her eyes in mute appeal to a higher power making Annie laugh.

'The photo is very evocative.' Annie put on her best thespian voice. 'Two historians... looking back through time... searching for the stories.'

Lauren snorted, biting noisily into her breakfast and chewing ferociously. She knew that irritated Annie and felt it a suitable punishment for the unnecessary early morning enthusiasm.

'Fine,' Annie said throwing her hands up in defeat. 'Have it your way. I think this is good for the project. It might tempt a few more visitors to brave the crossing of the Forth and venture into Alloa.'

Lauren poured the tea and sat back as Siggi padded over and stood with his head in her lap. She ruffled his ears and began to read the article. It was in the culture and arts supplement and was very positive. Lauren read on with interest and surreptitiously fed her crusts to the dog under the table.

New Director of Engagement for the History of Scotland Trust, Hazel Rankin, put out a request for submissions to the academic community. Renowned local historian, Dr Lauren McDonald of Stirling University, answered that call with her proposal called 'Fractal Lines'. Together with their team, they hope to bring to life the stories of the ordinary people who lived in these places during extraordinary times.

The dean will be delighted, she thought, *although a few others probably less so. Oh well, that is their problem*. Looking at the photograph of Hazel she felt a twinge of guilt. Had she gone too far the previous afternoon? The woman was so hard to read though, and her acerbic comments had gotten under Lauren's skin. It was exhausting, all the jostling for position and worrying about what others think. *One of the real perks of middle age*, she thought, *is that I no longer gave a flying fig about all that*. She wasn't going to try and bend herself to anybody else's expectations nor was she going start playing the role that Leinster and his ilk seemed determined to cast her in. She just hoped that he hadn't been pouring his poison in Hazel's ear.

'Penny for them?' Annie asked as she pulled out the chair next to Lauren.

'I was just thinking about the project,' Lauren said. Knowing there was little point in trying to hide anything from Annie she continued, 'I just can't read Hazel.'

Lauren went quiet for a moment, trying to put her finger on what it was about the other woman that rubbed her the wrong way.

'She's just so... prickly,' she said, pushing Siggi down from the table where he was foraging hopefully for crumbs.

'You've been feeding him at the table again!' Annie said. 'No! Bad boy, away you go.'

Lauren, caught red-handed, gave the dog an apologetic look and changed the subject back to Hazel.

'One minute I think we are getting on famously and the next she's getting uptight about the evidence,' she said.

Annie turned the newspaper around and looked down at the picture.

'She looks... brittle...' Annie said searching for the right words. 'Sad almost. What's her story, do you know?'

'Not really, I think she was with an art consortium of some kind before in York,' Lauren said, her brow furrowed. 'Came back here to take the job at the History of Scotland Trust.'

'She's a local then?' Annie asked.

'I think so, her father is a well-known scientist, I heard,' Lauren replied.

'Well, go gently, love,' Annie said softly. 'I'd bet she has a story to tell too.'

Lauren knew that Annie was right but there was something off between the two of them. It needed to be addressed. Perhaps some neutral ground and a decent coffee might help. She would suggest they have a catch up. *Maybe at that lovely little bakery in the town where they did the most amazing scones*, she thought.

CHAPTER 18

LAUREN

The late September day had a definite autumnal feel. A heavy downpour of rain bounced on the pavement and drummed on the cars parked along the street. Lauren entered the coffee shop, shaking the rain from her umbrella. She placed it in the holder by the door and scanned the room for Hazel. The warm, sweet smell of scones baking filled the air. It transported her back to another time. She was six again, sitting at the wooden table in the kitchen eating the left-over dough from the ceramic bowl as the scones baked in the aga. It was her reward for helping to cut the scones by pushing the crinkle edged ring down with both hands, seeing how many she could make from the rolled-out mixture. The bowl was heavy and had a diamond pattern. It was the same colour as the eggs she had collected earlier that morning from the hen house. Nana, in her blue gingham apron hummed to herself as she folded the washing.

Hazel called her name and the room returned with a rush.

'Sorry, I was miles away.' Lauren slid her cardigan off her shoulders and shook her head.

The wave of nostalgia left her feeling slightly disconnected from the here and now. The warm glow of the memory lingered. Her childhood had been a happy one and Nana's solid, dependable presence had always been a source of comfort to Lauren. They had been so close. The house had that same feeling now with Annie in it and Lauren counted that blessing every day.

'The seasons are on the change now, eh?' Lauren said with a determined cheerfulness.

'Could do without the rain at the moment though,' Hazel said. 'We are hoping to get the temporary exhibition centre onto the site in the next couple of weeks and the area at the back of the tower is like a mud bath when it rains. It drains so slowly.'

'I wonder what's under there,' Lauren began. 'There'll be the foundations from the manor house and the other buildings that were destroyed in the fire I suppose.'

Hazel eyed the cakes and scones on the counter and offered the menu to Lauren.

'No need, I'll have a pot of tea and the scone of the day,' she said, catching the attention of the young waitress.

They ordered tea and scones for two and continued to talk about the tower and the progress of the research as they waited for them to arrive. As they both relaxed and the conversation felt easier Lauren knew this had been a good idea. Hazel explained that the Archaeological Society had asked if they could carry out a geophysical survey of the grounds before the structures are built. It was part of their survey of all the History of Scotland Trust sites. Lauren agreed, the timing was excellent, and it would add another layer of detail and data to their own project. It was an exciting chance to find out what might be hidden beneath, and Lauren knew that the graduate researchers on the team would be keen to see it in action.

'Well,' said Lauren, 'I have more good news. We have been invited onto Radio Scotland Women's Hour to talk about Fractal Lines. The email came in this morning.'

'That's excellent!' Hazel said, leaning back as the waitress placed the teapot on the table between them.

'Are you okay with this though? I think they'll want to look at it through the lens of the women's experiences,' Lauren asked as she cut open her scone.

'About that...' Hazel cleared her throat. 'I've been thinking. You were right. I am getting in my own way and I'm sorry.'

Lauren looked at the other woman with her neat and well put together appearance. Hazel Rankin was a careful woman who considered things from every angle. Lauren could tell she was fiercely intelligent and very driven. She had even more respect for her now and wondered if Hazel might share more.

'I can be a bit full on, I know,' Lauren said with an apologetic smile. 'I admire you though, I can tell you have real integrity.'

Hazel looked away quickly but not before Lauren saw the flash of pain. Stirring the cloud of milk into the tea she took an educated guess at the cause.

'Integrity doesn't always make one popular though does it?' she said gently.

'No, it doesn't,' Hazel replied, studying the cherry blossom pattern on the tablecloth. 'Although it makes it simple to know what the right thing is, it doesn't make it any easier to do it.'

'I'll drink to that.' Lauren raised her teacup in salute. '*Ileigitimi non carborundum,* as the saying goes.'

They laughed and returned to planning out the next few days. By the time they had finished the pot of tea they had identified some key points to highlight in the radio interview. There were some interesting stories about the women who had called Alloa Tower their home. They certainly hadn't stayed at home spinning or embroidering.

The final topic of conversation for the afternoon was the update meeting with the subgroup of the board. There was a lot of progress to report and both women felt it should be fairly straightforward. Tickets were selling for the initial two events planned at the tower and the media interest would go down well. Lauren made a note to mention the dates of these and how to purchase tickets in her interview. The first event was an evening of fireside storytelling themed around the timeline of the events that the tower had seen and looked to be very popular. The second was a family treasure hunt planned for the closing weekend at the end of October, and they still had a month to finalise the plans. There would be clues to solve with actors playing some of the tower's previous occupants and opportunities to dress up in different costumes. If these went well, they could be the first link to the next property in the project.

Hazel pulled out some of the marketing materials to show Lauren. They looked great and, with a strong advertising campaign, they should do well. Making the project itself part of the engagement strategy was exciting and both the historians and the team at History of Scotland Trust were enthused. The trick would be in keeping up the momentum.

When Lauren left the coffee shop, it had stopped raining, and the sun was dazzling as it reflected off the wet pavements. She felt sticky in the humidity as she made her way back to her car, peeling her cardigan off. Catching her reflection in the window of a hairdresser's shop, she saw that her hair had doubled in volume and was now an unruly mass of tight coils. She sighed, there was nothing she could do but embrace it. *Typical Scotland*, Lauren thought, *the unpredictable weather is entirely predictable. At least it gives people a surefire topic of conversation.*

Lauren was pleased with herself as she drove home, the meeting with Hazel had been a success and it felt as if something had shifted in their relationship. It was a step forward. She really did admire Hazel, recognising in her a woman who very clearly lived life on her terms. Carving out her niche on the edges. She knew exactly how hard that could be. In a lot of ways, they weren't so different and this project could be excellent for both of them. They could be quite a formidable team. With a flash of inner revelation Lauren realised how much she wanted that.

CHAPTER 19

JEANNIE

Jeannie woke to the rumble of a passing wagon and rose quickly. Her eyes were gritty and she fumbled with the laces of her skirts as she dressed. She had found little rest again last night and dozed fitfully, awake at every sound. The swelling in her cheek had lessened but the skin felt tender still and she winced as she swilled her mouth with salted water. Her thoughts were of her sons and their fates in what was to come. They would have to make a choice, she supposed. Answer the call of the laird, the man to whom they had pledged fealty to when they came of age, or remain loyal to the King they served now? There had been, she knew, families who faced each other across battlefields before and she gave a silent prayer that her boys be spared that terrible ordeal.

The square around the well was busy again and a wagon was being loaded with goods bound for the market. Judging that she had a few minutes to spare, Jeannie crossed the little square to look in on Johnny. He was up and playing on the earthen floor with a rough-cut wooden soldier. The splint remained intact, and his eyes were bright and clear. Jeannie smiled as she listened to the prattle of the boy giving orders to his soldier and seemingly none the worse for the events of the previous day. She advised the lad's mother to give him more willow bark at bedtime to help him sleep and again through the day if he should need it. Satisfied that danger from the blow to the head had passed, Jeannie left them.

The day was set to be warm again and she paused a moment under the dappled shade of a tree, enjoying the whispering breeze. The horses were being saddled and Mistress Erskine's fine roan mare stamped impatiently as her halter was strapped. The grey beside her chewed hay from the bale and flicked its ears, content to wait. Stirling Market was always well attended by those who had wares to sell and the household was busy preparing to leave. Usually there would be an undercurrent of excitement within the party but not today. Today the soldiers on guard duty remained watchful and now bore their swords and weapons close at hand. Another sign of the rising tension and readiness within the tower.

As she entered the great hall, she saw Gavin speaking with another of the household retainers. His stoic presence reassured Jeannie. He was a man who thought quickly and kept a level head. Despite the limp, he was a competent rider and would do his best to keep his mistress out of harm's way should it be needed. He acknowledged her with a nod of his head.

The horses were brought around and Mairead stepped out into the sunshine, her braided hair shining like burnished copper. The high collar of her green cloak accentuated her long neck. Mairead swung herself gracefully up into the saddle and sat tall and straight-backed, looking like an image of a Celtic goddess from the tapestries in the solar. There was little chance their party would go about their business unremarked today, it seemed. Jeannie was offered a hand up into the stirrup and it was only as she straightened from adjusting the rein she noticed it was James standing by her horse. He looked at her and winked.

'Try to keep your mistress from beggaring us at the silk merchants today.' His eyes were full of mischief and his voice was pitched to reach his wife on her horse in front.

Mairead turned indignantly in her saddle, ready to rebuke him, but he went to her side and disarmed her with a smart bow. He took her hand, lifted it reverently to his lips and kissed her knuckles. Mairead giggled and shook her head at him. He remained looking up at her adoringly, his face wearing an earnest look and his manner every inch a chevalier from a ballad.

'Looking as bonnie as she does, they'll be falling over each other to sell her the finest colours,' he laughed as Mairead pulled her hand away and swatted him.

'I'll make you no promise,' Jeannie replied, smiling indulgently at the playful affection between the couple. The three riders coaxed their horses through the village and out onto the road. Those working in the surrounding fields paused to watch them pass and acknowledged Mairead by removing their caps or dropping a small curtsey.

The road opened out and ahead of them they could see Stirling with the castle on the hill to the west. Mairead, impatient to be away, kicked her horse into a trot and then, with the flash of a brilliant smile over her shoulder, into an easy canter. Jeannie looked to Gavin, who raised his eyes heavenwards and urged his own horse to match her pace, leaving Jeannie to follow suit. Jeannie shifted her weight in the saddle as her grey gelding settled into an easy, rhythmic stride. Although a competent enough rider, Jeannie was out of practice and the jolt of the movement through her marrow reminded her that she was not as young as she used to be.

The road was busy with other travellers who stepped aside to let the party go ahead and they exchanged greetings with a waved hand or smile as they went. Gavin scanned the road ahead, constantly alert to their surroundings. As they reached the outskirts of the city they slowed back down to a walk. Threading their way through the press of people, carts and livestock as they wound their way up towards the merchant quarter. The heat intensified the acrid smell, making Jeannie cough and her eyes sting as they passed by the cattle pens and continued to wind their way upward. The earthen streets of the lower parts of the citadel gave way to grey cobble stones which rang under the hooves of the horses.

They veered left off the main thoroughfare and the throng began to ease. Gavin led them along Castle Wynd and they stopped at Mar's Lodging, the earl's Stirling lodging. At the arched entrance way, Gavin spoke with the guards and Jeannie, patting the neck of the horse, looked up at the building. It was imposing and at regular intervals along the stone frontage, there were shields bearing the family crest and references to their ancient lineage. There were also statues. Some looked like the gods of the Romans or the Greeks. She noted the one set into a recess above the archway. It was taller than the others and depicted a woman draped in a winding sheet, she held a sword to her chest. As Gavin's horse turned to rejoin them, he followed her gaze.

'Her name is Jeannie Dark,' he said.

'Jeannie Dark?' Jeannie looked up at the sad and beautiful face of the statue thoughtfully. 'Joan of Arc? The French peasant who led an army into battle?'

Gavin nodded and Jeannie saw he was surprised by her knowledge. Duncan had told her the tale of the young martyr and her visions. He had accompanied the laird to France on a visit to her grave in Rouen. The folk of the city left little offerings and prayers for her in the grand cathedral. As they passed through the vaulted archway, Jeannie looked up again at her namesake and had the uncanny feeling the statue's sightless gaze looked right back at her.

The archway opened into a courtyard filled with men and women about their business. The farrier stood by a wooden post outside the stable with a bucket at his feet and the hind leg of a huge black horse between his thighs as he prized the shoe from its hoof. It was the largest horse Jeannie had ever seen, and she was impressed by how still it stood. *A horse that well trained was for riding into battle*, she thought as the shoe dropped into the waiting bucket.

They drew their horses to a standstill and a stable hand rushed forward to hold the reins and help Mairead down from her roan mare. Gavin swung his leg over and dismounted neatly before throwing the rein over his horse's neck and coming to offer Jeannie his help. She stepped down into his waiting arms gratefully and stroked the long nose of the grey which stood glistening with sweat in the summer heat. As the stable lads led the horses to the shade of the feeding nets and water trough, a man strode confidently toward them. He grasped Gavin's forearm in greeting and then turned to welcome Mairead. The man introduced himself as Hugh and offered them wine or ale in the hall. Mairead declined the offer, insisting she was keen to take in the sights of the city and visit the market.

'I'll send an escort with ye, mistress,' Hugh said.

'Do not trouble yourself,' Mairead replied. 'I have Gavin here and Jeannie who know the city well enough.'

'But mistress...' he began.

'No, no,' she interrupted. 'I have calls to make on behalf of Lady Frances and that is no errand for your men.'

The sweep of Mairead's arm encompassed the building work and piles of stone lying within the courtyard. Jeannie and Gavin exchanged a glance behind her, their look acknowledging that the young mistress was a force to be reckoned with. Hugh cast a questioning look at Gavin who nodded subtly to him. If Mairead had seen it, then she chose to let it go unremarked.

The three walked the short distance from earl's lodging down the broad street towards the Market Cross. The bright fabrics of the stalls lined the street and Jeannie caught the bitter and aromatic scent of spices as they passed by. The spices were displayed in bowls and woven baskets. The pungent golds and reds drew her attention and they wove their way along. Passing the egg seller and the barrows loaded with vegetables they moved away from the food stalls and on towards the fabrics and house-hold wares. Mairead stopped to admire the ribbons on display at one stall and the merchant rushed to offer her a fine length of ribbon the colour of a fir tree. He held it up beside her hair and Jeannie knew the man had chosen well. The colour suited Mairead and she laughed delightedly at whatever compliment the merchant had given. Mairead nodded to Gavin who with a dour expression reached into his jerkin and removed a few coins from the leather pouch.

Eager to get on Gavin herded them towards the apothecary to replenish the stores of herbs, tinctures and medicines that Jeannie needed. The window of the shop was filled with brown glass jars and bottles. In one large jar there was a fluid and what looked like large floating beans. Mairead lent in close to examine them and recoiled when Jeannie informed her they were lamb kidneys and good for cleansing the blood of poisons. Jeannie approached the counter and handed her list to the shopkeeper. His greeting was warm and he kept up a steady flow of conversation as he collected jars and bottles from crowded shelves behind. As he weighed and measured the items, he shared the latest news – the city was busy and trade was good. There was an outbreak of a coughing sickness in Edinburgh and the Duke of Argyll was in residence up by the castle. Jeannie felt Mairead's attention fix on the conversation and remembered that the Duke was her uncle. The shopkeeper continued to talk and his chest puffed up with self-importance at Mairead's attention.

'The Duke arrived with many men, my lady,' the shopkeeper said earnestly.

'He is an important man,' Mairead said, her eyes lowered modestly.

'Aye, the King's representative in Scotland,' the shopkeeper continued as he wrapped their purchases into a parcel. 'Here to reassure the merchants that they are getting a fair bargain in their trade with the English I'd wager.'

'Good day to you,' Mairead said, her voice honeyed and her expression sweet.

Jeannie wondered again at the guile of the other woman. She had played down her interest well and given the impression that she had become bored of the topic when strayed into politics.

Gavin stepped forward to pay as Jeannie picked up the parcel from the counter and bid the shopkeeper farewell.

With purchases from the linen merchant and orders for sugar and spices placed, Gavin led them back up to the market cross. A crowd had gathered around as a man dressed in black breeches with a black cap was speaking. The long face with its grey beard and fierce eyes was animated and he shook his fist to underline the point. Not yet close enough to hear his words, Jeannie was struck by the reaction of the crowd. Often times the crowds would heckle or jeer those who chose to come here and speak. Today they were quiet, many were listening closely and agreeing. There was something almost hypnotic about the intensity of the man's rhetoric and the undercurrent was of anger being stoked and banked. Uneasy, she drew back towards Mairead.

The crowds within the market behind the cross moved aside as two soldiers on horseback picked their way through. *Redcoats*, Jeannie thought, *government soldiers*. Many of the looks they got were unfriendly and more than one man spat on the ground behind them as they went. The man at the cross looked around as the attention of the crowd shifted. Seeing the soldiers approach, his face contorted with anger and he continued to speak with renewed vigour. The tide of the crowd ebbed as some onlookers began to melt away but most stayed. They stood their ground, looking defiantly at the approaching soldiers. Close enough now to hear fragments of the speech, Jeannie knew it was about the treatment of the Scots since the Act of Union. Betrayal and broken promises. Beside her, Gavin had his hand on the dagger at his waist as he steered them round towards the edge of the stalls. Jeannie, heart racing, moved herself in front of Mairead and Gavin behind as they went forward.

To her horror, a cabbage sailed through the air and hit the back of one of the soldiers. A hush fell across the crowd and the young redcoat did well to control his horse as it danced sideways and threw its head. In streets this busy, there was no way for the soldier to know where the insult had come from and he remained resolutely upright in his saddle watching the speaker and the crowd. Gavin took advantage of the sudden surge of activity around them and took Mairead by the arm. He steered the women quickly up one of the side streets and back onto Castle Wynd.

The city is like a tinderbox, Jeannie thought, and the mixture of heat and feelings of anger towards the King and his government was potent. It wouldn't take much for it to catch alight. The gathering storm she had sensed in the tower was being felt here too.

CHAPTER 20

MAIREAD

They made their way to the house of the merchant Murray. It stood in a row of fine houses with a thatched roof and a dark wooden door. Mairead insisted that this was a social call on behalf of Lady Frances and that Gavin should take their purchases back to the lodging. He was reluctant but left after eliciting promises that they would remain within until he returned. Mairead smoothed back her hair and straightened her skirts whilst Jeannie knocked on the door. They were shown to the reception room by a young maid who welcomed Jeannie with a flurry of exclamations about the health of her mistress and the growing babe. When introduced to Mairead, she curtsied, hurriedly turning pink at her impertinence. Mairead assured her there had been no insult and the girl backed out of the room. The clatter of her steps filled the house as she rushed to tell her mistress about their unexpected visitors. The wood-panelled room was elegant and comfortable with upholstered chairs and a couch the colour of bitter orange. Mairead stroked the sumptuous fabric. On the wall was a portrait of a couple, the merchant and his wife, she presumed. He was seated on the same couch and his slender wife stood behind him, her hand on his shoulder, eyes cast demurely downwards. The merchant Murray was wealthy, and the room spoke of a comfortable life.

The door opened and a young woman entered. Her gown was plain but Mairead took in the quality of the fabric and the fine lace at the cuffs. Isobel Murray looked shyly at the women and then presented herself first to Mairead.

'Welcome Mistress Erskine, you do me an honour with your visit,' said Isobel as she risked a look at the face of her visitor before turning to Jeannie and taking her hands.

'Mistress Murray.' Mairead inclined her head in acknowledgement. 'The Lady Frances asked that I look in and hopes to find you and the babe are in good health,' Mairead said.

'That is a kindness indeed mistress, please call me Isobel' the woman said warmly. 'We are both well thanks to Jeannie's skill. We owe Lady Frances much and will not forget it.'

There, Mairead thought, *this is how it is done.* A system of kindnesses and favours, of obligations and debts. No blistering oaths sworn in blood were needed. A simple reminder of what is owed and to whom. Perhaps there was much to learn from the lady after all and the web of alliances she had woven.

'How does the babe?' Jeannie asked.

'He is strong and feeds well,' Isobel said proudly. 'A fine pair of lungs on him too,' she continued as a cry began from above.

The door opened again and the young maid carried in a tray with tea and a plate of dainty confections. Isobel stood to pour the tea and Mairead could see a slight tremor in her hand. She looked closely at the woman and saw the dark circles under her eyes and the light sheen on her pale forehead. Mairead looked to Jeannie and saw that she was already on her feet taking the teapot gently. Jeannie looked questioningly as she handed Mairead a cup and she answered with a very slight incline of her head.

'Might I see the babe, Isobel?' Jeannie handed the woman a cup.

'Oh yes, he'll be feeding.' Isobel went to stand.

'No need to trouble yourself,' Jeannie said, 'I dare say I can find my way.'

Mairead saw that Jeannie had a way with people and began to understand why her aunt by marriage was so fond for her. The woman seemed able to earn their trust and respect easily. That was a useful trait to have.

Isobel and Mairead faced each other across a beautiful carpet depicting an orange tree in full fruit. They made small talk about the heat and the price of goods. As they talked, Mairead weighed up the choice that now faced her. Lady Frances had suggested this visit and she was keen to know why.

'Lady Frances will be pleased to hear you are recovering well,' she said, 'I will write to her on our return.'

'I am grateful to her for sending Jeannie to tend me,' Isobel said. 'My husband and the earl trade often and have certain *interests* in common.'

Catching the emphasis Mairead understood that the merchant was sympathetic to the earl's cause. Mairead smoothed her skirts and relaxed a little further into her seat. She felt herself on surer ground.

'Is your husband out at the market today?' Mairead ventured.

'No, he is not.' Isobel looked directly at Mairead and said, 'He is away in France. There is a shipment he must secure.'

Mairead caught the words and the cautious tone in which they were spoken and her mind raced. *What is in France?*

'Well then, I hope his voyage is successful,' Mairead said brightly. 'You will have much to do in his absence.'

'Aye, but that is the lot of women is it not?' Isobel sighed 'We go or stay as we are bidden. I trust you will find much to occupy you at Alloa Tower? 'Tis a large household.'

'That it is,' Mairead agreed. 'The command of the garrison does my husband honour.'

'It does you both honour.' Isobel inclined her head. 'May both our husbands have fair winds and calm seas.'

Mairead raised her teacup in salute and they smiled warmly at one another. Mairead saw the fierce intelligence behind Isobel's smile and felt a spark of kinship. *Is this a woman in whom I might find a true friend?* Used to forging her own path and finding the company of other women dull it surprised her how much she wished for that.

Jeannie returned and the conversation shifted to the baby who was now sleeping soundly. The moment had passed. Isobel returned to the quiet and proud mother she had been when they entered, clearly devoted to her child. Jeannie wrote out a receipt for a tincture to help with the pain from Isobel's milk coming through. When the maid entered announcing Gavin had returned, the three women were sat in easy companionship.

'Thank you for your hospitality and do forgive us for arriving unannounced.' Mairead stood to take her leave.

'You are welcome here, *Mistress Erskine*,' Isobel said, 'my husband is proud to hold the patronage of the Argyll.'

'I will send Jeannie to look in again,' said Mairead wondering at the slight emphasis on the Erskine name. 'Send a messenger to me if she can be of further aid.'

'Please give my thanks to Lady Frances,' Isobel said, 'her patronage is valued and we owe her much. You, too, are welcome here mistress should you require anything.'

The air was stifling as they stepped out into the street and Gavin led them back to Mar's Lodging. It seemed that there had been no further incident at the market cross, and the city buzzed with activity. From the flashes of red visible here and there, government soldiers were stationed across the city, under her uncle's command. She wondered if her nephews and cousins would be part of the force. What was her father doing now? A jolt of guilt pulsed through Mairead as she realised that her loyalty to her husband and his clan would set her against her family. A restless pit opened deep in the centre of her being and began to send up sparks of unease. Images of those she loved flashed across her mind. She pictured her father and uncle deep in conversation by the fire in her family home. Their heads bent close together, so alike in their mannerisms. Then she saw James commanding his garrison of men at the tower. The fatigue etched deep in his face and shoulders squared to the burdens. Her heart ached at the thought that they might be called to face each other across a battlefield. *Perhaps it wouldn't come to that?* Deep down she knew that was a feeble hope, the wishful thinking of a child. She would have to endure whatever came and do her duty. Keep the tower and those under her protection safe.

Hugh had found her a comfortable chair in a shady room. The heavy door served to muffle the sounds from outside but Mairead was relieved to be out of the sun and mull over her meeting with Isobel Murray. She drummed her fingers lightly on the arm of the chair as she tried to piece it together. Merchant Murray must be a supporter of the Stuart King, in league with John Erskine. Perhaps he and his wife were close to the centre of these events. The thoughts swirled round in her head.

'Mistress?' Hugh said, startling Mairead from her musings.

'Oh, thank you,' she said as a jug of ale and platter of cheese and meat was placed at her elbow.

'I'm afraid it is the best we have at present.' Hugh looked at her curiously and she gave him a bright smile.

'It will do just fine,' she said, then sensing some explanation was required, she added, 'I was wondering if I had spent too little or too much with the merchants today.'

'If there is more required then we can send along for it. Merchant Murray is always very accommodating for the Argyll,' Hugh said. 'Lady Frances insisted that Isobel Murray had the finest eye for silk and lace outside of London and would have them brought from nowhere else.'

Her aunt had encouraged the connection. Mairead thought of the caution she had sensed in Isobel. Neither sure of the other and both with much to lose. She must be canny now. *Je Pense Plus*, she reminded herself.

CHAPTER 21

JEANNIE

J eannie sat in the shade at the edge of the courtyard and watched the goods from the market being unloaded in front of her. Barrels of ale and sacks of flour were being sorted and taken down into the underground stores under the watchful scowl of the quartermaster. Jeannie recognised the transformation that the lodgings were undergoing, she had seen something similar take place at Alloa Tower. The lodging was becoming a barracks and every available room and space was being turned over to sleeping quarters and stores. Walls were being reinforced with iron and stone all around her. This would pass unnoticed from the street, and the bustle of a market day would make the comings and goings of provisions and men less obvious. From her vantage point, she could see an urgency to the work but it had been carefully planned. Each man and boy knew their task and was about it efficiently. Stonemasons, smiths, soldiers and retainers all worked with purpose.

As she watched, Gavin came out of the hall and secured his pouch across his shoulder and chest. He tucked in folded missives, looking grave as he too surveyed the changes taking place around them. He beckoned to a young lad, gave an instruction and sent him hurrying towards the stables. Jeannie stood to make herself ready for the return journey, thinking about filling her water skin at the well before they went. She skirted the outer edge of the courtyard, taking care to stay out of the way of the men and animals that filled it. The well was in the western corner of the square, sat under a wood and thatch shelter and she untied the goatskin from her waist. A small group of soldiers and stonemasons washed their faces and hands in buckets of water to help cool them and acknowledged Jeannie as she began to work the pump and held the skin under the faucet. She peered down into the stone-lined darkness, the air had a fresh sweetness that contrasted with the hot bodies of men and beasts around her. She lingered, enjoying the moment until the water began to spill from the neck of the skin and run down her sleeve. She straightened and tipped the skin over her mouth. The water was fresh and soft as she swallowed and wiped the drops from her chin with the back of her hand.

Seeing the horses were being led across the square, Jeannie looked around for Mairead. She would see if the mistress needed anything before they mounted again. Hugh had offered a private room inside for Mairead to take her meal and rest. Jeannie had still been in the hall and had helped herself to bread and ale at the common tables. Coming outside to find a space to rest out of the way, she did not know where to look. Seeing Hugh still with Gavin, she made her way towards them and stood ready to catch their attention. The men were absorbed in their discussion, unaware of her presence.

'The laird's orders are to be given by word of mouth only,' Hugh said. 'He dare not risk a written message.'

Gavin stood, hand resting on the hilt of his sword and brow furrowed as he nodded to indicate he understood

'Most of the northern clans have joined with the laird and will send a man to Braemar to bear witness. A muster at Inverness will follow,' Hugh said. 'The English Jacobites will push up from Lancaster north as the earl pushes south. All being well they will meet here in Stirling.'

Jeannie smothered the gasp she felt rising. English Jacobites too? This would mean a war in both countries.

'James is to hold the tower and the crossing. He must not be drawn into the fray at Stirling.'

Gavin's eyebrows rose in surprise and he looked down at the cobblestones before him. It was clear he was trying to make sense of the information and anticipate the next move.

'The Stuart King will cross the North Seas from France and along the Forth to be crowned here?' Gavin asked.

'It would seem to be so.' Hugh shrugged his shoulders.

Gavin rubbed at his chin looking worried. He bid farewell to Hugh and the men clasped hand to elbow as soldiers had always done. Hugh rested his other hand on Gavin's shoulder in a gesture that Jeannie read as a wish for good fortune. She cleared her throat and walked forward.

'Where will I find Mistress Erskine?' she asked. 'I will see what she needs before we leave.'

Hugh led her into the lodging and she noticed the look of worry he cast back over his shoulder towards his friend as they turned.

The lodging was unrecognisable as the elegant residence of the earl. The furniture and tapestries had gone, leaving the stark stone of the bare walls. Every available space had been turned over to house the soldiers. Hugh continued to lead Jeannie up towards what had been the earl's private rooms and here at least there remained some vestiges of comfort. *These rooms must be reserved for the officers,* Jeannie thought as Hugh stopped outside one such room. Jeannie thanked him and knocked on the door, announcing herself loudly to be heard over the noise of the hammers on the stonework below. Mairead called for her to enter and she stepped into the room.

'We will be ready to leave soon,' Jeannie said. 'Do you have need of anything?'

'No,' Mairead sighed as something outside hit the floor with a loud crash followed by the raised voices of men. 'I will be glad to leave the city and all this...'

Jeannie glanced at the door and then stepped closer to Mairead. She wanted to be heard over the din but not by anyone who might be passing.

'The English Jacobites are rising too,' she said urgently. Mairead's eyes widened in shock. 'James needs to hold the tower and control the crossing.'

'How do you know this?' Mairead asked.

'Hugh passed the orders onto to Gavin.' Jeannie caught Mairead's sharp look and said, 'I wasn't listening in, mistress, I was looking for you.'

Mairead nodded.

'Isobel's husband is in France,' Mairead whispered urgently, 'to fetch a special cargo... aid perhaps or soldiers?'

'The King!' Jeannie exclaimed far too loudly then clamped her hand over her mouth.

'James Stuart is coming to Scotland?' Mairead muttered as the understanding dawned. 'That is what she was trying to tell me. Then I can put my trust in Isobel?'

The door swung open and Gavin hurried them out to the courtyard. Jeannie looked thoughtfully at her young mistress as she guided her horse along behind. Her love for James was beyond question and she knew her duty. Any lingering doubt about the woman's loyalties evaporated and Jeannie knew that, for better or for worse, she would bind herself to Mairead Erskine.

CHAPTER 22

HAZEL

The History of Scotland Trust project board met at Airthrey Castle in the grounds of the university. The castle had been many things over the years, from a convalescence home for soldiers in World War One to a maternity hospital. Since the university had acquired the land, it had become a teaching space and now the beautiful building was used to host events and exhibitions. Castles like this told the story of the fortunes of the clans and landowners in Scotland. This version of the castle had been built in the late 18th century and as she looked around her Hazel was glad to see it retained many of the original features. Hazel had never been inside before and her eye was drawn to the ornate cornicing with either an alabaster lion or unicorn in each corner. The national animals of England and Scotland and together they were symbolic of the union of crowns. She smiled to herself at the synchronicity of that and leant across to point it out to Lauren who looked up and grinned in response. They were seated around a large round oak table which was filling up with members cups in hand.

Hazel felt at ease and smiled as Chris opened the meeting with a discussion about Lauren's radio interview. A few of the people present had listened and it had been a tremendous success. Lauren was a natural teacher, and she had held the presenter and listeners captivated. She had skilfully slotted in the upcoming events as part of the project and as a result, the storytelling evening had sold out with enough demand to put on a second. Hazel looked around the table. Only one face wasn't smiling. Klaus Leinster sat watching Lauren intently as she spoke about the radio interview. A slight twitch of the muscle in his cheek gave away his disgust. It looked to Hazel that the man was jealous of the attention. Chris, the chair of the board, asked Hazel her thoughts and she looked hurriedly away from Dr Leinster, suddenly aware that she had been staring. Hazel agreed that between the article in the Scotsman and the radio interview, the media exposure was gathering pace. The marketing team were already looking at how to keep the momentum building.

Hazel began to relax as she gave an overview of the public's engagement to date and her plans for growth over the coming weeks. Her last meeting with Lauren had cleared the air and she felt that they were truly on the same page. Experts in their respective fields, together they were building a vision for the next phases of the project. The board members peppered her with questions and offered ideas with enthusiasm. A buzz of excitement spread through the room. Spending so far had been minimal, which always went down well with the trustees who were accountants and businesspeople. The dovetailing of their Fractal Lines project and the Archaeology Society's request to survey sites opened up many new possibilities for the project and the trust as a whole. The external advisors were impressed and keen to highlight where other links could be made.

Hazel kept an eye on Dr Leinster, who had said barely a word so far. She could tell by the faint trace of a smile on his lips and his hands folded neatly in front of him that he was biding his time. There was something hawk like about the way he waited, eyes hooded but alert and watchful. *Well, let's see what he has to say shall we*, she thought to herself as she steered the conversation around.

'Dr Leinster, is there anything that we should consider at this stage? Given your position as a trustee at the National Library I'd be interested in your perspective,' she asked.

Hazel, aware of Lauren beside her noted that the other woman seemed to remain completely relaxed. Dr Leinster took his time to consider the question and appeared to be savouring the tension she felt begin to build.

'Well, I'm sure you will already have this in hand, of course, but for the benefit of my trustee colleagues,' he gave Hazel a tight smile, 'it is imperative that you keep an eye on the terms of the World Heritage Trust grant. They are strict about the projects staying on brief and the detail of how the money is being spent.'

Before Hazel had time to answer, Chris took the initiative.

'You are absolutely right, Klaus,' he said with a hint of annoyance, 'the grant was awarded with specific criteria. The Archaeological Society have their own funding and there is nothing that would rule out the projects dovetailing.'

'Excellent,' Klaus said. 'If that is all in order then I suppose my only other caution would be to ensure that the focus remains on the project as a whole and not any one... erm aspect.' His eyes met Hazel's as he sat back in his chair.

As the meeting ended, Chris caught Hazel for a conversation about an upcoming event at one of the trust's other properties. When she turned, she saw that the room was emptying. Lauren's bag and cardigan were still hooked over her seat and she decided to wait and have a quick debrief. Hazel moved the cups and glasses from the table back onto the catering trolly, not liking to leave a mess for others. As she turned back, Klaus Leinster appeared. She could see him in the reflection of the picture frame on the wall in front of her. He stood uncomfortably close and she was aware of the slightly spicy scent of his cologne. Her grip tightened imperceptibly on the cup she was lifting as she straightened up and prepared to face him. *He must know he's too close*, she thought and felt a cold sweat bead between her shoulder blades.

'Dr Leinster,' she said, 'am I in your way?' Her voice sounded high and shrill in her ears. She swallowed hard.

'Call me Klaus, please,' he said without moving. 'I was hoping to catch you.'

'Oh,' Hazel said, 'how can I help?'

A prickle of unease spread down her arms as she realised her predicament. If she stepped to the side and round him, he would be between her and the door. If she stayed as she was, he still had the upper hand.

'I'm trying to help *you*, actually,' he said, his tone dripping false concern. 'With some friendly advice. Be careful with Lauren, she doesn't play well with others.'

His features settled into self-satisfied look at Hazel's shock. He continued.

'This project is about building her reputation and forging her career,' he said and reached out to touch her arm, voice now condescending. 'She will use your idea as her springboard and think nothing of it.'

Hazel's outrage overrode her unease and she turned her body to the side and moved past him, shrugging off his hand.

'It is possible for two professionals to work together without it being a competition,' Hazel said, feeling a flush rise to her cheeks.

'You cannot afford another scandal, Miss Rankin,' he said.

At that moment, footsteps approached the room and Klaus leaned in close, sneering at her.

'You were warned...' he hissed under his breath and turned to walk out of the room. 'I wish you luck Hazel,' he said as he passed her, his voice now cheerful and light.

Lauren stood aside at the doorway to let him leave. She appeared to have a handle on the situation from the expression of concern on her face.

'That man,' Hazel said shakily, 'is a pig.'

Lauren nodded in agreement and asked, 'Are you okay?'

'Yes,' she replied, knees weak with relief. 'He wanted to warn me about you.'

Lauren's laugh surprised Hazel and she looked at the other woman in confusion.

'Well, we are getting a lot of positive publicity and exposure,' she said, 'that he will think should have been his, and you did rather pull the tiger's tail.'

Hazel couldn't disagree with that and it was her turn to laugh.

'For what it's worth,' Lauren began, pulling on her cardigan, 'in a fist fight... my money would be on you!'

Hazel knew that it wasn't the fear that had made her angry, it was the fact that he had tried to intimidate her, to use what he thought he knew against her. She was angry at herself for allowing him to make her feel that way. It was unacceptable and the behaviour of a career bully. *What could she do about it*, she wondered? He worked on this campus and had a legitimate reason to be there after the meeting. He hadn't overtly threatened her. No, he was far too subtle for that. Hazel replayed the interactions between Lauren and Klaus in her mind and felt a new sense of understanding and solidarity growing. Lauren was quietly and simply standing her ground and refusing to be intimidated. There was something she could learn from that and she admired the way Lauren stayed in her personal power. It was clear, though, that he would continue to seize any opportunity to make things difficult and would need to be handled carefully.

The thought circled through her mind as they made their way out of the building. Her car sat alone in front of a dense clump of trees. In the gloom, she thought she saw movement and felt a wave of nausea rise. *Just the adrenaline wearing off*, she told herself. She hurried to her car, unable to stop herself glancing around nervously. Climbing in, she locked the door. The silence closed in around her. She turned the key and pushed herself back into the seat and slowed her breathing.

CHAPTER 23

HAZEL

M etal screens had been erected around the area that the geophysical survey team would be working on first. Their function was primarily to allow the team to work without disturbance but it was fair to say that they had certainly attracted interest locally. As the van containing the equipment pulled onto the gravel path, Hazel could see a number of the workers from the council office gather in the corridor of the building which overlooked the tower. The archaeologists climbed out of the van, and she went to greet them. They made their way up to the charter room where Lauren, Tom and the HoST guides waited.

The first order of business was to look at the drone survey information and the plans for the tower and manor house. Hazel was looking forward to this. She had heard a lot about the 3D modelling software the Archaeological Society had developed with colleagues from across the globe. The lead archaeologist, Iain, had agreed to give a demonstration for the historians working on the Fractal Lines project using the work they had carried out at Skara Brae in Orkney to help them understand how the information gathered was interpreted and how that might be used in projects like their own.

Iain began to lay out the pictures taken by the drone on the table. It struck Hazel how different the site looked from the true bird's eye perspective compared to the view she could see with the naked eye from the roof of the tower. She leant in close to study the photo showing the area behind the tower. The manor house once stood in part of it. The rowan tree caught her eye, even from above, the knot of branches showed the age of the tree and the ripening berries were vivid crimson. Hazel knew from the plans that the tree was all that survived from the original gardens of the manor house. It must have seen such change and it was incredible that it still continued to thrive year after year. From the image in front of her, she could see that the wall curved round to accommodate the tree and she traced the line of it with the tip of her finger. Isobel, the guide for the tower, came to see what she was looking at.

'It has always been considered bad luck to cut down a rowan,' she said. 'They're supposed to be a tree that protects the home.'

'I've seen this before.' Iain picked up the photo. 'Lots of superstition about trees. There are often rowans on the site of stone circles, too, and because of that they are associated with the Druids. It is a bit like yew trees in churchyards.'

'It is a really gnarled old tree,' Hazel said, 'and old, even for a rowan.'

'We'll be starting with that part of the grounds,' Iain said. 'I wonder what has survived of the house down there.'

The geophysicists, Claire and her colleague Sam, set up the laptop and began to load up the software. They had also brought in small models of the magnetometer and an earth resistance meter which the tight huddle of historians were excited to play with.

The group assembled around the table and Iain explained the project that the Archaeological Society were working on. The geophysical and drone surveys for all of the designated sites of historic interest would not only provide an accurate overview to enhance the information and records but would help identify what could be explored next. There was a real buzz in the archaeology world because the 3D modelling software didn't disturb the ground. It was a technological leap forwards that protected the ecology and environment too. It took the idea of seeing under the soil to a new level and it dovetailed perfectly with Fractal Lines.

Hazel was fascinated as Claire took them on a virtual walk-through of Skara Brae, the neolithic settlement on Orkney. The site was critically vulnerable and could be washed away or recovered by the dunes at any point so it was a race against time to record and learn what they could. The focus in the room was palpable as the historians considered the possibilities of technology like this in their own fields of interest. It was a startling contrast to cutting-edge programming and graphics against the backdrop of such an old space. In a moment of fancy, Hazel wondered what the people in the portraits around the room would make of it if they could see this unfolding. John Erskine would have approved, she imagined, given how he enjoyed modernising his properties. Hazel looked around for Lauren who watched from the side like a proud mother as her students bombarded their visitors with questions and gave her a thumbs-up when she caught her eye.

Lauren managed to round up the historians and shepherd them back to their tasks so that the work on the survey could begin. Hazel set up her laptop at the table and began to work through the plan for moving the project to the temporary outbuilding during the winter. Lauren, Tom and their team could still access the tower but there was an ongoing schedule of maintenance and conservation to accommodate. She hoped that the temporary home of the project would keep the project visible.

The next email in Hazel's inbox was an invitation to appear as a guest on a podcast to talk about the project but also the importance of trusts in protecting the heritage of Scotland. The podcast was hosted by a well-known historian and one of her favourite authors. Hazel liked to listen to this particular podcast when driving long distances and replied with her acceptance immediately. Excited to share the news with somebody she sent a text to her father. It was only 11 a.m. and she knew he would be in his study, a place where he did not permit mobile phones or laptops. She could picture him sitting in his worn leather chair with his journal in front of him, a cup of tea at his elbow and his glasses pulled down onto his nose. Perhaps he had finished writing for the day and was now reading or studying one of the old scientific books from his collection. The thought made Hazel smile. Her father was a creature of habit who, like her, took comfort in his routines. It drove her mother to distraction that the two of them were so alike.

At lunchtime, Hazel went down to the small staff kitchen to make herself a coffee to have with her salad and took it outside to see how the survey was going. Iain watched the monitor in the back of the van carefully as Claire and her assistant took slow and methodical steps. They worked their way around a grid marked out with bamboo posts and red ribbon. Hazel sat on the bench with her face upturned to the sun, enjoying the warmth after the cool interior of the castle. A shadow crossed her vision, accompanied by the scent of oud and amber. Lauren sat down beside her to watch the progress of the geophysicists. The repetitive movement and pace were almost meditative and the women sat in companionable silence. Hazel was the first to move as she opened the tub which sat on the bench beside her. The peppery smell of rocket and the sherbet sweetness of watermelon wafted up. Hazel pulled the little fork from the lid of the tub and began to eat.

'Tom is doing a good job of leading the field teams. It suits him.' Hazel took a sip of her coffee.

'Yes, he had a tough start to his doctorate before he transferred to my programme. I keep telling him to get out of the library and into the real places,' Lauren said. 'He's thriving on this project—How does that even fill you?' Lauren peered doubtfully into Hazel's lunch box before thrusting a white cake box at her. 'Here, have a strawberry tart.'

When Hazel hesitated to take the proffered tart glistening with sauce, Lauren held it closer and pointed to the strawberry.

'Fruit, see?' she said. 'Life is all about balance. Live a little!'

Hazel took the tart and bit into it, closing her eyes to savour the creme patisserie and the satisfying snap of the pastry case. It was heavenly and she discarded what was left of her salad to give it her full attention.

They looked on with interest as Iain called across to Claire to stop for a moment. She was working on the area at the roots of the rowan and carefully passed the magnetometer she was using to her assistant and made her way over to the van. To Hazel, the device looked like the handle of a lawnmower with a strip light at the bottom. Like the kind of invention created by an eccentric engineer in his garden workshop from random things he had lying around. Hazel watched as Claire perched her sunglasses on her head and peered in close at the screen. She couldn't hear the conversation but Iain was tracing around a shape with the tip of his pen and they were in deep discussion.

'I wonder what they've seen,' Hazel said, brushing pastry crumbs from her lap.

'Maybe they've found some of the legendary Jacobite gold,' Lauren whispered dramatically.

Laughing, the women watched as Claire took the other machine out of the side of the van and began to set it up. Hazel was enjoying her break and to her surprise, she was enjoying Lauren's company too. Checking her watch she saw she had only a few minutes left of her break and a looming deadline for a report she'd need to work on this afternoon. Reluctantly she gathered her things and made her way back up to the charter room.

Hazel was looking over the monthly visitor and revenue figures from the summer period and making notes for her quarterly report when she heard footsteps echoing up the staircase. Iain was red-faced and slightly breathless from the exertion. She stood to pull out a chair for him but he shook his head.

'Have you found something?' she asked.

When he nodded, she called up the stairs to Lauren and Tom who were working through the paper archives in the solar. They appeared, looking expectantly at Iain who cleared his throat and rested his hands on the back of a chair.

'We think we might have found a body,' he said simply.

'A body?' Lauren repeated incredulously. 'Where?'

'Under the rowan,' Iain replied softly.

There was absolute silence for a moment as they took that information in. Hazel sat down heavily on the chair as the room swam around her. There was a rushing in her ears as she struggled to process what that meant. Lauren took charge.

'Okay,' she said turning to Iain. 'Is there a procedure for this?'

'Yes,' he confirmed. 'We notify the police and then they will decide what happens next.'

'Any idea how long it's been there?' Tom asked, clearly bewildered by the sudden turn of events.

'Well, from the density of the earth above, it isn't recent,' Iain said, then taking in the expressions on their faces, he shrugged his shoulders. 'But that's what forensics are for. I'm sorry.'

'Right,' Hazel said, 'who is going to call the police? Probably best be you Iain as you know what you've seen on the screen.'

Iain returned to the van to make the call and Hazel remained sat at the table with Lauren and Tom. The shadows in the room lengthened as a cloud moved across the sun. The warmth and colour seemed to seep from the room and Hazel began to feel a dark hole open deep in her solar plexus. She needed to be busy. She stood abruptly to gather the tower staff and break the news to them. The need to try and stay ahead of whatever was coming now consumed her.

Lauren stood beside her as she explained to the team that, what looked to be, a body had been found and that the police had been notified. The team were stunned and listened attentively as she talked them through closing the tower to the public and waiting for further instruction from the police. As they went, talking quietly between themselves, Lauren began to gather her things.

'Tom and I will get out of your way,' she said gently.

'You aren't staying?' Hazel asked, surprised.

'Not unless there's anything you need us to do here?' When Hazel shook her head, Lauren continued, 'Then we will go back to the university and keep working on what we have.'

Hazel felt a sense of irrational betrayal. That awful and familiar feeling of being isolated and left to face the consequences alone. A rush of bile erupted in her throat. She swallowed it down and tried hard to push those thoughts away.

'It might not be as bad as all that.' Lauren put her hand on Hazel's back. 'All publicity is good publicity.'

Lauren and Tom collected what they needed and left with Lauren trying to put a positive spin on the situation. Her forced brightness grated on Hazel's nerves and she was almost relieved when their voices faded out at the base of the stairs.

Hazel sat alone with her head in her hands and made a mental list of who needed to be told and what needed to be done: organise for the grounds to be secured, get her team on a press briefing, let Chris and the Chair of the Board know. There was a procedure for events like this and a crisis management briefing would be held. For now, it was Hazel's job to liaise with the police and close the site down as quickly and efficiently as she could. *First things first*, she thought as she picked up the phone with a shaking hand, she had to call Chris.

CHAPTER 24

HAZEL

Hazel woke drenched in sweat and drew a gasping breath in. Sitting up, she reached for the bedside lamp and clicked it on. The glow from the lamp made the darkness surrounding her feel deeper and she hugged her knees up to her chest, wrapping her arms around them and trying to slow her breathing. In through her nose and out through her mouth. Slowly, slowly, her terror was beginning to subside. Artemis jumped onto the foot of the bed and padded her way up to sit beside Hazel, nudging her hand with a cool nose and rubbing an arched back against her leg. Hazel stroked the back of her neck and the cat settled in close to her, yellow eyes unblinking and remaining watchful. Fragments of the dream lingered around her like thick fog. She could still feel the pressure of hands around her neck beginning to tighten. The darkness. The rough voice as she was dragged from her bed. It was the same nightmare she'd had since York. Although it had been months now since the last time, it had lost none of its potency.

Glancing at the clock, Hazel saw it was 4.30 a.m. and knew that all chance of sleep was gone. With a sigh, she got out of bed and headed to the bathroom. The light felt harsh bouncing off the white tiles and copper sink. She turned on the shower and looked herself in the mirror. As the steam filled the room, she peeled off the grey vest top and cotton shorts she slept in, throwing them into the laundry basket. Opening the shower door, she paused as she was about to step in and turned and locked the bathroom door. Under the shower, she faced the flow of water and closed her eyes, letting it cascade down her face and shoulders. She drew in a shuddering breath and began to cry, letting the tears fall unchecked along with the water. It was happening again. Would she ever be free of it? Of him? Stupid, stupid, stupid, she had allowed herself to relax and start to believe it was all coming together. Her guard had come down and now this.

In the kitchen, she made herself a strong black coffee and focused her attention on the scent whilst it brewed – it grounded her in the present. Artemis gave a plaintive meow circling her food bowl expectantly.

'At this time, you usually prefer to be out catching your own breakfast, don't you?' she asked.

Hazel opened the cupboard and pulled out a small tin as the cat's meows became more urgent.

'So much for the goddess of the hunt, eh?' Hazel joked, emptying the tin into the waiting bowl.

She stood by the window, looking out over the garden watching the sky begin to lighten. The blackbird in the hedge was awake too and his calls trilled out into the stillness. As she sipped her coffee, her mind returned to her cottage in York. On another morning, when dawn broke and the cloudy sky was streaked with reds and pinks.

***

She struggled to open her left eye and slowly, deliberately willed her hand to move towards her face. The effort was exhausting and her limbs felt like lead. As she walked her fingers up from her chin, she felt a viscose wetness. She poked her tongue out and recoiled at the metallic taste and sharp pain. Her lip was bleeding. On up her face, her finger probed the hot swelling around her eye. A wave of panic overtook her and she let out a harsh, painful sob. Pulling herself slowly up the bed to a sitting position, she turned on the light and twisted to see herself in the mirror. The broken skin on her lip and swollen eye, and the red marks around her neck had bile burning her tender throat. Helpless, she vomited onto the floor beside her, tears stinging her face.

She froze as she heard a noise. A frantic scrabbling and then a yowl. *Artemis.* She forced her feet over the side of the bed and tried to stand. The room spun and her legs refused to hold her. The sounds of yowling became more desperate, and she slid down the bed to the floor. On her hands and knees, she crawled across the floor toward the sounds of scratching. She had no sense of time in the fog of dizziness and pain, moments or hours passed as she moved inch by painful inch. At last, she got her hand to the door and pulled the chrome handle down. Artemis pushed her head through the gap and into her face, pacing around her, agitated. Hazel tried to speak to reassure her, but her tongue was stuck to the roof of her mouth and her voice wouldn't come. Artemis came to a halt at her side and nudged gently.

Everything went black.

The next time Hazel awoke, it was to full sunlight streaming through the roof light and her head was pounding. Artemis lay with her head on her white paws and two slits of yellow visible under her half-closed eyelids. Hazel stretched her arms out gingerly and found they moved with greater ease than before. She pushed herself up to sitting with her back against the wall. The room tilted and spun in a kaleidoscope of light and colour. Another wave of nausea hit, leaving her breathless. She remained still until the sensations passed and began to crawl forward again towards the stairs. With tears of sheer frustration streaming down her bruised face, she made her way down. Seated she dragged herself one slow stair at a time, gripping tightly onto the spindles as she went. On the last stair she paused to catch her breath and fought another round of dizziness. The sound of a bird singing reached her, its notes painfully high in her ears. Following the sound, she looked through the kitchen to the patio doors. They were wide open. Her heart lurched and she tried desperately to think back to the previous evening. Then she saw her phone. It lay charging on the white counter-top. She needed help.

The call handler had asked Hazel to stay on the line until the police and ambulance arrived. She felt displaced, as though she was observing the world from outside of herself, as she listened to the reassurances of the voice on the line. A blackbird on the sandstone flags of the patio hopped close to the door, head cocked to one side. For a second, they watched each other until the call handler spoke again to say that the paramedics were outside. As the line went dead, two women in green suits appeared through the back gate and Hazel's world filled with strangers, noise and touch.

The paramedics were almost silent apart from a softly spoken instruction and exchanged glances she pretended she couldn't see over her head. With gentle hands, they helped her change into a blue forensics suit. A white blanket wrapped around her shoulders. It was stiff and had NHS Yorkshire written in blue letters as a boarder. Behind them, a detective spoke quietly to another forensic suit with a camera. Hazel allowed herself to be led into the back of an ambulance as the police officer promised her again that Artemis was going to be just fine with the local vet. The harsh light and motion inside the vehicle made her feel sick and she squeezed her eyes closed, fighting the flood of sensation that threatened to overwhelm her.

In the hospital, she was taken to a private room with soft lamps and a rug on the floor. Hazel took it in as if watching a scene from a film, distant and detached. The door opened and a woman stepped in carrying a box marked forensic samples. The woman was in her 50s, Hazel guessed, and wore blue surgical scrubs. She introduced herself as Sarah, a doctor who worked with the police. Hazel listened impassively as Doctor Sarah explained that she needed to examine Hazel, take some photographs of her injuries and collect some samples. Her hands were folded in her lap and her gaze was on the floral pattern of daisies and roses on the curtain. She nodded her consent and stood for the photographs. Hazel remained silent through each stage of the examination. Her throat felt as though she had swallowed a razor blade, and the edges of her vision sparkled. She felt a sharp scratch in her arm as a cannula was placed.

When the doctor had finished, a nurse joined her and together they helped her out of the forensic suit and into the blue and green hospital gown. They hooked up a saline drip to help with the dehydration and offered her something for the pain. Hazel shook her head. The red aura of pain around her was all that kept her anchored to the room and the present. Darkness waited on the edge of her vision along with her fear. The nurse asked if there was anyone she could call, and Hazel shook her head. She didn't want anybody to see her like this. She had no words. No voice. She just wanted to curl up and let the exhaustion engulf her.

Hazel was woken apologetically by a detective who introduced herself as Amanda. Although she tried to focus on the questions she was asked, it was like she was underwater, everything was echoing and unclear. From the light outside, it was now evening but Hazel had no sense of time passing. Amanda was asking if she had anywhere to go, the forensics team would need to go back to the house tomorrow and continue their work. She had nobody to call. Her loneliness broke like a storm wave on a rock and something deep inside her cracked open. The fear, the anger, the pain all welled up through it and came out as a raw wail. She rocked forward and Amanda caught her shoulders to hold her steady, then hit the button on the wall for help.

This time when Hazel woke, she knew there was only one choice. She asked for a phone and dialled the number etched into her memory since childhood.

'Mum?' she whispered, voice thick with pain and emotion. 'Can I come home?'

***

The chime of the doorbell summoned Hazel back from the past and she glanced at the clock on the wall – 7.30 a.m. She made her way to the door and opened it wide, knowing there were only two people who thought that this was an appropriate time to visit.

Her mum breezed past her with two shopping bags in her hands and made her way to the kitchen. Her father remained on the doorstep, taking in the dark circles and her red-rimmed eyes. She turned towards the kitchen, and he followed shutting the door.

'Breakfast, darling.' Her mother was rooting around the cupboard looking for the frying pan.

It was an instruction rather than a question and Hazel, knowing there was no point in protesting, began to prepare a fresh pot of coffee. Her father placed a newspaper on the table and her eye caught the headline she knew was coming.

Historic Investigation Turns Up Body.

'It could be worse,' her father said, opening the paper to the article.

'It'll mean we lose weeks of access to the site for visitors,' Hazel said. 'The events will all have to be cancelled.'

'They can be rescheduled,' he said, scanning the text. 'This might even be good for the project in the long run.'

'Not if we lose the funding.' Hazel pushed the plunger on the cafetiere down slowly.

'Now, don't jump to conclusions,' he said gently as he watched her carefully.

Hazel stared out of the window again, avoiding her father's eyes. Her hands wrapped tightly around her mug, inhaling the warm chocolatey aroma of the coffee.

'Be rational,' he said. 'This is not a disaster, it is a setback.'

Hazel said nothing. How could she explain that this was history repeating itself? It was all going to fall apart now. She knew it.

'This isn't York,' her father continued, as though he had read her thoughts. 'You just need to pivot.'

Her mother brought bacon and egg rolls to the table, and they ate quietly. Hazel understood that her parents had been worried for her when she had called them last night and that this was their way of trying to help. It had been for as long as she could remember; if she hadn't placed in a competition or hadn't been selected for a team, when she was preparing for exams, when her first and only serious relationship ended. Her mother would feed her, and her father would be cool, collected and rational. It infuriated her as a teenager. Now she truly appreciated the effort and gratefully took the comfort it offered.

CHAPTER 25

LAUREN

Lauren let go of the breath she had been holding as the door shut behind the last of the trustees. She sagged against the black leather of the chair. The atmosphere in the boardroom of the History of Scotland Trust had been tense and it had drained her. The police and archaeologists were still carrying out their investigations so the grounds around the tower were still off limits. Leinster had been positively gleeful.

At the moment all they could say for certain was that the body was female and not recently deceased. Now there would be further tests to establish how old the corpse was and see if a cause of death could be established. Security had to be set up at the site to keep the social media sleuths out. Tom had shown Lauren one of the videos full of wild speculation. Lauren swithered between amusement and annoyance. Apparently, this was common now in situations like this and in missing persons cases too. The hashtag 'bodyinthetower' was trending. With a bit of luck the frenzy would die down soon. The additional security measures were a huge cost that the trust was having to front. Combined with the loss of revenue from the cancelled events, the trustees were becoming concerned about the finances.

The opaque glass wall that separated the meeting room from the corridor cast a grey light and in front of it, Hazel sat twisting her ring, deep in thought. Lauren was worried about Hazel. The dark circles under her eyes were obvious although, from where Lauren sat, she had handled the meeting beautifully.

'I think we have persuaded them that we can make up for the lost time,' Lauren said.

'Hmm?' Hazel looked towards her. 'Sorry, I was miles away.'

'I said that we have persuaded the board that we can still make it work, it'll just take more time,' Lauren said again.

'Yes. Hopefully, we can get the site back soon and minimise the security costs,' Hazel sighed and tucked her hair behind her ear.

Lauren's phone beeped and she pulled her glasses from the top of her head to peer at the screen. The message was from the radio producer from BBC Scotland looking to have them back on the show to discuss the discovery. This would be a good opportunity to keep the public interested in the project.

'We've been invited to give a radio interview with BBC Scotland,' she explained. Hazel looked exasperated and opened her mouth to, presumably, object and Lauren held up her hand.

'Hear me out,' she said. 'It's a good opportunity to keep people interested.'

'It's morbid!' Hazel shook her head.

'Well, yes, I suppose it is really.' Lauren shrugged her shoulders. 'Although it is an opportunity to keep the narrative factual and dampen some of the wild rumours and speculation.'

Eventually, Hazel agreed, and Lauren texted back to accept the invitation. She suggested they head into town and get a coffee but Hazel wanted to stay and get some work done. As she readied herself to leave, Lauren noticed that Hazel was once again twisting her ring round and round her finger and recognised it as a sign of anxiety.

'Hazel, are you okay?' she asked.

'Just tired,' Hazel responded distantly, hunching her shoulders defensively.

Lauren remained unconvinced but decided not to push further. There was a distant look in the other woman's eyes and she could sense the heaviness. *An ocean of pain is behind that elegant façade*, she thought, *and she looks like it might well drown her.*

***

In the studio Lauren and Hazel sat facing the host with a huge red tipped microphone between them. The producer had given them headphones and as Lauren slipped them on she could hear Rebecca Walker introducing the next hour.

'Next we are joined by Dr Lauren McDonald and her colleague Hazel Rankin whose fight to save historic properties has taken a rather macabre turn.' Rebecca smiled at them encouragingly. 'Welcome to you both. I know we've had a number of questions about the mysterious body at the tower.'

'Thanks Rebecca,' Lauren replied lightly and glanced at Hazel waiting for her to speak and then to fill the awkward moment she continued, 'Thank you for inviting me back.'

As the interview progressed Lauren warmed to the topic but beside her Hazel remained tense, twisting the ring on her thumb. The answers she gave about the project were short and sharp.

Rebecca probed about the impact of the recent discoveries and delays. Lauren supplied what details she could whilst casting worried glances at Hazel who gripped the edge of the desk.

'So Hazel...' the host began, 'what can you tell us about the body?'

'Erm... we know very little at the moment.' Hazel looked startled but rallied a little to add, 'We know it is a woman and that it is not a recent grave.'

'Okay,' Rebecca continued, 'so what made the geophysics team start their search there?'

Lauren was alarmed to see a flush starting to creep up Hazel's face. The host noticed it too and pushed a glass of water towards her which Lauren slid to Hazel as she began to answer.

'Well, according to the old maps it is an area of the grounds that has remained untouched since the tower was built,' she said trying to sound conversational. 'When we looked at the plans from the construction of Erskine's tower house this was a wooded area at the edge of the village.'

'Oh really, wow,' Rebecca said, her interest sparked. 'So what were you hoping to find?'

'Evidence from earlier settlements. It would be interesting to know what the site was before the tower,' Lauren replied switching into her lecturing mode. 'Especially here in Scotland where there could be Viking, Pictish or even Celtic roots to a place.'

As the interview wound up Rebecca thanked her guests and asked for any final thoughts.

'We know there is a lot of interest about the body and it's great that so many people are excited about the history,' Lauren began, 'but please let the police and the archaeologists do their jobs.'

Beside her Hazel had recovered and looked embarrassed. Rebecca gave her a thumbs up and a smile of encouragement.

'And from you Hazel?' she asked. 'How can people get involved if they want to?'

'Well, they can send their theories and thoughts to the History of Scotland's social media pages.' Hazel's voice sounded a little hoarse and she cleared her throat gently. 'Our experts will discuss some of them in a live stream on Friday.'

As they left the studio Lauren watched Hazel carefully. The other woman had barely said two words and was now pulling the collar up on her coat and avoiding eye contact. Lauren let the silence stretch between them. She knew what it was like, after all, to feel as though you are unravelling. In the weeks before Leinster published the Douglas papers, she had thought she was going mad. A spark of fury ignited at the memory of those times.

***

In her office uncharacteristically early Lauren was trying to catch up on the essay marking she'd ignored all weekend. As the campus began to come to life she watched as the first-year undergraduate students began to walk up the path towards the lecture theatre. Subdued by the early start and the rain they were huddled together in groups. Klaus was due to be lecturing today but had delegated it to one of his PhD students instead. That had irritated Lauren, too busy with final touches to his latest research to bother with the undergraduates. The hype around it had been building for months. Klaus was convinced it would change the view of the importance of Scotland's nobility in shaping the modern world.

She lifted her cup to take a sip of tea and realised it was empty. *Well, that won't do I'm at least one cup under par as it is.* With a deep sigh she got up and headed to the faculty kitchenette. As the tea infused she wandered over to the notice board and read the latest updates from across the faculties. This meant she was out of sight of the door when she heard Leinster's voice. She had been about to step round and wish him a good morning when his tone stopped her.

'What do you call this?' Leinster was seething

'It's my synopsis of the information in the clan archives...' The female voice sounded close to tears.

'Who told you to do this?' he raged. 'I didn't set you this task!'

'I thought...'

'No, my dear. You didn't think. That much is clear from this rubbish.' The ripping of paper punctuated his words.

Shock propelled Lauren out from behind the wall.

'Is everything OK here?' Lauren asked her eyes fixed on the woman she recognised as Grace Lenzie, one of Leinster's post graduate research assistants.

'No. The standards in this university are falling. I expect *my* research assistants to be at the top of their game.' Leinster shook the torn document at Grace. 'Don't ever bring me research of this quality again.'

Grace flushed red and looked at the floor wordlessly as Leinster stamped out of the room and down the corridor.

Lauren poured her own tea and another for Grace. She offered the cup, and the woman shook her head.

'What was all that about?' Lauren asked gently.

'It is nothing Dr McDonald,' Grace said, shifting uncomfortably.

More of the faculty entered the break room and the moment passed. Grace turned and hurried out. Lauren watched her leave. She had a hunch and followed it along the corridor to the toilets. Pushing the door softly she could hear the muffled sounds of sobbing. Making up her mind she took the cleaning in progress sign from the storage cupboard and placed it outside the door. *That should buy a little privacy.* She tapped on the cubical door.

'Grace? It's me, Dr McDonald.'

The bolt slid backward, and Grace came out wiping her red rimmed eyes on a folded piece of tissue.

'You do not have to put up with that kind of behaviour you know. It's bullying.' Lauren leant her weight on the sink studying Grace's face carefully.

'Oh, it isn't just me...' Grace sighed. 'I knew he wasn't going to like what I'd found. I saw the way he treated Tom...'

Grace looked at her uncertainly as though unsure she should say more. Lauren silently willed her to continue, she certainly wasn't going to add to the issue by browbeating Grace.

'I thought if I showed him the research he might at least consider it before he finalised the papers...' Grace looked at her pleadingly. 'I was trying to help...'

'Help who?' Lauren was almost sure it wasn't Leinster.

'Tom.' Grace's eyes filled again with tears. 'Oh Dr McDonald... it's awful. He is always criticising Tom and making fun of him for being too slow. When Tom found evidence that cast doubt on the Douglas Theory Dr Leinster called him out in front of all of us and made him defend it. Poor Tom couldn't get a word in edge ways... he just kind of... crumbled. Dr Leinster said if he made such claims again, he'd not only embarrass himself but all of us too.'

Lauren could well imagine the scene as Grace's words came tumbling out.

'The synopsis you pulled together was based on Tom's theory?' Lauren asked.

Grace nodded.

'That was brave... considering.' Lauren squeezed Grace's arm

'I think Tom was right and if he is then it calls parts of Dr Leinster's work into question. It makes the leap a little more difficult to support. That the Douglas family had a Machiavellian influence on the events in England, Europe and America too. I just want him to know that before he publishes.'

Lauren was thoughtful. There were two separate issues here. All research was subject to peer review and, of course, to challenge by other historians. It was never an absolute science, but Klaus was bullying his researchers. She remembered Tom from his postgraduate studies. He was quiet and thoughtful. He had a brilliant mind but always played it safe until he was sure. Easy prey.

'You can make a complaint about the way you were treated today,' Lauren said. 'I will support you.'

Grace looked panic stricken.

'I know it takes courage to speak up, but the university will protect you.'

'I'll think about it...' Grace checked her reflection in the mirror and rubbed at a smudge of mascara and then guiltily. 'I'd better get back...'

Lauren shook her head as she watched Grace leave. It had to stop.

CHAPTER 26

MAIREAD

A weight on Mairead's chest like a rock pinned her on her back. She fought to breathe. Her muscles burned and her body was rigid. She kicked her legs, tangled in her skirts, as she fought to get free. Unable to cry out, she beat her fists desperately on the floor beneath her. The shouts of men and footsteps thundering down the corridor drowned out the noise as hot tears stung her eyes, and the darkness sucked at the edges of her vision pulling her under.

Mairead bolted upright in the bed and kicked at the tangled mess of sheets to free herself. Her heart pounded in her ears and the sounds around her were confused, as though she was listening from under water. With a shuddering breath, she pushed the nightmare from her mind. She steadied herself, feet on the cool stone floor, and took in the room around her. The wooden frame of the bed was solid beneath her and not the cold earth of her dream. The tapestries and drapes a wash of reds and creams that drove away the lingering darkness. Her hand rested on her chest as she felt the tension begin to leave. The steady gaze of Lady Frances watched her from the portrait across the room. Through the opaque glass of the window, a blue sky emerged. The sun was low, it was still early. Clarity began to return as she realised the tower was full of activity. Heavy footsteps echoed and worried voices passed the door. *Something is amiss*, Mairead thought as she began to dress hurriedly. As she pulled her stays over her head, Murren entered the room, her eyes wide and close to panic. The woman laced her in with clumsy fingers as Mairead wound her hair into a tight plait, her deft fingers moving urgently. With her skirts fastened, she thrust her feet into her shoes and rushed, breathless, down to the great hall.

The room was filled with men roused from their beds with sleep still heavy upon them. They continued to gather, some with shirts undone at their throats and others strapping sword belts into place. The cooks and kitchen boys edged their way around the outside of the hall and stood in hushed conversation, glancing anxiously towards the dais. The quiet in the room felt heavy, broken only by the shuffling of feet and whispered questions. Her gaze found James, his red head tall amongst the knot of men. Their eyes met. His grim expression made her heart thump as she pushed her way through the throng of bodies towards him. Reaching his side, she squeezed his fingers. Stiffening her spine, lifting her proud chin and trying to lend him her strength. He walked forward, all eyes fixed on him.

'The laird has mustered at Braemar.' His voice carried clearly across the silence of the room. 'He has raised the standard of the Stuart King.'

A ripple of shock swept the room. Mairead, hands hidden, clutched the sides of her skirt trying to keep her face impassive. James waited, his back to her, for the room to quiet.

'Our laird has charged us with holding safe his ancestral seat,' James said. 'The heartlands of our clan. Our orders are to watch the crossing and to hold the tower.'

The clansmen roused by the honour of defending their laird's keep responded with a chorus of 'Aye' and shouts of 'For Erskine'!'

'For Erskine! *Alba Gu Brath*!' James roared.

As the cries of response settled back to silence, James nodded approvingly. Mairead saw his shoulders drop a fraction. The waiting of the last few days had been intolerable. Now it would begin.

The captains stepped forward and began to give orders. James, taking her by the hand, led her out of the hall. Her heart, swelling with pride, hammered in her chest as they climbed the winding staircase in silence. James closed the heavy oak door to the solar firmly and stood with his back against it and head bowed. Mairead went to him and cupped his face in her hands, raising his chin to look him in the eye. His face was rough with stubble growing in red and glinting in the morning light from the windows. She kissed him softly on the brow and he pulled her closer. Their heads met brow to brow.

'What are my instructions?' she asked softly. 'What would you have me do?'

'Keep the men fed and well quartered,' he said decisively. 'There will be watches and scouting parties day and night.'

She nodded.

'Messengers coming and going too. They must be fed and offered rest. Gavin will see that the harvest is brought in quickly.'

'I'll have Alais keep the kitchens working. The women of the village can help with the harvest. Jeannie is well stocked with herbs and ointments.' Mairead set her shoulders back and counted the tasks off on her fingers.

James began to laugh, and the age of responsibility fell away for a moment as his eyes sparkled.

'Well, wife!' he said, 'you give orders like you were born to it.'

Mairead kissed him then rested her head on his chest. She felt safe in his arms as though he were a tree to cleave to during the storms. They had this moment of peace, they had each other. And that, right now, in this moment of anticipation was all she wanted.

***

In the charter room, Mairead and Gavin poured once more over the lists of provisions and the yields from the barley and wheat crops. Written in Gavin's cramped hand, the columns of tithes and orders placed marched down the page. Alais had the kitchens working in shifts, they would need more flour and oatmeal ground. Gavin explained to her how much the yield would produce in sacks of flour and oats, pulling across the ledger with the provisions needed for the garrison. Gavin was patient and seemed pleased that she was keen to learn. He beamed at her as she began to make the conversions for herself and write the new figures on the provisions lists. Mairead marvelled at this gentler side of Gavin, she had been accustomed to seeing him stamping around the tower with a deep furrow in his brow. She dared another question, this time about firewood and peat, wanting to hold this moment of lightness a while longer.

The seriousness of the position could not be held at bay for long and the conversation returned to what they may need. The tower must prepare to face anything in the coming months. Mairead had listened closely as the men discussed the likelihood of government soldiers firing the crops if they made it this far north. A siege or raid might mean they faced starvation in the winter if their supplies were unable to get through or the country was at war. Fear of that threatened to overwhelm her and she cast it aside, keeping her mind busy with the task at hand. They must get the last of the harvest in and some of the men garrisoned at the tower could help in the fields. With determined authority she gave the orders and Gavin rose to convey them. The tower shifted into a mood of watchful readiness. Mairead knew that they had done all to prepare for King George's response. Fragments of her dream returned to her. The fear, the feeling of being held down and unable to escape. A burning rose in her throat and she took a large gulp of ale. Rubbing her temples she tried to ease the tightness. Keeping her mind in the present and keeping it busy would leave no room for worry and fear. That is what she must hope.

Feeling the need for air, she rounded the last curve of the staircase onto the roof and took a turn of the walkway. The thick walls felt safe, and she leant against the cool stone, looking out towards the dark shape of the river Forth below. The Erskine flag flew proudly and, billowing gently in the breeze, would be visible for miles. It would be a reminder to those approaching of whose land they were now on. The man at arms on watch passed close behind her and peered out at an approaching column of dust. Mairead rushed to follow his gaze. Riders! As they approached, she began to make out the colour of the banner the lead rider flew. Campbells. Messengers from her uncle. Mairead lifted the hem of her skirt clear of the floor and descended as fast as she could. Breathless she stopped at the foot of the stairs and tried to compose herself. She could hear the hall filling for the second time that day. James stood on the dais, chin high, ready to face whoever entered. As she crossed the hall, he beckoned her to his side. *A wife from a Campbell family might be a useful symbol*, she thought as she walked forward.

At a nod from James the doors opened, and three messengers were led into the hall. Their blue and green kilts stark against the sea of red in the Erskine colours. Silence fell as a path through the hall opened. The Erskines stood proud and, without any obvious signal, at least that she had seen, closed in behind the party of messengers. Mairead recognised her cousin, John, his Adam's apple bobbing nervously, at the front of the group. She remembered him from their childhoods as a cocksure bully who used to pull her hair. With satisfaction, she saw the shock of recognition cross her cousin's features, followed swiftly by discomfort. James had seen it too and glanced in her direction looking for her response. Mairead forced herself to remain steady and calm beside him.

The men at arms halted at the foot of the dais and the messengers approached the stairs. James, a tall man anyway, looked down on them, his feet planted wide and hands on his hips. He was a formidable figure. The necks of John and his companions stretched up to look at him. John removed a letter bearing a heavy wax seal from his pouch and stepped forward.

'James Erskine, I am...' John began.

'I know fine well who you are, lad, and I know who sent you,' James said, his voice carrying clear to the back of the room. 'Say what you've come to say and be gone.'

A number of barely stifled laughs echoed around the room. Mairead saw the jaw of one of the men accompanying John tighten at the insult and his hand moved toward his sword. The man regained control of himself but the look he gave James was murderous.

'The Duke of Argyll, commander of the government army in Scotland, bids you to surrender Alloa Tower to his command.' John's tone was composed although Mairead could see the flush on his cheeks which betrayed his anger.

Shouts of 'Never!' and 'Erskine!' filled the room along with the thud of stamping feet on the floor. James raised his hand without taking his eyes from John's face. Silence fell. John flushed red. Mairead's eye was drawn to his companion. A muscle began twitching in the jaw of the angry messenger whose hand now gripped the hilt of his sword. The tension rose another notch and every person in the room looked to James. Unhurried, he took a step forward and down onto the first step, his hands at his sides. He gave the air of a wolf ready to leap.

'For God's sake man, be still,' John hissed to his companion as the third messenger laid a restraining hand on his colleague's arm.

'Anything else?' James asked.

'The Earl of Mar stands accused of treason as will those lairds who stand with him and the false king, James Stuart,' John raised his voice to be heard clearly. 'His Grace offers you a choice, James Erskine. Offers these men a choice.'

Another roar from the clansmen echoed through the room.

'I'd say you've had your answer, lad,' James said grimly. 'If Argyll wants this house then he's welcome to try and take it.'

John shrugged his shoulders and shifted his attention to Mairead.

'Mairead, your father also sends a message,' John said. 'Should you wish it, we will see you escorted to safety.'

James turned to his wife, expression carefully neutral. He took a step away from her, showing all present that she was free to make her own decision.

'It is Mistress Erskine, I'll thank ye,' Mairead said coldly as James now stood in front of John with the hilt of his sword loose in his scabbard. The whisper of the steel as it moved was more of a promise than a threat. 'And as you can see, I have all the protection I need here,' she continued.

'I believe that is your business concluded then gentlemen,' James said with a bow of mock politeness.

At a nod from John, the messengers were escorted from the hall. Mairead let out her breath as the doors banged closed behind them. James kissed her hand and then addressed the room.

'Argyll won't ask politely a second time,' he said. 'Stand ready'.

Amid the surge of activity Mairead retreated to her room. The feeling of bravery and triumph coursing through her in the hall seeped away with each step she took. She and James were pieces of carved ivory on a gaming board commanded to do the bidding of the players. *Who would make the next move?*

CHAPTER 27

JEANNIE

The days since the earl's declaration passed in a haze of exhaustion. Jeannie had been working in the kitchens at first light, overseeing the ovens and the kitchen lads so Alais could get some sleep. Her afternoons were spent in the fields helping to bring in the late summer crops. The weather held fair, a blessing to the folk of the tower as the future was full of uncertainty. The long sunny days of toil and company made the time pass quickly but the work was hard and made her back ache. Threshing had made the joints in her fingers swell and she steeped them now in a bowl of lavender and wormwood sitting at the doorway in the cooling evening air. As she lifted her face to the last of the sunlight, she heard footsteps approaching behind her. Alais appeared at her side and peered into the bowl, giving Jeannie a sympathetic look.

'Gavin is asking for you,' Alais said.

A sigh escaped Jeannie, and she prepared to rise.

'Stay as you are,' Alais said, her hand on Jeannie's shoulder, 'you've surely earned a rest. I'll tell him you will be along shortly.'

'Can it wait?' Jeannie asked.

'As there is no sign of news, and the men are playing dice in the hall, I dare say it can,' Alais replied.

Jeannie gave her a grateful look and dipped her hands back into the bowl up to her wrists. The warmth of the water and the scent of the lavender were soothing, and her fingers moved a little more easily.

Jeannie found Gavin seated in the charter room with the household ledgers open in front of him. A haze hung thickly in the air formed of smoke from the hearth and the tallow in the candles. Laughter and voices rose from the hall below. The tower had adapted, and it struck Jeannie that they settled into their new situation naturally. With so much to do there was a shared purpose and all except the very old and the very young had a part to play. Yet as the leaves began to turn the threat of danger grew. It was only a heartbeat away now, looming like a storm cloud on the horizon. Gavin looked up and pulled out the chair beside him, inviting her to sit. He pushed a list across the table and Jeannie scanned it. More provisions would be needed, and a portion of the harvest was to be sent to Hugh at Mar's Lodging in Stirling.

'The mistress has asked that we travel to Stirling,' Gavin said, 'to deliver the food and collect the provisions.'

Jeannie nodded her understanding.

'We will travel with guards,' Gavin continued. 'I do not know what we may encounter on the roads.'

His expression was grim, his tone radiated disapproval and Jeannie thought he might say more. When the silence stretched uncomfortably, she cast around for a clue to his mood.

'The mistress has things she wishes me to procure?' Jeannie asked.

'It would seem that there are particular items the lady has need of, and she is quite insistent that they are required urgently.'

Jeannie picked up the paper with Mairead's writing and took her leave of Gavin. Assuring him she would check the list and let their mistress know if the items could be found closer to home. Several of the items, she noticed, would require a visit to the Merchant Murray, giving her an opportunity to check in on his wife, Isobel, and their babe.

Jeannie woke with the rising sun and dressed to travel. Stopping as promised to check in on young Johnny. The bruise had disappeared now, and his arm was healing well. He ran round her skirts, chasing an imaginary foe and waving a stick grasped in his pudgy little fingers. She smiled to see him so full of life. His mother looked harassed, there were purple smudges under her eyes that told a story of worry and lack of sleep. Jeannie's heart squeezed in sympathy. She remembered well the boundless energy of her own sons and the worry when there was war or unrest. Gently, she reassured the woman that raising laddies was a sore trial but one day she would miss the constant noise and stickiness. Neither of them mentioned the soldiers and the threat of attack. Those who lived around the tower house knew to make their way within at the first sign of trouble. They were more fortunate than those on the outer reaches of the laird's lands who would need to fend for themselves. As she approached the stables, she saw two carts loaded with sacks of provisions. Eight horses waited saddled and ready. She stroked the velvety nose of the pony she had ridden last time. His nostrils flared and he nuzzled her shoulder in greeting. She held out her hand, offering a small apple, and then checked the tack, making sure the buckles were tight. Gavin gave the order to the soldiers to mount up just as she was letting down the stirrups. One of the stable boys brought over the stool and she stepped up, settling herself in the saddle. The carts began to move, flanked by the guards. James had ordered that weapons were only to be drawn if there was an attack and so the men rode with swords at their backs. Jeannie saw the hilts of daggers glinting at the top of boots within easy reach. Gavin gestured for her to fall in behind the carts and he rode at her side with two guards behind. The red and green of the Erskine colours stood out stark against the yellow and gold of the fields. The pace was brisk and the mood one of vigilance as they rode.

On the crest of the rise to the north of the tower, the silhouettes of two riders were clearly visible. The guard at the front of their party had seen them too and he turned to give the order to proceed as planned. The riders, whoever they were, remained on the crest and made no move to either follow or to depart. Jeannie glanced in their direction as they passed beneath the rise, but the bright morning sun made it impossible to see their colours. The message was plain enough, though. The tower was being watched.

The city walls loomed ahead as the carts laboured up the hill towards Mar's Lodging. A group of small boys who had been playing at the side of the road stopped to watch them pass and Jeannie realised that a strange quiet accompanied them. At a harsh word from one of their mothers, they moved back from the road. The city had a different feeling than it had on her last visit. People were wary. Aware of the redcoats patrols their escort took pains to avoid directly crossing paths. The façade of the lodging came into view and Jeannie loosened her grip on her reins, relieved that part of the journey was over. Once the heavy door swung open they entered through the archway. As she moved forward, she looked up at the solemn face of the statue of Jeanne D'Arc. Inside the walls much had changed since her last visit. The lodging was now unrecognisable and instead there was a barracks with makeshift stables and stores. Despite the brightness of the day, it felt oppressive to Jeannie. So many men and horses cramped together made it dry and airless. It felt like a fire waiting for the spark. So it was to her great relief that Gavin was anxious to get on with their task.

They left quietly through a small door at the outer edge of the wall which led to a narrow passageway. The guard closed it firmly behind them. The city's great Kirk basked silver in the sunlight, but its long shadow fell over the narrow close making it blessedly cool after the lodging. Neither Jeannie nor Gavin wore Erskine colours, they were simply dressed as befit their positions in the household. Hugh had agreed they would be safe enough in the city and allowed them to go unaccompanied by liveried guards.

The streets with the merchant and burghers' homes were bustling with activity and the Murrays looked to be doing a steady trade. Once admitted, Gavin was ushered into the store along with his list of goods leaving Jeannie standing in the hallway. After a moment, a maid approached to lead her into the room in which they sat on her previous visit. Isobel Murray greeted her warmly and they spoke of the health of the baby. A pink glow had returned to the woman's cheeks and the shadow of pain had lifted from her fine features. The baby was also doing well, and Jeannie gave silent thanks for that blessing. The first months of life were precarious for both mother and child but the woman before her looked hale and hearty. Conversation turned to trade in the city and the comings and goings of the clan chieftains, then Jeannie brought out her list.

'Mistress Erskine has need of these,' Jeannie said as she handed the paper over.

Isobel looked down the items, nodding to herself as she checked them off against a mental inventory. Most of the items were textiles needed for clothing and the household linens, but Mairead had been very specific about the French lace.

'Aye, this will be no problem,' Isobel said. 'Although I will need a few days for the linens and lace.'

'Can they be delivered with the goods for the tower?' Jeannie asked.

'I'll see them delivered safe for your mistress,' Isobel said, 'but I am curious about the lace...'

Jeannie remained silent.

'A babe of her own perhaps?' Isobel said softly.

'That I cannot say,' Jeannie said. 'Perhaps it is only that she doesn't know for how much longer the roads will remain safe to pass and wants the linen chests full.'

The women returned the conversation to safer topics until a light knock at the door signalled that Gavin was ready to leave. Jeannie watched the crowds as they went about their business. She noticed flashes of steel at the sides of men who were dressed in their clan tartans. Patrols of government soldiers were easy to spot in their coats, the bright red of the rowan berries. The clansmen did not turn aside or try to hide their weapons. That wasn't the way of the clans and there was not yet an open war. Bearing arms was their right although she knew that been removed by English King Edward once before in the wake of a different uprising. The uneasy peace of the moment felt brittle.

Passing one the narrow closes on their way towards the Kirk a movement in the shadows caught Jeannie's eye. A prickle of apprehension crept up her spine. There it was again, a flash of blue and green. They were being watched! She quickened her pace muttering her suspicion to Gavin. At his nod they crossed the street and ducked into a narrow passageway. There they waited. Gavin positioned himself, dirk in hand, with a view onto the thoroughfare. Just here it widened out into a bend for horses and carts to turn up towards the castle esplanade. A dark figure in Campbell colours doubled back and then with a sour expression moved on. Jeannie let out a sigh of relief and Gavin returned the knife to its sheath concealed within his belt loop.

'I'll get a message to Mistress Murray,' Gavin said as they stepped back out into the busyness of the street. 'It may be that they, too, are being watched.'

'Does Argyll know the Murrays are in league with the laird?' Jeannie asked, her concern for Isobel and the babe rising.

'Perhaps,' Gavin said. 'But I think it is we who are watched.'

'I would be sorry to bring trouble to their door.' Jeannie looked back towards the row of merchant houses lower down the hill.

'Well then, you and the mistress should have a care before you decide on any more urgent errands.' Gavin's tone was gruff.

Jeannie looked at him and seeing the tight-lipped expression thought better of the retort that sprang to mind. Instead, she nodded and glanced around looking for more signs of the man in the shadows. With careful steps they looped around and approached Mar's Lodging from the other side. Though watchful Jeannie saw no more of the shadowy figure.

Once within Mar's Lodging, Jeannie went straight to the stables and stood resting her head on the flank of her horse. A wave of tiredness washed over her, and her body ached. The memory of the figure in the shadows had set her nerves on edge. Despite her fatigue, she was keen to be home, back within the thick walls of the tower. The horse seemed to sense her discomfort and tossed his head. The warm breath was sweet as he whickered gently to her. She scratched behind his ears and spoke softly to him of his hay net and the sweet apples waiting for him at home. A stable lad led the horses out and Jeannie was helped into the saddle, gritting her teeth as her back complained about the long miles ahead.

CHAPTER 28

JEANNIE

Jeannie drew her shawl tightly around her shoulders. Autumn dew glistened on the grass and soaked into her skirts as she knelt to cut from the herb beds in the medicine garden. The deep menthol woody scent of rosemary filled the morning air as she worked. There was a coughing sickness spreading in the tower; breathing the vapours from rosemary and hyssop steeped in boiling water could help ease the chest. With so many people living in such close quarters Jeannie hoped there would be nothing more serious to contend with in the coming months. Her gaze landed on the rowan tree within the copse, leaves vivid hues of red and yellow. It had borne fruit early this year, the sign of harsh winter to come and the weather was already turning. She had harvested what she could from the garden over the last few days and set it to dry.

In the chill of the still room, Jeannie set a kettle over the fire and began to strip the leaves from dried stalks of chamomile. She would use the flowers in infusions and the stalks went into the pot for her soaps. Nothing was wasted. The change of season had brought with it a change in the atmosphere in the tower. As the leaves turned, news of the earl's progress had reached them often. The lairds of the Highlands and Islands had, on the whole, rallied in support of the Stuart King. A great force had swept south and was now making for Stirling. The civil war that Jeannie feared had not yet come to pass and she dared to breathe a little easier, the heat and tension of the summer giving way to hope and optimism.

She thought again of her sons, picturing them as small boys running round the still room riding their imaginary horses or building castles from sticks and stones. She could almost hear Angus' raucous laughter and the endless prattle of Collum as he toddled after the older boys, so desperate to be included. Her heart ached at the memories, and she threw a sprig of rosemary onto the fire. As the rich herbal smoke billowed up the chimney, she sent with it a silent prayer for her boys to be kept safe.

***

The metallic smell of blood reached Jeannie as she entered the charter room carrying her medicine box and she knew then why she'd been summoned. James beckoned her forward and a flicker of relief crossed his face. He ordered the men down to the great hall to give her space to work. Seeing him stood now, silhouetted in the window with hands clasped behind him, Jeannie noticed the change in him. He'd grown into his command. The man more serious than the lad he had been but still a gentle heart. She bent now to focus on the man in front of her. A bandage tied round his thigh oozed blood. It was none too clean, and Jeannie shook her head as she began to untie it as gently as she could. Underneath, a deep gash revealed bone. She looked up into the man's face, grey with pain and fatigue.

'It is deep and will need to be sewn,' she said, careful to smile reassuringly at him. 'It will need to be cleaned first.'

The man nodded in response, a fine sheen of sweat covered his brow and upper lip as he sank back into the chair. Jeannie reached up to feel his forehead. It was cool to the touch. *No fever. That's a good sign.*

'A sword cut?' she asked him, then turned to James. 'I'll need whisky for the pain, and it would be best to move him to the guardroom now.'

James gave the instructions and returned to stand behind the wounded man.

'Widow Kellie has great skill,' he said, 'she'll see you well-tended.'

As the men came to lift their wounded friend, James caught her arm.

'There was a skirmish on the road,' he said. 'The rest of the wounded are being brought here. What do you need, Jeannie?'

'Clear some room to tend to them and I'll need fires lit,' she said.

As James went to see to her requests, Jeannie returned to the still room. Collecting what she may need, she picked up her basket of bandages and a jar of honey. The sounds of the kitchen were intensifying as preparations for the midday meal began. The smell of fresh baked bread from the oven reminded her that she had not yet eaten but it seemed that would need to wait.

There were now four men in the guardroom and Jeannie moved between them, assessing who needed her help most urgently. The young rider lay on the freshly scrubbed table with sweat pouring from his brow. His breaths came in rapid gasps. With sympathetic hand on his shoulder, Jeannie took a strip of leather from her box and put it between the lad's teeth. He bit down hard as she began to pour water over the wound flushing out the dirt and darkened clots.

'Hold down his shoulders and legs,' Jeannie ordered two of the onlooking men. 'Keep him steady whilst I sew.'

Jeannie splashed whiskey over the needle and passed the thread through the eye. Moving quickly with sure fingers she pulled the edges of the wound together. One of the men winced in sympathy as she tied the end of the thread and tugged it tight. Jeannie stepped back satisfied at the neat row of stiches. A clean cut and deep though it was the wound should heal well. Jeannie cleaned her hands thoroughly as the dozing lad was moved onto a cot brought from the billet. She wiped the sweat from his forehead gently. He was ashen faced but there was still no sign of a fever.

The others had an assortment of broken ribs, black eyes and missing teeth. Their swaggering arrogance and ribald humour were wearing her patience thin. Jeannie tutted loudly as they congratulated themselves on blows landed and blows withstood. She took hold of the bearded chin of a man with cuts to his lip and above his cheekbone, tilting his head none to gently to better see the injury. The man winced and opened his mouth to complain. The steely look that Jeannie gave him made him close it again quickly and lower his eyes. She cleaned him up, moving her finger lightly over the bone around the cheek and eye. Nothing was broken there but from the way the man was hunched over, there was pain in his back and ribs. She lifted his shirt to see large red welts and the beginning of bruising. Tutting again she applied a salve of comfrey to the area and promised to return with a yarrow tea to ease any injury inside.

Mairead crossed the room with Murren trailing reluctantly in her wake. Judging by the way she was dressed in a plain woollen tunic with an apron tied at her waist, Mairead had come ready to assist.

'Can we be of use here, Widow Kellie?' Mairead asked.

A glance at Murren's pale face told Jeannie that only one of the two women before her would be of help.

'Perhaps Murren could take the soiled linens to the wash house,' Jeannie replied, 'there will be need of clean cloths and bandages.'

With a grateful look at Jeannie, Murren hurried away.

Mairead rolled back her sleeves and listened attentively as Jeannie gave instructions.

'There is a cloth steeping here,' Jeannie indicated with a tilt of her head as she examined the livid bruising on the back of the man sat hunched before her. 'The water contains comfrey and linseed stalks.'

Mairead wrung the excess water from the warm cloth and following Jeannie's lead she pressed it gently to the man's back. He hissed at the pain.

'Bind it good and tight now. I think the ribs are broken,' Jeannie said handing her a long piece of cloth.

'I'm sorry. I'm almost done...' Mairead whispered as the man whimpered in pain. She wound the length of cloth around his torso pulling to keep it taught. 'There.' She gently tapped the man's shoulder as she tied off the ends and tucked it in.

Jeannie nodded in approval and gave Mairead a warm smile. The other woman looked pleased and returned her smile almost shyly. Their attention turned to the next casualty, this man was older, his face bloody and missing a front tooth. As she inspected a deep gash over his brow, he retched and vomited blood and ale at Mairead's feet. Jeannie was surprised to see that Mairead barely flinched. It seemed the mistress had a strong stomach too – the makings of a healer in her own right perhaps. The women worked in companionable ease until all the wounds were dressed.

Mairead spoke softly as she sat at the side of the young rider who was awake again and moaning with pain from his leg. Between them, they lifted him as gently as they could and persuaded him to drink the tea prepared by Jeannie. It smelled of liquorice and the lad pursed his lips before forcing himself to swallow it down. The effort had exhausted him and his eyes fluttered closed as they eased his head back down onto the makeshift cot.

'What was the cause of this?' Mairead asked the eldest of the men laying a cool cloth on the lad's head.

'We had ridden south of the Forth Crossing, mistress,' the man said. 'Looking for news of the rising in England. We came across the lad being run down by riders in Douglas colours.'

Pausing often as coughing sent a jolt of pain through his ribs, the man told of the fight that broke out as they gave the injured lad time to get clear. The lad's wound had come from the wild thrust of a sword as the Douglas men attempted to unseat him from his horse. The patrol, Erskine men under James' command, had stood their ground giving the lad time to get away with his message.

'What of the Douglas men?' Mairead asked.

'They turned tail when it became clear they had lost the messenger,' the man said. With a grin at his fellows he continued, 'Had no stomach for another taste of Erskine steel and muscle.'

The men laughed and Jeannie allowed herself a smile at the victory. As rough as they were, these men had upheld the clan honour and probably saved the lad's life. She poured them each a dram of whisky from her box, for medicinal purposes she assured them. They drank it gratefully toasting the health of the earl, the King and the honour of the Erskines.

Having pronounced the others fit enough to return to their own quarters, Jeannie busied herself cleaning down the benches. The room was hot with the fire blazing and so many bodies within, but the lad's teeth were chattering. Mairead pulled the blanket up to his chin and smoothed it tenderly over his shoulders. Jeannie saw the crease deepen between the woman's eyes.

'It's the blood loss,' Jeannie said. 'The cut was to the bone.'

'It is a wonder he stayed in the saddle all the way here,' Mairead said quietly.

'Terror probably kept him riding.' Jeannie shared her thought aloud. 'Then when he could see the tower, the desperation to reach it.'

'He must have ridden hard before that too. With a message Douglas didn't want him to deliver,' Mairead said, echoing Jeannie's own thoughts.

As she bent to place another log onto the fire, Jeannie stumbled. Bracing her hand on the mantle to steady herself she stood up slowly. Mairead looked at her sharply and sent her for food and rest with the assurance that she would stay with the lad.

Reluctantly Jeannie left persuaded by the promise to send for her if there was a change.

At Alais' table in the kitchen, Jeannie sat with a bowl of mutton stew steaming before her. She tore a piece of bread and dipped it into the thick gravy, the garlic and thyme made her mouth water, and she savoured the richness of the meat. Alais placed a bowl of stewed apples and blackberries on the table and instructed Jeannie that she must eat if she was going to nurse the lad through the night. Jeannie knew her friend was right and could feel the stew and bread fortifying her frayed nerves even as she ate. Alais distracted her with talk of the great hall. The lad had brought news from the English lords who had joined the Stuart cause – they were mustering and beginning to push north.

The mood in the hall has changed again, Jeannie thought, as she folded the blankets, brown wool rough between her fingers. Men spoke with conviction about the earl's victory. He held the north of Scotland for the Stuarts, and the south was rising in support. James Stuart would land in time to lead them to a great victory. *How could it be otherwise now?* they reasoned. Jeannie shared their pride in their clan chieftain, but a kernel of unease still rested deep in her belly. It whispered caution to her, counselling her to stay prepared. *This is not over yet. Nothing was certain.* Jeannie smothered the thought into action as she strode decisively back towards the makeshift sickroom.

CHAPTER 29

HAZEL

Hazel tracked the descent of the red line along the graph. Removing her glasses, she massaged her temples trying to relieve the tightness. Visitor numbers were falling across all the properties and the cost of maintaining the sites was skyrocketing. Marcus had run the financial projections, and it was grim. She knew it was time to make the hard decisions. What could the trust let go? There were always offers from developers who would turn the sites into hotels or golf courses. She paced now between the map on the wall and the window, her loafers squeaking on the polished concrete of the floor with each turn.

Pausing at the map she looked at the sites in the more remote places. The iron age broch Dun Troddan in the wilds of the Highlands. It made no money and was maintained with the income generated by memberships. Would these be the sacrifices? Left to community groups or to the wilds? She resumed her pacing, trying to find another way, another idea. She twisted the ring on her thumb as thoughts whirred. *Breathe*, she told herself. *Just breathe.* At the window she paused and began to trace a square on the glass. In for four, hold for four, out for four, hold for four. Box breathing was a technique she'd learned from her therapist, an anchor to the present when the panic threatened to overwhelm her. She hadn't been keen to try it until she'd learned that the military and world class athletes use it to help regulate their heart rate in high stress situations. It worked. The intensity of her senses receded, and she felt her shoulders start to drop.

In the harsh light of the toilet, Hazel ran the cold water and splashed her face. Meeting her own green eyes in the mirror she saw how blood shot they looked. Her cheeks were pale and there was a deep crease of worry on her brow.

'Come on,' she said aloud, hands gripping the rim of the copper sink. 'Get a hold of yourself.'

She smoothed her hair back into a ponytail and yanked the bobble tight. Tucking the black edge of her tank top into the high waistband of her linen trousers, she checked herself again in the mirror. *Better*, she thought, *more like a functioning adult.* Still, her tongue felt thick and her mouth dry.

Filling her glass at the water cooler, Hazel saw Marcus making a beeline for her. She'd been trying to avoid this, knowing he would see straight through any attempt to pretend she was okay. They had known each other too long for that. The narrowing of his eyes told her she was right, and she groaned inwardly.

'Well, you look like you've not slept in a week,' he said.

'Gee, thanks friend,' Hazel said, taking a sip of the water.

'Do you want to talk it through?' he asked. She tensed, and he added, 'The options appraisal for the board?'

Hazel shook her head. Her independence had always been her armour and her shield. Relying on herself meant she didn't need to rely on others. It had served her well in the past and so her walls of defence rose around her.

'I'm still working up the options,' she said, 'but thanks.'

'Sure. Just shout if you need a sounding board,' he said.

Hazel stayed quiet, feeling awkward at his discomfort, a hot lump of emotion rose in her throat made it impossible for her to speak. Lifting the glass to her lips, she took a sip and swallowed hard.

'You've got friends you know. We'd like to help...' he tried again, his earnest face furrowed with lines of sadness.

Hazel remained silent and could only give a slight nod. Marcus' eyes were full of compassion. It was more than she could bear so she returned to her office quickly and shut the door firmly behind her. A message flashed up on her screen from Chris asking her to give him a call. She had been expecting this but the pit in her stomach deepened nonetheless.

The World Heritage Organisation had frozen the funding for Fractal Lines until the police and forensic archaeologists finished their investigation. The project committee would convene to discuss the best way forward. She'd failed. The nightmare was repeating. Why could she not break free? Hazel stood at the window, the room spinning around her. She squeezed her eyes closed and dug her fingernails into the palms of her hands, blocking out the world around her. Adrenaline surged through her, crackling like lightening along her arms and legs. She forced herself to be still. Rigid. Fighting the urge to run. Stepping forward, the floor tilted sharply beneath her as though she were on the deck of a ship. Panic closed her lungs, and her hands flew to her neck, trying to loosen its grip. She dropped to the floor, her knees crashing to the concrete, and slid round onto her backside. Pulling her knees into her chest, she rested her head on them. Behind her eyelids, the world flashed red and black.

Pain flooded in as the tide of panic receded. The sweat between her shoulder blades cooled to an unpleasant stickiness. Her knees throbbed and a band of tightness sat across her brow. On shaking legs, she made her way to her chair and took a gulp of water.

'Come on, Hazel,' she whispered to herself. 'Get a grip. You need to focus.'

Rolling up the legs of her trousers to look at her knees, she could feel the heat coming from the angry red patches that had taken the brunt of her fall. Her palms held half-moons of blood where her fingernails had broken the skin. She concentrated on her breath, its rise and fall like waves on sand. Slowly, breath by breath, she pulled the ragged edges of herself back into the centre. Brought herself back under control and turned the lock in her mind. *There's no time now for this*, she thought.

From the drawer beside her, she took a highlighter and the list of the trust's properties and sites. She made her way methodically down each page, cross referencing against Marcus' finance report, highlighting the places where the trust was losing money. Staying focused on just this task, she lost track of time until a tap at the door startled her.

'It's nearly 6 p.m.,' Marcus said as he leaned against the doorway.

'I'm nearly done,' Hazel said. 'I'll just finish this page.'

'Mei called. Said she messaged about a run?' Marcus said gently.

'Oh.' Hazel grabbed her phone and saw the notifications. 'I've been totally engrossed in this,' she said guiltily.

'I'll let her know. Don't worry, I'm sure she'll forgive you.' Marcus pulled the door closed softly.

In the silence of the office Hazel finished her list. She flipped the document back to the first page. Her eye caught by the highlight on Alloa Tower. *Could they still save it*, she wondered?

'I can damn well try,' she said aloud.

CHAPTER 30

LAUREN

It was blessedly cool down in the bowels of the university library where Lauren had set up her research room. Outside, the sticky humidity had made her hair wild and untameable. Today she hadn't even tried, and the copper ringlets floated around the nape of her neck in the breeze of the air conditioning unit. With her flowing tunic and Celtic knot work necklace, she looked every inch the eccentric academic and knew it. The climate down here was carefully controlled to protect the manuscripts and old books, kept at a constant twenty degrees centigrade. Today it was perfect.

Making notes about the Alloa parish records from 1712 to 1714 she glanced at her watch and decided it was time for a break. Putting her gloves back on, she closed the heavy book with its yellowing pages and ancient leather cover. The musty smell of old parchment and the bitterness of the binding glue intensified with each movement. Wrapping it carefully back into the cloth jacket, Lauren placed it gently into the Perspex box. Removing the cotton gloves again, she placed them neatly beside it palms up and thumbs folded as though in salute.

The glass fronted room contained only a table and four chairs. In the centre of the table were four adjustable lamps and clear Perspex cradles for the books to sit. The room felt harsh, clinical even, despite not having a single sharp edge or corner that could snag and damage the precious books. Lauren waved to the librarian tapping her watch to indicate she was taking her lunchbreak. The stacks were floor to ceiling cabinets that concertinaed together to store the most fragile and valuable books. In the more advanced libraries these were now robotically accessed, the librarians only needed to remove and replace each item as it was presented to them. Here, though, they were still operated by the turning of a wheel at the end of each row. This moved them apart for access or back in to save space. Lauren had tried this a few times and it was hard work. *The librarians must have arms like Popeye*, she mused.

As the lift ascended to the main entrance of the library Lauren felt her senses assaulted by the busyness of the food court and concourse. After the white quiet of the stacks this was a lot to process, and Lauren wished she'd thought to bring lunch with her.

Having grabbed a pasta salad and water, she found a quiet area off the staff lounge and picked at it without much enthusiasm. Scrolling through emails, she saw the invitation to attend a meeting with the Project Advisory Board. The attached agenda had a motion proposed by Dr Leinster to discuss the future options for Fractal Lines. She would put money on one of those options being to close it down and replace it. *Well, well, well*, she thought sitting back as she read on, *the old leopard doesn't change his spots.* If Klaus wanted to force a debate or motion to end the project, she was ready for him. The picture they were building using the surviving household letters, the Erskine papers and now the parish records were a vivid account of life in the tower house in the early 1700s. Some of the characters coming to the fore were intriguing. One of her research graduates had been rooting out old folk stories and songs from the area that might well tie in nicely too. Lauren was determined that this project wouldn't go down without a fight. She typed out a message to Hazel, inviting her to meet.

Back down in the stacks, Lauren read over her notes. These records were a rich source of information and filled in gaps in the Erskine documents left by the fire of 1800 which destroyed the mansion house attached to the tower. The team had been lucky as these were unusually detailed records and the cleric, a man named John Dunn, had been meticulous. The second book was wrapped in black cloth. Her gloved hands placed it carefully in the cradle and undid the metal clasp holding the leather covers. There were stains on the cover, water marks she guessed peering at it closely. In patches it was more faded. She imagined that it must have been a vivid red once upon a time but exposure to sunlight had aged it to the colours of rust.

Turning the pages gently, she noted that that this volume was dated between 1715 and 1716. It was in the same hand as the previous text. Lauren pulled the lamp over and settled down to study the writing carefully. She found what she had been looking for in August 1715. The earl and his family had departed the tower for their estates in Braemar. In charge of the tower was his nephew James Erskine and niece by marriage, Mairead. An influx of men followed over the month, swelling the numbers of Dunn's congregation. *Clansmen sent to defend their laird's ancestral home and to hold the strategic advantage of the crossing at the river*, she thought. The names of the women were fewer, and most had been in the earlier record. Members of the household were named along with their occupation. There were two besides Mairead Erskine who were not in the latter records. Murren MacArthur had appeared in 1715 and Widow Kellie. Still, that was not significant in and of itself. The natural order of births, deaths and marriages might account for that.

The tap on the glass brought her back to the present as the librarian apologised for interrupting her but said she would be finishing for the day soon and needed to sign the books back in. Lauren scribbled the last of her observations and began to pack the book carefully away.

'I'm sorry to rush you Dr McDonald,' the librarian said, taking the Perspex boxes from the counter and checking their reference numbers against the list.

'I'd lost track of time,' Lauren replied. 'I'll book them back out again if the room is free tomorrow?'

The librarian confirmed that it was, and Lauren posted the gloves through the slot to be laundered.

Emerging again into the throng of the main library, she checked her phone for a reply from Hazel and was surprised to see her own message remained unread. Lauren was worried for the younger woman. She seemed to have retreated within and her walls had gone up. Unbidden, the image appeared in her mind of the meeting room at Airthrey Castle and what she had interrupted between Klaus and Hazel. Klaus had been too close and his honeyed tone had oozed false concern. A realisation crept over her. Hazel had been furious, and rightly so, but underneath that had been something else. Fear. Lauren recalled how tightly the other woman had held herself. Like a hare. Quivering with tension, alert and ready to run. Her own fury rose. How dare he? How dare Leinster behave in such a way and swan off with that smug smile on his face. Hazel had stood her ground and good for her. Lauren had too when she'd faced a similar affront. Men like him were less common now but still likely to get away with it. Women were more likely to defend themselves now. They shouldn't have to, but these characters had always existed. Believing they were superior and acting with impunity. There would be a reckoning for Klaus Leinster she vowed. *What would it cost though? What price would Hazel pay?* Lost as she was in her thoughts; her feet made their own way along the hillside path toward home.

The late afternoon air in the garden was cooling and Lauren sat on the sloped grass under the shade of the old ash tree. A breeze danced through the branches above and cast a shifting pattern of light onto the blanket beneath her. Siggi lay beside her with his head resting at her hip and she stroked his velvety ear as she made her way through the day's emails. Stopping abruptly, she read and re-read the heading of the email from Chris at the History of Scotland Trust. The interim forensics report was in. A jolt of anticipation ran through her as she waited for it to download.

Pulling her reading glasses from her head, Lauren scrolled down the document scanning the text for the key points. *Adult female*, well they already knew that. *Age still to be determined. Carbon dated to early 1700s, confirmed by analysis of fabrics and the coins found in the grave site. Evidence of multiple injuries but the cause of death was still to be confirmed*. She skipped forward to the conclusions at the end of the document. The woman's hands had been bound but her body had been arranged for a burial.

Lauren rolled the details through in her mind again, making sense of what it meant for the project. The body was from around the time of the uprising. *Perhaps the fabric and clothing would shed more light into her position in the community?* The woman had sustained significant injuries, and her hands were bound but she had been buried with care rather than thrown into a hole in the ground and left to rot. No evidence of a grave marker had been found but that didn't mean it had never existed. Old photographs, drawings and artwork might hold some clues, she would get a team onto that research in the morning. They would be able to resume their research again now, too, because the body wasn't recently deceased and so it wasn't an active crime scene. This was another thread to follow back to the past and she felt a tingle of intrigue tug at her.

CHAPTER 31

LAUREN

B ack in the study room down in the stacks, Lauren's white gloved finger hovered above the text as she made her way down the list of dates and names in the census records. Her search of the burial records had yielded nothing. She hadn't expected it to given that the body wasn't found within the boundaries of the kirk yard, nor was it on the site of the family mausoleum, but it always paid to be thorough. Now her attention turned to cross-referencing the names of the members of the household against Tom's list from the Erskine papers. Paying particular attention to the women her mind kept returning to the body under the rowan tree. The woman would be here somewhere, Lauren was sure, waiting just out of sight. All she needed to do was follow the threads of connection and be patient. Patience was not a virtue that came easily to her though. She sighed shifting her weight to the other leg pushing her knuckle into her lower back to relieve the ache.

The hairs on her neck rose as she felt a shadow behind her and was unsurprised to see Klaus Leinster. He stood with his hands in his corduroy pockets watching her through the window. Suppressing her irritation, she opened the door to the study room.

'Hard at it, I see,' Klaus said, peering over her shoulder at the book in the reading cradle. 'I thought that this kind of leg work was what graduate students were for.'

His brash voice reverberated within the emptiness of the space yet, she remained in the doorway, blocking his entrance.

'I've always enjoyed the research,' she said, deliberately softening her own voice. 'It keeps the mind open and the skills sharp.'

'As I recall, it also gives you a 'mightier than though' attitude,' he hissed. His flushed face now just inches above hers as he loomed over her. 'Enjoy the time you have left in the limelight before it withers and fades.'

Lauren bit the inside of her lip, forcing herself to remain outwardly calm. Her dignified silence only served to rile him further.

'As the faculty darling your fall from grace will be a blow. It will be hard on you when your little project at the tower folds, and it *will* fold,' he sneered at her and tiny flecks of furious spittle hit her face. 'Still, I'm sure the dean will find you something to do. If only to keep you from causing any more *trouble*.'

Lauren clenched her back teeth together, steeling herself not to react as a writhing ball of fear, anger and disgust rolled deep in her gut.

'It is your acolytes I feel for,' he continued, straightening up and rearranging his features into a mask of scholarly concern. 'Not the most promising start to their careers stranded in your long shadow.'

She met his condescendence with a little smile. Refusing to be intimidated, she shrugged her shoulders.

'Our *little project* will be just fine, students learn as much from what doesn't work as what does,' she said smoothly with a perfect imitation of his accent.

His cheeks flushed and his fists clenched at his side. Through the window, Lauren could see the librarian hovering uncertainly and watching their exchange.

'But thank you for your concern,' she continued and began closing the door. 'Do excuse me, Klaus, I have more to do here before the project board meeting. It promises to be an interesting afternoon.'

The door made a satisfying click as she closed it firmly. She turned her back and returned to the book.

When she was sure he had gone, she slammed her hands down on the thick plastic of the table. Shaking as the adrenaline drained from her body. *That man is an odious boar*, she thought furiously, letting out the pent-up tension, *throwing his entitled weight around and stamping his feet when he doesn't get his own way.* The irony of it was that he was a relic of the past. The best way to deal with a bully like that is to prove you're right. She heard Annie's voice in her head and knew she wouldn't tell her about today's skirmish. Her gentle wife would only worry and there was nothing to be gained from that. Although today, Lauren decided, she would allow herself a moment of dark amusement in knowing she enraged Leinster by simply daring to be his equal. She returned to her place on the page and tried to focus on the task in hand.

Perhaps I should be more worried about Klaus, she thought. His dislike of her had crystalised into something deeper. She knew why of course. Grace had made a complaint about Leinster's behaviour and there had been an investigation. Lauren had given a statement and then a couple of weeks later she had been summoned to the dean's office. There she heard that Grace had dropped the complaint. There had been mediation he said and Grace was transferring to a university in Wales. Tom, on the other hand, would need to repeat the year as his work did not meet the academic standard. Lauren had been furious. Poor Tom had been hung out to dry. Places on doctoral programs were highly competitive, and it was a small world. The dean could barely meet her eye. Lauren had insisted she would take Tom into her own team. Despite the dean's reluctance she had refused to budge.

When Leinster published his research Lauren had reviewed and challenged it. She followed the research trail Tom and Grace had begun. They had been right, and she had proved it. Klaus, true to form, had played his ace and painted a picture of professional jealousy and rivalry between them. She, the cold ambitious loner, and he the popular and respected professor. She regretted nothing. Her mind replayed the conversation and she felt her unease deepen. It had become apparent that he was now fixated on ruining her career and his fury today had been barely controlled. It frightened her more than she wanted to admit, and she'd have to take more care going forward.

***

The project board had gathered in the meeting room in the History of Scotland Trust's headquarters. The windows were opened wide and tinkling glasses of iced water were being handed round the table. Lauren sat down next to Hazel who was tracing out a pattern in the condensation of her glass, deep in her own thoughts. With concern, Lauren noticed how loose the rings on Hazel's fingers had become. She saw the Finance Director, Marcus, also studying her. His brow creased with a worry that echoed hers. The meeting was beginning, forcing Lauren to put her niggle to one side for the time being.

Chris gave an overview of the current position and confirmed that the police and archaeologists were happy to turn the site at Alloa Tower back over to the trust. The trustees were pleased and keen to re-open as soon as it was possible. Lauren listened with interest as the impact on visitor numbers was discussed. Chris made the case for a press release containing some of the details about the body to reassure and encourage visitors to return. Lauren tucked her hair back as she listened, nodding in agreement with Marcus as he wondered aloud if the mystery might attract more attention to the project going forwards. That would have positive impact on visitor numbers surely. The live stream discussing the theories and questions the public had submitted got more engagement than anything the trust had ever posted. People loved a good mystery, she knew, and more so if it came with a tale of gruesome murder or tragic accident.

Chris moved the meeting on to the geophysical survey reports and invited Iain from the Archaeological Society to take the floor. The room was dimmed and an image of the grave, taken from above, was projected onto the screen. Lauren, like others around her, leant forward to better study the detail. The red dot of a laser pointer darted across the screen whilst Iain highlighted out the points of interest from the report.

'We found coins *in* the grave, so they were most likely buried with her and not dropped by somebody at a later date,' Iain explained. The audience's attention sharpened, and he added, 'Just the two though so probably not the infamous Jacobite gold, sorry.'

'A pity,' said Chris, 'that would have solved a few issues.'

There were chuckles and Iain nodded to his colleague to move to the next slide.

A second image appeared. It was a cross section of the grave and showed the woman lying on her back with her arms, hands together, along her torso.

'This is a 3D model of the grave and the immediate area,' he said as his colleague rolled the cursor showing different views. 'This area here is where we found the coins.'

'At the head?' Lauren asked, standing and walking towards the screen, her head tilted side to side as she studied it, fascinated.

'Yes, right here... and here.' Iain circled the laser at the top of the head and to the left side of the cheek.

A ripple of excitement rose from the historians and there were murmured exchanges. Iain held his hand up for quiet.

'As some of you have guessed, the placement of the coins is consistent with other burials particularly in the Highlands and Islands,' he said.

A collage of images of well-known burials and tombs now flashed onto the screen.

'The coins are found placed over the eyes.' Iain pointed them out on the images.

'Silver to pay the ferryman. That's an ancient custom. This woman was someone important,' Lauren whispered, turning to Hazel.

The noise in the room rose as people broke off into smaller groups to discuss the findings. A small group were crowded round the screen asking questions and exploring the 3D model with Iain.

'Her hands were tied together, she'd been hurt,' Hazel said slowly working through the information in her head, 'and the grave is outside the kirk yard. Yet somebody has buried her with dignity and placed coins on her eyes?'

'Yep, it is a bit of a mystery,' Lauren agreed. 'We'll keep looking for her in the records and the forensics report should tell us how she died.'

'This could save the tower,' Hazel said, and Lauren noted the feverish look of hope in the other woman's eyes.

'It could be the making of the project,' Lauren leant forward, her own excitement growing.

Hazel, eyes bright, grinned back at her and squeezed her hand. This was a gift. The breakthrough they had been waiting for. Lauren stole a look at Klaus who sat alone, arms folded, stoney faced. He caught her watching him and she raised an eyebrow in response. Klaus turned his head away but not fast enough to hide his venomous fury. *Ha*, she thought, *checkmate!*

CHAPTER 32

MAIREAD

Mairead inhaled the crisp air and watched her breath billow softly as she exhaled. Pulling up the hood of the green woollen cloak around her, she walked the paths of the garden seeking a moment's solitude. Fallen leaves crunched under her feet and somewhere nearby a blackbird called to her mate the sound carrying sharp and clear. She stopped under the golden leaves of a horse chestnut tree resting her back against the rough bark. Lifting her face toward the pale morning sun she sought comfort. The clansmen were restless, and James' temper was on an ever-shorter fuse. Message after message reached them of Erskine's victories and the immense size of his growing army as he swept south. The men were eager to join the fray, but their laird had stopped at Perth. As the days turned to weeks there were mutterings and then questions which James couldn't answer. Her husband was angry and there was little and less she could do to ease that.

The sound of footsteps approached and she groaned inwardly. A few minutes to take the air and a turn around the gardens was all she sought. Was that too much to ask?

'Mistress.' Gavin bowed apologetically. 'There are messages from the laird with a proclamation to be read. James has asked for you.'

Mairead sighed and followed him towards the house. The deep lines of tension around his mouth and the exhaustion in his eyes worried her. She had grown fond of Gavin. He was loyal to the Erskines and his stoic presence was a comfort. Although his manner could be brusque Mairead had seen in him a genuine affection for James, and she was glad of that. As he walked ahead of her, she saw his gait was laboured and stiff. *The cold and damp of the season have seeped into his bones*, she thought. She would ask Jeannie if there was a poultice or tea that might help.

The household were crowded in the hall. Conversing in groups, they waited, their anxious chatter rising to the vaulted ceiling like so many crows in a rookery. Mairead had changed into a green gown and hastily twisted her hair into a plait. It hung between her shoulder blades like a rod that kept her straight. There had been no time to speak with James but the set of his jaw and steely expression made the know in her stomach tighten. Gavin held a parchment in his hand carrying the thick wax seal of John Erskine. He looked to James, ready for a signal to begin. Stepping forward, James raised his hand, and the room fell into a heavy silence. Mairead sought Jeannie in the crowd, and they locked eyes for a moment.

'We have orders for the tower,' James said. 'They arrived this morning from Perth with the instruction that they be heard by all.'

James gave a nod to Gavin who broke the seal. The snap echoed loudly in the waiting silence of the room. Unfolding the parchment Gavin cleared his throat.

'James Stuart, rightful King of Scotland's army is mustered at Perth,' Gavin read. 'The army is commanded to bring the City of Stirling and the crossings of the River Forth under the King's control.'

Cheers went up around the room from the soldiers. Mairead's breath hitched in her throat. Beside her, James stood like a rock and she saw a flash of anger cross his face. There was more to come and James did not like these orders.

'It is my command that the garrison of Alloa Tower stand firm,' Gavin continued, his voice rising to be heard over the confused din.

Shouts of anger and disbelief now rose from the soldiers. Mairead felt a wave of relief course through her and as she looked out saw it reflected in the faces of the wives and daughters before her. Looking to Jeannie, she saw the other woman's face drawn into a deep frown. She glanced towards James, whose teeth were clamped together in an effort to control his emotions. With icy clarity, she understood what Jeannie had been quicker to grasp;

Argyll has a sizeable force of his own in Stirling and reinforcements from England would surely come. The tower stood between the government armies to the south and Stirling. They were in the path of the coming storm. The chill spread through her and she swallowed hard, forcing herself not to vomit. She looked again to Jeannie, whose sharp eye had missed nothing, and felt a current of understanding pass between them.

'Silence!' Jame's roar brought the room back under control so Gavin could continue.

'We must hold the advantage of the Forth,' Gavin continued. 'Signed John Erskine, Earl of Mar, on the day of our Lord, 9 November 1715 at Scone Palace.'

'We have our orders,' James said, his eyes hard as he scanned the room.

'Are we to sit here then? Hiding behind the walls of the tower like bairns behind their mother's skirts? Where is the honour in that?' a bearded man asked as the men around him muttered in agreement.

Mairead held her breath, unsure how her husband would react to the blatant defiance. James remained still a moment looking at the parchment he now held. He descended the stairs. Those around stood back, clearing a space, eyes fixed on the floor. The men respected their young commander, and he was an easy man to like, but Mairead sensed their uncertainty now. *What will he do*, she wondered, *now the orders of his laird are challenged*? From her place on the dais, she was unable to read his expression but his shoulders were firmly squared and his steps were steady and determined. Her heart began to race. For so large a man, he was light on his feet and made no sound now. He approached the man who had spoken and laid a hand upon his shoulder.

'You are proud to be an Erskine,' James said, 'and that does you credit.'

James raised his voice to be heard in the furthest corners of the hall.

'We are Highlanders. Sons of warriors.' He turned and pointed at several of the men. 'There is to be a battle and your hearts are heavy at the thought of not fighting side by side with your kin. For honour and for pride.'

Calls of 'Aye' and stamping of feet erupted. James waited for it to subside.

'Our laird has commanded us to hold this tower and house. The jewel of the estates and the ancient seat of the Erskines. Come what may, that is what we shall do. What more honour than that can we seek?' he said, addressing his final question to the man in front of him.

As the cries of 'For Erskine!' and 'For the Stuart' shook the walls, Mairead's heart filled with a fierce pride. As James moved through the hall, the soldiers clasped his forearm in the manner of warriors and brothers in arms. They patted him on the back, and he spoke words of encouragement to some and shared a joke with others before returning to her side.

Without a word James took her hand, raising it to his lips, kissed her knuckles and led her from the hall. Once in the relative privacy of the house, James lengthened his stride. Mairead gathered her skirts in her free hand, lifting them slightly to allow her to keep pace. At the door to her rooms slammed closed behind them, James slammed his fist into the solid wood and cursed. Mairead hesitated, reaching toward his back and then changing her mind. No words of hers would soothe him just now, she knew. Instead, she opened the door of the ornate cabinet. The light caught the diamond lines cut deep in the decanter, throwing rainbows onto the walls. She poured a generous measure of the amber liquid into a glass and offered it to her husband. He took it from her with eyes still dark and furious. Draining it in a single gulp, he gave it back.

'Tell me.' she invited gesturing to the chairs before pouring another large measure of whisky for him and a much smaller one for herself.

As James sat Mairead raised her own cup to take a sip, but the peaty smell was nauseatingly strong. She waited as the darkness ebbed slowly from her husband's features.

'He will not allow me to join him at Stirling,' James said. 'I asked him to relieve me of my command here and allow me to join the Erskine army with my brothers and cousins.'

Mairead bit back the bitter words of anger and rebuke racing through her mind and smoothed the green folds of her skirt to hide her hurt. He had not told her. He wanted to ride out. To adventure and danger, without a word. Abandoning her here.

'My uncle has wasted precious weeks in Perth while Argyll has mustered in Stirling. More and more men have come. Now, when it comes to it, he commands that I stay here" – he waved his arm contemptuously around the room – 'and defend his keep. Ensure his precious house and gardens are safe.'

'But as you told the men in the hall...' she began in confusion.

'Christ woman!' he roared. 'What else could I say? We have our orders and he is my laird.'

She flinched back in her seat at the venom in his voice and gripped the arms of the chair, knuckles white. She'd never had cause to fear him but she had never seen him so angry.

'This is a job for old men and cripples,' he said after a time, voice now hoarse with emotion. 'Have I not led the men well? Not proved worthy of a place at his side?'

Torn between the desire to rebuke and console him, Mairead sighed.

'Show him what you are worth.' She unclipped the ring of keys from her belt and pulled out the one for the stores. 'The larders and stores are filled. There are bags of grain and barrels of vegetables in the tunnels.

He frowned at her, not yet comprehending.

'There is wood and peat cut for fuel. Tallow for enough candles to last the winter and cloth for cloaks,' Mairead said locating another key. 'The tower and village are well provisioned.'

James' mouth opened in surprise as she spoke.

'Under your leadership we can survive a winter under siege and cut off,' she spoke with a deal more certainty than she felt.

A harsh laugh escaped James and he leant forward to kiss his wife. She sent him back to the charter room and his men with as much lightness as she could summon.

The door closed behind him and she sank back into the chair. The room wheeled and spun around her. The moment of danger at last was upon them. It had been so long in the coming that she had hoped perhaps it could be avoided. The endless preparation. Watching and waiting. Unable to fight it any longer she succumbed to the heaviness. Her limbs felt like lead as she kicked off her shoes and lay, still fully clothed, on the bed. Staring at the embroidered scene of unicorns and maidens on the canopy above her, she drifted into a fitful sleep.

CHAPTER 33

JEANNIE

A red sunrise crept over the tower as she emerged onto the rooftop walkway and she shivered. Was it an omen? Although what it might foretell, she dared not even think. Jeannie drew the hood of her cloak over her hair. A bitter north wind swept in gusts, stinging her cheeks and carrying the promise of snow. Across the tower, James and Mairead stood side by side their hands clasped tightly. They had been stationed here since the wee hours, looking east towards Dumyat. Behind the hill and hidden from their view was Sheriffmuir. The desolate heath on the slopes of the Ochils was where Erskine and the Stuart King's army were at this very moment making their stand. The last few days had brought a stream of messengers carrying news of the skirmishes and the positions of the armies.

Other than the low moan of the wind, the rooftop was quiet. It was the same below where the men sat to break their fast. They huddled together in groups with barely a word exchanged. Even the kitchens, usually a hive of cheerful business, were subdued.

'Mistress,' Jeannie said as she approached.

Mairead turned, her face red from the biting cold.

'There are cots made up in the guard rooms with fires ready to light,' Jeannie said. 'The women are making bandages and blankets.'

'The women and children are all within?' Mairead asked.

'Aye, they are,' Jeannie confirmed.

'All is prepared, my love, shelter and room for any who may be injured.' Mairead turned back to James taking his other hand.

'Go below now,' he said and then when he thought she might refuse, 'You'll catch your death of cold up here. Others have more need of you than I at present.'

Jeannie drew her gently away by the elbow, feeling the other woman trembling with the cold.

'Come, mistress,' she said trying to sound confident, 'Alais may need more help in the kitchens and the women from the village want to be useful. They await your word.'

As they descended the stairs, Mairead entered the charter room door and stood with her hands held out to the fire, trying to rub some feeling back into them. Jeannie removed the woman's cloak, stiff and damp with the morning chill, and replaced it with a blanket from the back of the settle. A frustrated sigh escaped her mistress, and Jeannie withdrew to a more discrete distance, mindful of the woman's fierce dignity. Jeannie thought that perhaps she understood. Waiting for word from the battlefield and watching the crossing for redcoat reinforcements was wearying. The worry and uncertainty gnawed at her too, but she had the distraction of her work to keep her occupied. Her mistress was not the type to find peace in homely tasks such as spinning. *Not unlike Lady Frances*, Jeannie thought. Mairead would do better with a purpose that used her mind.

A map lay spread across the table held down at the corners by silver candlesticks and a pewter ale jug. Jeannie looked down on the landscape of central Scotland. Markers laid out the known positions of each army like pieces on the board of boys playing at soldiers. The army under Erskine's command were marked with blue. There were more of them than the red markers of Argyll's forces, almost half as many again by her reckoning. *Are my sons somewhere on that board? Perhaps Angus was right now at Sherrifmuir facing the man he used to call his laird across the battlefield?* A wave of horror rooted her to the spot.

'My brother and cousins will be here. Playing pieces on a board.' Mairead's long and slender finger reached onto the map and touched one of the markers.

The thought had so closely echoed her own that a lump rose in Jeannie's throat.

'My laddies too, I think,' Jeannie said, her voice thick with fear.

Looking down at the map, it was plain to see how important the ferry crossing was. A jewel for the victorious commander and a sore temptation to a retreating and vengeful one.

'It will not end here.' Mairead's voice was quiet and far away. 'No matter who wins the day. There will no peace now. We will be caught here until it is over.'

'Caught, perhaps, but not trapped,' Jeannie said thoughtfully. 'Come, mistress, there is something you should see.'

Jeannie took a candle and wedged it carefully into a holder from the small alcove within the stone of the tower. She handed it to Mairead and lit it with her own from the taper.

'Mind your footing,' she said, lifting the candle high in front of her, 'the floor here is uneven.'

Jeannie's eyes stung at the bright point of light in the blackness. Her nostrils filled with the smell of damp. Once her vision had become accustomed, the rough-hewn stone of the walls became visible. She led the way forwards, her hand brushing the wall to steady herself.

'Where do they lead? Mairead asked curiously.

'This one comes out by the river,' Jeannie answered. 'The entrance there is concealed by the stones of the bank.'

'There are others?' Mairead asked curiously.

'One other that is still open,' Jeannie replied 'it comes out in the forest beyond the walls. The others are gone now with the foundations of the house.'

They paused as the passage had become narrower and the floor slick. Jeannie moved the candle this way and that, illuminating the green moss covering the walls around them. It was cooler now and the air felt heavy.

'Are they secret?' Mairead asked, running her hand over the wall where her candle had picked out names carved into the stone.

'Your husband knows of them as do most of the lads of the garrison,' Jeannie said. 'They would dare each other to venture down here as bairns.'

'I can well imagine it,' Mairead laughed.

'It was worth the thrashing they risked if they were caught.' Jeannie remembered the swaggering and bragging as she had tended their bruises. 'We should return to the tower, mistress, the floor grows treacherous underfoot.'

As they stepped back into the cellar room, Jeannie brushed the dirt from her hands and then lifted the rough spun sacks of grain back into place against the doorway.

'Should you ever have need then you can get out here without being seen. I have checked both ways, the entrances have been cleared,' Jeannie said. 'The other tunnel lies under the eastern tower, hidden like this.'

'Escape like a princess from a bard's tale?' Mairead said. 'I used to dream of such things as a lass.'

Mairead gave Jeannie a smile full of mischief and mirth. It was good to see the younger woman smile. Her cares had lain heavy on her of late. Jeannie was glad she had thought of this. The secret of the tunnels had brought some spark back to her mistress.

***

The light had faded to muted grey as the messenger approached. He was mud splattered and grim. He leapt from his horse whose sides heaved from the effort of the ride. Jeannie watched, insides churning, as Gavin led him hurriedly into the tower. There had been no word since the early morning. As the day wore on, the atmosphere in the tower had become a string on bow drawn taut and now waiting for release. James had prowled the rooftop walkway, refusing to let anyone else take the watch.

Jeannie, having done what she could to prepare, was ready to tend the wounded. Two large rooms on the eastern side of the house had been turned over as a makeshift hospital. Each could hold a dozen men if needed. The women from the village had brought large jugs of water which now sat ready to heat. Rolled strips of linen for cloths and bandage filled woven baskets stacked neatly against the wall. Once content with the rooms, she had turned her attention to her own safety. James had instructed the people in the village to move themselves within the walls of the tower and the house. Although a portion of the house remained unfinished, it was roofed and so provided shelter. Jeannie carried her bedding towards the still room. Although she had been content to bed down with the other women from the village, Mairead had insisted, arguing that it made sense for her to be on hand in a place that others knew to look for her.

A fire blazed in the hearth and for that kindness she was grateful. The thick stone walls of the tower on the lower floor kept the rooms cool even in the heat of summer but now as winter began to bite, they were frigid. She unrolled her blankets in a nook close to the fire. She did not expect sleep to find her this night but a place to rest would be a welcome retreat. By the flickering light of a candle, she opened the wooden chest which contained her precious treasures. From it she lifted a carved figure of a soldier that had belonged to her boys. She turned it around in the light looking at the features. They were still visible despite the little chips and scuffs it bore from much play. Underneath it sat a long ribbon in green cloth. She and her mother had embroidered it with a vine of flowers in yellow thread. Then each woman in the village had added a stitch to the border. For luck. The ribbon bound her hand to Duncan's during their wedding. Jeannie ran her fingers over the fabric. His death had opened a hollow space deep within her that would never close. She missed him, missed their life together. She missed Angus and Collum too. Carefully, she folded the ribbon and placed in on the chest. She laid the carved figure gently on top and closed the lid of the chest firmly.

At the evening meal, word passed along the tables that the battle at Sherrifmuir had been won. Some said it had been a great victory and that the Argyll's redcoats had been routed. The tale grew bolder with each retelling. It seemed to her that news was less than certain. Four more riders had arrived since the first, looking to change horses before taking the ferry across the river. With each piece of news, the story had become more confused. What did seem certain is that both armies had sustained heavy losses.

Jeannie looked to the table where Mairead sat alone. James had been present barely long enough to eat before the arrival of another rider had drawn him away. Mairead sat straight, her face unreadable, picking at the bread on her plate. She had reduced much of it to crumbs and, if Jeannie was any judge, had done little but push her meat around with a fork. Gavin appeared on the dais and bent to speak into Mairead's ear before handing her a note. Once she had opened it, Mairead put her down her fork and stood abruptly. The hall grew quieter as she left in a swish of skirts.

Murren rushed down the row of benches between the long tables and people turned to follow her progress. Jeannie caught her eye and Murren beckoned her urgently. Jeannie followed the girl to the corridor at the foot of the stairs away from the many listening ears.

'The mistress has asked you to attend her. There are men on the road who will need your help,' Murren said breathlessly, wringing her hands in her apron.

'And where is your mistress?' Jeannie asked sharply.

'Gone to her rooms to change,' the girl replied.

Jeannie hurried along the corridor, unsure of what news awaited her. The door was ajar and she knocked before pushing it open.

'You sent for me?' she asked.

'Two messengers arrived,' Mairead said as she braided her hair into a single long plait to keep it from her face. 'The first from Stirling to say the town is awash with rumour and both sides are claiming victory. The second from the laird with orders for James.'

She handed Jeannie a note. The handwriting was cramped and the ink smudged as though the writer had been rushed. She moved into the light of the candelabra. The note, from Isobel Murray, urged Mairead to caution. Her husband was certain that Erskine had withdrawn further north to try to stop any more of his forces melting away with the morning mists. Argyll was awaiting reinforcement from the redcoats and was almost certainly headed back to Stirling to bolster his defence of the castle and the city.

'Both messengers passed a train of men in Erskine colours some riding and the most badly injured on carts. They will make their way here,' Mairead said. 'If we know they are coming then so will Argyll.'

'I'll light the fires and gather the women to help tend them,' Jeannie said.

'I will aid you. I have no mind to sit idly by the fire.'

Jeannie saw the determined set of the woman's chin and knew there was no discussion to be had on the point. *Neither of us can influence the events that follow*, Jeannie thought, *but we can do the work in front of us now. We must trust to hope for the rest.*

The first rider into the courtyard had a young lad in the saddle before him. His arms hooked under the lad's oxters to keep him upright. The lad was unconscious and his head rocked forward as the horse came to a stop. Two of the soldiers rushed to lift him from the horse. Jeannie, holding a torch aloft, looked the lad over and sent the men to the hospital room. The rider was also helped down and, although covered in dark red blood, had no obvious injury. His face was tight with exhaustion and he leant into his horse's flank to steady himself.

'Who is the lad? Surely he's too young to be on a battlefield?' Jeannie asked him.

'A drummer with the Erskine foot soldiers,' the man mumbled. 'He was trapped under a fallen cart, crying. I couldnae leave him mistress, I have a laddie his age...'

She nodded her understanding. The soldier's haunted eyes were unable to focus. Jeannie stopped a passing guard and bid him take the man to the great hall and find him food and a stiff drink.

The ragged stream of carts and men had at last slowed to a trickle in the square. The moon, just past full, arced westward in the early hours. James had dispatched men to offer what help they could to their exhausted kinsmen and stood now beside Jeannie, silent and brooding. She wiped a stray lock of hair, damp with sweat, from her forehead and surveyed the scene. Those able to walk had been sent to the great hall where Alais had the large cooking pots bubbling with broth and gruel. Those who needed their wounds tended but could wait awhile had been taken to the larger of the hospital rooms and into the care of Mairead and some of the village women. Some, more than she would have liked, were seriously injured and needed either a surgeon or a skilled healer. In the absence of the former she would do her best.

A shout for help echoed across the square and both Jeannie and James ran towards it. On a cart lay a man sweating and moaning in pain. The foam around his mouth was tinged black with blood. Jeannie lifted the blanket covering his stomach and the rancid smell engulfed her. She did not need the torchlight to know that the man's guts had been opened and there was nothing she could do to save him. She shook her head ever so slightly at James. His shoulders sagged and he muttered a quiet prayer.

'Jock!' The man's eyes fluttered open as James said his name. 'What's to do with ye man? Lying about here when there is good ale to be had inside.'

They manoeuvred him onto a blanket tied around poles and carried him as gently as they could to a bed in the warmth of the house.

Jeannie washed her hands and began to mix herbs and liquids from the jars and bottles on her makeshift work bench. Around her the beds were filled and the stench of vomit and stale sweat was nauseating. The pungent willow bark made her eyes water but was a welcome relief as it over-powered all other odours for a moment. She added opium to dull the man's pain and perhaps even speed his passage. James sat beside Jock, who writhed in agony and cried out. Not words now. Just sounds from the depths of his horror. James spoke to him gently as she worked. From the corner of the room another soldier, one who had accompanied Jock, watched her with hooded eyes. His intensity made Jeannie uncomfortable, and she pulled her shawl tightly about her as though it were a shield. She asked James to sit Jock up and poured the draught. Jeannie's gentle hands cleaned his mouth and bathed his brow as he slowly drifted into sleep. Within a few minutes Jock's breathing became less laboured. It slowed and then stopped. The soldier in the corner spat onto the rushes and crossed himself throwing Jeannie a black look as he left.

As morning broke, Reverend Dunn moved between the beds offering comfort where he could. He stopped at Jock's bed-side and offered a prayer for his soul. His face was solemn and eyes full of compassion. Jeannie knew his wouldn't be the only death this day. Deep down, she railed against the futility of it. All this suffering. All these lives cut short. To what end? She gripped the handle of the spoon she was holding and forced those thoughts away from her. *Just see to the work laid before you*, she told herself.

CHAPTER 34

MAIREAD

The rain fell in sheets and bounced off the crenelations. Although it was barely midday, the sky was inky grey. Mairead squeezed around the soldiers on the roof, looking for James. It had been days since he had done more than doze and goodness only knew when he had last eaten. He would surely collapse if he didn't stop soon. *That is if he doesn't drown first*, she thought. Shivering as icy drops worked their way through her hood and down her neck, she found him at last, his hands braced on the wall brooding into the gloom. Rain poured from his hair and face in rivers. His fingers were cold to the touch as she placed her hand over his. He glanced at her and then frowned. Standing on her tip toes, she shouted to be heard above the roar of the deluge.

'Please my love, come in now.' She turned his face to hers. 'There is nothing to be gained from this.'

His eyes were ablaze and Mairead knew that, for now, anger was keeping him upright. Gavin and the most senior of his men had tried to persuade him to rest to no avail. She was not certain he would heed her now, either, but she had to try.

'You are needed below. There are matters to attend to,' she tried. 'James!'

Her shout caught his attention, and she sagged with relief as he nodded. He kissed her forehead and led the way inside, pausing at the doorway to order a change of watch. She tugged his shirt over his head and threw it to the floor where it pooled water. She had sent Murren to the kitchens for a hot meal and banished Gavin and the others until James had taken food and rest. He rubbed his hair dry and drank the warmed wine she offered.

'Have you nothing stronger in here?' he asked as he drained the goblet.

'Perhaps. After you have a proper meal in your belly,' she said in the tone her mother had used with her and her siblings when they were being thrawn.

He made a sour face at her but said no more as Murren returned with a mutton stew, thick with gravy and chunks of neep and carrot. It was served with a basket of fresh bread still warm from the oven. Mairead ate sparingly. The heaviness of too much meat turned her stomach of late. Instead, she ate the bread with a thick curl of butter and watched James devour his meal. His eyes were growing heavy now and a wide yawn escaped him.

Mairead poured him a whisky and placed it on the table at the side of her bed. She gave him a pointed look.

'Am I to be put down for a nap like a mewling babe?' he said, feigning outrage.

'If you will not look after yourself,' she said in her best matron's voice, 'then I suppose I must.'

'Lie beside me, wife.' James pulled off his boots and stretched out.

He took her hand, lacing his fingers with hers and they stared up at the embroidered canopy.

'Your uncle will come,' he said, 'now mine has retreated.'

Mairead knew he was right. She stayed quiet. There was no more to be said.

'He will demand our surrender and we will not give it.' His voice was soft.

The frustrated anger of the last few weeks had, for now, abated and she heard tired acceptance in his voice. Her heart ached and she rolled to her side to face him.

'Will he come himself? Or send a force to set a siege?' she asked.

'Truthfully, I do not know,' James sighed. 'My orders are to hold the tower no matter the cost.'

'Well,' she rested her head on his chest, 'then that is what we will do.'

Mairead lay listening to his breathing lengthen as he drifted into a deep sleep. She got up and padded softly to her writing desk. Drawing out parchment, she began to pen a short note. She dipped the nib and swirled it thoughtfully in the ink. She must tread carefully now. Should her letter be intercepted then there must be nothing to implicate her or James. It must seem to be a letter between two acquaintances swapping housekeeping tips and laments about the weather. Bending her head to the task she chose her words with care. She folded the parchment and pushed the seal into the red pool of wax. The seal was a simple carving of a tree its roots and branches reaching. If she could get this to Isobel Murray, she hoped, they may yet get some support. She slid the drawer of the small desk open quietly and pushed the letter into the green velvet within. Softly she crept back to the bed and curled herself around James.

Three harsh bangs woke her from a fitful doze and she shook James by the shoulder. The door opened revealing Gavin who gave her an apologetic glance as he spoke over her shoulder to James.

'John Campbell has returned,' he said, 'with another message for you.'

'A visit from your cousin, Mairead,' James said his voice dripping sarcasm, 'how pleasant.'

'This time Campbell would prefer a private audience,' Gavin said.

'I would wager he does.' James pulled on his Jerkin. 'I will see him in the charter room. I do not want him within the house.'

James splashed his face with water from the basin and ran his hands through his hair. Mairead helped him into his overcoat and tied the leather thongs of his Jerkin at the neck. Although he was unshaven and still looked weary, her husband was formidable. She stood up on her tiptoes, kissing his cheek. He seemed to transform as he crossed the room from her gentle husband back into the fierce leader of men.

The charter room was crowded as Mairead entered and James stood at the hearth looking into the flames. Around the table, the men listened as the missive from the Duke of Argyll was read aloud. He offered terms for the surrender of the tower. The men here had played no active role in the rebellion and King George could be persuaded to accept their allegiance. Perhaps even grant the Erskine lands to a more loyal subject. He urged James to be pragmatic. His laird was in retreat and the English rebellion was now in disarray. There was nothing to be gained by defiance of the crown now. As the words were read aloud, Mairead could well imagine her uncle sat in his rooms at Stirling Castle dictating them. Her uncle was a commander of armies, but she did not think he relished the violence of war. If a way could be found that he could deliver a victory without it, then he would avoid needless deaths. She said as much when one of the men asked what kind of man her uncle was.

James had thanked John Campbell and sent him on his way with the promise of an answer delivered to the castle. With that gesture, he had bought time.

'A messenger has been sent to Perth,' Gavin said. 'The scouting parties have not reported anything beyond the watchers we already had sight of.'

'No word from the laird?' James asked.

'It would be brought to you immediately.' Gavin's tone contained the merest touch of reproach.

With a heavy sigh, James faced the assembled men.

'Our standing orders are to hold the tower. In the morning, a message must be taken to Argyll to politely decline his terms,' he said evenly.

Some of the men with hotter tempers argued for a less measured response but, to her relief, James held firm.

'We will not fight unless attacked,' he said. 'We must trade patience for the hope that the tide might turn again.'

As they left the charter room, Mairead saw her opportunity and waylaid Gavin. Knowing the man was as sharp as a tack, some honesty but not the whole truth would be prudent now. She prevailed upon him to convey her message when he carried James' to the Duke of Argyll. Isobel Murray was her only friend here, she had said, and a social connection would lift her spirits. There could be no harm in that, surely? Gavin, shuffling uncomfortably at her emotive pleas, eventually agreed.

Having dispatched her letter Mairead could only hope Isobel understood the true meaning of the questions within. *What news had she from her husband*? *Would aid be sent if the tower fell under attack?* She sent a fervent prayer that if it was read by other eyes that it would appear to be a letter from a lonely woman to her only friend within reach.

CHAPTER 35

JEANNIE

The rain continued to lash the tower for days following Argyll's message and the mood of the occupants confined within grew ever darker. The scouting parties who patrolled the ferry crossing and the roads during the scant hours of daylight returned soaked to the bone and raw from the storms of hail. The tower was now watched closely, and Argyll's redcoats were massing. They were surrounded. With still no word from their laird, the men began to lose heart. More than one of the soldiers injured at Sherrifmuir had slipped away, creeping from the tower during the night and vanishing into the hills. Jeannie's days had continued to be filled with caring for the wounded. Four more men had died in the two weeks since the battle. She hoped now that those who had survived so far were out of immediate danger.

In the still room, she prepared the poultices for changing the bandages. *The rain may be a curse for many things*, she thought, *but it had meant an abundance of the sphagnum moss that healed wounds so well.* James had allowed her out to the peat bogs to collect it on the condition that she took an escort. Her gallant companion had complained loudly about the weather. Exasperated, Jeannie had insisted the man make himself useful and she had filled her leather pouch twice over. They had been aware of the riders who sat high on the ridge, the scarlet of the coats visible despite the drifting mist. The redcoats made no move, but she had thought it best not to tarry longer than necessary. The oppressive feeling of threat had been growing steadily closer in her mind for days now. It seemed to lurk in the corners and just beyond her sight in the shadows of the cold room. Jeannie glanced in that direction now, the hairs rising on her arms. *No time for that*, she chided herself. There was much to be done.

The hospital room had been cleaned and sluiced thoroughly when Jeannie returned. The last of the linens were now being changed on the box frames by two young girls whose idle chatter fell silent when she entered. The room smelled of lavender and lye soap. It was warm with the fire and the large cast iron candelabras. With only six patients remaining, there was more space to work. Laying out what she needed on the table by the wall, Jeannie prepared. Mairead entered the room, tucking her hair up under the rim of a white cap and joined Jeannie as she washed her hands. It had become a habit of late for them to change the dressings together. Jeannie had been surprised by the other woman's curiosity and her way with the men. A perfect blend of firmness and cajoling. She would need that today as the task before them was particularly gruesome.

The man laying face down reeked of spirits and his body was tense with fear. The other three patients took deep swigs of the strong liquor from the skin they passed between them. Jeannie spoke softly to him as she peeled off the bandage and removed the padding. It was tinged with green and gave off a bitter smell of decay. Mairead held a candle close as Jeannie explored the edges of the burn. More of the flesh on his lower back had blackened and died. It would need to be removed but, mercifully, it was far less than she had feared. Mairead readied herself at the man's head to hold his shoulders down if needed. She crouched and offered him a leather strap to bite down on. Jeannie took tongs and carefully removed the knife blade from the fire, placing it onto the tray alongside the bowl for the waste and a bowl of clean water. Urging the man to be as still as possible, she bent her head to work as quickly and carefully as she could.

The man lost consciousness at the second cut of the knife, which Jeannie knew was a mercy for all of them. His screams had brought the guard running the first time she had needed to do this. With nerves on edge she'd been lucky there wasn't more blood spilled.

'What is in this?' Mairead asked as she picked up a jar of salve and sniffed it. 'I can smell the rosemary.'

'Only honey and rosemary,' Jeannie said, 'it can be applied to a wound or cut to help seal it.'

Jeannie spread the salve across the man's back, taking it out as far as the skin was red and then covered it with the moss she had gathered earlier that day. Mairead held it in place as Jeannie placed another bandage over it. She would wrap it around his torso when he awoke and was able to sit.

Jeannie stood back as Mairead unwrapped the bandage from the upper arm of another of their patients. She smiled to herself as the other woman carefully ran through the checks Jeannie had taught her. Just as she was about to suggest it could be left to the air for a while, Murren burst into the room.

'We are to be attacked, mistress!' she shouted.

The men around them began to struggle to get up and peppered the girl with questions. She turned her eyes pleadingly to Mairead who held up her hand for quiet.

'What do you mean attacked?' she asked, putting down the dressing she had been holding and slipping back into her role as mistress of the household.

'There are soldiers all around the tower,' Murren said.

'Go!' Jeannie urged Mairead. 'I'll finish here.'

She bit her lip anxiously as the other woman pulled the cap from her head and hurried after her serving woman.

In the great hall, all was in uproar. Men stuck dirks and carabines into their belt loops. The ringing of broadswords being drawn filled the air. Soldiers ran back and forth, mustering for James to give their orders. Jeannie skirted the edge of the room, keeping close to the white of the walls, looking for Mairead. She stopped at the foot of the spiral stair. The thud of footsteps echoed, and James rounded the final turn with several men on his heels. Behind them came Gavin and Mairead. From the red rims of her eyes and the spots of high colour in her cheeks, Jeannie could see that Mairead had been crying. She reached out and squeezed the woman's hand as Mairead hurried past, following her husband to the dais.

Weaving through the press of bodies now filling the hall, Jeannie moved forwards and, staying close to the wall, found a space at the front. James was easy to spot as he was a good head taller than those around him and his shock of red hair glowed as it caught the light. Mairead stood off to the side a little way behind him and her face was now pale but impassive. Jeannie suspected that an effort of will was being required and felt a stab of sympathy. She realised she was twisting her apron tight in her own hands as she waited.

James faced the hall and a hush fell. Jeannie saw him take a breath in to steady himself.

'I will ride out and hear what Argyll's men have to say,' he began, voice level. 'This is a show of force meant to goad us.'

There were murmurs of confusion around the hall and Jeannie saw the surprised look that passed between the captains who flanked James. The tower was surrounded by armed men, that was plain for them all to see, but the Erskine men wanted to fight.

'The soldiers outside are wearing clan colours,' he continued, 'this, for now, is a matter between clans.'

The men listened attentively as James explained that the redcoats would no doubt be close at hand but their absence was a message. Argyll would avoid bloodshed between the clans if he could and they didn't want a siege through a bitter winter. The messengers James had sent had been waylaid and their letters taken but the Campbell soldiers were disciplined. The messengers had returned to the tower. The mood amongst the crowd in the hall was beginning to turn. Heads were nodding and shouts of 'Aye' punctuated his speech.

'So, I will ride out and meet John Campbell.' James' voice rose passionately. 'We will show them what discipline and honour look like!'

Roars of agreement and stamping feet met this and Jeannie's eyes met Mairead's. She saw just a flicker of fear.

'For Erskine!' The rallying cry from James sent the hall into a cacophony.

With blood running so high, the tower house felt like a powder keg primed to explode. It would only take the merest spark. Their young commander had done well so far to keep a tight rein on the men before him. *How much longer would that last?* She sent up a silent prayer that the men James had chosen to accompany him were steadfast and level-headed.

From the door of the still room, Jeannie heard the horses' hooves fade into the distance as James rode out. He rode with a white banner, the age-old symbol of truce, but she knew they would be armed to the teeth. She was fond of James and felt fear for what might become of him.

The pine log she had tossed onto the fire hissed and spat as she worked filling the room with a sharp scent. Left with little choice other than to stay busy, she rolled back her sleeves and began to scrub the table, the bristles of the brush working in little circles as she went. The room around her faded as the memories surfaced in her mind. Duncan, Collum and Angus, the faces of those she'd tended seemed to swirl before her. Alan. The dark stain of blood on the pale of the hearth. The image shifted, a dark stain of blood on the ground. A dusting of snow and flakes falling. The wind. So cold. She shivered and a cry of horror rose in her throat.

The shouts of men outside broke through Jeannie's daydream. The brush fell from her hand and clattered onto the floor as she tried to orient herself in the here and now.

'Widow Kellie!' She heard her name being called frantically and rushed out to the square.

The red heat of anger was palpable as soldiers prepared their weapons. Some worked quickly to fit saddles to horses who danced and stamped nervously.

'Widow Kellie, please hurry!' cried the voice she now recognised as James.

He knelt on the floor cradling the body of a man in his arms. A knot of men pressed round him. Jeannie pushed her way through and dropped to the floor at his side. The man's eyes were rolling and there was a round wound to his shoulder. The scorch marks on his clothing and the smell of gunpowder that mingled with the coppery scent of blood told her this was a musket shot. Feeling behind him she could not tell if the shot had passed all the way through or remained lodged somewhere in the body.

'Take him to the sick rooms,' she ordered and added, as the men rushed to help, 'Gently, gently.'

As James rose, she could see the red splatter on his face and the blood stains on his shirt collar and sash.

'Are you hurt, lad?' she asked turning his chin to better see his face.

'No, it isn't my blood.' His voice was small and distant as he looked at the scenes unfolding around him. 'I pulled him across my saddle as he fell. Dinnie fash yourself, Jeannie.'

'Are there more injured?' she asked.

'Not now but there will be before this day is through, I'll wager.' His eyes clouded with anger. 'They offered insult, and he drew his weapon. The shot was fired before John Campbell could get his man under control.'

Jeannie watched James as he ran a weary hand across his face.

'I'll not be able to stop it now,' he said, 'and neither will Campbell.'

The desolation in his voice chilled Jeannie to the core. Around them the men of the tower formed ranks and readied themselves to fight. James squeezed her hand and turned his attention back to the command of the men.

Jeannie gathered her skirts and hurried to the sick room. The man was one of the young captains who had arrived with James.

'Let's have a look at ye, lad,' Jeannie said soothingly as she used her knife to cut through his clothing.

The shot had passed right through his shoulder his body was slick with blood. Making a wadding she pressed down hard at the wound on the front trying to staunch the flow. The lad's eyes flickered closed. Slivers of information and news had reached her as she fought to keep the captain's body and soul together. His breathing became ragged and Jeannie, knowing she could not save him, did her best to make him comfortable. Holding his hand and speaking softly to him her anxious gaze returned time and again to the windows.

As the light began to fade, Jeannie made her way to the kitchen. In the dim corridor she heard a soft weeping and, raising her candle, saw Murren. The girl sat tucked into an alcove in the wall, head rested on her knees. Murren looked up at her with tears rolling down her cheeks. Putting the candle on the sill of the window above them, Jeannie knelt beside the girl who threw herself forward into Jeannie's arms and began to sob in earnest. When the storm of tears had passed, Jeannie eased herself down onto the floor beside her.

'What is it, lass?' she asked, wondering if harsh words from her mistress had sent the girl running for cover.

'The mistress says I must be brave,' the girl said as the tears filled her eyes again, 'but I am very afraid.'

Jeannie nodded her understanding.

'That is the lot of women,' Jeannie said, 'waiting to see what will become of us.'

'Aren't you afraid?' Murren asked wiping her eyes on her sleeve.

Jeannie took a moment to think.

'Yes.' She looked down at her calloused hands and the blood staining the linen of her shift sleeves. 'I am afraid of what will come. But my work is to look after those within the tower. Your task is to serve your mistress. That is what we must do now. Being brave means doing that even though you are afraid.'

As the girl returned to her duties, Jeannie's thoughts turned to Mairead. The rash and arrogant girl who had arrived here had been forged into a strong leader in her own right. She had proven herself more than able to run a household and ensure a garrison was well provisioned. Jeannie admired her spirit and her determination to set her own path. She would need that strength for whatever was to come next.

A clatter of hooves and shouting filled the night. Jeannie followed the noise and tried to make sense of the scene before her, a group of Campbell soldiers rode to the entrance to the tower. Behind them, hands bound walked James with the muzzle of a musket pressed between his shoulder blades. The door opened and Mairead ran forwards. Gavin gripped her by the waist and held her tight. Jeannie pushed her way to her mistress and whispered to her urgently, 'Hold yourself!' Then more gently. 'You are watched.'

Mairead went rigid and shook Gavin off. He stood ready beside her with his hand on the hilt of his sword, with Jeannie stood at the other side. Behind James the rest of the Erskine men were herded into the square. The villagers stood around the edge of the square shocked and terrified. In the crowd a woman's sob was stifled. The mounted Campbell soldiers got down from their horses and John Campbell stepped forward. He issued an order in sharp tones and the man behind James gave him a vicious jab to the kidneys and shoved him forwards. Jeannie winced at the blow, and her heart thundered in her chest.

'After you, madame.' John gave Mairead a mock bow.

For a moment Jeannie thought Mairead might leap at the man clawing but with an effort she mastered herself. Instead, she drew herself to her full height and walked through the large wooden doorway into the tower.

In the centre of the great hall, James stood with John Campbell behind him. His eye was swollen almost shut and blood covered his forehead and nose. His hands were bound in front of him, yet he stood tall and proud despite the barrel of the musket pushed firmly into his lower back. The hall continued to fill as word spread, and people shuffled in shocked silence. Several men in Campbell colours stood with their swords or dirks drawn. A scuffle as the door to the hall drew the attention of those present, and Jeannie saw Gavin shoved roughly onto the dais with a knife held at his side. Behind him, Mairead shook off the arm of another Campbell soldier. She strode forwards, tall and defiant, her fury evident in her tight lips and hard glare. John rammed the musket butt hard into James' back and he began to speak. Mairead went to go to James, but Gavin caught her arm and shook his head.

'The tower is now under the command of the Duke of Argyll,' James said, his voice slow and clear in the silent space. 'You will remain here for now with a garrison of Campbell men.'

Somewhere in the room, a child began to wail and was shushed by its mother. James locked eyes with Mairead.

'Dinnae make it hard on yourselves,' he said. 'I have the word of the Duke of Argyll that there will be no retribution against those who didnae fight.'

The atmosphere in the room grew dark as James' words began to sink in.

'Who will have command of the garrison?' Mairead asked. Her voice sounded unnaturally high to Jeannie's ear.

'I will, Cousin,' John responded with a mocking bow. 'The men will be taken to the castle in Stirling and held awaiting the King's judgement.'

A gasp escaped her and Jeannie felt the room spin. *What would become of them now?* she wondered. Uncertainty coursed through her veins. Steeling her mind against the worst of possibilities, her words to Murren returned to her. She would need to be brave. To walk the path laid at her feet and do what good she could. Even though she was afraid.

***

Delicate feathers of frost climbed the windowpane in the laird's audience chamber as Jeannie stood with Gavin and Alais. The room had the musty scent of disuse, and the fire had not yet lifted the chill. Mairead had given instruction that this was to be offered to John as befit his station. It was in the furthest wing from the Erskine's private family suite and the contrast was stark. The wooden panelling stained with ox blood made it dark and austere. Everywhere she looked, Jeannie could see the marks of rank and status displayed. The high wingback chair with its red velvet upholstery and the family coat of arms in white plasterwork which gleamed in the candlelight.

John Campbell entered the room and cast a hard glare around those assembled. Mairead, her knuckles white on the back of the cherry wood chair, attempted to break the tension.

'The rooms in this wing have been prepared for you and your retinue,' she began. 'Is there more you require, Cousin?'

John took in the opulence of the room and the beginnings of a satisfied smirk rose at the corners of his mouth. Jeannie looked from him to Mairead, silently willing her not to rise to his bait.

'I will take my meals in here and not in that draughty byre you call a hall.' He then looked to Jeannie and Alais and said, 'Which of you is the cook?'

'I am, my lord.' Alais stepped forward, her eyes fixed on the floor just in front of John.

'My soldiers will need a decent evening meal. With bread and meat. Ale too.'

Alais simply nodded and curtseyed before stepping back. John then glared at Jeannie.

'What is your business here, woman?' His voice was cold and Jeannie felt a jolt of defiance rise within her.

'I help the sick and wounded. Deliver the babes and tend to the medicinal gardens,' she said, noting the distaste that crossed his features.

'Good. Some of my men will have need of you. Tend to the wounded.' He dismissed her with a flick of his wrist,

'All of the wounded, my lord?' Jeannie asked raising her chin.

Behind her she felt Gavin tense. Alais placed a warning hand on her back. John's cheeks reddened and he slammed his hand down upon the table causing his glass to rattle. Jeannie held her breath. Had she gone too far? Been too bold? Then he seemed to consider his options.

'Yes. Tend to the Erskine wounded too. They will be marched through the streets of the city tomorrow for all to see,' he said with a cruel smile, taking delight in the thought of that.

Jeannie let out the breath she had been holding and curt-seyed. Alais gave her a small push into action as they left the room.

In the still room, Jeannie bathed the cuts and bruises on James' face. The skin around his eye was tight and hot and the cut on his lip was deep. Both would heal well if kept clean, but the lip would scar. The soldier, set to guard James, stood by the door, looking sullen. His friends were in the hall at their supper, and he had drawn the straw for the first watch. Jeannie, with her back firmly to the soldier, poured a glug of whisky from a small bottle into the tisane she had brewed hoping that the smell from the herbs would mask the peaty scent. She handed it to James who took a grateful sip.

Mairead entered the room, followed by a scurrying Murren. The girl carried a tray with bowls of stew and a dark loaf of bread. The smell of the stew opened a pit in Jeannie's stomach. When had she last eaten?

Addressing the guard, Mairead said, 'Here is your dinner, why not sit in the room out there and enjoy it?'

Her tone was all honey but the guard eyed her suspiciously. She sighed and, removing a key from the ring, she locked the door that led to the garden then offered the guard the key.

'He cannot go anywhere un-noted in this house,' she said, 'and with you outside that door there is nowhere to go. Your stew grows cold.'

The guard nodded and followed Murren out. As the door closed behind them Mairead threw her arms around James. Jeannie was about to leave also when James called her back.

'Jeannie, you need to hear this too,' he said. 'The household and those from the village must do as ordered by Campbell.'

He put his finger on his wife's lip to stifle the protest.

'Heed me, Mairead,' he said urgently. 'You, most of all must give him no reason for retribution.'

'My cousin has made that as clear as glass,' Mairead said bitterly. 'It will be the men in Stirling's jail who pay the price if we are troublesome.'

Mairead's colour rose and her eyes filled with tears that she dashed away quickly.

'John has always been a bully,' she spat.

'Jeannie, the folk of the village will listen to you. They will follow your example,' James said.

'I'll do what I can to keep the peace.' Jeannie's eyes pricked with tears.

'Do nothing rash,' James pleaded with both of them. 'Promise me!'

The fear and anger burned as it welled up from her chest to her throat and all she could do was nod. Jeannie left quietly to allow the couple a few last moments of privacy. Weary now to her bones, she wished Duncan was still here. Wished herself back at Kildrummy. Wished herself anywhere but here.

CHAPTER 36

JEANNIE

The ground was frozen solid and glistening beneath her feet as Jeannie walked through the village. The blacksmith's wife was with child and her time was close now. The light from the forge escaped under the heavy doors and she heard the voices of women within. Shona was being supported on either side by her neighbours as she walked to and fro, pacing a path between the wall of the forge and her own front door. She paused and bent forwards as another pain wracked her body. Jeannie blew on her hands to warm them then placed them on Shona's belly. Feeling the solid curve of a head and another of a bottom she knew the babe had not yet dropped into the birth canal. As this was the woman's third birth, Jeanie wasn't worried. Shona's body knew what to do and shrugging off the woollen shawl a low moan escaped through the woman's gritted teeth.

'That sounds like the babe is making good progress,' Jeannie said, taking in the film of sweat on Shona's face. 'You'll be ready for the stool soon, I'll wager.'

The women nodded in agreement and continued their slow walk, each supporting Shona under her arms. Jeannie picked up the shawl and draped it back over the woman's shoulders just as she began to shiver.

Inside the low-ceilinged room of the house, Jeannie set the horseshoe shaped stool in front of the fire. How many babes had this chair seen safely into the world she wondered as she set a kettle of water to boil. The seat of the chair had worn smooth with use as it went to whichever woman had need. With four legs, it remained solid and sturdy. Sounds of another birthing pain carried in from outside and this time a cry rose from Shona. From deep within the woman it was fierce, almost wild. Jeannie knew the sound well. It meant the baby was almost here. As the women led Shona into the house, Jeannie prepared the room with clean rushes for the floor and blankets. Shona was helped onto the stool. The four women in the room were all experienced with birth and they worked together with a quiet efficiency. As Shona laboured to push the baby into the warmth of the room, Jeannie rubbed her back and pulled a wooden comb from her bag. Shona bit down hard as the crown of the head appeared followed at the next push by the rest of the baby.

Jeannie rubbed the little thing dry and wrapped it, now howling indignantly, in a blanket. Shona was cleaned up and helped into her bed where Jeannie handed her the bundle. She pulled back the blankets and laughed at Shona's delight. A boy at last. As reality returned to the room the tears of joy then became bitter sobs of fear and desperation. The smith had been taken in chains to Stirling with the others.

***

These days were dark and icy cold. The tower existed under the long shadow of the King's justice. News reached them sporadically and the latest messenger brought tidings of the fate of the Englishmen who'd risen in support of the Stuart cause. The room was heavy with anger and resentment as the folk of the tower gathered at John Campbell's order. An uneasy silence fell as John took his place on the dais. To Jeannie's disgust he held his hand out to Mairead.

'Join me, Cousin,' he said with mock politeness. 'Let us hear how the King deals with rebels.'

Mairead did as she was bidden and fixed her stare on the floor before her. Jeannie felt her own terror rising and swallowed hard. The messenger was beckoned forwards and cast a pitiful glance at Mairead. He cleared his throat and opened the declaration.

'In accordance with the laws of the land and of King George, the rebels were tried and convicted of treason'

Jeannie felt her knees go weak. Around her there were cries of shock and despair. John bellowed for silence.

'At Lancaster the men were sentenced and hung by the neck until dead.'

A wail of despair rent the silence and Jeannie saw Shona sink to the floor, the babe still in her arms. On the dais Mairead was frozen, pale as marble.

Jeannie's loathing for John Campbell grew with each passing day. For her own part, Jeannie sensed his unease in her presence. He watched her with suspicion as she went about her work tending to the men. He was a cruel man. It seemed to be his pleasure to torment and belittle Mairead at every turn. If he hoped to destroy her spirit, he had misjudged his mark. The folk of the tower watched their mistress bear each insult with her back straight, red hair gleaming. Her beautiful face, thinner now, was cool and impassive. Her eyes, though, were sapphires of defiance.

Jeannie had yet greater reason to fear John Campbell and a cold prickle travelled from the crown of her head down the length of her spine whenever he was near. Unlike Mairead, she did not have connection to a powerful family to evoke. Nor did she have the protection of a husband. She was careful now to keep only to the common herbs and remedies, mindful that she walked a hairs breadth line. It had been trodden by so many women before her, the balance of being needed for her skill and despised for it. Yet Shona's baby seemed to Jeannie proof that life must go on. No matter the circumstances, a new life offered hope. Arriving just as the year prepared to turn it felt like a sign.

Flickering and precarious like a flame in a draught though it was, she must look for these rays of light now.

She worked in the still room, preparing a salve of goose fat and pine to soothe the cough of a guard. Crushing the dark green needles under the blade of her knife released the menthol oils she would use. It wouldn't mask the rancid smell of the rendered goose fat, but it would soften the edges of it. Mairead entered and shuddered with revulsion covering her nose with her sleeve.

'It will smell less vile as it sets,' Jeannie said.

'It surely must or how would anyone stand it?' Mairead asked, removing her sleeve as she became more accustomed to the stench.

Jeannie looked the woman up and down. Her cheeks were pale and pinched and the red rims of her eyes told a story of tears being shed. She led Mairead over to the chair by the fire and bade her sit.

'What ails you?' Jeannie asked gently.

'I cannot settle to anything,' Mairead said, looking down at her hands. 'I cannot sleep, and food turns my stomach.'

Jeannie, her head cocked to one side, left a quiet space for Mairead to fill. The woman had borne the trials of the last few weeks with a reserve of grit beyond her years, but their toll was becoming clearer and clearer. The edge of Mairead's nails were red and ragged and the skin of her fingers was chapped and rough.

'I am afraid for him,' Mairead whispered and a single fat tear rolled down her cheek.

Jeannie had no words that would lessen that fear, and neither would she treat the woman before her like a bairn to be soothed. Yet, she knew something of the pain and frustration she saw so plainly before her. The dark well of anger and longing that Duncan had left behind was only ever a heartbeat away. There were times even now, especially now, that it threatened to swallow her whole.

Jeannie handed Mairead tea as the other woman laid bare her fear and worries. They came out in small parcels. Little words and thoughts forced their way through her armour. Feelings of helplessness. Of not knowing. The terror at the thought of losing him. In the tense moments of stillness, Jeannie simply listened. These were her fears too. The fears of all the women folk of the tower. Yet they must endure. Must continue to bake the bread, waulk the wool and tend to the livestock. Waiting for the next message, the next event that would tilt their course again. If the laird, even now, was gathering his strength and planning another push in the spring then the fortunes of the tower may turn again.

Mairead is not completely powerless, Jeannie thought and knew that she, herself, refused to be. Could a message be got to Isobel Murray? From there to Lady Frances? Mairead was too precious a jewel for John Campbell to risk, but *she* was not. Her pulse quickened at the thought, and she looked around her. This still room was her domain, with its strong walls and order. She had carved out this place for herself, but it balanced now on the edge of a knife. Life was cruel to those with no protection and no power. Widows starved in towns and villages each winter having to rely on the pity and charity of their neighbours. Shona and her babe cast out to fend for themselves. She had seen the fates befall other women when she had travelled with Duncan to collect the rents and it haunted her still. Was she brave enough to risk what little she had?

What other choice did she have?

Mairead let out a deep sigh as she began to regain her composure, giving Jeannie the moment she had been waiting for. Her throat felt tight and she cleared it, knowing that if the other woman agreed there would be no turning back.

'There may be a way to get a message out,' she said very quietly. 'You are not forbidden from writing letters?'

'No... I am not,' Mairead said, 'but everything I write will be read by John Campbell.'

'It will,' Jeannie agreed, 'so the words must be carefully chosen.'

Jeannie knew that a wife would be expected to write to the powerful friends of her husband to plead for aid. Her uncle is the Duke of Argyll, surely a plea for leniency might be indulged.

'Not all of the messages need be written.' Jeannie's voice was barely above a whisper.

Mairead leant forward and took Jeannie's hand as she considered this.

'It is too dangerous.' She shook her head. 'If we are caught it will be visited on James and the men. On us too.'

'Which is why it must be me,' Jeannie said.

Mairead stood and paced the room, her indecision clear in the way she caught her lip between her teeth.

'Whatever happens, we will need help.' Jeannie's voice was level. 'The next man given charge of the tower may turn us all out.'

'Our laird may yet prevail. It is not done yet and my cousin remains alert to an attempt to retake the tower,' Mairead hissed at Jeannie, her temper flaring and two red spots bloomed on her cheeks.

Mairead closed her eyes and took a deep breath. The weight of her worries made her look for a moment fragile, and Jeannie felt a pang of sympathy for the woman. Caught between hope and fear, Mairead seemed frozen. To act was a risk but so was doing nothing. She had never been one to shy away from what must be done. Over the last days and weeks, resentment had formed like a stone in her shoe. Resentment at the injustice of their situation, at the way John Campbell behaved but most of all at her own reliance on the actions of others. She felt small and her vulnerability had hit her hard. Jeannie felt a spike of agitation rise at Mairead's hesitation. She pushed it down. Disharmony between them would serve nobody. Jeannie changed tack.

'As mistress of the tower, it is for you to see to the welfare of those loyal to Erskine within these walls,' she said, hoping that an appeal to the woman's sense of duty might get through. 'I serve you and will help you where I can.'

'I sent word to Isobel Murray,' Mairead whispered. 'A message hidden within a letter. No aid has come. Perhaps we are abandoned?'

'Perhaps we must try another way,' Jeannie said softly.

The colour had drained further from Mairead's cheeks and she raced to the door. Wrenching it open, she vomited. Jeannie rubbed her back until the retching ceased and then fetched her a cool cloth to wipe her face. Leading her, arm around the shoulder to Duncan's chair, she began to wonder.

'When did you last have your courses?' Jeannie asked.

Mairead looked up sharply and a look of wonder crossed her face as she realised. She placed her hand on her stomach.

'Now?' she asked. 'After all this time, I am with child now?'

'It is often the way of it,' Jeannie said, handing Mairead a cup of water. 'A summer birth?'

A new generation, she thought, *and so the wheel turns*.

CHAPTER 37

HAZEL

H er phone rang again for the fourth time that afternoon. Since word had spread of the unusual burial, it had been impossible to get into the flow of the project with so many interruptions. The emails, messages from colleagues and people popping by to talk about the project had been incessant. Bristling with irritation, Hazel picked it up, intending to send the call to her voicemail along with the others. She paused. Unlike the previous calls, this one had a caller ID. It was the journalist from The Scotsman newspaper looking to do another feature piece on the project. Hazel knew that the opportunity for more publicity was sorely needed and answered.

By the end of the call, she had sent a calendar invite for an interview and photo shoot to Lauren and to Tom. The photographer would be back and had requested images from the geophysical study to use as part of the article. Hazel fired off a quick email to Iain asking if there were any he was happy to share.

She opened the report again and scrolled through the pages, pausing at the image generated by the modelling software. The bones found in the grave had been fleshed out and the woman lay looking peaceful. She was clothed in a simple dress dyed in a deep blue colour and dark apron. The fragments of cloth found on the body had been tested and the homespun cloth had been dyed with elderberries. Her arms rested across her abdomen, still tied at the wrists, and her eye lids covered with the silver coins. Hazel read the description of the condition of the body. Broken ribs and a nasty fracture to the cheek bone. This woman had suffered violence and injury. Left broken and alone in a grave outside the cemetery. That wasn't the whole story though, was it? Somebody had cared for her. Laid her gently to rest under the rowan. Hazel reached out and gently touched the magnetometer image on the screen as though reaching back across time.

A memory resurfaced for Hazel. In the courtroom, she had sat next to her father. His shoulder pressed close into her side, a solid presence lending her the strength to listen as this room full of strangers discussed her injuries. The x-ray image of her own skull had been projected onto a large screen. It showed a hairline crack running across her cheek bone. Hazel had glanced at it and then fixed her eyes resolutely on the wooden carving of the royal seal above the chair of the magistrate. She explored the lion and the unicorn holding up the royal coat of arms as the doctor described the force it would take to cause such an injury. She needed no reminder. The ache and discomfort had lasted weeks, months even. Chewing had been painful and running caused the ache to pulse from the crown of her head to the tip of her shoulder.

Her thoughts returned to the body they had found, and goosebumps appeared on her arms at the strange sense of connection she felt, as though they were bonded by the hurt inflicted on them. A fractal line between this woman's past and her own. Her determination for the project to be a success had awoken feelings of frustration and helplessness. She had tried so hard to move past this but here she was again, caught in the web of her own despair. Only physical exertion kept it at bay when the walls closed in, pounding it out of her mind with each run. Her determination to prove to herself... prove to herself she could move on. She sighed. She was trying too hard and holding on too tight. Hazel could see it. The concern in Marcus and Mei's faces. The sidelong looks Lauren gave her. They didn't understand. They couldn't.

The chime on her inbox dragged her attention back to the present. Lauren had received a call from an old colleague who now worked at the University of Columbia in New York. He wanted her to appear on his podcast. *All to the good*, thought Hazel. She had known that the public interest in the mystery of the body would be high. International coverage would be the icing on the cake for the project. With a quick call to Lauren, she made arrangements for them to meet the following day back at Alloa Tower. She began closing the windows on her computer until she was left once again with the image of the woman in a grave. *Who are you? And how on earth did you end up there?* Solving this mystery would now become the focus of the project, Hazel reflected, realising that caused a flutter of excitement. There would be no way to ignore it even if she wanted to. Hazel was surprised by how badly she wanted answers to her questions, like a tug on an invisible rope that bound her to this other woman.

The charter room was filled with light streaming in through the windows. The table covered with documents, books and dusty box files. Tom had propped a huge whiteboard up on the wall beside the fireplace and was adding Post-it notes to different sections. The lurid colours were jarring in the faded splendour of the room. Hazel hung her black wool coat on an antique stand which had been liberated from the entranceway downstairs.

'We've told him there are apps that do that these days,' Lauren said, following her gaze.

'But this is better,' Tom said with a note of protest. 'It lets us all see the bigger picture.'

'It's an eyesore, is what it is,' Lauren said.

This appeared to Hazel to be the latest skirmish in a long running dispute between the two and she decided the best course of action was to remain neutral.

'We're historians,' Tom said brightly, 'supposed to do things the old-fashioned way otherwise we'd be the Modern Studies Department.'

Hazel couldn't help but laugh. She tried to hide it by crouching to read the notes on the board. Following the lines which connected the information and dates. Her eye was drawn to a sketch of the gardens dated 1713 and, beside it, an image generated by the geophysical survey. On the sketch, there was a small copse of trees, her eyes tracked across to the other image where only the roots of the rowan could be seen. A sliver of something she had read as a child tugged at her memory.

'What is the folk lore about rowan trees?' Hazel asked.

'It used to be considered very bad luck to cut down a rowan,' Tom said.

'In some places it still is,' Lauren said, joining them to look at the picture. 'Rowans are trees of protection. They were never used for firewood. My granny refused point blank to have the one in her garden cutdown when it dropped a branch on the shed roof during a storm in the 80s.'

Hazel looked closely at the sketch again then pulled off her glasses, resting the leg of them against her lips thoughtfully. At the table, Hazel laid out the site plan and found the spot where the trees had been and where the rowan now stood.

'What are you thinking?' Lauren asked with interest.

'The wall curves out here.' She pointed to the map. 'It skirts around the roots of the rowan. If it hadn't, then our body would have been dug up when the wall went in. I can't help wondering who she is and what happened here.'

'Yes, it is very unusual,' Lauren said. 'Buried with such care but in an unmarked grave. Under a tree that was thought to protect places from evil. We've been looking for her in the church records.'

'That must be like looking for a needle in a haystack,' Hazel said.

'The archaeology report gives us approximate dates to work from. The coins are dated 1711 and Iain reckons they were not very old when they went into the ground,' Lauren said, 'but we should know more when the forensics report comes in.'

With a lingering look at the site plan, Hazel and Lauren sat down to prepare for the upcoming interviews.

***

A whirlwind of media interest in the body gathered pace over the following days, Hazel found herself at the centre. She had just been interviewed by Rebecca and Martin from BBC Scotland's weekend news and current affairs programme. The Scotsman had run a feature piece which had sparked a flurry of requests for television and radio interviews. The events at Alloa Tower had sold out. History of Scotland Trust had to bring in staff from other properties to keep up with demand. It was all happening so fast that Hazel had barely drawn breath. She was almost glad to be on the slow train between Glasgow and Stirling. Although it stopped at every small station along the route, it gave her time alone.

She put her headphones over her ears and pressed play on her 90s playlist. The low sun streamed through the window and Hazel yawned, her eyes heavy. The nightmares had persisted. A face visible in the shadows, watching her. Sometimes it was Matt and sometimes, of late, it was Klaus Leinster she saw, mixed with incoherent fragments of memory. She woke with sweat cooling on her body and adrenaline coursing through her veins. After each occurrence, she checked both the doors were locked and bolted. It had become a ritual, reassuring herself that she was safe.

Last night, her long run with Mei had done her body and soul good. Some of the tightness in her shoulders had unwound as the miles spooled out behind them along the paths at the feet of the hills. The shapes of the Ochil's rising out of the early evening darkness sheltered them from the wind, and it was not yet so cold that they needed to cocoon themselves in thermal layers. Mei had commented that it was good to see Hazel looking less stressed but was still worried that she was exhausted. Mei had teased her about her dreams being haunted by the mysterious woman in the grave and Hazel had laughed it off. But it was closer to the truth perhaps than she liked to admit, even to herself. The sixpences from the grave had bled into her dreams too, their cruciform shields with tiny crowns in her hand – the fare to cross the river.

With her laptop open on the white granite worktop, Hazel poured herself a glass of Rioja. Pulling herself up onto the stool, she curled her toes around the cool metal of the foot bar, savouring the spicy depth of the wine. Artemis sat on the windowsill staring out at the dark of the garden, her tail swishing contentedly. Her parents had just left after their usual Sunday lunch which had been pushed back to an early dinner this week so they could watch her interview together. Her Mother had brought a beef wellington to cook, knowing it was her favourite comfort meal. They had dissected the news of the day with their meal and then watched her interview over coffee. According to her father, the manner of the woman's death was a hot topic of speculation at the golf club, and he was being treated like a minor celebrity in the hope he had insider information. She didn't usually work on a Sunday, but the emails were piling up and she hadn't even read the monthly finance report yet.

She worked her way through the inbox, dealing with the calendar invites and deleting those that were unimportant. As she was opening the finance report, another message pinged in. It was from the Coltrane Institute and contained the forensics report. Hazel leant forward on her elbows and read it slowly. At the end, she sat still in the pool of light from the spotlight overhead. Artemis rubbed herself along Hazel's feet as she wove in and out of the chair legs. A cold heaviness descended as she digested the information in the report.

The woman had several more injuries, some old and some newer. One sentence stood out: *Of particular note on the MRI scan were fractures to the vertebrae (C1 and C2) and the hyoid bone.* The sanitised and clinical language felt so at odds with the horror that it described when she looked at the body map included to see that these were bones in the neck.

Artemis' plaintive meows roused her from her thoughts, and she put out fresh water and kibble for her before getting ready for bed. The final line of the report ran over and over through her head.

This leads to the conclusion that the most likely cause of death is strangulation.

CHAPTER 38

JEANNIE

As she entered the hall, Jeannie saw the garlands of holly and ivy strung out in readiness for Hogmanay and the turning of the year. They left her cold, there was no appetite for celebration amongst those who lived in the tower. Heaviness had settled and people went about their business with drawn faces and only hushed conversation. She remembered the feasts of years gone by. The marking of the old ways with a yule log and the storytelling on midwinter's eve. The dizziness of dancing reels after too much honeyed wine or fire cider. In the north these festivals still were observed, she knew, but here in Alloa they were only a faded memory. Outside, frost had crept over the landscape laying claim to the trees and paths. Colours blanched in the mist that lingered on the fields. Jeannie stiffened as a cold finger of foreboding drew down her spine.

James and the men of the tower had been tried and they now awaited judgement. Gavin had attended and reported that many had fallen sick in the icy damp of the gaol. She had watched as Mairead pleaded to be allowed to send them food and medicine. They were traitors to the crown, John had refused. Instead, he counselled her that a prudent woman would seek to distance herself. He would hear no more of it. When word reached them that two of the Erskine prisoners had succumbed to a fever, Mairead had fallen into a rage, kicking and tearing at her bedlinens, cursing John Campbell. She and Murren had closed the shutters around the bed and locked the door, trying to ensure their mistress' grief and desperation didn't attract attention. Jeannie felt real fear now for the fate of James and his men. What hope remained to them? What bonds of kinship or loyalty could they call on for aid or to intercede? From their laird, they had heard nothing. Jeannie struggled to believe it of the man she had served for over half her lifetime. Yet, here they were. Forsaken. *Would John Erskine really abandon his nephew to his fate?*

At the table in the still room, Jeannie stripped berries from the stalks of juniper, preparing for the saining of the tower and house. The berries clustered in threes within the silvery needle. Their deep purple skin worked its colour under her nails. She tied the stalks tightly into bundles and placed them into a basket. Later she would hand these round the women to be burned on *Ne'eer Morn*. Tears began to fill her eyes as she thought of saining her home. Cleaned and sprinkled with water from the burn, they closed the door as the room filled with the heavy sweetness of the smoke. Coughing and with eyes stinging, Duncan would open the door to let out the old year and welcome in the new. A fresh start. Even as she worked, it seemed a hollow promise. Wiping the falling tear away, she tried to rid herself of the thought. That had passed now and the choice that faced her was how best to endure.

The summons to the great hall came as Jeannie worked alongside Alais preparing the clootie dumplings. The warm scent of cinnamon and spices rose from the bowls they stirred. Gavin called to them from the doorway that the household were to bear witness to the King's Justice. Jeannie steeled her nerves as she and a crowd of the kitchen workers followed Alais. They entered through the serving room door at the side of the dais and shuffled along by the wall to make room for those still arriving.

Alais gasped and grabbed Jeannie's arm. She followed her friend's gaze to the group of men in their riding cloaks and leather boots. Her breath hitched in her throat. Knees turning to jelly, she leant her weight back onto the wall, steadying herself. As though aware of her stare, the dark-haired man turned and met her eye.

'Collum,' Jeannie whispered.

His serious face was older than when last she'd seen it. Always quieter than his brother and slow to anger, his eyes now were cast downwards, his countenance filled with the darkness of a heavy weight. Jeannie knew then what his errand was and swallowed hard. Her heart felt as though it would fly from her chest torn as it was between her horror at what was about to unfold and her empathy for her son. Her youngest who must deliver this terrible blow. Here. In the place he once called home. She pressed her hands into the wall behind her, fighting the urge to run to him. Alais looked from her to Collum, her face going pale as she too made the leap of understanding.

The King's message was delivered by a man who, judging by the greying hair and weather lined features, was well into his middle years. The soft burr of his Edinburgh accent was at odds with the sour expression he wore. Used to his task, he stood unmoved as he read the proclamation.

James Alexander Erskine and those who stood with him did raise up in arms against King George, their rightful King,' he said. *'They have been found guilty of treason...'*

A clamour rose and John strode forwards, bellowing for silence to no avail. His guard drew their weapons, encircling the group of messengers. Jeannie elbowed her way closer to the knot of men her fear for her son overriding all else in the moment, but it was Mairead who restored order.

'Peace!' she commanded, holding up her hand. 'I will hear the sentence passed by King George.'

The room quieted and heads turned to her. Standing tall and alone with her head held high. She glared at John, who bade the messenger to continue.

'Treason,' he said, *'is a capital crime and punishable in law by death. The leaders of this rebellion will be taken from Stirling to London and there, will be executed.'*

Jeannie's hand flew to her mouth to stifle the cry. She saw women turn to each other, clinging close in their hushed terror and anguish. Mairead seemed to sway a moment on her feet and then catch herself. Jeannie took hesitant steps toward her and stopped. John's arm shot out to steady his cousin, his own shock evident on his face.

'I will see this order,' Mairead said to John. Her voice was so hoarse it came out as a low hiss.

John gave his cousin a worried look then nodded to the group of messengers. The man who had spoken coughed and nodded. Collum stepped forward as though his feet were iron. He held out a document bearing the heavy red seal of the King. Mairead reached for it.

'Collum Kellie?' a man shouted from the crowd and pushed his way forward.

Mairead's eyes narrowed as she looked from Collum to Jeannie. Jeannie's mouth went dry as the ripple of shocked recognition spread. She froze.

'Gallus of ye to show yer face here. Have ye no shame, man?' he said and spat at Collum's feet.

A lad of twelve or thirteen years ran at Collum, fists flailing and landed him a blow to the chin before the guards drew their swords. Gavin stepped between the swords and the boy, gripped his shoulder and shoved him roughly back into the crowd where his mother caught a tight hold. Jeannie found herself held tightly by an iron grip on her upper arm.

'Be still now,' Alais whispered to her as though reading her mind. 'No good will come of it.'

Mairead gave Collum a look so cold it might turn him to stone and broke the seal. The crack seemed to echo too loudly. With lips pressed into a thin line, she read the decree and nodded in resignation as she handed it to John. A keening noise broke the silence of the hall and Jeannie saw Shona, the blacksmith's wife, fall to her knees, holding her baby and two small girls close. The noise was like a punch in the gut to Jeannie, who felt that deep pit of loss and despair begin to spin. Darkness flickered at the edges of her vision. She turned back to her son who was now at the centre of the knot of men as they left the hall. His eyes met hers like a stormy sea. They were filled with regret and sorrow.

Alais pulled urgently at her arm and led back towards the serving room door. As they approached, it was barred by two of the kitchen men. Alais gave them a fierce look and tried to push them aside, but neither would budge. The impasse in the door- way was attracting more attention and Jeannie's panic began to overwhelm her. Gavin pushed his way through to the doorway and took in the situation before him.

'Out of the way, man,' he said, 'Widow Kellie has done no wrong here.'

His voice was raised and both reluctantly stepped aside. He went ahead and Alais pushed Jeannie along behind. Jeannie felt as though she were wading through thick mud and stumbled, unseeing, into one of the men. She felt the gob of spit spray her face and heard the word 'bitch' hissed into her ear as she righted herself and hurried forward.

Jeannie swilled water around her mouth and then spat it into the hearth. She cupped her hands and splashed her face. Pressing her hands into the base of her neck to cool herself, she drew a shuddering breath. Shaking from the events in the hall, she had vomited over and over until she'd laid exhausted on the frigid stone of the floor with hot tears streaming. Now feeling numb, she rested against the table trying to make sense of it. Collum had come bearing that horrible news. Her kind-hearted and gentle laddie. Her heart ached for him. *The King would be merciful*, she thought, *surely he would not make such a public show of punishing James. James who had done nothing but defend his laird's keep?*

A voice raised in the corridor outside the door sent Jeannie's pulse racing and she slid the bolt across to bar the door to the still. If it had not been for Alais' quick thinking and Gavin's solid presence, she did not know what might have happened in the hall. She took the paring knife she used for cutting herbs, the cool bone handle smooth in her hand and slipped it deep into the pocket of her skirts.

***

A tight band of pain throbbed in her head when she awoke the following morning. She had slept only fitfully, alert to every sound. As she swept the hearth and laid a new fire, she dipped the wooden ladle into the pitcher of water and found it almost empty. She would need to refill it. Hoping to use the well unseen, she pulled the hood up of her cloak and took her pail. She unlatched the door to the medicinal garden and slipped quickly outside. A heavy snow had fallen overnight and with the sun only just rising in the square at the centre of the village, all was quiet. She hurried to the well and pulled on the chain to draw her water. As she turned to leave, she came face to face with Shona. The woman's eyes hardened when she recognised Jeannie and she turned her back resolutely. Jeannie lifted the pail, pausing with the indecision of trying to reason with the woman but as she heard voices approaching, she thought better of it and strode quickly back through to the gardens. *This is a living nightmare*, she thought. A woman did not last alone when those around her turned their backs. *Where could she turn now*, she wondered? Those who offered her friendship risked the same treatment.

Alais stepped from the shadows behind the doorway as Jeannie entered the still. Water sloshed over the side of the pail in her hands and splashed onto the floor between them as Jeannie stopped. Gently, Alais took the pail from her and led her to Duncan's chair.

'You've had a terrible shock I dare say,' her friend said softly. 'I've brought you bread and porridge to break your fast.'

Jeannie opened her mouth to refuse and Alais waved it away.

'Ye will eat,' she said. 'Ye have tae.'

Jeannie felt the words and the fear rush up her throat and she began to sob. Alais held her tightly and let her cry it out. When she had quieted, Alais patted her hand.

'The mistress has asked to see you,' she said.

Jeannie gave her a questioning look but Alais shrugged, not knowing what was wanted of her. She pushed the bowl and bread into Jeannie's hands and left quietly.

***

Murren answered the knock on Mairead's door, her eyes discs of astonishment as she saw Jeannie. Murren turned to her mistress for instruction.

'Let her in,' Mairead said, 'and take these to the kitchens.'

The two women faced each other across the room. Jeannie looked at the floor and waited for the other to speak, unable to meet her red rimmed eyes. After a moment, Mairead sighed.

'I have some bleeding,' Mairead said, her voice flat and distant.

'How much?' Jeannie asked, crossing the space between them and reaching out to Mairead who stepped aside.

'Only spots so far,' she said.

'Any aches or cramping?' Jeannie put her hands back at her sides and moved back as Mairead shook her head.

'It is not uncommon,' Jeannie tried to offer comfort, 'but you will need to rest. To stay as quiet as possible until it passes.'

Mairead sagged and sat heavily on the bed. Her eyes were dry now and desolate. She hadn't slept either, Jeannie was sure. She wanted to offer the woman some comfort, to ease her fears and suffering but there was nothing she could do.

'Is there anything you need?' Jeannie asked.

Mairead looked at her.

'He was your son,' she said, voice shaking, 'the man who brought the decree from King George. He was James' friend. They played together in the tunnels as children. You told me that.'

Jeannie lowered her eyes again at the pain the memory now held.

'He served at King George's court with Laird Erskine. Travelled with him to London and was offered a place serving the old King's justices.' Jeannie kept her voice level.

Mairead looked thoughtful for a moment.

'Will you take a letter for me to James?' she asked. 'If I must rest then you must take it.'

Jeannie hesitated, caught between her fear and her pity for the woman.

'There will be no objection from John or my uncle to a condemned man receiving a letter from his wife,' Mairead said, her voice cracking.

'I will take the message for you,' Jeannie said her voice shaking with emotion.

Mairead moved to the bureau and pulled a sheaf of paper from the drawer and began to write. Jeannie pulled the door closed quietly behind her with a glance over her shoulder at the anguished woman.

CHAPTER 39

MAIREAD

Looking out over the thick blanket of snow lying on the gardens, Mairead sat rubbing some feeling back into her cold hands, her furs pulled up to her neck. The winds of the night had roared around the house, finding every little gap and way in. Even with a fire blazing in the grate the chill lingered and bit at her nose. The winter had been particularly harsh and all through Hogmanay the wind had driven sleet and snowstorms across the country. The roads were all but impassable. Mairead began to wonder if she would ever feel warm again. Although Jeannie believed it safe for her to take walks outside, the biting cold far outweighed the boredom at her confinement. The smell of warm bread and honey filled the room as Murren unloaded the tray and she felt a pang of hunger. Blessedly, the worst of the sickness seemed to be behind her and she sat down, eager to eat. Breaking the round loaf in two, she spread each side thickly with butter and honey. Wrapping her hands around the cup of warm ale and closing her eyes, she savoured the sweetness.

The knock at her door intruded on her peace and she swallowed down her irritation when Murren opened the door to John.

'I am sorry to disturb your meal, Cousin,' he said. 'I have come to see if you are well?'

Since the verdict of the trial had been delivered, John had kept his distance from her. Being spared his little cruelties had been a blessing of her current condition. This change in his tone however made her wary. 'I am much improved,' she replied stiffly, unwilling to offer more.

'I will be attending our uncle at Stirling Castle and he will want a report,' John said and paused for a moment as though trying to choose his words with care. 'I am obliged to tell him of your... circumstances.'

Mairead's anger flared and she faced him, her colour rising.

'Why ask, Cousin?' Mairead said. 'You already have your answer.'

'It is my business to know!' John pinched the bridge of his nose. 'I will not justify myself to you. I came to offer to bear a message on your behalf. Why must you always be so thrawn and unyielding?'

She dropped down onto the chair, abruptly pulling back the reins of her temper. This was a familiar battle in an old war and she had no strength left to fight it again. John had come to them as her father's ward when she had been seven and he nine. He had followed her and her sisters, always watching. Like a shadow. In games he was rough and did not like to lose. She remembered a day when they had raced along the sand of the beach to the sea to jump the waves. The sea spray on their faces and her sisters laughing and cheering. Both determined to reach the water first, John had been fast, but she was faster. He'd been so enraged that he'd pushed her into the water, ruining her shift and new dress. Mairead had been thrashed for that and he had stood watching slyly from the corner. He had enjoyed seeing her suffer even then. When she complained, her mother had reasoned that he must be lonely at Dunotter with only lassies for company and suggested they should play games that he could win. She bristled even now at the thought of that. Why should she let him win? Yet, here and now, John had the upper hand. What sense was there in making it worse? Might it even be more to her advantage to soften a little?

Mairead gestured to the chair opposite and John sat. He placed his thick leather gloves on the table and poured himself a cup of the warmed ale.

'The baby should be born in the summer,' Mairead said. 'James has been told.'

John's brow furrowed. His fingers steepled under his chin as he thought.

'Your father may offer you shelter if you ask it,' he said and she shook her head vehemently in response.

'No, the baby is an Erskine,' she said simply.

'Without a father,' John replied.

The pain of that statement brought stinging tears to her eyes. John took a sip from his cup, allowing her time to compose herself.

'The Earl of Mar may give us shelter for his nephew's sake,' she said.

'The Earl of Mar?' John spluttered and slammed his cup back on the table. 'You cannot think our uncle will allow you to leave his custody?'

'This war is not over yet.' Mairead knew she was goading him but was unable to stop herself. 'Erskine holds the Highlands.'

John's lip curled in a sneer, and he barked a harsh laugh. He pushed back his chair and began to pull on his gloves.

'Erskine is finished. His army melts away with the winter snows. He is a traitor to the crown.' He shook his head at her. 'He will lose his wealth and his estates. His head too, when he's caught.'

Mairead stamped to the window turning her back to him.

'For the sake of our kinship and the time we spent together as bairns,' John said. 'I offer to carry a message for you. If you don't have the wit to use the opportunity to plead for yourself or for your child, then I can do no more.'

Mairead felt an agony of indecision as he strode to the door. His words hit their mark. For herself, she didn't care, she'd stood before John in the great hall and had chosen to remain an Erskine. Her love of James meant she would hold to that. But for the child, *their* child, should she plead? Would she get another chance?

She called to him as the door opened. 'I have a request for my uncle.'

John turned back expectantly. There was no affection between them but the bonds of kinship in the Campbells ran deep. They had been raised to duty, both schooled to keep their word. She wondered if he might even find respect for what she must do.

'I would like to see my husband,' she said, 'before he is taken to England. I would like to say goodbye.'

John's eyes widened and he bit back whatever rebuke had been on his lips. Instead, he gave her an appraising look as if wondering what move she was planning to make. To her satisfaction, she caught a glimmer of uncertainty which was quickly masked.

'As you wish, Mistress Erskine,' he said with a bow, closing the door behind him.

***

The still room was empty when Mairead entered. The fire was lit but the water pail was missing. Jeannie would be at the well, she guessed. She had watched as the woman bore the suspicion and anger of the people in the village. Fearing she would make things worse and reassured by Alais that the dark cloud would blow over, she had said nothing. Mairead looked around the room at the few possessions and trinkets. *Will this be my lot too?*

Shall I live my life relying on the forbearance of others? Pushing the thought away, she paced around the table then stopped and picked up a wooden bowl. The bottom was smooth, worn by use and inside it was pitted with dents and gouges. The contents were dark green and had been ground down too finely for her to identify them by sight. She sniffed the contents, recoiled, and returned it quickly. Her sense of smell was so much stronger now and the sharp scent that came from the herbs in the bowl was overpowering.

'It will pass when the baby is here,' said Jeannie, stamping the snow from her shoes. 'Can I help you, mistress?'

'I have been granted a visit to James in the gaol.' Mairead saw Jeannie's alarmed expression and continued quickly, 'My uncle has insisted that I must be accompanied. Will you attend me?'

'Aye, if you wish it,' Jeannie said. 'It will be a hard ride in this weather and perhaps unwise for you travel back and forth in a day.'

'I will take a room at an inn and John will provide an escort to see we do not find any... trouble.' Mairead gave a tight smile. 'I have petitioned my uncle that we may be able to deliver food and blankets to the Erskine prisoners.'

'What was his answer?' Jeanie asked as she hung her hood and cloak in front of the fire to dry.

'That I was riding my luck,' she replied, watching the melting snow fall pooling on the dark stone of the hearth. 'As he did not go so far as to forbid it, I do not mean to let that stop me...

Gavin suggested that the gaolers may turn a blind eye if they are sufficiently rewarded for their efforts.'

Jeannie agreed and Mairead was struck by the woman's quiet courage. She wondered if it was concern for her well-being or for James that drove the decision but either way was grateful for it. She planned to visit Isobel Murray whilst in Stirling too but, fearing that Jeannie would refuse or try to change her mind, kept that to herself. *There will be time enough to tell her.*

Mairead spent hours stood on the roof walk, wrapped in her furs, watching the snow falling and searching the road for riders, for any sign that the roads would open, and she could go to James. There were moments of hope when she convinced herself that Erskine would prevail. Waking dreams where a great force took Stirling Castle and James was returned to her. She imagined him lifting her high in the air, spinning her around as the snow settled on his eye lashes. When the reverie passed and the horror of reality returned, she sank under the weight of it, lost and unable to do more than weep. Caught between the need to see James and the red ball of fear about what she would find, she maintained her vigil. Murren had been unable to persuade her to eat or to rest and began to fear her mistress would throw herself from the roof.

Finally, the snow stopped and a spell of fine weather thawed the roads. Mairead was helped into the saddle and John, holding her horse by the bridle, gave instructions to the men he was sending as escorts. White ears flicked back and forth as the horse tossed his head, mirroring Mairead's own impatience.

'You will be accompanied at all times, Cousin, and a room has been arranged for your comfort,' John said sternly.

He eyed Jeannie suspiciously and opened the bag she had tied onto her saddle. Seeing the ointments and small bottles, he closed it again pursing his lips.

'Go carefully, Cousin,' he said sternly.

As she turned her horse towards the road, Mairead wondered what John had meant. His voice held an edge of threat. She had been careful and told nobody of her plans. If he thought that she had a channel of communication to Lady Frances she would not be given this boon. Unless he hoped that she might give herself away. Her letters to and from Isobel Murray were read by John. He made no effort to disguise it as he delivered them unsealed. Their discourse was carefully bland.

***

The rank smell of the gaol was so thick it burned Mairead's nostrils, and she wrapped her cloak around her nose and mouth as she was led along the maze of dark corridors. In one of the cells to the side, a man reached through the iron of the bars and grabbed at her skirts as she passed. Jeannie wrenched them free for her but she shuddered at the echo of his vile insults. They stopped at last outside a heavy wooden door and the guard looked at her expectantly. After a moment, Jeannie pressed a coin into his hand and he held it up to the light. A sixpence, it seemed, was not enough. Mairead took another from the small purse she had tied deep within her pocket and held it out to him. Her heart hammered in her chest as he snatched it from her. The realisation that there was nothing to prevent him taking her coin and throwing her back out into the cold. She met his eye, seeing the frank appraisal as he weighed his options. After a heartbeat pause, he gave the door a violent kick.

'On your feet. You have a visitor,' he growled and then turned the key in the lock.

The room beyond was icy cold and the wall by the narrow window was slimy with mould. Mairead hesitated in the doorway as her eyes adjusted to the gloom. A figure stood in the far corner.

'James?' she asked uncertainly. The man before her was too thin to be her husband, surely?

At her voice, a look of despair crossed his face which he hid as he tried to stand tall. Her legs shook as she moved towards him and raised her hand to touch his face. James recoiled. She took his hand instead and drew him forward into the silvery thin beam of light. His face was ravaged with pain the skin hung loose from his cheeks. *He looks so old.* Mairead's heart cracked open but when his eyes met hers, they were the same deep blue.

'You should not have come,' James barked. 'Why are you here?'

The venom in his words cut Mairead to the bone and her cheeks reddened as the guard laughed at her discomfort.

'The Duke of Argyll granted me a private visit with my husband.' She glared at him.

He shrugged his shoulders and left. Jeannie reached deep into the depths of her skirts and brought out a carefully wrapped bundle of food. She handed it to Mairead and then followed the guard out of the door, closing it behind her.

'Did my letters reach you?' Mairead asked.

'Aye, lass, they did,' he said, his voice thick with emotion. 'When will the bairn be born?'

'Before midsummer, Jeannie says.' Mairead pressed her head to his chest and his arms encircled her. 'What will I do?'

James held her quietly and she squeezed back tears at the feel of the bones in his chest and back where there used to be muscle.

'Do what you must,' he said. 'Ask your father for shelter.'

Her protests fell on deaf ears. In a rush of words, she told him of her plan to get word to Lady Frances and ask for her help now. He raised her chin and put a finger over her lips to silence her pointing to the door.

'No, my love, what matters now is you and the bairn,' he said.

Despite the wave of frustration that threatened to engulf her, she held her tongue. She would not argue with him now, not in their final moments together. Instead, she nodded and softened back into his arms, feeling as though her heart was being wrenched from her chest.

Mairead felt Jeannie's hand under her arm as she stumbled out into the bright daylight. Unable to see through her tears and shaking from head to foot, she was led gently to the edge of the street. Her mind whirred in a desperate panic, searching for a way to save him and coming up with nothing. She wanted to scream and tear at the stone of the walls. Drawing shuddering breaths, she tried to compose herself. John's guard stood impatiently tutting as the women drew curious glances from passers-by.

'Steady, lass,' Jeannie murmured in her ear as she bent forward, retching. 'To the inn now and we can get you warm.'

'I cannot bear to leave him.' Mairead's voice was an agonised whisper as she forced herself upright.

'You must,' Jeannie whispered urgently as the guard now looked ready to drag Mairead along the broad street.

The room at the inn had dark panelled walls and a low ceiling. With a small wooden table and meagre fire in the hearth, it was a far cry from the comfort and luxury of the tower. The noise from the yard below carried through the room but the linens on the bed were fresh and the room was clean. Mairead unlaced her sleeves and removed them as Jeannie poured water into a bowl for her to wash. The stench of the gaol clung to hair and stuck in her nostrils, she wanted to scrub herself raw to be rid of it. For now, this jug of tepid water and rough lye soap would need to be enough. As much as she loved James, she could not obey him in this. She needed to know she had done everything she could. For James and for their child.

'I need to see Isobel Murray,' she said in a low voice to Jeannie, aware of the guard at the door.

'I am not sure that is wise...' Jeannie whispered.

'Wise or no I have to try,' she insisted.

Jeannie sighed and nodded her agreement. Mairead dressed quickly and secured her purse once again in her pocket.

Getting past the guard had been difficult and he had refused at first to take her. Mairead had been insistent. The household required supplies, she'd argued and Murray serviced both the tower and her uncle's residence. What objection would John have to her ordering the necessary goods for the kitchen? She produced a folded list and waved it at him. She knew exactly what was needed and it would not take long. The items could be on their way to the tower whilst the weather held and the roads were open. The exasperated guard had eventually relented and now stomped ahead of them towards the market cross.

The Murray's shop was busy and as Isobel approached with a smile Mairead gave her a pleading look. Understanding her meaning, Isobel greeted her politely as she would any other customer.

'Mistress,' she said, 'will you take your ease by the fire away out of the cold? I'm sure your man here and your servant can gather what is needed.'

The guard gave Isobel a black look, but Mairead handed Jeannie the list and followed Isobel across the room. As she took a seat by the fire, Isobel kept up a steady stream of chatter about the weather and the price of wool. Mairead gave Jeannie a grateful look as she drew the guard along with her, searching for the items on the paper.

'Are ye well, Mairead?' Isobel asked softly, her back to the room as she poured a cup of hot tea. 'We've had no way to get word to you.'

'Have you heard anything from my aunt, Mistress Murray?' Mairead asked, keeping her voice light as other customers drew close.

'No, we have not. The weather has been harsh and the roads are not safe,' Isobel replied and then, as the group of customers moved on, she dropped her voice to barely a whisper and added, 'James Stuart has landed in Scotland not three days ago.'

Mairead kept her expression carefully bland and sipped her tea. As another woman joined them at the fire, the polite passing of time resumed until Jeannie approached to say they had placed the order and were now ready to leave. The guard, keen to be on his way, glowered behind her. Mairead took her leave of Isobel, and they stepped back out into the freezing air. She walked quickly back to her lodging, needing time to consider this news and knowing that it would reach the tower soon enough.

***

The door to their lodgings had barely closed behind them when Mairead drew Jeannie close and drew her to the centre of the room. Away from prying ears she took the other woman's hands and squeezed them

'The King is here!' Mairead exclaimed giddy with excitement. 'James Stuart has arrived from France.'

'Are ye sure?' Jeannie's eyes widened in surprise.

'So says Isobel Murray,' Mairead continued. 'Surely now the clans will rally once more behind the laird?'

Jeannie bit her lip as though considering the news.

'Aye, they may. If the Stuart can raise an army then Argyll might be forced to negotiate at least.'

'It will save James!' Mairead's eyes burned bright amber. 'It must...'

Jeannie turned away. She took the cloaks and set them to dry on the chairs by the measly fire. Mairead felt a needle of irritation that Jeannie did not share her joy.

'Jeannie,' she said sharply, 'are you not glad of this news?'

'I do not know what will unfold now.' Jeannie's tone was uncertain. 'I am only certain that the danger has not yet passed. You must be cautious, mistress.'

Mairead nodded, her hand resting on the swell of her belly. She knew there was wisdom in Jeannie's words, yet a spark of hope had taken root within her. The first she had felt in many months.

CHAPTER 40

JEANNIE

A nother group of soldiers arrived at the tower, soaked to the skin and faces ruddy from the march. Argyll knew the Stuart King was in Scotland and preparing for a second push south now the roads were open. Their arrival had meant a morning of cleaning and hasty preparation as rooms were made ready to garrison them. Jeannie sat at a table next to Gavin at the edge of the hall, taking in the scene. The newcomers wore the redcoats of the English army and even the Campbells eyed them with cold hostility. Their captain was a man named Morton. Fair-haired and in his early twenties, he sat back into his chair, lifting his feet up onto the table. Jeannie saw Mairead bristle with indignation. Looking around the hall, here and there were more experienced soldiers. They sat in smaller groups eating and talking together, keeping themselves apart from the rest of their cohort. The rest were rougher and louder. As one of the kitchen boys passed by holding a platter of roasted chickens, a soldier snatched it from

his hands and when the lad protested, he fetched him a stinging blow to the side of his face. Outraged, Jeannie made a
move to stand. Gavin, with a warning look, gripped her wrist
tight, pinning her to the bench. He inclined his head toward
the dais and John, who sat tight lipped and furious.

Captain Morton called Mairead forward and Jeannie
found herself holding her breath as the young woman stood
tall and pale, like a marble statue.

'Although you are the wife of a condemned traitor,'
Morton began, giving her a look of disgust, 'your cousin here
insists that you be allowed to keep your rooms.'

Mairead met the captain's eye but, to Jeannie's relief, said
nothing.

'You will be treated as befits your station,' he said, 'until
Argyll decides what is to be done with you.'

As Mairead returned to her seat, Morton stood and addressed the hall.

'The Earl of Mar is a traitor. The men folk of this tower
await the gallows,' Morton's clipped English tones carried
clear across the hall. 'If this were England, you would find
yourselves sharing their fate.'

'Aye, well, this is not England,' John said, his voice shaking with anger, 'and the Duke of Argyll gave his word that
non here would be harmed as long as they remained peaceful.'

'As long as they remain *obedient*,' Morton corrected. 'Come now Campbell, show me the hospitality the Scots are famous for.'

The noise in the hall rose again slowly. From the worried glances exchanged Jeannie knew the threat had been well understood by the folk of the tower.

***

Jeannie stooped over the bench cutting herbs for tea to ease the coughing of men in the sick bay. She jumped in fright as the still room door swung open and three men entered. The first of the redcoat's sword hissed as he drew it from the sheath.

'Stand aside woman,' he demanded, 'Captain Morton has ordered this room searched.'

Jeannie felt hot bile rush up her throat as he pressed the tip to her collar bone. She placed the herbs and paring knife back on the bench forcing herself to make slow and deliberate movements. Heart thundering and her mind racing she tried to make sense of what was happening. *What were they searching for? Did they know about the letter to James? To Isobel?* Jeannie stood mute as bottles and pots were opened then tossed aside. Her dried herbs poured from their burlap bags and strewn across the floor.

'No! Please!' Jeannie cried out and felt her hair grabbed from behind.

'Quiet!' the soldier growled wrenching her head back.

She watched in horror as the blanket was torn from the bed and it was turned over. Next the soldier kicked at the metal cooking frame over the fire. The pot fell to the floor and cracked tipping hissing tea onto the hearth stone.

An older soldier strode into the room alarmed by the noise. He took in the disarray and began to shout. The soldier holding her hair let go and shoved her roughly forward.

'Can you not see that these would be needed if a sickness spreads through the tower?' he roared pointing to the spoiled ointments and pouches of herbs. 'Has not one of you the sense they were born with?'

With sharp words ringing in their ears, the rest of the search was conducted with more decorum. The soldier who had held her was a small man, his furtive glances and movements reminded Jeannie of a stoat. He caught Jeannie watching him and cast her a filthy look. The man forked his fingers and spat on the floor at her feet. She shuddered with revulsion as she watched him leave. With shaking hands, she began to put the still room right salvaging what she could. Jeannie took a fresh pot and poured water to begin brewing the tea again. The scent of rose hips and hibiscus a bright contrast to her dark mood.

***

In the kitchens, Alais was wrapping hunks of yellow cheese in cloths and one of the kitchen girls packed them carefully into waiting saddle bags.

'Master Campbell is summoned to Edinburgh,' she said in response to Jeannie's questioning look.

'Captain Morton with him?' Jeannie asked and, at the shake of Alais' head, murmured, 'Oh dear.'

'There is a fever amongst the English, the kitchen boys are saying,' Alais said. 'Have a care Jeannie, these men are pigs.'

Jeannie gathered what she needed from the cold store at the back of the kitchen, intending to check in on Mairead. Across the room, she saw one of the women point in her direction.

'Widow Kellie?' the redcoat asked.

'Aye,' Jeannie replied recognizing him as the soldier who interrupted the search of the still room. 'What do you have need of...?'

'Jenkins,' the man supplied. 'I'm told you are a healer. Some men started with a fever yesterday. More today.'

Jeannie followed him to the rooms in the east wing of the house. The rugs had been rolled up and the furniture stacked to make way for the beds laid in neat rows along the room with packs and lines of boots. Several of the beds were occupied by soldiers who lay sweating.

With her cool cloths and soothing teas, Jeannie moved amongst the soldiers. The cold and wet weather of Scotland had seeped into their chests and settled heavily in bones. Fevers, she knew, were unpredictable and she must be vigilant. Jenkins was the quartermaster and agreed with her suggestion that the sick men be roomed apart. He gave quiet orders for the move to be undertaken. Jeannie saw the sour expressions of some as they were roused from their rest to see to it. Amongst them, the soldier from the still room who had put her in mind of a stoat muttered and swore under his breath. Feeling his eyes upon her like two hot coals, Jeannie tried to stay focused on the man who lay before her, exhausted after a bout of coughing. She eased him up to sitting and encouraged him to drink.

As the day wore on, Jeannie began to see the rhythm in the soldier's day. The changes of the watch were frequent and those who were not on watch were given other tasks to keep good order. Again, Jeannie noticed the difference in those soldiers who were veterans of other campaigns. They carried out their tasks with care and pride.

As the light faded, Jeannie left the soldiers quarters. She needed more herbs for her teas and still intended to look in on Mairead. In the still room, she scrubbed her hands, arms and face. The sour smell of sweat and vomit clung to her still so she changed her apron. Carrying an earthenware jug into which she had ladled rose hip tea, Jeannie made her way towards Mairead's room. She used the servants' corridor, unwilling to draw attention to herself.

Opening the door onto the main corridor she heard raised voices. She stopped dead, trying to work out where the sound

was coming from. The crash of breaking glass and the beginning
of a scream that ended abruptly drove her forwards and she ran
towards the noise – it was coming from Mairead's rooms. The
door stood ajar and the scraping of furniture and furious cursing
indicated the struggle within. As she entered the room, Jeannie
saw Murren white and shaking, cowering in the corner. Behind
the door, Mairead was pinned with a man's hands around her
throat. Her face was red and eyes rolling as she clawed at him in
desperation. The man's knee at her stomach prevented Mairead
from kicking out. Mairead's frantic movements began to falter.
She was close to losing consciousness. Without hesitation, acting
only on instinct Jeannie swung the jug with all her strength. It
cracked off the back of the man's head with a sickening thud and
he crumbled to the floor.

Mairead slid down the wall gasping for breath and Jeannie
stepped over the man to catch her. She eased her to the floor
checking the extent of her injuries. Red marks stood out livid on
her white neck and her eyes were bloodshot.

'Murren,' Mairead managed to croak, searching the room
for her servant.

Jeannie turned and only then saw the way the girl cradled
her arm. She knelt in front of her and with gentle hands took the
injured arm. The skin was hot and purple and the fingers white.
There was certainly a break and a nasty one at that. Blood welled
up in the teeth marks on the girl's neck. With white hot fury,
Jeannie knew what other injuries she would find on Murren's

tiny body. She lifted her gently to stand and the girl began to weep at the sight of the man on the floor. Jeannie pressed her hand to her head as the tightness there grew. She must think clearly now and act quickly. She closed the door. Hoping it might buy them time until the guard changed. Time to see what must be done.

Kneeling over the man on the floor, she put two fingers to the side of his neck feeling the steady jump of a pulse. She was relieved to find one. Turning his head, a shock of recognition flooded her. It was the stoat man. His mean little features pinched even as he was out cold. Mairead must get to John and tell him what had happened. Hope sank when she remembered that John was not here. That was no doubt what had emboldened this man.

Mairead's colour was returning as she sat hand protectively over her belly. The swelling was visible now under her skirts. Whether the babe had been harmed by this day's trials, only time would tell.

'You must act quickly, lass,' Jeannie said urgently. 'He may wake at any moment or he may be missed.'

Jeannie's words seemed to snap Mairead back into herself and she looked with distaste at the man. Seeing Murren still rooted to the spot, mute terror etched on her young face, Mairead pushed herself up the wall and back to her feet. She staggered and steadied herself before aiming a savage kick at the man on the floor. It connected with a thump like meat hitting the butcher's slab. Jeannie squeezed her eyes shut. Not a noise had escaped the man. *He might never wake*, she realised.

'Mairead, no!' she said as the woman stood over him with a knife in her hand. 'Do that and we'll all swing.'

Jeannie caught her wrist and as their eyes met Mairead released her grip on the knife. Hooking it with her foot Jeannie kicked under the bed and out of sight. Drawing shuddering breaths Mairead took in the disarray in her bedchamber.

'I came from the solar,' Mairead began, her voice still a horse whisper and the words painful. 'He was on top of Murren. She was crying in pain. I threw the glass at him. He slapped my face. Grabbed my neck.' Her hands went to the welts at her throat.

Murren made a keening noise behind them as her shock gave way to the pain. Casting an anxious look towards the door Jeannie went to the girl, trying to quiet her with gentle words.

Mairead dropped to her knees and began rifling through the man's clothing. Jeannie watched her in disbelief. *What is she doing?*

'A letter,' Mairead said, meeting her eye. 'He wanted payment for a letter. He threatened to take it to Morton.'

Good God! If anyone else knows of this, it is over. Jeannie looked desperately at the door, straining to listen for approaching steps.

'His pockets,' Mairead whispered, tears filling her eyes as she pulled frantically at the man's arm, trying to move him.

Jeannie knelt beside her and they heaved. Between them, they rolled the weight of the man onto his back and, gasping with the effort, they searched. Tucked inside his jerkin was an envelope, damp and sour with sweat. With a shiver of revulsion, Jeannie handed it to Mairead who tore it open with shaking hands.

'Lady Frances,' Mairead said, her voice harsh with pain.

Jeannie held her breath as the other woman's eyes flew across the words. Mairead shook her head. Eyes dark with fear and grief, she handed the letter to Jeannie. The earl was with the Stuart King in Perth but the promised French army had not arrived. Her advice to her niece for the sake of the bairn was to throw herself on Argyll's mercy or come north. They must rely on their own wits now Jeannie realised.

Jeannie shivered as the heat of the anger drained from her body. It was replaced by horror at the futility of their situation. She looked around her as though watching from outside of herself. Murren huddled against the door. The pinched face of the man lying prone. Mairead's red welts vivid against her pale skin. The cold in her veins turned to stone as the weight of it all fell around her. Her thoughts came now with a hard clarity. There was only one choice.

'We will need to save ourselves,' she said, 'we must act now whilst there is still time.'

Striding to the fire, she threw the letter into the grate and watched until she was sure it was ash.

'I will take Murren to the kitchens,' Jeannie said.

Murren began to weep and shake her head.

'Sweet lass, this must be done in the light. Others will need to bear witness. I will let no more harm come to you and neither will Alais,' Jeannie said softly. Then she turned to Mairead. 'You must find Captain Morton and tell him what happened here. Demand that he takes action and that your cousin is informed. John still has command of the tower.'

'Then I must tell him that you hit the man...' Mairead said. 'You will have to answer for that.'

Jeannie knew it, but what other way was open to them?

'Go now!' she said urgently, 'before we are discovered.'

'Thank you.' Mairead clasped Jeannie's arm.

She drew Murren close to her. The girl turned her trembling cheek into Jeannie's shoulder as she led her past the man on the floor. Quickly, she led her to the servant's corridor and to the relative safety of the back of the kitchens.

CHAPTER 41

LAUREN

The whirlwind of media interest and interviews showed no sign of slowing and Lauren floated on a cloud of happy exhaustion. She had to admit that she was looking forward to the spotlight being on somebody else at the next two events. The Fireside Evenings had sold out twice over and would be live streamed as well. A first for the History of Scotland Trust and for her. She had managed to persuade Tom to introduce the event, knowing that he deserved recognition for the work he had put in. She smiled to herself, feeling proud of her student. Her vision for the project had been to breathe life into these places and their history. Tom had taken that concept and run with it, finding ways to not only connect people to the past but to let them experience it.

Lauren walked along the tree-lined avenue to the tower and paused to take in the moment. The place was full of light and life. She closed her eyes for a moment listening to the thump of the hammers and the buzz of drills as the marquees were constructed, the beep of a van reversing and somewhere a loud peel of laughter added to sense of industry. At the doors she saw Isobel, the curator, anxiously shepherding in a huge ornate mirror, her shoulders hunched. Concern about how they would manoeuvre the valuable antique up the stairs was evident even from a distance.

Lauren walked around and slipped into the tower through the side entrance to avoid adding to the congestion and angst. She climbed the stairs to the charter room and found herself in all the splendour of an eighteenth-century castle with the silk covers of the carved chairs and the portraits watching on from the walls. The sixth earl's plans for the house and gardens were laid out on the table at the centre of the room. Taking it in, Lauren knew the team from the History of Scotland Trust had done an amazing job of setting the scene. It was easy to imagine the laird sitting in his highbacked chair with the white powdered wig on his head pouring over the details with the master builders. Lauren felt a sense of satisfaction as she looked around. It was all coming together.

In the late afternoon, members of the board of trustees and invited guests began to arrive for the dry run of the Fireside Evening. Hazel had been insistent and, at first, Lauren had been irritated. Over planning risked the creative flow of an event like this and it was not in her own nature to micromanage every detail. Yet she knew that Hazel had given everything to this project and now, with so much interest, she wanted it to be to be perfect. Lauren thought about Hazel and how low she had been during the darkest days of the project. It had gotten under the other woman's skin and the pressure from the board had been intense. There was more, though. Her mind drifted back to the meeting at Airthrey Castle and the interaction between Leinster and Hazel that she had interrupted. Whatever had happened to Hazel in York had been dredged up along with the body here in Alloa. Stories of the past had that power. Running deep within cultures and societies, shaping the views people held and the decisions they made. It was why history fascinated people, connecting them with invisible threads they couldn't see but seemed, on some level, to feel. The rattle of cups interrupted her thoughts and reminded her that she was supposed to be up in the solar with the storyteller running over the plans for the sessions.

Theatrical tension had been building from the moment the guests arrived. The experience began with the Archaeology Scotland virtual model of the tower and house. Guests seeing it as it once stood then watching it evolve through 700 years of history into 1715. Next, they moved onto Tom's research which pulled out the stories and details of life at the tower during the '15 Uprising'. Then there was the exhibition called 'The Kist' which was where the investigation surrounding the body, and its unusual burial, was housed.

In the flickering light of LED candles, the guests took their seats and an expectant hush fell in the room. Melissa began by describing the role of storytellers, or bards, in Scotland's history and how they were like the celebrities of the day. Not only did they tell stories but they also collected them as they travelled from place to place. Lauren warmed to her instantly. Drawing the hood of her long woollen cardigan up over her head, Melissa morphed into the character of an old woman at the fireside spinning tales for the amusement of the laird and his household. Around her the anticipation built and Lauren felt a sense of satisfaction at a job well done.

In spite of herself, Lauren leant forwards in anticipation as Melissa told tales of the eerie will' o-the-whisp lights said to be seen from boats travelling along the Forth. Lured into the marsh and wetlands by the fey lights, the boats would become stuck and when the dawn broke and the lights vanished, the captains would find their crew half mad and their cargo missing. Next was the Curse of Alloa Tower cast by the angry monk which promised blind heirs, deaths and the ruin of the tower in fire. Lauren admired Melissa's skill as she ramped up the tension telling of the ghostly woman in black who was often seen rocking the empty cradle in the solar.

'Of course,' Melissa said, 'you are all drawn here this evening by a story... a mystery to be solved. I was intrigued too and turned to local legends and folk tales to look for clues.'

Beside Lauren, Hazel fidgeted in her chair. It had taken some persuading from Tom and the team to let this unfold as part of the experience alongside the foods to try and the trades.

'Many of you are familiar with tale of Flora MacDonald,' Melissa began, 'the woman who helped bonnie Prince Charlie, disguised as her serving woman, to escape after the battle at Culloden. Well, Flora is not the only woman who is said to have risked it all in the battles for Scotland.'

Lauren looked around at the rapt faces of the audience as Melissa began to weave her tale. Local stories of a woman who killed a guard whilst attempting to carry a message to her husband in Stirling Castle Gaol. The brave and beautiful young bride had come to Alloa with her husband who served in Erskine's guards. After the Battle of Sherrifmuir, her husband was imprisoned and sentenced to death for treason. Having escaped her own confinement by rendering her redcoat guard unconscious, she and her serving woman made for the tunnels under the tower.

'What happened to her next is lost to the mists of time,' Melissa said dramatically, 'but some believe she may be the woman in black who haunts this very room. Others believe she made her escape and returned north to her kin. Some versions of the tale tell us she died during the escape. The redcoats, not wanting it to be known they had been bested by the young woman, buried her in secret in the grounds of the tower.'

Delighted laughter and applause filled the room as Melissa brought them back to the present. Lauren caught Hazel's eye and saw the relief and pride that echoed her own emotions.

***

Lauren sat in front of the fire with her legs curled underneath her and piles of notes fanning out around her. This was the part of any project that Lauren enjoyed most. When all the research was done, and the story unfolded, revealing itself glimpse by glimpse through the months of slowly, carefully, peeling back the layers. This time, though, it felt different. Heavier somehow. Every answer in this tale only led to more questions. Her instincts told her that they were close, though. Tantalisingly close. Siggi whined at her at, hopeful of a crust from her plate.

'Well, my boy,' she said, stroking his ears. 'We know what killed her, don't we? But who is she? What happened to her?'

She slipped him a piece of her sandwich, deep in thought about the tales Melissa had told. There was always a grain of truth at the heart of folk tales. It was what made them so relevant and compelling. It was easy to imagine the young bride and her servant fleeing through the tunnels by torchlight. The skill of the storyteller had made them so vivid. The Fireside Evening had been brilliant, and she knew it was going to be a real hit with the public.

CHAPTER 42

MAIREAD

Mairead's body quivered and her breath came in rapid gasps as she waited to be admitted. The soldier who had opened the door looked her up and down and his eyes widened when he saw her neck. Trying to calm her racing thoughts, Mairead looked around her. Captain Morton had taken rooms in the eastern wing of the house which John Erskine had intended for the use of important visitors. Gavin had brought her to see these rooms when she first arrived at the tower. He had explained that they were influenced by the palaces of Versailles. She remembered how she had stared in wonder at the lavish gold leaf on the wallpaper and the ruby and saffron rugs. It was as though that was a different lifetime now. The door opened and the soldier beckoned her in.

Morton and two other men stood and watched her expectantly. *What if he already knows of the letter? What if he refuses to believe me?* Mairead waited from him to dismiss the others and when he did not, she looked down at her hands trying to hide her discomfort. It was too late for doubt now. She would know soon enough.

'Captain, one of your men attacked my serving woman.' Her voice was still harsh and it was painful to get the words out clearly. She coughed and continued, 'When I interrupted him, he did this.' She indicated to her neck.

Morton stepped towards her, fingers cold on her chin. He turned her neck from side to side, looking at the marks. His hair was long and tied back in a black band at the nape of his neck. Flecks of gold reflected in his sandy hair and, this close, she could smell the sourness of last night's wine. Her stomach clenched.

'Ask Jenkins to fetch the man here and we will hear what he has to say,' he said and then to Mairead, 'I am assuming, *madam*, that you can identify him?'

'No!' the shout escaped her. 'You will not able to bring him here.' Her voice cracked painfully with the effort and she stopped.

'And why would that be?' Morton asked his grip tightening painfully on the top of her arm.

'Widow Kellie...' She closed her eyes tight and sent up a silent prayer for forgiveness and croaked, 'Widow Kellie hit him. With a jug. He was going to kill me. In my rooms.'

Morton gestured to one of the men who hurried to do as bidden. He turned back to her, angry and suspicious.

'You will sit here, madam.' He pulled a chair around and forced Mairead down into it. 'We will get to the truth of this.'

Mairead's throat burned. The wave of fear and anger she had been riding began to crest. Her vision blurred and hearing only snatches of the conversation around her, she fought to stay awake. A cup was pressed into her hands, and she looked up to see the soldier who had answered the door. His concern was evident in the anxious look he gave her, and she was grateful for it.

Hurrying footsteps pounded down the corridor and Jenkins entered the room. He saluted Morton. Mairead could see that his sleeve was stained in blood. He gave an account of the soldier, Brown, out cold on the floor as Mairead had said. A wound to the side of his head but alive. More men entered and Jeannie was pushed into the room. Her arm circled protectively around Murren whose body was wracked with terrified sobs. Mairead met Jeannie's eyes and found her own silent terror reflected there.

'What am I to make of this? A soldier of the King's army accused but unable to speak for himself and the three of you. The wife of a convicted rebel, a serving girl and a woman my men tell me is a witch.'

The shocked silence that followed Morton's words was broken as Murren's sobs grew louder.

'Silence her or I will,' he snarled at Jeannie.

Jeannie turned the girl into her arms and held her close whispering into her ear. The sobbing quieted a little and Mairead saw her chance.

'My cousin, John Campbell, is the commander here' she said as haughtily as she could manage. 'It is to his justice that I will submit my complaint.'

Captain Morton threw back his head and laughed at her audacity but Mairead pushed on.

'He is due to return tomorrow is he not? I demand that he hears the complaints.' It was risky and she knew it.

Mairead stayed quiet now, allowing Morton to think.

'Very well, madam,' he said and then to Jenkins, 'Escort Mistress Erskine to her rooms and double the guard. Keep these two under lock and key.'

Knowing there was no point in pressing him further, Mairead stood to follow Jenkins. As Jeannie and Murren were pulled from the room, Morton stepped into their path. Looking at Jeannie with distain.

'You had better pray Brown does not succumb to his injuries,' he snarled and leant down close to her ear, 'or I will not be responsible for the actions of my men.'

Mairead stepped in front of Jenkins and led the way back to her rooms. She kept her head high and her pace sedate. Her fury at the pain and injustice had been tempered to steel by Morton's laughter. She was gratified to see the shocked looks on the faces of the household as they saw the red marks livid on her slender neck and the bruise now blooming on her cheek bone. Mairead knew that word of this would spread like fire through heather, reaching the ears of the Campbell soldiers. The redcoats were already disliked, and it was an uneasy alliance with the Highlanders. Morton did not treat John Campbell as his equal and that had been the cause of more than one ruck between the two sets of soldiers. With luck, Alais and the kitchen staff had seen Jeannie set the break to Murren's arm and enough of her distress to know what the cause of it would likely be. She hoped it would be enough to hold the redcoats in check until John returned. She continued her slow progress across the house, taking the most circuitous route despite the irritation of Jenkins behind her. It was a petty act of defiance. The only one open to her now.

At the doors of her room, Mairead paused as panic started to churn in her stomach. *Would Brown still be lying there?* She wasn't sure she could bear that. To her relief, he was not but the room remained in disarray. The pieces of the jug and the broken glass lay where they had fallen. The table that held her toilette was on in its side where she had knocked it when she was thrown against the wall. Worse still was the dark pool of sticky blood that soaked into the rug. The coppery smell of it caught in her nostrils and she swallowed down the bile rising in her throat.

'Your keys, madam,' Jenkins said holding out his hand. 'I will take them for safekeeping as you will have no need of them at present.'

Mairead unclipped the silver ring from her skirts, feeling their weight as she handed them over.

'The door will be locked for your protection and two guards posted outside,' Jenkins said as she turned her back to him. 'Can you manage without attendance?'

She continued to ignore him and, after a few moments, heard the lock turn and click. Only then did Mairead let out the shuddering breath of tension and sink onto the bed. She cried her despair into the pillow, determined that the guards outside would not hear.

She must have dozed eventually and woke feeling groggy as the last rays of sunlight fell onto the floor. She heard a soft tap on the door and wondered if this was what had woken her. A woman's voice. She relaxed a little as the door opened and Alais entered, carrying a tray. With care, she placed it on the table and looked around the room.

'We'll light this fire, shall we, mistress?' Alais asked gently. 'The cold is not good for you or the bairn.'

Mairead agreed. Her whole body ached and her tongue felt too big for her mouth. She watched as Alais lit the fire and set a kettle on the hook above it. Next, the woman turned her attention to the room and she began setting it to rights. Mairead stood to help but pain shot like lightning along her spine and she lowered herself back to the bed. Alais kept up a soft babble as though soothing a poorly child and Mairead let it wash over her, realising that she preferred it to the silence.

'I can do nothing about this tonight,' Alais said indicating the blood-stained rug, 'but I can cover it.'

As the kettle began to hiss and bubble, Alais made her a pot of tea and sweetened it heavily with honey. With her hands wrapped around the cup, Mairead allowed Alais to draw her to a chair by the fire and wrap a blanket around her. An impatient thump at the door made Alais curse softly.

'Aye alright, I'm coming,' she shouted over her shoulder.

'Murren...? Jeannie?' Mairead's throat was so painful the words were barely a whisper.

'I'll see them warm and fed,' Alais replied as the hammering on the door got louder. 'Gavin will do what he can to see them treated gently.'

With an apologetic look back over her shoulder, Alais hurried out. The key scraped the lock and Mairead knelt on the floor sweeping her hand under the frame of the bed. She felt the smooth handle of the knife and withdrew it. The knife was small and the blade kept sharp. It wasn't much but it was all she had to defend herself. She pushed it under her pillow. Drawing the chair close to the warmth of the fire she sat. Her hand resting on the swelling of her belly felt the first flutters of life, like the wings of a butterfly. Relief and fear washed over her in waves and tears began again to roll down her cheeks. *I am sorry little one*, she thought, *there is little we can do now but wait.*

CHAPTER 43

JEANNIE

The earth floor leeched the cold from Jeannie's bones as she sat resting her back against the uneven stones of the wall. The thin layer of straw added nothing to her comfort, but it was fresh and clean. Murren lay curled in a tight ball with her dark head laid upon Jeannie's lap. From the change in her breathing, she had finally found sleep. Jeannie knew there would be no rest for her tonight. So far, the guards had kept their distance, wary of the Scottish witch they had heard such fearsome tales about. These two were young though and the guard would change with the watch. She would need to keep her wits about her. With no windows to track the light and so far away from the doings within the tower, she had no way to tell the time. By her reckoning, though, it must be the middle of the night. Gavin had brought them blankets along with broth and bread. The guards watched every move and forbade him to speak to the women. He would, he'd said, return in the morning with breakfast.

Looking down at Murren's swollen face, the events of the day played once again in her mind's eye. Mairead's frantic struggle and the way her eyes rolled, the thud as the jug met his head and the way he hit the floor. On her instincts she had acted, knowing that Mairead had been moments from death at his hands. Seeing the echoes of fear etched deep on this young face before her now, she would do the same again. There had been no time for thought and there was no regret. Would there be justice? If so, then whose? Captain Morton had no ties to the tower or it's people and clearly no love for the Scots. John Campbell took delight in making others uncomfortable, but he at least kept order and commanded the tower with discipline. Mairead was his cousin and her protection was in his gift. *Who might speak up for me?*

The candles guttered as the two guards approached to take the next watch. Jeannie moved her hand to shield them, afraid of them going out and leaving her trapped in the darkness. A hammering on the door began and one of the new guards, older by the sound of him, shouted to her.

'The fever has claimed two of the men this night,' he snarled.

The voice of the other guard was indistinct but whatever was said moved both men away from the door. Jeannie's heart thundered in her chest. Surely, they did not blame her for that too? Oh... but they would. They were calling her a witch. Every stubbed toe and curdled pail of milk would be her doing. There was a time she would have laughed off that slur. She was a healer and midwife. Her skills were trusted by the laird himself. She had delivered every man, woman and child born at the tower and village for the last twenty years. They all knew her. Now, though? She still saw the looks of suspicion on the faces of some since Collum had delivered his terrible message. With Morton's redcoats and the Campbell soldiers, she could not rely on her position. As the possibilities for her fate crossed her vision the candle burnt out. In the blackness she began to shake.

The guard changed again as a chink of pale daylight crept under the door. This time, the pair were Campbells with their Highland lilt. The door opened and Jeannie blinked as her eyes adjusted painfully to the brightness. She reached out and shook Murren's shoulder and the girl cowered, pressing herself back into the wall. One of the men placed a jug of water on the floor.

'Might we have a candle?' Jeannie asked humbly.

The soldier returned a moment later with two tallow candles and lit one before passing it to Jeannie. As he came forward, she recognised him as one of those wounded when James' men were defeated. Beside her, Murren whimpered and, seeing this, the soldier took a slow step backwards. In spite of herself, the gesture of kindness touched Jeannie.

'Thank you,' she whispered, and the man gave her a nod of acknowledgement.

They drank thirstily from the jug. Jeannie poured a little cold water into her hand and splashed her face, trying to shake off the heaviness that clung to her. In the candlelight, she checked

Murren's injuries. The physical ones would heal, she knew, but those in her mind may not. The girl had not spoken a word, and her eyes had a faraway look that troubled Jeannie. It was as if the girl had gone to a place deep within and had locked herself there in her fear and torment.

Gavin brought porridge sweetened with honey in a blackened pot. It was wrapped in a cloth to keep the heat in. He handed Jeannie two wooden spoons and with a glance back towards the door, he leant in close.

'Captain Morton will send for you shortly,' he whispered urgently. 'Two of the men have died of fever and it spreads through the English soldiers.'

'He will not wait for Campbell then?' Jeannie murmured.

'Not for this. The men believe the sickness is your doing,' he said and held up his hand when she began to protest. 'Be careful. Do nothing to anger him further.' The note of caution in his voice betrayed his fears.

The guards were becoming impatient, and Gavin left reluctantly. He cast a worried look over his shoulder that sent a cold shiver of fear down her spine. Jeannie's stomach turned over, but she knew that she must eat. There was no telling when her next meal might be. She unwrapped the pot and handed a spoon to Murren, encouraging her to eat as though she were a bairn. The porridge was thick and Jeannie had to force herself to swallow each mouthful, all the time listening for more footsteps.

Her wait ended as she heard the voice of Jenkins, the quartermaster, ordering the door open. He strode into the room.

'On your feet, Widow Kellie.' His deep voice was used to giving orders and Jeannie found herself obeying without thought.

As she stood, Murren grasped her arm and Jeannie turned, trying gently to reassure her. Jenkins nodded to the guard behind him who took Jeannie's other arm. Murren's screams of fear filled the space and the guard raised his hand to strike her.

'No!' Jeannie gasped stepping between them. 'Please, she's frightened. Let me talk to her.'

Jeannie crouched down and brought Murren's face close to her own trying to get her to attend.

'Hush now, lass,' she said softly. 'It's me they want. You stay here and I will return soon.'

Pulling her arm free of the girl's rigid grip she gathered her courage. Jeannie straightened, every muscle in her body ached from the cold damp of the stone floor. She forced her numb feet to follow Jenkins out of the door.

The tower had no gaol and with so many garrisoned the only space they had found to confine them was in the cellars of the new part of the house. People stopped and stared as Jenkins led her into the tower. She looked around her, the tower looked so different to her eyes now. The elegance of the rooms designed to host royalty fading into the mud of the winter roads from so many boots. She saw Captain Morton seated with several of his men and theroom fell quiet as she was led before him. Looking around, there was no sign of John or the Campbell soldiers who had ridden with him and her heart sank.

'Widow Kellie.' Morton turned to face her. 'Fever spreads through my soldiers and there are those who believe you are the cause of it.'

'I am not, sir.' Jeannie fought down her panic and tried to keep her voice from shaking. 'I have done what I can to help.'

'Yet two of my soldiers who arrived here hale and hearty are now dead.' Morton stood and paced a circle around her as he spoke. 'Another lies unconscious by your hand.'

The tension in the room rose sharply. The remedies she used to treat the fever were known to many and grew in abundance.

'Willow bark and yarrow to help a fever are all I have used. There is no secret to that. Why some recover and others do not is beyond my ken,' she said.

Morton's face was mere inches from hers and the loathing she saw there made her blood run cold.

'I will not have my men live in mortal fear of a witch.' He raised his hand and Jeannie tensed, ready for the blow.

'Captain Morton!' a voice rang across the space and, with surprise, Jeannie recognised it as belonging to John Dunn, the minister. 'Widow Kellie speaks true. Willow bark and yarrow are remedies used by many. That does not make her a witch.'

Jeannie, frozen, watched as the indecision flickered across Morton's face.

'Bind her hands and gag her,' he said. 'We will get to the truth of this.'

Rough hands shoved a ball of cloth into her mouth and wrapped it tight across her face. Rope bit into the skin of her wrists as they were tied in front of her. Retching and blinded by stinging tears, she was dragged from the hall.

Jeannie was shoved roughly into the makeshift cell and stumbled blindly landing heavily on the floor. As the cellar door banged shut behind her she struggled upright onto her throbbing knees. Murren peeled herself from the wall and, sobbing, loosened the gag. She worked it free enough that it slid down to Jeannie's chin. Jeannie spat out the cloth, followed by burning bile. Jeannie trembled and the room whirled as she continued to void the terror from the pit of her stomach.

'Water,' Jeannie rasped. Her tongue was thick as though coated in moss.

Murren lifted the jug and she swilled her mouth, trying to rid herself of the bitterness left by the cloth. She spat it out into the straw and took a painful swallow. Dread like a lead weight pressed in on her, heavy and suffocating. Exhausted she edged herself into the corner, knees pulled up close to her chin. Murren crawled to her side and leant her tiny, fragile body against Jeannie's. There, huddled together and shivering, they waited.

CHAPTER 44

JEANNIE

Startled awake by the creak of the door, Jeannie was blinded by the light from a burning torch. Unable to make out anything in the shadows beyond she pushed herself up to sit. Back pressed tight into the cold stone of the wall. Rough hands grabbed her, pulling her to her feet. The men were doing their best to move quietly. Fear clenched in her bowels. They did not want this to be discovered. Murren was mute with terror and Jeannie prayed she stayed that way. It was her that they had come for and if the girl drew no attention, they may leave her alone.

With a man either side, they hauled her out of the doorway and into the gardens. The cold air hit her all at once and she began to convulse. Terrified and disorientated Jeannie tried desperately to get her bearings. Her feet, already numb with cold, slid and skidded on the icy ground as she was dragged forwards. The tower was a dark shadow to her left. The pale glow of the moon reflected on the heavy blanket of snow and she could make out the copse of trees ahead. They were taking her to the wood.

One of the men at her arm stumbled and brought her down with him. She pushed herself up to her knees, and the man jumped to his feet, cursing her furiously under his breath. A sharp crack echoed as he kicked her face. White heat exploded in her vision. She tasted the warm rush of blood and salty tears on her lips. Another kick broke her ribs and forced the air from her lungs. She fought for a shuddering, agonizing breath. Lifting her hands over her head and curling forwards, her torso on her knees, she cowered. Jeannie focused on the space that seemed to stretch between one heartbeat and the next. Willing herself to stay conscious. Her senses pulsed, alive to every detail. The grunts of the men as the blows continued. The sourness of their sweat. The glint of moonlight on the melting snow under her. Her fear alchemised into something hard and sharp as soft flakes of snow fell in her hair and clothes. A pool of crimson spread before her. She saw again the vision she had all those months ago as Alan lay on the hearth in the kitchens. A realisation hit her. She had known it would end in blood, just as it began.

An owl screeched in the darkness and the men fell silent. She could hear the flapping of wings as the bird took flight. The moon appeared again through the inky grey clouds as she chanced a look up.

'Not here!' One of them looked around anxiously. 'We'll be seen. Get her into the trees.'

A hand in her hair yanked Jeannie to her feet. Under the cover of the trees, she felt a rope pushed over her head. One eye was swollen shut and she could feel the globs of snot and blood freezing to her cheeks. She forced the other eye open and through the haze she focused on the face of the man in front of her.

'Why?' Through swollen lips her voice sounded as though it was far away.

'You murdered Brown...' the man hissed and spat at her. 'Witch!'

His face twisted in rage as he threw the rope over the branch. It dug into the bark with a creak as he gave it a savage yank. The rope bit into her neck lifting her to her tip toes. Her body, broken and bleeding, shuddered as she clawed frantically trying to loosen the rope. Through the fire burning in her chest she gasped, sucking air into her lungs. She did not cry out and, as the noose bit deeper, she knew she could not. She was in a place beyond fear now. Locked in a raw and visceral fight to survive. Her legs kicking desperately at the air beneath her. The moon appeared once more from behind the clouds and in its silvery light she surrendered.

In her mind's eye she saw Duncan. His broad shoulders and slow smile. His hand bound to hers by the cloth she had embroidered with yellow flowers. She saw the faces of Angus and Collum and her nose filled with their sweet newborn scent. She could feel the weight of them in her arms, their tiny fingers wrapped around hers. Precious moments of the love she had shared filled her memory pushing away the fear and pain. An eerie calm descended on her. Her heart filled with joy leaving no room for anything else. Jeannie let go with a sigh and floated away into the snowfall and moonlight.

CHAPTER 45

MAIREAD

Mairead sat enclosed by the shutters of the bed. Her body ached and it was hard to turn her neck. She had slept only fitfully between the pain and was unused to being alone. She jolted as the door to her room flew open with such force that it slammed into the wall. Struggling to sit up she drew the letter knife from under her pillow and held it tightly.

'Mistress!' Although muffled by the wood of the shutters, she realised it was Alais.

The wooden panel opened and the terrified cook pulled her to the edge of the bed.

'Mistress please! Quickly. They took her. They took Jeannie!' Alais was breathless and her eyes were wide with fear.

Mairead pulled on her shoes and threw a shawl around her shoulders. At the doorway, she saw Campbell soldiers with swords drawn, looking anxious. The fog of tiredness was pushed aside by the panic in those around her. She hurried after Alais, thoughts whirring, trying to make sense of what was happening around her.

Mairead was led out into the pale dawn. The white carpet of snow had been churned to a slush that sucked at the soles of her shoes. Her eyes followed the path made by so many boots across to the cluster of trees. Her stomach dropped as she began to understand. *Oh, dear God no!* Her legs felt like lead as she moved forwards. Alais was beside her, the woman's hands clutching her skirts, repeating the Lord's Prayer over and over.

A horse chestnut tree stood guard at the edge of the copse, barren branches spread to form an archway. There Gavin stood, gripping the hilt of his sword and covered in smudges of mud. His knuckles were bruised and bloodied. Recognising Mairead and Alais, his hand relaxed. Mairead went to step forwards and Gavin blocked her way.

'Mistress, we were too late,' Gavin's face was grey with shock and his voice raw with anguish, 'there was nothing to be done.'

This cannot be. It must be a mistake. Disbelieving, Mairead ran forwards and Gavin caught her by the arms. She struggled, trying to pry herself away and craning to see around him. He held her firmly and with eyes filled with tears shook his head. She pushed him away and spun round to face the watching crowd.

'Who did this?' Mairead demanded her shrill voice piercing the stillness.

Casting her eyes around her seeking an answer. She turned to the Campbell soldiers. None would meet her eye.

'The man, Brown, died in the night.' Gavin's anguish overcame him and he swallowed hard. 'His friends took her from the cellars and brought her here.'

'Captain Morton?' Mairead spat. 'He allowed this?'

'He did not, mistress.' A Campbell soldier Mairead recognised from her father's household found his courage and spoke up. 'The men came back to the guard rooms drunk and boasting. If Morton was too afraid to deal with the witch, then they were not. The quartermaster heard them. A fight broke out...'

'What have they done to her?' Mairead wailed unable to hold back the tears.

Dealt with the witch? Oh God! What have they done? Mairead's spine felt as though it were dissolving, and she sagged, Gavin catching her. Her body shook with shock and cold and her teeth chattered. Gavin removed his coat and wrapped her gently in it. Mairead took a shuddering breath and forced herself up straight, meeting his eye.

'What have they done?' she repeated her voice like iron.

Gavin's head bowed and he sagged forward to his knees in front of her.

'They hanged her, mistress.' Gavin closed his eyes as if trying to block out the image. 'I came as soon as I heard and found the redcoats at the tree. They would not let me cut her down.'

Mairead struggled to her feet and faltered. Her heart thundered as she stood, torn between the horror of what she would see and the need to see it. Taking sobbing steps she walked under the boughs of the horse chestnut. Under the rowan, a figure lay covered by a cloak. She knelt beside it aware of the silence that now settled around her. With a trembling hand she pulled back the hood. Beside her Alais gasped. Reaching out numb fingers, Mairead smoothed back the white streak of hair from Jeannie's swollen and bloody face. She brushed her fingertips tenderly across the pale forehead. It was the only place she could see that was not broken and violated. The tears streamed hot down her frozen cheeks.

Alais knelt at Jeannie's head, resting her hand on the forehead of her friend. Mairead, unable to hold back the tide, wept. Beside her and through her own tears, Alais whispered the words of an old blessing.

'And may the blessing of the earth be on you, soft under your feet as you pass along the roads, soft under you as you lie out on it, tired at the end of day; and may it rest easy over you when, at last, you lie out under it.

May it rest so lightly over you that your soul may be out from under it quickly; up and off and on its way to God.'

It is my fault, Mairead thought with icy certainty. *My fault she is here. She died because she acted to save me.*

'She cannot stay here,' Mairead cried to the watching soldiers. 'I will not leave her out here.'

'For now, you must,' Gavin said gently. 'John Campbell is commander here and it is he who must decide what will be done.'

'She will not be alone, mistress.' The Campbell soldier looked down at her with compassion. 'We will guard her.'

***

Mairead allowed herself to be guided back to her rooms and helped out of her wet shift into warm dry clothes. Caught in her grief she neither knew nor cared who it was that attended her. Surrendering to the ministrations of gentle hands, she was dimly aware of the shock as her own marks and bruises were made visible. The warming pan was lifted sizzling from the hearth. Voices now insisted she lay down to rest and she was helped, hobbling and numb, to the bed. Smelling of woodsmoke and peat, the pan was placed under the white linens to warm her. Instead of offering comfort, the heat stung and made her itch as the feeling returned to her toes. Mairead stared at the canopy, too afraid of what she would see to shut her eyes. In the room two women sat, one was knitting, and the clack of the needles ran like a drum beat through their quiet conversation. Mairead's senses felt as though they were aflame, and her heart lurched at every creak of the floorboards and noise from outside.

John's knock was soft and he entered the room, mud spattered and still in his riding attire. The women from the village, wee Jock's mother and the blacksmith's wife, had helped her to dress when the guard at the door told them John Campbell had returned. He took in her grief ravaged face, her red rimmed eyes and the bruises now deep blues and black at her neck. The look of pity he gave her was more than she could bear, and she lowered her eyes to avoid it.

'I had hoped to bring you some good news, Cousin.' John paced back and forth as he spoke checking off the items on his fingers. 'But I have returned to find the place in an uproar and completely lawless. Four people are dead. You are accused of murder. Morton has demanded that half my men be flogged for sedition. Christ's bones, I was gone but four days!'

Mairead watched as he pinched the bridge of his nose in agitation. It was the same thing her father did when he was trying to hold onto his temper. She had seen it often as a child but had never thought of he and John as alike until that moment.

'I have heard Morton's account.' She was surprised by the venom in John's tone at the man's name. 'And now I will hear yours.'

Mairead knew she had little choice but to trust him. Yet now, in this moment, she felt easier about it. Perhaps it was how he reminded her of her father or the flicker of anger at the bruises she bore that softened her. Or perhaps it was because the things that were important before no longer seemed so now.

She began her account slowly, the words coming in short bursts. She described the behaviour of some of the redcoats, their abuse of the rules of hospitality, their casual disregard for the house. The searches of her rooms and then the attack by Brown on Murren. She told him of the girl's strangled scream of terror as the bone in her fragile arm had snapped. Mairead told him of how that sound had sickened her and driven her forwards to help. Clawing and pulling at Brown, she had fought. He had her by the throat, her back pinned to the wall as he had tightened his grip. Her lip trembled as she described the burning of the air being squeezed from her lungs. The odd sense of being outside of herself she had felt as she had known she was dying. Then just as the blackness began to engulf her, he had hit the floor like a sack full of tatties. Jeannie had hit him with the jug she had been holding. He was bleeding and unconscious but breathing when she had gone to Morton.

John had not interrupted once whilst she spoke. He stood now resting his hand on the mantle above the fireplace. His face serious and inscrutable.

'Jeannie,' she whispered. 'Morton's men believed her to be a witch. They took her in the night to the wood and hanged her. From the rowan tree. This is my fault...'

As she subsided into grief filled silence John tilted his head to one side as though weighing up a decision.

'Widow Kellie's death is not of your doing and the men responsible will answer for it. They are government soldiers and under Morton's command. They are his to deal with as he sees fit,' he said, choosing his words with care. 'My men will answer for disobeying the order to keep you under lock and key. They will answer to me.'

'John, please...' she begged. 'Jeannie cannot be left out in the snow. She must be decently buried.'

'There will be time for that. For now, I will need to do what I can to restore some order and discipline before you meet the same fate.'

***

Gavin and some of the kitchen boys had dug a grave under the rowan tree where the frozen ground had given way to softer soil around the roots. It seemed fitting to Mairead. Jeannie would lie at peace, beyond harm, under the protection of the tree. She would be safe from further insult. Dunn had been sympathetic, but church law was clear. The minister has regretfully decreed that she could not be buried in the kirk yard. She had died accused of murder and witchcraft. He had prayed for her soul and would lead a service on the theme of forgiveness, he'd promised.

The red light of the setting sun kissed the tops of the trees as they gathered. The body had been cleaned and wrapped in simple white shroud. Alais, with great care and tenderness wound around Jeannie's neck an embroidered cloth. The yellow flowers stood out bright in the gloaming.

'I found this in the still room,' Alais said her eyes shining. 'She wore it at her marriage and always kept it close. She should have it now...'

Mairead listened as those gathered by the cold grave spoke warmly of Jeannie in happier times. The babes she had ushered into the world and those souls she sat with as they had left it. Even in the short time Mairead had known her she recognised the fierce courage and warm heart Jeannie was known for. Wiping the tears from her face Mairead took two silver coins from her purse.

'Go well, my friend,' Mairead whispered.

She leant forward and laid the coins gently over Jeannie's eyes in the old way. Her payment for the ferryman, to carry her safely across the river between the lands of the living and the dead. As the earth was shovelled into the grave Mairead prayed silently for the soul of the woman who had given all to protect her. Hoping that she might find peace now.

The sun disappeared and the trees faded into inky darkness. Mairead gave a last lingering look at the grave then, her heart aching with every step, led them back to the tower by torchlight.

***

In the days that followed, Captain Morton's redcoats left the tower, returning south to England. The Stuart King had returned to France escorted, she was told, by the Earl of Mar. The uprising was over. Mairead sat under the trees at the foot of the rowan. She came here often now to sit in the quiet of the copse, away from the constant buzz of the tower. A shaft of yellow sunlight reached through the canopy and fell on a patch of snowdrops almost ready to open. The little white flowers hinted at spring and her hand rested on her belly where the baby kicked contentedly.

'Are you well, Cousin?' John's shadow fell across the clearing and Mairead squinted up into the light. 'Forgive my intrusion.'

Mairead smiled and John eased himself down onto the ground beside her.

'There is news of James.' John hesitated. 'The man who brings it is Collum Kellie.'

Mairead's heart leapt, and she felt breathless. News had reached them of the execution of the English rebels who had fought at Preston and since then Mairead had feared a messenger bringing a date for James' execution. Each new day since had brought peaks of hope and troughs of despair. Now at last the news had come.

She got to her feet as the tall young man entered the copse. She steadied herself against the tree for a moment drawing strength from its solid presence. Mairead faced the messenger, her mouth dry and fear coursing through her body. His eyes were so like his mother's that she felt the sting of tears.

'Mistress Erskine.' Collum gave a small bow. 'The Duke of Argyll petitioned the King to show mercy and grace to those involved in the insurrection. His Royal Highness agreed and the death sentence has been commuted.'

James would live. Mairead was engulfed with a tide of relief forcing her to her hands and knees. Her hand covered her mouth as the tide broke free with a cry. Somewhere between a roar and a sob it wrenched free the fear and pain of the last few months. It opened a chasm deep in her soul and left her shaking.

Collum turned away discreetly as she gathered herself. She took John's offered hand and rose with effort to her feet. Light-headed she listened as Collum explained that James would remain at Stirling Gaol and that all lands, estates and titles would be removed under the terms of John Erskine's Writ of Attainder. They would have no home and no position. *But he would live.* It was enough. Mairead gathered herself. Her heart heavy with the weight, knowing that what she had to share was no fair exchange.

'I must answer your kindness in bringing this news with a tragedy,' Mairead said thickly.

Seeing his confusion and concern she laid a gentle hand on his arm. John withdrew to a tactful distance.

'Your mother...' she began her voice breaking, 'was a friend to me.'

'Was, mistress?' Collum said, eyes wide with alarm.

Mairead took his hand and told him the tale of the soldiers Jeannie had nursed and the death she had prevented. Through tears and voice shaking, she described his mother's death and her burial here under the trees.

'Your mother was a remarkable woman. She was brave and fierce and loyal,' Mairead said gently. 'She showed me kindness when I arrived here a stranger. She became my friend.'

Collum thanked her solemnly and asked to be left alone with his thoughts. As Mairead walked away from the copse, she felt as though she had been released from some invisible cage. The future was far from certain but whatever came she would stand and face it. That was the debt she owed to Jeannie.

CHAPTER 46

LAUREN

F lushed with the success of the first of the live events at the tower and with her head a little sore from the celebratory bottle of wine afterwards, Lauren flopped into the chair. Her pigeonhole outside her office had been overflowing and the room was stuffy from being unused for a few days. She opened the window, wincing at the brightness as she pulled the beaded cord for the blinds. *I'm getting too old for this now*, she thought. A late night took days to recover from and left her feeling fuzzy. Tea, she needed tea. The cup which had been sitting on her desk had started to grow an interesting bloom of mould and she made a face as she put it to one side to deal with once she had fired up her computer.

The emails from the national archives had been sitting in her inbox for a few days and the flag now blinked reproachfully at her. Lauren just hadn't had the time in the last few days but she sat now at her desk and opened the file. More letters and papers from Lady Frances' personal papers had been located. Not knowing what might be of most interest, the archivist had taken the liberty of scanning and sending all those dated between September 1715 and March 1716. There were fifteen files in all. Lauren made herself a fresh pot of tea as the files downloaded. She took a long sip of the strong brew and sighed in relief.

As she worked her way down the list, one immediately caught her eye. It had been found tucked between the pages of Lady Frances' commonplace book. The writing was faded and hard to read. Lauren zoomed into the file. On one side was a receipt of sorts, detailing the linens and fabrics which had been sent and then on the other was a much more personal note. The writing looked cramped and laboured, a far cry from the confident and elegant pen strokes of Lady Frances and her circle of correspondents. Lauren leant in closer to the screen, trying to decipher the faded text. The author apologised for being the bearer of sad news. It told of the rumour her husband had heard of events within the tower. To Lauren's frustration the next two lines, where the paper had been folded, were unreadable. She picked up the thread of the text again as it described a woman being accused of murder and hanged without trial by men from Captain Morton's guard. Morton and his soldiers, she knew, had been garrisoned briefly at the tower to guard it against any rallying of the Jacobite's. She read on. The Widow Kellie was taken from her cell and hanged.

Lauren felt a jolt of recognition at the name. She had seen that before. She grabbed her notebook and flicked through the pages. There! There it was in the kirk records. Widow Kellie had been recorded as a parishioner in the 1715 records but did not appear in the 1716 pages. She had written the name on her list of names that might belong to the body they had found. Her hands shook. This had to be their mystery woman. The note described her being hanged. The body had broken neck bones. She was important enough for Isobel Murray to write to Lady Frances about. It had to be her. Could they prove it though?

***

As the lift took them from the main floor of the crowded library down to the sterile coolness of the stacks, Lauren filled Hazel in on the contents of the letter. She tapped the button impatiently as they waited for the doors to slide closed.

'Even if you're right, this still might not be enough to prove it conclusively,' Hazel said, turning to Lauren. 'The bar for evidence is high.'

'We must try, though. She deserves that.' Lauren swiped her pass to take them through to the security area and they put their bags through the scanner.

'It does feel somehow... unfinished,' Hazel said as they made their way to the call desk.

The librarian had been following the story at the tower with interest and was eager to help. Two leather bound record books lay ready in their white trays. In the reading room, they put on the white cotton gloves and Lauren lifted the first volume into the cradle carefully. She leafed through the delicate pages to find the one she had noted. Her finger hovered just above the page as she made her way down the list.

'Here we go,' she said.

Hazel stood at her shoulder, reading the neat little lines of names. It was certainly there – Widow Kellie. The women exchanged a look charged with excitement. They combed through each line of the rest of the records and the name did not appear again.

'If we could corroborate this with a third source then it would be a compelling argument,' Hazel said thoughtfully.

'I've requested access to Lady France's papers at the National Archive,' Lauren said. 'The commonplace book might give us something.'

'The trust are liaising with the coroner about possible dates for a reburial,' Hazel said, 'and an appropriate memorial.'

That was good, Lauren thought. They could lay her to rest somewhere peaceful and have a marker at the rowan. If being a historian had taught her anything, it was that life was messy and often cruel. Doing the best with what life presents was the common thread. People were so much more than just the events that happen to them and this woman deserved to be remembered for more than just her death.

Lauren turned at the tap on the glass of the door. Her eyes widened slightly as she saw the dean standing there. She gestured for him to come in and raised her eyebrows at Hazel apologetically.

'Lauren... and this must be Ms Rankin, yes?' the dean exclaimed thrusting out his hand.

Hazel shook it awkwardly.

'Pleasure to meet you,' he said then turning to Lauren, 'I wonder if I might have a word...?'

'We think we might know who the woman under the rowan tree is,' Lauren said. Still caught up in the excitement she tried to lead the dean towards the books on the table.

'Good. Good news...' The dean remained by the door looking uncomfortable. 'There is something else I need to speak with you about. University business I'm afraid.'

'Oh, okay,' Lauren said flustered. 'I'll finish up here and pop up to your office.'

Lauren was distracted, she stood looking down at her notebook trying to work out what the dean wanted so urgently. She hadn't heard the librarian's offer of help to put the books away. Hazel gave her a side long look.

'We'll see to these,' Hazel said decisively, shooing her towards the door. 'On you go and find out what he wants.'

Lauren gathered her bag and glasses and made her way across the campus to the dean's office. She pulled out her phone and guiltily checked her emails searching for a clue she might have missed. She'd been completely absorbed by Fractal Lines for weeks and felt disconnected from the faculty.

The administration block sat in the original part of the university in an ugly breezeblock building. It had not yet been relocated to the new campus building and it was depressingly beige and tired. The only thing it had going for it was the beautiful view of the loch to the Wallace Monument. Lauren looked out of the window pulling her sleeves down into place and pushing an errant curl off her face. It was like being back at school having been summoned to the headmaster's office and not knowing why. Her palms began to sweat at the thought.

'You can go straight in Dr McDonald,' said the dean's PA putting the handset down.

Lauren turned the handle and strode in, trying to look calm and collected. The dean smiled at her and gestured to the sofa. She perched on the edge of the ancient brown leather as he took the chair opposite.

'It is about Dr Leinster I'm afraid.' The dean shifted uncomfortably in his seat.

Lauren's heart gave a warning thump, and she clasped her hands together in her lap.

'He will be taking a leave of absence,' he continued. 'It is unexpected, and we will need to think about how we cover his teaching load.'

Lauren nodded but wasn't sure she understood at all. The dean was looking at the floor between them. She chewed the inside of her lip as she spun through the possibilities for one that made sense. It wasn't unusual for academics to take sabbaticals or visiting fellowships at other universities. But that wasn't what he had said was it? A leave of absence? What was going on? Even for the dean this was taking an age to get to the point.

'What do you need me to take on?' Lauren asked unable to bear the pregnant silence any longer. 'And for how long?'

'Um... indefinitely...' the dean sighed and seemed to reach a conclusion.

He removed his glasses and polished them on the sleeve of his jacket. Lauren saw how old and tired he looked and felt a twinge of sympathy. It couldn't be easy, trying to navigate the funding situation and the ever-evolving priorities for research.

'There is an investigation into Dr Leinster's conduct.' The dean spoke slowly as though choosing his words with care. 'We need somebody to head up the department who has the trust of the students. A steady hand at the tiller.'

Shocked, Lauren sat back in her chair. What on earth was happening?

'You want me to run the history department?' Lauren swallowed hard.

'It is an acting position for now... until things... settle.'

'What about Fractal Lines? We have the plans in place for the next phase.' Lauren's mind raced through the practicalities.

'Yes,' the dean nodded, 'excellent publicity for the university. We will make sure you have all the support you need. You won't be expected to teach of course.'

'But I will keep my post graduate program?' Lauren's tone was insistent.

The dean gave assurances that it could all be worked out. They would have a meeting to discuss the details in the next few days. He would let her focus on the events at Alloa Tower.

***

Lauren entered the kitchen and sat down at the table. There was so much to think about, and she wasn't really sure where to start. Annie was making tea and bustled around the kitchen getting cups and the teapot.

'Lauren?' Annie called her name again.

'Hmm, what was that?' she asked with a jolt.

'I asked if you wanted a piece of the flapjack...' Annie rested her hand on Lauren's shoulder. 'Are you alright, love? You are miles away.'

'Sorry. It's been a big day,' she replied, patting Annie's hand.

Annie sat down opposite and listened intently as Lauren recounted the conversation with the dean. When she had finished

Annie squeezed her hand. Lauren looked into the concerned face of her wife and felt a wave of gratitude. Annie knew her better than she knew herself and understood that what she needed now was to make sense of it in her own head.

'I think this calls for something stronger.' Annie collected two glasses from the Welsh dresser and poured a measure of brandy into each.

Lauren swirled the glass around and watched the iridescent ring form on the crystal.

'If it is another investigation into bullying then surely he'll be sacked?' Lauren asked still staring into the glass.

'He certainly should be, yes,' Annie replied evenly.

'They won't just sweep it under the carpet and let him fade away with his reputation intact?' Lauren's sat back in the chair angry now. 'Surely they can't be thinking that?'

'They might.' Annie's voice remained level.

Lauren slammed her hand down on the table and yanked off the silk scarf she was still wearing. She threw it onto the chair beside her and took a glug of the brandy. Annie watched her silently.

'I could have stopped him sooner!' Lauren raged. 'I *should* have stopped him sooner!'

'You tried,' Annie said softly.

Lauren thought of Grace and Tom and how much influence over their careers he held. Could she have done more? No, perhaps not. She knew she was a good teacher though and could bring out the best in her students. Here was an opportunity to show how it can be done differently.

Her thoughts turned to her run in with Leinster in the stacks. She had stood up to him but he had frightened her. That had taken something from her, and she was still furious about it. He had no right. It was the sense of entitlement that angered her most of all. The same one that echoed through the ages. The same one that allowed women like Widow Kellie to be accused of witchcraft and murdered. She put the glass down decisively.

'I can bloody well do something now.' Lauren's head raised determinedly. 'I'll take the acting head of department role, and I'll do it the right way.'

'That's the spirit,' Annie said approvingly and raised her glass in salute.

Lauren's fire had returned, and she pulled her laptop from her bag. *She could do one more thing too*, she vowed. She could give Jeannie Kellie her name back.

CHAPTER 47

HAZEL

Hazel stood at the window, looking out at the labyrinth of streets in the old town curving their way up to the castle. Her hands curled around the mug, savouring the smell of her freshly ground coffee. It was one of the true treasures in her life and she relaxed back into the window frame watching a tourist bus try to navigate a hairpin turn. She had a few minutes before the monthly leadership meeting. Her report had been a long one. Fractal Lines was really taking off now and she needed to plan for the next location. Mei had suggested she take a holiday first, perhaps she was right, some time off would do her good.

The last few weeks had been difficult. The discovery of the body had brought back feelings of that hellish time in her own life she had tried to bury deep. Then when she had been forced to face it, she had felt as though she'd unravelled. Still trying to make sense of it and who she was on the other side. Realising that in fighting so hard against it becoming what defined her that is exactly what happened, she had kept herself in that prison.

The chime of the church bells reminded her that she had somewhere else to be.

Marcus nudged her shoulder as she sat down next to him and gave her one of his mega-watt smiles. Clearly, he knew something she didn't and she made a little face at him behind her laptop as she opened the cover. Chris had left her until last on the agenda and as they went through the reports from each department, Hazel felt a sense of anticipation rising. *What is going on?* she wondered. She really hoped that they weren't going to make a huge deal of the project. At last, Chris came to her report.

'Shall we just take this as read?' he asked the room. 'We have a very important development to discuss.'

Hazel pitched forward in her seat, she had not been expecting this and looked at him in confusion.

'It's okay. Relax,' Marcus whispered seeing her anxiety.

'The trust had had an approach from the BBC to make a documentary series following Fractal Lines.' Chris handed her a copy of the proposal.

Hazel's palms felt slick with sweat and her mouth went dry. It was beyond anything she could have imagined, and her mind ran through the possibilities it opened up.

'I don't know what to say...' she stuttered. 'I didn't expect this.'

As the meeting ended, and the others left, Chris sat down beside her.

'Take some time. Get your questions down on paper,' he said. 'The producers have suggested that the crews follow you and Dr McDonald.'

A thousand reasons why that was a terrible idea crossed her mind. She was about to start listing them when Chris stood up.

'Don't underestimate yourself, Hazel. You can do this. This project was a brilliant idea. *Your* idea.'

She sat in the meeting room and read over the proposal. She tapped the lid of her pen thoughtfully against her lip torn between her discomfort at being in the limelight and the benefits of the offer. She reasoned with herself that it would generate enough income to secure the future of these places. Wasn't that what she had set out to do? How could she say no?

***

The kirk yard was full as Hazel and Lauren walked side by side through the funnel of barriers to the open grave. The coffin looked so small as it rested on wooden blocks. A hush fell as the minister began, his voice magnified by the small microphone pinned to his collar. The wind picked up as the minister read, carrying his voice away as it whipped through the trees. At a nod from the undertaker, Hazel stepped forward. She took the small thistle and heather corsage, tied with the Erskine tartan, and placed it onto the lid of the coffin.

'I hope you find peace,' she whispered softly realising just how deeply she meant it.

Lauren followed, crouching to add a cutting from the rowan tree with a cascade of red berries on the leaves. Hazel's shoulders felt tight with emotion as she lifted the green velvet chord and looked up at Lauren and Tom. Lauren's eyes were filled with tears as they began to lower the coffin – it was so light. Hazel had been braced as the wooden blocks were eased out but the six pall bears lowered it easily to rest gently on the bottom. They stepped back, heads bowed as the final prayers were said.

In the charter room of the tower, the project team gathered around the table all dressed in dark colours. The room felt heavy. She continued up the stairs to the roof of the tower and round the walkway to look out over the hills. Lauren joined her, pouring tea from her flask and handed Hazel a China cup with a ring of roses around the rim. The burial had felt appropriate, and it had surprised Hazel how personal it had felt. She and Lauren had been resolute about the dignity of it and not allowing it to become a media circus. There would be time for that when the memorial stone was laid. The stone mason had been working on a design and Hazel had seen the sketches. It was simple and beautiful. The science meant that they knew so much about her – the injuries she suffered, the clothes she wore and what was happening in the world around her.

'It would be good to be able to give her back her name,' Lauren said as though reading Hazel's thoughts. 'All we have is the end of her story.'

'Maybe we aren't meant to know,' Hazel replied.

Lauren opened her mouth to respond and closed it again, confused, as Tom handed her a manilla envelope.

'This arrived earlier,' he smiled, 'from Argyll's papers at the National Library.'

'Argyll's papers?' Lauren was bewildered. 'Who asked for these?'

'I did,' Tom said shyly. 'I had a hunch. Campbell must have been sending reports back to Stirling. Especially with redcoats garrisoned alongside him.'

Lauren laughed delightedly and untied the string and slid the document out. It was a photocopy of part of a letter. The writing was small and cramped. The words crowded the page making them hard to read. Lauren squinted taking it to the centre of the room under the light then began to read. Hazel reached into the envelope to pull out the cover slip that had come with the document. It read:

Military report from John Campbell to the Duke of Argyll dated February 1716 concerning the court martial at Alloa Tower of three English soldiers under the command of Capt. Morton.

Hazel's hand flew to her mouth. Tom's instincts had been right! Could this be it? Did this report have the answers they had searched for? She watched Lauren closely. Their eyes met and Lauren nodded handing her the document.

'The body is Jeannie Kellie!' Lauren whooped and the team crowded around her. 'Three soldiers were court martialled for murder. Their defence was that they were drunk and under the influence of witchcraft from the woman,' Lauren continued.

'John Campbell and a man named Collum Kellie pressed Morton for a court martial. He refused and they appealed instead to Argyll.' Animated with the excitement Tom took up the story.

As the excited chatter and celebration rose in the room Hazel climbed the stairs towards the roof walkway. She needed to be alone. A moment to think. She pushed the heavy door open and felt the breeze, cool on her cheeks and neck. She leant against the parapet staring at the letter still in her hand. Tears began to fall, becoming sobs, as the relief flooded her. There was sorrow too. For Jeannie and the brutal way she had died. As grief coursed through her she covered her face with her hands weeping for herself too. For the hurt and horror she had experienced. The futile fury because it was pain and suffering forging a connection. Her to Jeannie. To so many others. The weeping subsided and she drew shuddering breaths. Leaning on the stone of the wall drying her eyes on the sleeve of her blouse she felt a gentle hand touch her shoulder. For a moment she almost expected it to be the spectral figure of an eighteenth-century woman. Instead, she turned to find Lauren who held out a bottle of whisky and in her other hand two chipped mugs.

'I'm sorry...' Hazel began shakily.

'Don't be.' Lauren silenced her with a wave of her arm. 'That will have done you good. You needed to let it go.'

Hazel took the proffered mug and smelled the peat and heather. Side by side they stood looking out over the river and hills. Comfortable in the silence that stretched between them Hazel took a gulp of the whisky. It burned her throat and she stifled a cough. Beside her Lauren laughed and unscrewed the lid from the bottle pouring them each another generous measure.

'We did it,' Lauren said triumphantly raising her cup. 'And so, to the next one!'

'To Fractal Lines,' Hazel replied clinking their cups together in a toast.

EPILOGUE

MAIREAD

Three years later

Mairead smoothed an errant strand of hair behind her ear and returned her hands to the folds of her skirts. In the opulence of the parlour, she was ashamed of the broken nails and callouses form the work with the wool at the mill. Across from her, Isobel Murray smiled gently.

'You are still a beauty, Mairead Erskine,' she said lightly, 'and your husband willnae have eyes for anything but you and the bairn.'

Mairead looked over at the sleeping child. She lay curled up with her russet head resting on a cushion, her chubby thumb stuck in a rosebud mouth and her face completely at peace. Mairead knew she was blessed. With an easy nature since birth, the bairn was full of joy and wonder which had carried Mairead through the last two years.

'She's tired from the journey,' Mairead said, 'too interested in the sights on the road to sleep.'

'Well let her rest here a while, there is time to spare,' Isobel said.

'I cannae thank ye enough, Isobel...' Mairead began, and Isobel shook her head.

'There is no debt between friends,' Isobel said. 'I did what little I could do gladly.'

'You found us shelter and work when others would turn from us.' Mairead met Isobel's gaze and she raised her chin proudly. 'A kindness I would repay if ever the chance arose...'

Isobel inclined her head and the silence spread around them as Mairead regained her composure.

She remembered vividly the last time she had sat in this parlour. She had been late in her pregnancy and John had announced that the tower was now under the stewardship of the Crown. Faced with an awful choice, Mairead had come to Stirling to visit James. Her father had offered her a place with him. The babe would be raised as a Campbell and she would live as a widow. It had been a gift, she knew, not many women would be afforded. Yet... after all they had faced together, she could not bring herself to turn her back on him. In the dank room of the gaol, James had first tried to reason with her, pleading with her to see sense and return to her family for the sake of the bairn. When she refused, he had become angry. When that had not moved her, he banished her from his sight declaring he would not see her again. The guards had led her from the cell and out into the heat of the city streets. Through stinging tears, she had made her way to Isobel Murray's door. The woman had listened and to Mairead's relief had not tried to persuade her to take up her father's offer. Instead, Isobel had spoken with her husband. They had interests in a woollen mill in Alva and were in need of workers. It wasn't what Mairead was used to, Isobel had said, but she would have a roof over her head and food in her belly.

Merchant Murray strode into the room and gave Mairead a slight bow. Older than his wife by many years, his hair was grey and thinning at the temples and he had a slight stoop. His face, florid in the heat, was kinder than it might have been for such a serious man.

'It is time,' he said simply.

Mairead rose to wake the sleeping child. She stroked the child's cheek and called her name softly. The girl's eye fluttered open and she sat up sleepily.

'Come now, wee flower,' Mairead said, her heart thundering in her chest. 'It is time to fetch your father.'

The girl climbed down from the chair and took her mother's hand. Isobel bent and straightened the girl's dress and tied her bonnet under the small chin. From the vase, she took a rose, it's velvety petals pale pink and handed it to the child.

'There now, bonny lass,' Isobel said, 'your father will be so pleased to meet you. Hold your mother's hand tight now.'

Mairead felt the chubby fingers resting in her clammy hand and gave them a gentle squeeze.

They followed the merchant along the street and up through the busy market to the doors of the gaol. Instructing them to wait, Murray removed the letter from his pocket and entered. Mairead stood uncertainly, listening to the excited babbles from her daughter as she spotted the goats and chickens in pens. *Will James be pleased to see us?* She had written. Whenever Merchant Murray had visited the mill, he had carried a letter from Isobel and had left with reply along with a message for James. She had received no letter in return. For her, the choice had been made the day they married and again at the tower when John had given her father's message.

Merchant Murray appeared in the doorway. A tall figure emerged behind him. James. Her pulse jumped at the sight of him. He was painfully thin and his handsome face was haggard. He stopped as their eyes met. Mairead wanted nothing more but to run to him, but her legs had turned to wood and taken root in the ground below her. She felt the little hand slip from her own as the child toddled forward, excited to show Murray the things she had seen in the market. The man took her arm gently and turned her to face James, who sank slowly to his knees.

'Jeannie?' he said, hoarsely reaching his arms out towards the girl.

Jeannie cocked her head to one side, her dark eyes taking in the man before her in a gesture so like her father's that Mairead's heart cracked open. The girl, now silent, thrust the rose to James. He took it from her, shaking as he tried to contain the emotion. Seeing them together now, they were so alike. The colour of their eyes and the set of their shoulders. Mairead took one uncertain step towards them and then another.

'I gave the flower, Mother, see!' Jeannie exclaimed.

James pulled them into a close embrace and Mairead felt the tension drain from her body. They were together. Whatever faced them now, that was all that mattered.

***

Wee Jeannie lay sleeping between them, her hand curled in his as James gazed at her in wonder. They had taken a room at one of the inns along the city walls. In the tiny room, they had begun the long process of becoming a family. Of getting to know each other again. Mairead took in the changes in her husband. The deep lines on James' brow had not been there three years ago, nor had the scar he bore on the top of his right arm. She had seen the effort it took for him to lift his daughter. The sorrow when the child wriggled from his arms and reached to her mother for comfort instead. He tried hard to hide it. His strength of character remained. There was much she had to say but now it came to it she couldn't fathom where to begin. Staring up at the bare ceiling with its black streak of soot from the tallow visible in the yellow flicker of the candlelight, she sought the words.

'A bonnie lass you've given me,' James whispered and it seemed he too felt the distance still between them. 'You've borne so much... alone.'

He shifted round to face her and the look of hesitation he gave her took Mairead back to the earliest days of their courtship.

'Can you forgive me?' His voice broke and he swallowed hard. 'I sent you from me because I didn't want you or the bairn to suffer needlessly.'

Seeing his pain, Mairead wanted to comfort him but the words would not come. Instead, hot, silent tears rolled down her cheeks.

'Ah, don't weep. Please dinnae do that.' He brushed a tear from her cheek with his thumb. 'It damn near broke me to say those things to you. I couldne give you the life you were promised...'

'I told you I had made my choice,' she said, breaking the heavy silence. 'The day that John came to demand the surrender of the tower. I meant it then and I mean it still. I love you. Not your clan. Not your position. My place is with *you*.'

Long after the candle had burned itself out, they lay awake. Their stories unfolded piecemeal as they struggled through long silences to say what was in their hearts. Mairead began with Jeannie's birth. What had come before was too painful. She spoke of the kindness of the women at the mill, taking her in when the Erskine household had been turned out. Of how they had held her through long hours of red pain. Her wonder at the wee scrap of a babe they handed her.

As the light of the dawn crept into the room, James smoothed Jeannie's hair and went to stand at the window.

'I had hoped you would have had Jeannie, Widow Kellie, with you...' he said.

She would need to tell him. All of it. There was no way to spare either of them the sorrow. Mairead swallowed hard.

'She could not be,' Mairead began. 'Sit by me here and I will tell you what passed.'

James sat with his back straight as though bracing himself for what was to come. He listened as she told of Captain Morton's arrival and the days that followed. When she told of the harm caused to Murren and her own injuries in halting it, she saw the muscle at the side of his mouth began to pulse and faltered.

'Go on my love,' he said reaching his hand out to her cheek. 'I want to hear it all.'

Mairead's eyes never left his as she described being kept under guard in her room and then the awful morning Alais had woken her. She shuddered at the memory of what had awaited her under the boughs of the rowan tree.

'Her grave is under the rowan. I pray every day that she is at peace,' she said.

'And what of Murren?' James asked.

'The minister John Dunn took her in,' Mairead replied. 'He has a new parish now with a bigger household. He swore he'd keep her safe.'

James bowed his head, his eyes betraying the storm of emotion and Mairead judged that was enough for now. There would be time enough for the rest.

Jeannie woke as the inn came to life around them. She and James played with the ball of twine on the bare floorboards, their heads close together. James smiled to himself as the girl prattled to the little cloth dolly that she prized above all her toys. The doll's clothes were made with the offcuts from the loom at the mill which Mairead had fashioned around an old bobbin. It reminded her of her own childhood. She listened as she put the room in order as James made the doll dance and Jeannie clapped along in delight.

'I'll see Murray this morning and give him my thanks,' he said. 'Afterwards I'll look for work.'

'I'll take Jeannie out into the city,' Mairead said, 'let her see the castle.'

After James had washed, she handed a clean shirt from the bundle Isobel Murray had pressed into her arms the day before. Mairead chewed at her lip as she watched James do his best to make himself presentable. He grimaced from the pain in his arm as he pulled the shirt over his head. Mairead winced at how prominent his ribs and hip bones were. She took a step forward to help him. With an effort she stilled herself. He was a proud man, she knew, and he needed to do this for himself. *How will he find work like this?* He needed time to build his strength back up, yet time would not put food on the table.

Returning to the inn after the midday meal had been served, Mairead set out the dark bread she had bought and unwrapped the small round of cheese. She tore the bread into small pieces for Jeannie and placed it on the wooden plate along with a cup of goat's milk. The earthy scent of the milk filled the small room, but Mairead couldn't bring herself to eat. Instead, she moved between the window and the small table like the bobbin on a loom. What now? She wanted nothing more than to be far from this place. Far from Stirling. But to where? There was nothing for them in the north, the Erskine lands belonged to the Crown.

Reaching into the deep folds of her skirt, she withdrew her purse and counted the small coins onto the table. Enough for a short while but not forever. She knew she was welcome back at the mill and in the small room alongside the river. Although it would be crowded with the three of them, it would be a place to start. Her work at the looms would be enough to feed them. The Murrays had done so much for them already, she did not know if James would accept further charity. Scooping the coins back into the purse, she sat deep in thought.

James entered the room with weariness etched on his face and hid it quickly as Jeannie leapt excitedly into his arms full of stories of her day. Her joy was infectious and swept James into it. He got Jeannie to close her eyes tight as he hid dolly behind the water jug on the chipped sideboard. Mairead joined the hunt, laughing as James gave his daughter clues for where to look next. *Our bonny wee lass is the healing James needs.*

Exhausted, they lay on the bed as their laughter subsided and James met her eye.

'Where will we go from here?' Mairead asked softly.

'I had hoped to find work with those who traded with my uncle...' His voice trailed off. 'I will cast a wider net tomorrow.'

'What news from Murray?' she asked, pushing away the uncertainty in the silence between them.

'It was my aunt who paid the bond to secure my freedom,' he said and removed a letter from his shirt.

Mairead knew well the confident stroke of the pen and savoured the weight of the silky paper between her fingers. The letter wished her nephew well and bid him to look to the care of his own family now. Mairead was grateful for this kindness. With the payment of the bond, James was also freed from a debt and was now at least his own man. Mairead knew the price would have been steep. Along with James' freedom, Lady Frances had gifted them the chance to choose their own path.

That night, the moon waxed full outside the window, casting a silvery beam into the dark little room. James began his tale. He spoke of the ague that claimed one after another of his men. It spread so easily amongst the wounded. With so many held together, he had succumbed. Through the fever and the thirst James had thought only of her.

'I prayed to see your face again,' he said. 'Then you walked my dreams. I saw you sat, heavy with child under the shade of a tree.'

Mairead took his hand and squeezed tightly, unable to speak. Jeannie shifted, flattening her tiny body into the curve of his chest, as though she too felt his sadness.

'I thought I was dying and God had granted my wish.' His voice sounded as though it reached her ears from far away. 'When I woke, they moved me to a different cell and then I received a letter.'

James spoke of the letter from John Campbell, telling him of her uncle's offer of a home for Mairead and to raise the bairn as their own.

'What choice was there?' James' voice cracked. 'My only thought was of you. Knowing you were cared for... perhaps even happy. I have nothing to offer you, my love.'

'We need *you*,' Mairead said, simply smoothing the cheek of the child between them.

'There may be another way,' Mairead said, keeping her voice steady. 'The mill has been our home for three winters and the master there is a good man.'

Beside her, James was silent. His hand clenched around hers and he nodded. The choice was made.

'We will find a way,' Mairead said, her voice certain. 'Together.'

'Together,' James agreed.

AUTHOR'S NOTE

Thank you for walking this path with me. I'm honoured you chose to spend time within the pages of *Echoes on a Fractal Line*.

One reader described my story as a love letter to Scotland, and I suppose it is. I consider myself very lucky to live here. The landscape is beautiful. Central Scotland is the crucible for so much of our history and characters. William Wallace, Robert the Bruce and Mary Queen of Scots all met their fate here. Before them were the brochs and hill forts of the Picts and Celts. I am surrounded by myth and legend. The perfect place to write historical fiction.

Writing this book was a weaving of the threads that connect us to the past. It explores themes of loyalty, survival, resilience and loss. I owe so much to the women who came before and their bravery in the face of terrible circumstances. This is for them, and for the women today who still need to be brave.

The work of my friend Senga Cree, leadership and empowerment coach, inspired the concept of a "fractal line". An image on one of her Portal cards got me thinking about how history loops and spirals, how our lives repeat patterns from generations past—never the same, but never quite different either. The science of fractals gave me a language for that. A desire to explore this connection in my storytelling gave me the rest.

Though the people in this book are fictional, the emotions they hold are not. They came from deep wells in history and my own lineage. If you found a reflection of yourself in these pages, I hope it brought some comfort, a spark of wonder, or even curiosity to follow your own fractal lines.

If *Echoes* moved you, I'd be grateful if you left a review or shared it with someone who might need it. That's how stories travel. And if you'd like to stay in touch, I'd love to hear from you. You'll find me at www.lee-annemcaulay.co.uk where I share news, upcoming books, and details about writing retreats and coaching for storytellers like you.

There's more to come. Always.

With gratitude,

Lee-Anne McAulay

HISTORICAL NOTE

Although Echoes on a Fractal Line is a work of fiction, its events unfold against the very real backdrop of the 1715 Jacobite Uprising. The '15 (as it is known) was one of several significant attempts to put a Stuart back on the throne of Scotland. Although both sides claimed victory, the Battle of Sheriffmuir, featured in the novel, was indecisive. The uprising ultimately failed and **John Erskine** fled to France with **James Stuart** (the Old Pretender) where he died in 1732.

The last major uprising took place 30 years later in 1745 centred on James Stuart's son, **Bonnie Prince Charlie.** One of the darkest and bloodiest moments of Scotland's past played out at the Battle of Culloden in April 1756 and marked the end of the Highland way of life.

I would like to take the opportunity here to thank James Erskine, Earl of Mar and Kellie as well as the team at Alloa Tower for their time and enthusiasm for *Echoes on a Fractal Line*. Their knowledge and patience were boundless and appreciated.

People

John Erskine, the 6th Earl of Mar, (c. 1675 to 1732) was nicknamed **"Bobbing John"** for his tendency to shift political loyalties. As the Secretary of State for Scotland, he initially supported the 1707 Act of Union. With his services no longer required under the Hanoverian king, George I, Erskine returned to Scotland, where he defected to the Jacobite cause in dramatic fashion. His legacy is complex: seen by some as politically astute, and by others as indecisive. He was also known for his determination to improve the local area of Alloa, and he established an industry, the glassworks, which still thrives today.

Lady Frances Erskine (nee Pierrepoint c. 1690 to 1691), the Countess of Mar came from a family of English aristocrats. She was philanthropic, a supporter of the Arts and also of the Alloa Glassworks. There are several striking portraits of her at Alloa Tower and one in the National Gallery but very little exists that tells her story and even less in her own words.

The Duke of Argyll, John Campbell, (c. 168 to 1743) is also mentioned in the novel. He is the uncle of both Mairead and her cousin John who are fictional characters. The Duke of Argyll was the general in command of the government army and had lodgings close to Stirling Castle, which are open to visitors now.

Places

Alloa Tower, the ancestral seat of the Erskines, **is** a real place and well worth visiting. It is in the care of The National

Trust for Scotland and is the largest surviving keep in the country. Dating back to the 14th Century the tower is strategically placed to guard the crossing of the River Forth and that is what drives the events in the novel. Sadly, nothing now remains of the magnificent house that existed in 1715. The tower's charter room features heavily in the story and view from the rooftop walkway is breathtaking.

Mar's Wark, the Earl's property in Stirling, lay in the shadow of the castle and although a ruin now, the facade and archway described in the book are visible.

Stirling Castle amongst many things, was the home of Scotland's medieval monarchs and is now in the care of Historic Environment Scotland. It is a beautiful castle and very popular with visitors. As an interesting aside, the current Earl of Mar holds the title of the Keeper of Stirling Castle.

Creative Licence

We do not know what was happening at Alloa Tower during or just after the uprising, which left me free to imagine it. I have tried to honour the spirit of the time, but invented characters and events to fill the gaps, and blended imagination with documented history. I do not mean this novel as a historical account, but as an emotional truth stitched from fragments.

If *Echoes on a Fractal Line* sparked your curiosity, I encourage you to explore the layered history of these places. Their stones still speak.

BEFORE YOU GO...

T hank you for reading this novel. I have a quick favour to ask you. As an independent author I don't have a team of people to support marketing or a to advertise my work. If you have enjoyed my book I would really appreciate it if you could leave a review on Amazon or Goodreads and help more readers to find it.

Lee-Anne

Printed in Dunstable, United Kingdom